Fertility

A Novel

By
Denise Gelberg

The characters and events depicted in *Fertility: A Novel* are fictional. Any similarity to actual persons or events is coincidental.

Grateful acknowledgment is made for permission to use an excerpt from "My Mother," by Abraham Sutzkever, *A. Sutzkever: Selected Poetry and Prose*, translated by Barbara and Benjamin Harshav. © 1991 by the Regents of the University of California. Published by the University of California Press.

Copy editing by Erica Midkiff
Cover design by Cal Sharp
Interior design by Charles R. Wilson

ISBN-13: 978-1482326222
ISBN-10: 1482326221

Yiddish Terms

A be kezunt — be well

Alter kocker — lecherous older man

Boychik — little boy

Brokh — misfortune

Bubbe — grandmother

Chutzpah —audacity, nerve

Efsha — perhaps

Essen — eat

Farblondjhet — confused, to wander aimlessly

Gevalt — oh my God

Gott in himmel — God in heaven

Kayn aynhoreh — knock on wood, spare us the evil eye

Kinder — children

Kleine kint — little child

Kleine mamela — sweet little girl

K'naker — one who self—aggrandizes

Kvell — to burst with pride

Landsmen — countrymen

Macher — a big shot

Maidel — girl; maidela — little girl

Mandelbrot — hard pastry, similar to Italian biscotti

Mazel tov — best of luck

Mein kint — my child

Mensch — an admirable human being; plural, menschen

Meshuggena — crazy person

Meshugge — crazy, mad

Mishegoss — insanity

Mitzvah — blessing

Momzer — bastard

Schlep — carry, pull

Schmuck — a bastard

Schpiel — story

Seichel — wisdom, street smarts, ingenuity

Shana — beautiful

Shankeit — a beauty

Shlong — penis

Shtarker — strong one

Tsoures — troubles

Tushie — rear end, bottom of a child

Vai iz mer — woe is me

Zadda — grandfather

Dedicated to my mother,

the Rivka in my life

ONE

The screams were a primordial code alert to the hospital staff, sending them sprinting toward the source. Entering the pediatric isolation room, the staff instantly understood the distraught mother's protests to the gods. Her two-week-old daughter lay bleeding from every orifice. With mounting dread, the parents watched the red stain spread across her tiny diaper. Had the physician on call been a man of faith, he would have prayed for help. As it was, he methodically set to work to save the tiny infant's life.

Sarah Abadhi opened her eyes to a cold, dark Monday in November. Listening to the wind howling outside the windows of her third floor walk-up, she decided to ignore the alarm, for a few minutes at least. Closing her eyes again, she drifted off, hearing nothing of the six a.m. news droning from the clock radio. Then a thought intruded: the phone call from Harry that had awoken her in the middle of the night. She threw off the covers and got out of bed.

Harrison Meinig, Sarah's boss, had a way of demanding attention. Harry, as he was known by everyone, led the health care practice in the white-shoe law firm where she was a fifth-year associate. His call was about the university hospital a few blocks from her Manhattan apartment. Apparently, there had been a medical error involving the child of a VIP. Sarah had to meet Harry there by seven; there would be no time for her usual Monday morning swim.

But not to worry. Sarah was, above all, a practical person. After being miserable for a long time, she reconciled with the life she led. She didn't expect to be happy — in fact, she swore off hope, particularly when it came to men, which gave her the courage to tackle each day. Few people would have guessed the lovely looking woman with the impressive *vita* worshipped at the altar of low expectations.

Right after hanging up with Harry, Sarah had gotten up and chosen her clothes for the early morning meeting. Now, as she struggled to rouse herself, she caught the forecast: a cloudy day with highs in the 30s. After a quick shower, she opted for textured black tights and the black pumps that wouldn't annoy the blisters she had earned during the NYC marathon the week before. With a dab of lipstick and some gold jewelry for her neck, wrist and ears, she was satisfied that she'd achieved the right look for an attractive but serious attorney. She shoveled a bowl of microwave oatmeal into her mouth, put her coffee in a travel mug and was out the door by 6:40.

Harry was already in the conference room of the risk manager's office when she arrived at 6:57. He wore the label "distinguished" like a birthright with his thick, silver-gray hair, steel blue eyes and still sharply angled jaw. He was tapping his fingers on the table as Sarah came through the door. Julie Bonner, the hospital's vice president for public relations, and an exhausted-looking John Mess, head of the risk management office, rounded out the group. An air of anxiety hung in the room as Sarah joined them at the conference table.

"Good morning," she said as she waited for the news that would undoubtedly make it anything but a good morning for either the hospital or the patient involved in the case.

John Mess didn't waste any time outlining the events that brought them together. "Yesterday afternoon the two-week-old infant of Mark Arkin was brought into the ER with what appeared to be a staph infection. After evaluation in the ER, the infant was admitted to an isolation room in our children's wing. The pediatric fellow, Dr. Richard Smith, followed protocol, ordering the antibiotic clindamycin, and the blood thinner heparin for the IV flush. The infant appeared to be stable when the parents left for a consultation with one of our lactation specialists. When they returned, the infant was in a medical crisis — bleeding from her eyes, ears, nose, mouth, rectum and vagina."

Sarah prided herself on seeming unflappable at work, but the image of a two-week-old baby bleeding out made her regret eating breakfast. The fact that the father of the baby was real estate mogul Mark Arkin only served to make matters worse.

Julie Bonner sensed the change in Sarah's mood straight away. "Are you all right, Sarah?"

"Absolutely. Please continue, John. How did the staff respond?" Sarah replied without hesitation.

Mess checked his notes and then looked up. "Dr. Smith immediately suspected a dosing error with the heparin. He attempted to counteract its blood-thinning properties by administering vitamin K and protamine sulfate. The attending physician, Dr. Esther Cho, was called in. She concurred with Dr. Smith's treatment. The bleeding was slowed. This morning the infant is in critical but stable condition. It is considered to have a good chance of survival."

Sarah noticed that Mess didn't use the child's gender when he spoke. She wondered if that impersonal approach allowed him to deal more easily with hospital-induced suffering.

"Where are you in your investigation of the dosing error?" Harry asked.

Now it was Mess's turn to grow pale. "Well," he began slowly, "we've discovered a couple of problems. It appears the floor was understaffed for RNs. You know, people have started their Christmas shopping and it's hard to get staff willing to come in for weekend shifts this time of year. Plus, a stomach flu has run through a lot of the staff over the last couple of weeks. I know, I know," he said, raising his hands, "no excuse that will help in a lawsuit, but that's the reality."

Sarah jumped in. "How short staffed was the floor?"

Bonner, as smooth as ice, had her story prepared. "As John indicated, the hospital was overtaken by a virulent strain of gastroenteritis last week. It decimated our ranks at all levels. Yesterday we were down three RNs on the floor where the Arkin baby was being treated. Some of the remaining RNs volunteered to work extra hours, but the nursing staff was still shorthanded. It is possible this unavoidable staff shortage may have contributed to the mistake in the dosage of heparin given to the baby."

"How big a mistake are we talking about?" Harry asked.

"A thousand times the correct dose," Mess replied.

All the air seemed to be sucked out of the room. Sarah couldn't get the picture of the bleeding baby out of her mind. Finally, she asked, "Could the overdose be the result of an illegibly or incorrectly written order?"

Mess was pleased he could put that question to rest. "We've just instituted computer entry for all medication orders. We have the order for heparin and it was correctly typed into our system." He quietly added, "We believe that perhaps someone misread either the order or the heparin label."

"So you think the dosing error can be traced to either the pharmacy or the floor nurse?" Harry asked.

Bonner offered up a possible culprit. "One of our most senior and trusted nurses, Joyce Hilker, was assigned to the Arkin baby. She administered the heparin. I hear she's inconsolable."

"Contrition doesn't usually help when there's a dead or damaged baby involved," Sarah pointed out as she shifted in her chair. "How could she have made the type of mistake we're talking about?"

"Well, that's the point we're at," Bonner said. "We think it's possible that the mistake wasn't entirely hers. As Harry speculated, it's likely the pharmacy was involved as well. That's something we hope you can figure out ASAP."

Then Harry asked the obvious question, given the father's tough-guy reputation. "So what is Arkin threatening us with? Did he have his lawyer crib-side through the night?" He posed the question only partly in jest.

"Amazingly, no lawyers yet and no threats to sue," Mess said.

"Arkin and his wife haven't left the baby. They are understandably upset. Well, that's something of an understatement. I guess the mother, especially, is beside herself. But Arkin isn't too far behind."

Harry's level of agitation — always at a simmer — was bubbling up. "Okay, so we've got to jump on this before Arkin has the chance to get his troops in position. Sarah will do some preliminary interviews of the staff today. Then we'll know more about where we stand."

Sarah nodded in agreement, but she had to wonder how Harry could be so cold in talking about a two-week-old baby. She knew there was some history between Arkin and him, though the specifics were sketchy. Something about a real estate deal where Harry and his client got clobbered. In any case, she knew what she had to do.

"I'd like to go back to our office, get some files, a digital recorder and a stenographer. I can be back here by 8:30 at the latest. Can I use this room for my interviews?" Mess nodded his assent.

"I'd like to sit in on the interviews," Bonner said.

"I'd rather you didn't," Sarah responded, without missing a beat. "I find I get a better result if I do the interviews without the employer in the room. The recorder and the stenographer are sufficient reminders that the stakes are high. You and John will have a full report of my findings after all of the preliminary interviews are completed — which I hope will be by the end of today."

Sarah could tell that Bonner wasn't pleased, but Harry backed her up. "You'll have your chance with them, Julie, but we find that the first interview right after the incident — conducted by an outsider — yields the best information."

Mess turned to Bonner. "Any sign that the media have gotten wind of this yet?"

"Not yet, but I figure that it's just a matter of hours, maybe a day at best. I'm working on a statement."

"Okay, so Sarah will be back shortly. And by the end of the day, we'll know better where we stand." Harry got up to leave. Sarah was right behind him.

"Thanks, Harry. I'd like a report — at least a verbal report — from Sarah by, shall we say, five o'clock?" he said, directing his attention now to Sarah.

"Of course," Sarah nodded. "You can facilitate my work by calling in the pharmacist that filled the order, and the nurses and doctors that treated the baby yesterday. Some of them may have the day off since they worked the weekend, but see what you can do."

"Don't worry about that. I'll round everyone up," Bonner assured her. They all shook hands before Sarah and Harry left.

Hailing a cab outside the hospital, Harry could hardly contain himself.

"What a cluster fuck. Cluster fuck, Sarah — a military term — when everything and everybody fucks up. Shit. No wonder we get paid so well. Defending a bunch of fuck-ups."

Sarah responded calmly. "We'll get this sorted out and figure out how to contain the damage. Let's just hope that baby makes it — and makes it intact." Settlements for damaged babies were often astronomical — rightfully so, Sarah thought.

The Ethiopian cabbie that picked them up drove like he was on a mission, which in fact he was. Sarah had called ahead to get a steno lined up. When she got to the office she quickly scanned the hospital's voluminous malpractice insurance policy, e-mailed her paralegal to highlight the provisions pertinent to a case such as this, canceled her noontime dental cleaning and headed back to the hospital with Doris Ostrom, the firm's most trusted steno, in tow.

TWO

Dr. Richard Smith must have been numb from exhaustion. There was no other way he'd miss the tall, attractive brunette coming in the hospital's main entrance as he was on his way out. But even a renowned ladies' man required sleep, and this ladies' man was anxious to get home and collapse. It was 8:24 a.m. and he'd been on duty since noon the day before. So much for his scheduled twelve-hour shift. This was Monday, his day off — funny how schedules became meaningless when a baby was bleeding out. Shit. He hoped that when he came back the next day, that baby would still be alive and, just as important, that she hadn't suffered irreparable harm at the hands of her so-called health care providers.

Rick Smith loved being a fellow in pediatric intensive care medicine. He'd been a decent student in med school, but had really hit his stride during his pediatric residency, when his tenacity in dealing with the very sickest patients won him notice. He was like a dog with a bone, unable to rest until he got to the bottom of what laid his patient low. Then he was relentless in his efforts to beat back the illness and return the child to a normal life. If his patient suffered a trauma by accident — or sometimes at the hands of a cruel adult — he was like a highly skilled craftsman restoring a work of art after an assault. He was a funny combination: carefree player on his rare days and nights off, and driven perfectionist the rest of his waking hours.

As he walked to his apartment he kept thinking about that baby, blood oozing even through the pores of her skin. With an overdose so large, it was nothing short of a miracle that she had stayed alive long enough for the antidote to kick in. He had a hunch she was a fighter. He had worked on babies whose spirits were so well defined that he marveled at their drive and, for lack of a better word, attitude. This baby was one of those. After only fourteen days of being on the planet, she already knew what she wanted and what she didn't. It could make a kid a pain in the ass, but for survival purposes, it was a real plus. Maybe she came by it honestly; the tabloids routinely portrayed her old man as a royal hard ass. From what Rick could see as he worked through the night, Mark Arkin was just a normal dad, scared that his kid wouldn't pull through, probably making private deals with his maker to save her life.

Just as he put his key into the deadbolt lock of his apartment door, his phone rang. It was the hospital. Shit. He'd made sure to bring the house staff up to speed — on the overdose case in particular. What the hell could they want now? He let it go to voice mail. Once inside he pulled off his clothes, peed, brushed his teeth and headed for bed. But then he thought better of it. Maybe he should just answer the call and get it out of the way. He called the number back.

"This is Dr. Smith on what's supposed to be my day off. This had better be good."

"Dr. Smith, this is Nancy Howland, Julie Bonner's assistant. Ms. Bonner asked me to let you know that you'll be needed for a meeting with the hospital's attorney today. The meeting is in reference to the Arkin infant's case." She attempted to sound authoritative while remaining pleasant. She knew how the fellows and residents guarded their limited time off.

"And who might Julie Bonner be?" he asked, making no attempt to hide his annoyance. Clearly, the hospital was getting its ducks in a row for a lawsuit while an eight-pound infant was fighting to stay alive. He was not alone in finding the bean counters and lawyers infuriating in the face of the life-and-death struggles that made up an average day in his department.

"Ms. Bonner is the hospital's vice president for public relations. She is assisting the risk management office and the attorneys in their investigation of the child's treatment. Every person involved is being interviewed today." Nancy Howland knew she had to stand her ground. Bonner had made it clear there would be no excuses accepted — even if a car service had to drive the staff member to the hospital for the interview.

"Well, that's just dandy...what's your name? Nancy? I've been on call since noon yesterday. I haven't had any sleep in over twenty-four hours. And as much as I'd like to help you, I'll be spending today between the sheets. Alone, I might add."

Howland knew she had to persevere and get him in for an interview, or Bonner would have her head on a platter. His address was displayed on her computer screen right above his phone number — he lived just a couple of blocks away. She decided to make a deal. "I understand completely, Dr. Smith. The interviews will be conducted throughout the day, and I am scheduling you last. We'll expect you at 4:30. That will give you a chance to catch up on your rest."

Rick was too tired to argue. And that would give him at least a semblance of a night's sleep. "That's very thoughtful of you, Nancy," he said, his voice heavy with sarcasm. "I am so glad you're taking my needs into account in this investigation. And will you be scheduling me another day off this week to make up for today?"   Howland wasn't getting into that rat's nest. She replied sweetly, "I'm sorry to say I have no authority to make those decisions or I'd be certain to give you another day off." She paused, waiting to see if he'd make another smart comment. Relieved when he didn't, she wrapped things up. "We'll see you at 4:30 in room 700."

Rick's fatigue led him to surrender. Had he some sleep under his belt, he would have kept up the repartee. Who knew? Maybe Nancy was a babe. And even if she wasn't, maybe she'd be an eager and enthusiastic partner, which held a charm of its own. But for now, all his desires were folded into his need to lie down and close his eyes. He hung up, set his alarm for 4:15 and got into bed. In less than a minute he was breathing slowly and rhythmically, enveloped in the rapture of long-deferred sleep.

THREE

Mark Arkin awoke that Monday morning with his arm around his wife. He and Catherine had succumbed to their exhaustion on a loveseat in the family lounge of the pediatric intensive care unit — the PICU. They'd been up with Ariel much of Saturday night as she fussed with what looked to be a nasty diaper rash. It was the nanny's day off, so they consulted the pile of baby books Catherine had amassed during her pregnancy. Then they applied ointment and kept her dry, but got no relief from the baby's incessant crying until four on Sunday morning. When she awoke around seven, the crying began again.

Mark Arkin didn't remember anything like this from when he had been married to Linda. Maybe that's because he had rarely been at home during their children's first years — or, for that matter, their later ones. He had never had any qualms about the long hours he kept. There had been no way to scale his industry's mountain while attending parent-teacher conferences and soccer games.

This time was different, though. Mark had never thought he'd be one of those fools — an *alter kocker* in his mother's parlance — who left a perfectly good wife for a new, younger model. He had been too busy amassing his fortune to chase skirts. Besides, he had been satisfied with Linda — who was both nice-looking and highly competent at running the family, the houses and their social life without any help from him. But when he met Catherine Malloy during an interview for an article she was writing for *Fortune* on his meteoric rise from the streets of Flatbush, he fell hard. At forty-seven he found himself besotted by the thirty-year-old natural beauty.

It took a year of pursuit, including a legal separation from Linda, before Catherine would even entertain the idea of going out for a drink. She refused to sleep with him until his divorce was final for over a year — something about the "one-year rule" that she had heard from a radio psychologist. The titan of real estate was powerless to sway her. The truth was, her unavailability added to her allure. Mark was fifty years old before he finally won Catherine over. And here he was, two years later, married to the woman he was crazy about, and scared that their baby would die fifteen days after taking her first breath.

As he sat on the loveseat, a terrifying thought crept into his consciousness: The nightmare with Ariel was retribution for what he'd done to Linda and their kids. But that was absurd. At the very least, it presumed some sort of balance in the universe, or, more improbable still, a wrathful god evening up the score. He had always pegged the notion of a "supreme being" as a scam, a way to keep the little people in line. He made big decisions every day, consequences be damned. When he walked away from his family, he had silenced the small but persistent inner voice of reproach by being generous. Linda got the houses in Scarsdale and the Hamptons, as well as alimony for the rest of her life. The kids got liberal child support until they were out of school, when their trust funds would kick in. Mark couldn't help but pat himself on the back, thinking that most first families would thank their lucky stars to get such munificent treatment from a husband and father who moved on in his life.

Still, here he was with Catherine. Through the night she had alternated between uncontrollable sobs and gentle crying until he finally persuaded her to try to sleep. It was his first victory at calming her, and he did it by telling her that if she got some rest, she would be in better shape to care for Ariel in the morning. Even as he made the case for sleep, he wondered if he was full of crap. Would Ariel even be alive in the morning? It was beyond him to understand how she could live to see another day after such an assault to her tiny body.

Try as he might, he couldn't shake the idea of retribution. What was happening to them and to their baby was too monstrous to be a random accident. For the first time since he was in grade school, he felt guilt. It was a sickening feeling. And the tears that fell silently on Catherine's hair frightened him as much as anything that had happened over the past day and night.

FOUR

Julie Bonner's office was nothing if not efficient. When Sarah returned to the conference room adjacent to John Mess's office, Nancy Howland, Bonner's assistant, was waiting for her. Howland informed Sarah that the pharmacist who'd filled the order and the baby's nurse, Joyce Hilker, would be coming in for interviews. Howland had left messages for the pediatric fellow, Dr. Smith, and the attending physician, Dr. Cho. She asked if Sarah wanted to interview the licensed practical nurse that had been teamed with Joyce Hilker on Sunday. Sarah thanked Howland for taking initiative and told her to contact the LPN as well as the charge nurse for the floor. She figured she could fit all of them in — and in cases like these, time was of the essence. She had to interview each of the major players before they had a chance to think too carefully about a cover, or to coordinate their stories.

After she and Doris Ostrom got themselves set up in the conference room, Sarah thought about how she could use the time before her first interview at 9:30. She decided to lay eyes on the pharmacy to see how orders were dealt with via the new computerized system. She asked Howland for directions and then suggested she let the pharmacy know Sarah was on her way.

The hospital pharmacy was actually smaller than she had imagined, but it hummed with what appeared to be the well-coordinated activity of about a dozen people in white jackets. Double doors led to the outpatient pharmacy, staffed by another four workers. Within the pharmacy there were row upon row of open shelves with more medications than Sarah had ever imagined possible. There was also a walk-in cooler for the medications that had to be kept refrigerated. As Sarah scanned the clean, well-lit room, a blond, middle-aged woman wearing a white jacket and white clogs approached.

"You must be the attorney Julie's office just called about. I'm Joanne Marsh, head of the hospital's pharmacy," she said, extending her hand. "Glad to meet you."

"I'm Sarah Abadhi," she said, shaking hands with the head pharmacist. Sarah noticed the Pharm.D. following Joanne Marsh's name on her ID tag, indicating her doctorate in pharmacology.

"Please, let me know how I can be of help in your investigation. This is the type of error I've spent my career trying to prevent. Believe me when I say I'm eager to know how this mistake happened."

Sarah was taken by her frankness and her straightforward demeanor. "I thank you in advance for your cooperation. It's clear that it's in everyone's interest to keep errors like the one that occurred yesterday to a minimum. You could help me by demonstrating how a doctor's order is processed by the pharmacy. I'd like to familiarize myself with the system."

"I'd be happy to. We put our Bar Code Medication System — BCMA — into operation just last week. We have orders constantly arriving on our system. Let me take you through the entire process from arrival of the order to departure through the pneumatic tubes."

Marsh was as efficient as she was confident when explaining the system. She used the first order of the incoming computerized requests as an example. "Let's see. A doctor on Four North has requested Effexor XR, 150 mg, for an eighty-nine-year-old female patient. I'll bring up the patient's profile to see what other medications she's taking. As you can see on the screen, there are no possible drug interactions, so we can fill the script without calling the floor to speak with the patient's nurse."

Then Marsh walked Sarah over to unit five of the large array of freestanding, open shelves and, using a stepstool, brought down from the highest shelf the large, brown, bubble-sealed Effexor capsules. Returning to the computer terminal, she scanned the bar code on the Effexor package and printed out a label with the patient's name and ID number, the prescribing doctor's name and ID number, the dosage and the date. Once the label was affixed to the cardstock portion of the Effexor packaging, the head pharmacist indicated on the screen that the order was filled. Before five minutes had elapsed, the order was put into a clear plastic capsule that would wend its way through the pneumatic tubes to Four North and the eighty-nine-year-old woman awaiting her antidepressant medication.

"That seems to be an efficient system. What if you had scanned in the wrong drug or the wrong dose?" Sarah asked.

"So glad you asked. Let me demonstrate how the system is set up to deal with those types of errors."

The head pharmacist went through the same steps with the next incoming script, Furosemide, 20 mg, for an eighty-two-year-old male on Seven West. She intentionally retrieved Furosemide, 40 mg, from the bottom of unit six of the open shelving. When she scanned the bar code for the incorrect dosage, the computer gave an error message in a large, red font.

"So you see, the computer will not print out a label for an incorrect dosage. It's as close to foolproof as a system can be," Marsh said, quietly triumphant and delighted with the system she had personally championed with the hospital brass.

"I see," Sarah said, reserving judgment. She'd been working on malpractice cases long enough to know that first appearances rarely told the whole story. Without a systematic investigation into what had happened fourteen hours earlier, Sarah would not be so quick to absolve the pharmacy of responsibility. "Thank you for showing me how your system works. It will help me as I conduct my interviews today."

"I'm glad I can be of help in the investigation. Don't hesitate to call if you have any questions."

Sarah thanked Marsh again and walked quickly out the staff door to the corridor. She trotted down the hallway and skipped the elevator in favor of the stairs, hoping to have a few minutes to herself before her first interview.

FIVE

Sarah could feel the blood pulsing through her body when she returned to the conference room at 9:20. She had missed her morning swim, and the bit of exercise provided by the seven flights of stairs felt good. She jotted down a list of general, open-ended questions that would give the baby's nurse the opportunity to tell her story. Doris Ostrom, the stenographer, nodded her readiness when they heard the knock on the door.

Sarah left her seat at the head of the long conference table and welcomed Joyce Hilker in, showing her to a seat kitty-corner to her own. She introduced herself and Doris and indicated that the interview would be digitally recorded, as well as transcribed. She started the recorder, stating who was present, the date and time of the interview and its purpose.

"Thank you for coming in, Ms. Hilker. I understand you were on duty last night and I know this is likely a scheduled day off for you."

"Yes. I'm actually supposed to be off today and tomorrow. But I understand this has to be done — this interview, I mean."

"We'll try to get through this as quickly as possible so you can have the rest of the day to yourself." Then Sarah gave her standard explanation for hospital employees being questioned after a medical error. "You understand that I represent the hospital. You, as its employee, are legally an agent of the hospital. So we are essentially on the same side — which is trying to discover the events that led to the overdose of the Arkin infant."

The attractive — albeit tired-looking — middle-aged, blond,

blue-eyed woman inhaled audibly and her cheeks reddened. Sarah wondered if she was going to break down. The nurse seemed to have a gentleness that Sarah hoped was something of a bona fide occupational qualification — a BFOQ in legalese — for the job of nursing. As Joyce Hilker struggled to compose herself, she said, "Of course. Everyone wants to figure this out."

"Okay then, we'll get started. Ms. Hilker, what were your duties yesterday, November tenth, in regard to the infant girl, Ariel Arkin?"

Hilker shifted in her seat as she began. "The baby girl was admitted to the floor from the ER around 3:45. I generally work a nine-hour shift, including a meal break. Given my hour commute each way, at my age that's about all I can reasonably handle. I was originally scheduled to work until four, but the charge nurse, Jeannie Lopez, asked if I could add another shift — or at least half a shift — because we were down a few nurses. Some people had called in sick. I felt bad for Jeannie. She was up against it; we had a lot of very ill children on the floor yesterday. And my own kids are grown — both in college now. My husband can make a meal for himself. And we can certainly use the extra money…," she hesitated for a moment, "…so I agreed to work until nine. I was assigned to the Arkin baby when she came up on the floor from the ER. That made her my seventh patient."

Sarah broke in. "How many patients do you usually care for?"

"Ideally, I care for four or five. But we rarely have ideal conditions with the nursing shortage that everyone — not just this hospital — is experiencing. So I'd say six is my usual patient load."

"Thank you. Please continue."

"The baby was put in isolation because it had not yet been determined whether her staph infection was drug resistant. I used universal precautions, introduced myself to the baby's parents and got her vitals, just as Dr. Smith came into the room."

Sarah interrupted her again. "Excuse me. Could you define 'universal precautions'?"

"Oh, I'm sorry," the nurse said. "I put on a gown and gloves that are removed when leaving the patient's room and disposed of in a special container for medical waste. The goal is to limit other patients' exposure to pathogens as doctors and nurses go from patient to patient."

"And do you recall what the baby's vital signs were?" Sarah asked.

"I don't recall exactly, but she had a temp and her heart rate was slightly elevated. I'd have to look at her chart to give you the exact information."

Sarah once again thanked Hilker and asked her to continue.

"As I was saying, Dr. Smith — he's a pediatric intensive care fellow — came into the room. He, too, was gowned and gloved as he examined the baby. When he took off the diaper and undershirt you could see the pus-filled lesions typical of an advanced staph infection. They seemed to originate in the diaper area and were spreading up the baby's abdomen and back.

"Dr. Smith asked the parents for some history. Apparently the baby had been born at term, two weeks earlier in another hospital. Until — I guess it would be Saturday evening — the baby had had no health problems. The parents said they first noticed what looked like diaper rash on Saturday night. She became very irritable. They spoke with their pediatrician on the phone on Sunday, who recommended they come to the ER and have the baby evaluated."

"What did Dr. Smith do after examining the infant and getting the baby's history?" Sarah asked.

"Well, he explained to the parents that the type of infection the baby likely had — community acquired methicillin resistant staph — seems to be on the rise in otherwise healthy newborns. He said they would treat the baby with antibiotics to stop the infection in its tracks — I think that's the phrase he used. The mother asked how she could continue nursing during the baby's hospitalization. Dr. Smith explained that she could stay in the hospital with the baby. The mother said the baby had been too fussy to nurse throughout the day, so she was very full with milk — uncomfortably so. The doctor suggested she try again right after he completed his exam. He said if the baby wouldn't take the breast, the mother could pump her milk. Then we could feed the breast milk to the baby through a nasal tube into her stomach."

The nurse stopped for a moment, took a drink of water and then continued. "The parents seemed okay with that and then Dr. Smith turned to me. He told me he was ordering clindamycin for the baby, as well as a heparin lock flush. He said he wanted me to monitor how the baby was nursing. In the event that she refused to nurse, I was to get the mother a breast pump. Then he turned back to the parents and asked if they had any questions. They wanted to know how long the baby would be in the hospital. He said it would depend on how she responded to the clindamycin; with luck she could be home in a few days. He also told them he would be on call until midnight and that they should feel free to have him paged at any time."

"Your ability to recollect the events is very impressive," Sarah said with a genuine sense of appreciation for the nurse's memory and cooperation.

"Well, I've been going over that scene in my mind all night, trying to get a sense of what could have happened...." Hilker trailed off and looked as though she might lose it again. Sarah asked if she needed a minute, but the nurse shook her head.

"Well, let me see. Just as Dr. Smith was removing his gown and gloves and disinfecting his hands, the mother asked how the baby could have gotten the infection. He said that the origin of the infection in cases like these is often unknown. There are theories as to how a baby can be exposed, but there is no definitive answer."

They were interrupted by a knock on the door. A tall, good-looking black man dressed in nursing scrubs popped his head into the conference room.

"Hello, is Joyce Hilker in there? I'm her union rep, Cletus

Jackson. Joyce has the right to representation in this interview."

Sarah knew that the union rep was legally correct, that under the Supreme Court's Weingarten ruling any unionized employee who might face discipline as the result of an interview with her employer had the right to have a union representative present. But Weingarten rights can be waived. The question was, would Hilker do so?

"I need to speak with Joyce before your interview continues," Jackson stated firmly. It was clear he knew the nurse's rights as well as Sarah did.

Although she was irked, Sarah showed no hint of her annoyance. "Of course." She turned to the nurse and said, "Ms. Hilker, as Mr. Jackson states, it is your right to have him present at this interview. You can also waive that right. Would you like a moment to think about it?"

"I'd like to talk with Joyce for a moment so she can make an informed decision — as is her right," he said to Sarah, emphasizing his last words. Then he turned his attention to the nurse. "Joyce, let's have a word out in the corridor." It was more of a command than a suggestion.

The nurse hesitated for a moment and then said to Sarah, "I'd like to confer with Clete. It'll only take a few moments." She left the conference room, closing the door behind her. Sarah turned off the recorder and gave Doris a "Who-needed-this?" look.

When the nurse returned, she had Cletus Jackson at her side. Sarah welcomed him to the table, suggesting that he sit next to Joyce Hilker. He unclipped a pen from his yellow legal pad and got ready to take notes. Sarah turned on the recorder and stated that the nurse's union representative, Mr. Cletus Jackson, had joined the interview. She hoped the tenor of the interview wouldn't be critically altered by his presence, all the more so now that they were getting close to the point where the heparin had been introduced to the baby.

Sarah asked Doris to read back the last paragraph of the

interview. Doris read the portion of Hilker's statement about Dr. Smith's discussion of the unknown origins of staph infections in newborns. That seemed to reorient both Sarah and the nurse. They were ready to proceed.

Sarah asked, "What happened after the doctor's explanation?"

"He reminded them again that they should feel free to contact him throughout the evening, and then he left to enter the orders for clindamycin and heparin lock flush into the baby's computerized chart."

"And what did you do?"

"Well, I asked the mother if she wanted to try nursing the baby. I could tell that she was getting quite uncomfortable. A nursing mother has to nurse — or pump — or she risks getting mastitis. I put a new diaper on the baby and swaddled her in a receiving blanket.

"As the mother opened her blouse and nursing bra, I saw her left breast was quite red — and apparently engorged with milk. I asked her if she had been nursing successfully until the baby became ill. She said she had, but that she usually had more milk than the baby seemed to need. I asked her if I could look at her breast more closely. The father got really jumpy then and asked if there was something wrong. I explained that a nursing mother who couldn't empty her breasts could run into problems and I asked again if I could take a look. The mother agreed. I asked her to remove her bra, which she did. And that's when I saw that she, too, had white pustules typical of a staph infection on the inside and underside of her left breast. Her right breast appeared engorged, but was of normal color."

The image of the inflamed, infected breast made Sarah squirm. It crossed her mind that she would have made a terrible doctor, given her aversion to suffering. She was only too happy to set aside the image of the diseased breast by asking Hilker what she did at that point.

"Well, the mother told me she hadn't noticed any white pustules earlier in the day. She seemed horrified, as did the dad. I knew Dr. Smith would want to see the mother's breast and would likely want a culture from one of the pustules. I also knew it was unlikely he'd want the mother to nurse the child, given her condition. So I rang the call button and Tracy, the LPN I was teamed with yesterday, came to the door. I told her to get Dr. Smith back ASAP, which she did."

Sarah thought to ask for Tracy's surname, but then she remembered Nancy Howland was already on the case. "And when Dr. Smith saw the mother?" Sarah prompted.

"He was very concerned, but calm and patient, as he generally is with the patients and their families. He said sometimes newborns get staph from contact with their mothers; some people carry staph on their skin or in their nasal passages. Babies and their mothers can have concurrent infections. Apparently, this was the case here."

"Had the baby's antibiotic — let me see, clindamycin — or the heparin been administered at this point?"

"No, Dr. Smith had left to order it, but it hadn't yet arrived on the floor."

"So what did Dr. Smith do, if anything, for Mrs. Arkin?"

"He said that the mother would also have to be put on an antibiotic regimen. He told the parents that he wanted to consult with one of the hospital's lactation specialists, but he thought it was probably best for her not to nurse the baby at that time. He said they could give the baby formula if need be. Then the mother got upset. Very upset. She said she couldn't believe this was happening. Her husband tried to comfort her. Then he got kind of pushy and told the doctor to get that lactation specialist in the room right away. Dr. Smith said he'd do what he could and asked me to page the specialist. I took off my gown and gloves, disinfected my hands and left the room to page the consultant."

"And where was the infant at this point?"

"She was in her crib."

"And had you or anyone on the floor administered any

medications to her?"

"The ER had started an IV for fluids. But we were still awaiting the clindamycin and heparin."

"And what time did you leave the baby's room to page the lactation specialist?"

Hilker thought a moment. "I really can't say exactly. I would guess it was around 4:15 or 4:30."

"Were you successful in paging the specialist?"

"Yes. She answered her page within just a few minutes. She said she would be at the baby's room in fifteen minutes — which was amazing, considering it was a Sunday. I thought to myself that at least that baby and mother had caught a little break."

Cletus Jackson interrupted. "Joyce, remember to just state the facts as you remember them." Sarah couldn't tell if the nurse appreciated the union rep's advice or found it a put-down. She nodded once and then waited for Sarah's next question.

"At what point did the heparin and clindamycin arrive on the floor?" Sarah inquired, drawing the circles of her questioning closer to the actual target of the investigation.

"Well, that was the thing. The pharmacy technician actually brought the two orders right up to the floor. He said the new computer system had a glitch and wasn't cooperating. The doctor had ordered them 'stat' so he ran them up to the floor himself."

Sarah couldn't help but think of Joanne Marsh's demonstration of the apparently foolproof system. "Is that an unusual thing for the pharmacy to do?"

"It happens from time to time, but it's fairly unusual. I thought the pharmacy tech was going the extra mile and I told him so."

"At what point were the clindamycin and heparin administered?" Sarah set her sights for the bull's eye.

Hilker looked at her union rep. Jackson nodded and the nurse proceeded, looking down at her hands. "I immediately gowned up and brought the meds into the baby's room. I told the father that Dina

Geissinger, the lactation specialist, would be in to see them very shortly. The mother was still sitting in the chair. She had the yellow paper gown covering her breasts and she was weeping. The dad was pacing around the room and talking to someone on his cell phone very quietly — almost in a whisper."

"And where was Dr. Smith at this time?"

"Dr. Smith was no longer in the room."

"And when were the clindamycin and heparin administered?" Sarah asked.

At this point tears began streaming down Hilker's face. She got a tissue from her purse and shook her head in resignation. "When I checked on the baby, she woke up with a start and began to cry. Both of the parents came to the crib to try to calm her down, but the truth was, they were so upset I'm not certain they were much help. I checked that both of the meds had the correct patient name. Then I hung the clindamycin from the IV stand and connected it to the catheter. As I was about to flush the IV with heparin, Dina Geissinger came into the room for the consultation."

Sarah interrupted her. "I understand the new computer medication system has bar codes that have to be scanned at every point. Did you scan the drugs before administering them?"

Still looking at her hands, the nurse explained what had happened next. "I attempted to scan the medications. The clindamycin scanned, no problem. But the heparin wouldn't scan. I remembered that the pharmacy tech said they were having a problem with the new system so I figured it was just a glitch. The system only started last Monday and we're all learning as we go. As I said, I visually checked the patient's name and medication name."

"And what about the dosage?"

Hilker looked up from her hands and stared directly into Sarah's eyes. "The label looked correct — 10 units per milliliter."

"So what did you do then?"

"I flushed the intravenous line with the heparin to keep it

patent — open."

"Who was in the room at this point?"

"As I said, the parents and Dina Geissinger. But then the three of them left for an examining room. I checked the IV one more time before I took off my gown and gloves and left the room. The baby had fallen back to sleep by the time I returned to the nurses' station."

"Do you recall the time you left the baby?"

"Yes, it was five o'clock. I remember because I knew the cafeteria would be open and I could get a takeout dinner to get me through until nine. Of course, with all that happened after I came back from the cafeteria, I never got to eat that dinner."

SIX

Joyce Hilker's blow-by-blow account of the events that followed her return from the cafeteria stirred both dread and awe in Sarah. The mother's screams brought Hilker running into the baby's room, where she found her wailing, "Oh my God, oh my God, help my poor baby." The nurse was joined by Dr. Smith, who immediately diagnosed the overdose and started treatment to reverse its devastating effects.

Hilker finished telling her story fifty minutes after she began. If the nurse had looked tired at the start of the interview, she was drained when it was done. Sarah thanked her for her cooperation. She also thanked Cletus Jackson, shaking hands with them both as she saw them out. Then the agnostic Sarah offered up a silent thank you. The union rep had not, in fact, prevented the nurse from giving what appeared to be a thorough account of the events of the previous night.

As she'd listened to Hilker's description of the quick response of the medical team, particularly the work of the pediatric fellow, Sarah wondered what it would feel like to have the skills and knowledge to save a person's life. Since her last boyfriend had taken a walk rather than entertain the thought of marriage, she had made work the center of her universe. Harry handpicked her to be his protégée last year and gave her more responsibilities than most associates — these interviews being a prime example. She knew she had a good shot at continuing to rise through the ranks of her firm. But she had no idea what it would feel like to prevent someone from dying. She had to be satisfied with protecting hospitals and their staffs from frivolous malpractice suits so that they could engage in their life-saving work.

But it was clear that if this family decided to file suit, it would be anything but frivolous.

She had just a couple of minutes before her next interview. How a mistake of such magnitude could occur was still an open question. From the scene described by the nurse — the frantic parents, the concurrent infection in the mother, the extra five hours tacked onto her shift — Sarah could imagine how an error could be made. She had to wonder if the nurse had really seen 10 units on the vial of heparin. Had it been mislabeled? And if so, who was responsible — the hospital pharmacy or pharmaceutical company? If it wasn't mislabeled, had Hilker checked the dosage as she said she had? Could she have misread it due to fatigue? And why didn't the computer system work? Were glitches really being experienced? Joanne Marsh led Sarah to believe the system was foolproof. Did the staff agree? She made notes to herself on all of her queries and was finishing the last one just as a pert, slim woman in her early twenties knocked on the open door. She introduced herself as Tracy Petersen, the LPN summoned by Nancy Howland. Sarah welcomed her into the conference room, showed her to a seat and excused herself, telling the young woman and Doris that she'd be back in a minute.

Sarah wanted to lay eyes on the heparin vial, and the sooner the better. She made a beeline for John Mess, who was in his office adjacent to the conference room.

"Excuse me, John. Where is the heparin vial that was used for the baby?"

"Actually, I have it."

"May I see it?"

"Of course, Sarah."

He got up from behind his large, cherry desk and walked to a closet next to the built-in bookcases. He opened the door to reveal a waist-high safe. Kneeling down, he entered several digits on the keypad, and the door opened. On the top shelf was a plastic zip-top bag. He handed it to Sarah. In the bag was a vial with a handwritten label showing the Arkin baby's name and ID number, her doctor's name and ID number, the date of dispensing and dosage of heparin: 10 units/mL. The label looked clear enough. However, when the vial was turned a bit there was a blue label from the manufacturer that read: Heparin, 10,000 USP units/mL. Clearly, Hilker never noticed the discrepancy. She handed the plastic bag back to Mess.

"Thanks. There appears to be some inconsistency in the labeling."

"Unfortunately for us, there does, indeed."

"I hope to get to the bottom of that by the time I finish up this afternoon. Having a picture in my mind of the medication is a big help. Thanks. I'd better get back; I have someone waiting for me now."

Sarah found Tracy Petersen and Doris chatting amiably about the weather and how they both hated it turning cold so early in the season. Doris was such a pro. She knew exactly how to put people at ease — not only in interviews such as this one, which were often fraught with tension, but at their frenetic, high-stress office as well. She was one of the few people at the firm who looked up from working to welcome Sarah when she arrived five years earlier. They hit it off from the start and Sarah always enjoyed teaming with her. Doris was the only one at work who could make Sarah's dimples show, a point Doris was only too happy to tease her about.

Sarah gave her standard introduction and then asked Petersen some questions to get a sense of her relationship with Joyce Hilker. Apparently, they had worked on the same floor for the last couple of years and were often paired together by the charge nurse, Jeannie Lopez. In Petersen's estimation, Hilker was a great nurse, maybe the best she'd worked with. She was also a great teacher, a plus for an LPN studying to become a registered nurse.

Clearly a fan of her partner and mentor, Petersen would likely hesitate to cite any faults or past errors. Sarah knew she would have to tread carefully when she went down that road in her questioning.

"Yesterday Joyce Hilker was supposed to finish her shift at 4 p.m. What was your schedule?" Sarah inquired.

"Well, lately I've been doing a noon-to-midnight shift. I know some people don't like getting out of work that late, but it works for my boyfriend and me," the nurse volunteered. "He gets off work at 11:30 and picks me up right at the front of the hospital. But this weekend I was just trying to get some overtime, so I took an extra shift yesterday, 7 a.m. to 4 p.m."

"Were you asked to extend your shift yesterday?"

"Oh, yeah. We were really shorthanded. That stomach flu hit a lot of us. I had it two weeks ago and I wouldn't wish it on my worst enemy. Anyway, yes, Jeannie — the charge nurse — asked if I would do back-to-back shifts. I didn't really want to because I'm on today at noon. But I could see she was really desperate so I said okay. Plus, the extra money always comes in handy."

"What was your interaction with the Arkin baby when she was admitted?"

"Joyce did the admission by herself because I was busy with another patient."

"Is that the usual procedure?" Sarah asked.

"Well, if we can, we like to introduce ourselves to the patient and the family together, but yesterday we were very busy and, like I said, short staffed," Petersen explained.

"So when did you start working with the Arkin infant?"

"The first time I came to the baby's room was when I answered a call that came into the nurses' station. When I got there, Joyce was at the door and she told me to get Dr. Smith right away."

"And what did you do?"

"Well, luckily he was at the nurses' station entering some orders into the computer. I told him Joyce wanted him in the isolation room — and that sooner rather than later would be better from the look that Joyce had given me. I know that sounds kind of pushy, talking to a doctor that way, but Dr. Smith is a good guy," Petersen said, smiling and nodding her head for emphasis.

Another vote for Dr. Smith. "And did you accompany the doctor into the baby's room?" Sarah asked.

"No. I had plenty to do and Joyce didn't ask for my help — just Dr. Smith's. We had a lot of very sick kids on the floor yesterday — I mean really sick — so there was no way I was going where I wasn't needed. Believe me when I tell you I had plenty else to do."

"When did you next assist Joyce with the Arkin baby?"

Petersen started twisting her light brown hair around her finger. She hesitated a minute and then began her version of the events of the prior night. "I think it was around 5:30 when all hell broke loose. I was with a little guy who was on a ventilator when I heard the screams and then the code alert. I realized it was the new admission's room, so I put on a gown and gloves and went in."

"Who was in the room at the time?"

"Let me see. Dr. Smith, Joyce, Jeannie Lopez and the parents. The mother was screaming, I mean hysterically. It wasn't until I looked at the baby that I understood what was making her act so crazy. God, I've never seen anything like that — blood coming from everywhere. Dr. Smith told me to get the parents out of the room. I mean the doctor can't think straight when people are screaming at him. So I did my best to get them out of there."

"What did you say?" Sarah was anxious to hear what this twenty-something LPN could have said to tear Mark Arkin away from his hemorrhaging infant.

"Well, I said just what I said to you. I told them the doctor couldn't do his best for their baby with them so upset — that he had to be able to work. The best way for them to help was to give the doctor space. The father started shouting at me, saying he wasn't going anywhere, that he wasn't going to leave his kid alone for a moment with such…incompetents. Yeah, that was the word he used, incompetents. Then Dr. Smith yelled at the father."

Sarah was intrigued. "What did he yell at the father?"

Petersen seemed to hesitate for a moment and her cheeks

flushed. "You have to understand how bad things were. I don't want to get him in trouble."

"It's best if you just tell me how things went. I understand it was an extremely stressful situation, Tracy," Sarah assured her.

"He said something like, 'Don't be an asshole. I am trying to save your baby's life — and unless you'd like to take over for me, I suggest you get the hell out of here and let me work.' Just like that. Then the mother shook her head like she couldn't believe what was happening. She was crying and she told her husband something."

"Could you hear what she said?"

The LPN tried to recall the scene. "I think she said something like the doctor was their only hope. Yeah, that's what she said. 'He's our only hope.' The father looked like he was about to go nuts, but the mother took his hand and led him out of the room. It was somehow one of the saddest things I've ever seen, and believe me, I've seen plenty of sad things working here."

"And what happened next inside the baby's room?"

"Everyone was so busy working on the baby, I figured I'd just do what made sense. I was going to get clean linens for the crib when Dr. Smith told me to get the pharmacy on the room phone and tell them we had an emergency, which I did. Then he said to put the phone to his ear. I did that, too. He told the pharmacy what he needed for the baby — stat — and that he was sending someone to personally get the meds. When he was done I took the phone from his ear. Then he told me to run down and get protamine sulfate."

"Do you remember the dose?"

"Oh, yeah. When Dr. Smith was still on the phone he said something like, 'This time, try not to send me a thousand times what I'm prescribing.' He told me to make sure I was getting 100 mg of protamine sulfate. He was very clear about that."

Sarah felt like she was hitting pay dirt. It was clear that Dr. Smith was certain the error originated in the pharmacy. Now Sarah had to nail down how the pharmacy's highly touted computerized medication system allowed these errors to occur — and with such calamitous results for two-week-old Ariel Arkin.

SEVEN

The interview with Tracy Petersen, LPN, was done by eleven o'clock. Sarah and Doris had time enough before Jeannie Lopez, the charge nurse, arrived to use the bathroom and get a cup of coffee. Coffee was Sarah's energy drink and comfort food. It also gave her something to do with her hands. Some people smoked cigarettes to keep their hands busy; Sarah generally had a cup or mug of coffee in hers. An admitted addict, she indulged with abandon.

Jeannie Lopez added little new information. She, too, heaped praise on Joyce Hilker, calling her one of the finest nurses she'd ever worked with, and describing her as smart and dedicated. She said Hilker was great with the patients and the families, too. Lopez's own interaction with the Arkin case began when the massive bleeding was discovered. She confirmed the steps that were taken to staunch the bleeding. When asked how she thought the overdose had occurred, she pointed the finger of responsibility at the pharmacy. She said she had no explanation, however, for how Hilker had missed the discrepancy between the labels on the heparin vial.

Dr. Esther Cho, the attending physician for the baby, was scheduled next, but she was late. Sarah used the time to begin writing up her preliminary findings. About twenty minutes later, a tall, slender woman in her late thirties appeared at the door.

"I was called to an interview. Is this the right place?"

"Dr. Cho?" Sarah inquired.

"Yes."

"Please come in," Sarah said as she showed her to a seat.

"Can we make this quick?" the doctor asked. "I have some very sick patients waiting for me on the floor."

Sarah skipped her usual introduction, started the digital recorder and nodded to Doris. "Certainly. I think we can get right to it. Dr. Cho, I'm interested in your account of the events surrounding the case of Ariel Arkin."

"Well, I came to room 405 after the code alert. As I was gowning up I saw an older man and a younger woman outside the door to the isolation room. I assumed they were family. Maybe the grandfather and mother. They were very upset.

"I entered the room and Dr. Smith brought me up to speed. It was a clear case of a massive heparin overdose. I personally had only read about so large an overdose, and I hope I never experience anything like that again.

"Dr. Smith and I agreed to administer 1 mg of protamine sulfate via IV for every 100 units of active heparin to reverse its anti-coagulating effects. He'd already put in an order for it. I reminded him to infuse it slowly to minimize hypotension, bronchial constriction and pulmonary hypertension. We also discussed using vitamin K to help stop the bleeding. We agreed on the optimal rate for infusing new blood into the infant to replace what she'd lost. Dr. Smith was on top of it. We were successful in our efforts to stop the bleeding. This morning, the baby is stable."

"Thank you, Dr. Cho," Sarah said. "Do you have an opinion on how the overdose occurred?"

"If I were you, I'd focus on the pharmacy."

"And what about the new computerized system for medications? How could it have failed to prevent the overdose?"

"It's beyond my purview to have an opinion on that," the doctor said curtly. "I think the person you want to talk to is Joanne Marsh, the head of the pharmacy. She was the new system's biggest booster."

"And the baby's prognosis?" Sarah asked.

"Given her response to treatment, I'm guardedly optimistic that she'll recover, hopefully without permanent damage."

*****

As Esther Cho left the conference room at ten minutes before one, Nancy Howland popped her head in to ask Sarah and Doris if they would like something from the cafeteria. Doris begged off, raised a Tupperware container from her bag, and asked Nancy for directions to the nearest microwave. Sarah, though slim, never willingly skipped a meal. Skeptical about the quality of the cafeteria's offerings, she answered that any vegetarian sandwich or wrap would be fine. As she started to reach for her wallet, Howland waved her off, saying it was on the house — and that she'd just brewed a new pot of coffee, which was welcome news for Sarah.

By half past one, the two women had finished lunch. Right on time, the person Sarah was now most interested in arrived at the door. Albert Cappelli, the pharmacist who had filled the orders for the Arkin baby, was a pleasant-looking man in his sixties. Cappelli was balding, mustached and carrying an extra twenty pounds in the midsection of his sturdy frame. He smiled as he extended his hand to both Sarah and Doris. He seemed relaxed. Sarah wondered how he could be, knowing the reason for the interview. She thanked him for coming in and wasted no time in getting started. She nodded to Doris, started the recorder and gave her standard introduction before posing the first question to the kindly looking pharmacist.

"Mr. Cappelli, how long have you worked at the hospital pharmacy?"

"That's a little complicated. I worked at this hospital's pharmacy for twenty-seven years before I retired two years ago. But when I retired I told Joanne Marsh — she's the head of the pharmacy — that I wouldn't mind coming in to help out when they were short staffed. I figured it would help keep me in the game, as they say, and the extra money couldn't hurt, either. So, to answer your question, I guess I'd say twenty-seven years full time and two years on and off."

"Could you give me an idea of how frequently you're called back to help out in the pharmacy?"

"Well, it goes in fits and spurts. Sometimes, nothing for a few weeks. Then, I can be called quite frequently. They've had a lot of pharmacists out lately due to some bug that's going around. Luckily, it's missed me so far. This month I've been in four times already, and it's only November eleventh. So I would say it's uneven."

Sarah's mind started to race. How much did Cappelli know about the new BCMA computer system? There had to have been training for all of the staff. Were Cappelli and other substitute pharmacists included? She decided to pursue that point before getting to his version of the previous day's events.

"Mr. Cappelli, were you given training for using the new computerized medication system, the BCMA?"

Cappelli smiled broadly, shaking his head gently up and down. "I guess you'd have to call me a twentieth-century kind of guy. I was a practicing pharmacist long before computers were part of the landscape. Yes, they gave me a little tutorial, I guess you would call it, when I came in last week. I'd been hearing about it for months and I read up on it at home."

Sarah persisted. "Did you attend any training sessions offered by the hospital before the BCMA was instituted?"

"Well, here's the thing. The full-time people were given time off from their regular duties to go to these sessions. The subs like me, well, if we came in for the training, there was no compensation offered. And to tell you the truth, it wasn't so complicated that I had to sit for hours to learn how to use it."

Joanne Marsh's demonstration had certainly made the system seem straightforward, so Sarah could see how an experienced pharmacist would think he could take a pass on formal instruction. However, yesterday's medication error exposed how wrong he was. She decided to get a sense of the depth of Cappelli's grasp of the system. Given her own limited understanding, she knew she was taking a chance, but she thought it was worth a question or two.

"So help me — as a layperson — and explain how the new

system works."

"No problem. It's really very logical. The order comes into the pharmacy by computer. The patient's medication profile pops up. We can see any interactions, contraindications, etc. If there are no problems with the medication profile, we get the medication from supply, scan it and the computer pops out a label. We put the label on and send it through the pneumatic tubes. Everything is bar coded and scanned. It's just like in the grocery store. Before the meds are administered, the nurse scans the patient's wristband to make sure everything is simpatico. Very nice. Helps to keep down medication mistakes."

Cappelli's explanation jibed with the one she had gotten from the head pharmacist. He clearly understood the broad outlines of the program. But a terrible error had still occurred, and current evidence indicated Cappelli could have been involved. It was time to find out how.

"Mr. Cappelli, I'd like you to recall the orders for the infant Ariel Arkin that came in late yesterday afternoon."

"Sure. I filled hundreds of orders yesterday, but I heard there was a problem with the baby, so I racked my brain to remember exactly what I did with those scripts."

"And what do you recall about filling the scripts for the infant?"

"The first thing I remember is that the orders came in as a hurry call, so they went to the top of the list of orders to fill. There were two: clindamycin — that's an antibiotic, often used for staph infections including MRSA, the drug-resistant kind of staph; and heparin for an IV flush every eight hours. Now this is new. We rarely were asked for heparin for most of my career. It was just stocked by pharmacy techs on each floor — near the patients. And I think it's still done that way in most of the hospital. But the powers that be decided that, as a way to prevent incorrect dosing, heparin would no longer be kept in the neonatal and pediatric patient care areas. I guess this was in response to overdoses that occurred around the country over the years. Personally, I couldn't recall an overdose in this hospital. Me, I figure why fix what's not broken? But I learned long ago that my opinion is not required when they change policy around here. I just follow orders."

"Mr. Cappelli, how did you fill the orders for the Arkin baby?"

"Well, just as I described. I got the clindamycin, scanned it, and the label popped out of the printer. The scanning system didn't like the heparin order, though. It refused to print the label, so I just handwrote a label with the patient's name, ID number, doctor, dose, etc."

"Do you remember the dose of the heparin?"

"Sure, for a baby's IV flush the doc would order a low dose — 10 units per milliliter."

"And did you fill the doctor's order for that dose?"

"Of course. I did what I've done hundreds of times before. I went to the shelf, got the blue-labeled heparin vial — blue is the 10-unit vial. Then I wrote out the label when there was a glitch in the computer system. I got a young tech, Alejandro — he's new — and told him to run the two orders up to the peds floor ASAP, which he did. He was back in the pharmacy in less than five minutes. Mission accomplished."

"And what is Alejandro's surname?"

"Let me think." His drummed his fingers on the table for a bit. "I think it's Avila."

"Thank you," Sarah said as she made a note to herself to have Alejandro Avila called in for an interview. "Mr. Cappelli, you said that you've filled orders for 10 units of heparin many times before."

"Yes, of course; after the heparin orders for peds and neonatal started coming through the pharmacy. It's used all the time for IV and catheter flushes."

"And you mentioned that the label for 10 units is blue, is that correct?"

"Yes, it's blue and the heparin 10 is stored on the third shelf — in the front — of unit eighteen in the pharmacy. After so many years I know that pharmacy like the back of my hand."

"Mr. Cappelli, do any other heparin vials have a blue label?"

The veteran pharmacist closed his eyes and thought for a moment. "Yes, 10,000 units also has a blue label — maybe a slightly different blue. But we store that on the top shelf at the back of unit nineteen. We use that full-dose heparin for anti-coagulation to prevent heart attacks, deep venous thrombosis and pulmonary embolisms."

"And you got the Arkin baby's script from unit eighteen?"

"Yes, just as I said."

"Well, Mr. Cappelli, the vial of heparin that was received on the floor was not 10 units. It was 10,000 units."

The pharmacist was clearly perplexed. "I don't see how that can be."

"Would you like to see the vial that was used on the Arkin baby?"

Concern crossed Cappelli's face for the first time since he had entered the room. "You have it here?"

"I can get it. Mr. Mess has it next door."

"Yes, I would like to see it, if that's okay."

"Of course." Sarah got up and excused herself. She wondered if Doris would engage the pharmacist in her usual chitchat while she retrieved the vial from the safe in John Mess's office. When she returned, she found Doris reviewing her transcription and Cappelli looking at his hands.

Sarah sat down and showed the pharmacist the vial in the plastic bag. He looked at the label with his handwriting. Then she turned the bag over to reveal the blue label with the clearly printed notation: Heparin, 10,000 USP units/mL. Cappelli took out a handkerchief from his back pocket, blew his nose and wiped his eyes. In no more than a whisper he said, "I'm sorry. I have no idea how this could have happened."

EIGHT

It was a few minutes after two when Sarah and Albert Cappelli arrived at the pharmacy. In a matter of minutes it became clear what had happened to result in the Arkin baby getting a thousand times the heparin Dr. Smith had prescribed.

The supply of heparin 10 was, just as Cappelli had said, stored in the front of the third shelf of unit eighteen, and the heparin 10,000 supply was stored on the top shelf of unit nineteen. Each location was clearly marked with a label and a bar code. However, behind the heparin 10 shelf label and next to a nearly empty box of 10-unit vials sat a new box of blue-labeled vials containing 10,000 units of heparin. Alejandro, the new pharmacy tech, had restocked the shelves yesterday. Sarah would have to interview him, but it seemed likely he had mistakenly put the look-alike 10,000-unit vials on the shelf where the 10-unit vials were supposed to go.

Cappelli took a long, hard look at the incorrectly placed box and excused himself to use the restroom.

As Sarah stood alone next to the shelf with the offending heparin, she surprised herself with the degree of sympathy she had for the people whose slip-ups had led to the catastrophic overdose. The veteran pharmacist had failed to catch the pharmacy tech's error when filling the rush order. He seemed to put less stock in the new BCMA system than in his decades of experience in the pharmacy. A nursing pro stretched thin, working with a sick, crying infant and her distraught parents, had failed to notice the discrepancy between the printed and handwritten heparin labels. Surely fatigue would have to be considered a factor in her error.

Just as Sarah was thinking how human — and even predictable — these kinds of mistakes were, the bathroom door opened. Cappelli emerged wearing a look of defeat just as Joanne Marsh approached, seeming to take two steps at a time.

"Joanne. It was me. I messed up. Look," he said, pointing to the incorrectly placed box of heparin. "I grabbed the vial from the new box just like this," he said as he picked out a vial from the 10,000-unit box, "saw the blue label and never double-checked the dose."

Marsh's face and neck turned pink. She shifted her weight from one leg to the other and folded her arms in front of her. "But Albert, the BCMA wouldn't allow you to fill the order with the wrong dose. You couldn't have scanned it. It wouldn't have scanned. That's the whole point of the system." She was almost pleading with him to tell her the system had worked.

"Joanne, you're right. It wouldn't scan. I just thought it was a glitch in the system. How long have the 10-unit vials been on the third shelf of unit eighteen? You and I both know that they've been in the same place for years. I just grabbed it. When it wouldn't scan I thought it was some kind of kink in the new system. And the label was blue. They're *both* blue, they're *both* blue," he said, raising his hands in the air. "That's why we always store the two doses on different shelving units."

"Who did the stocking of the shelves yesterday?" the head pharmacist asked.

"The new fella, Alejandro," Cappelli replied. As soon as Cappelli said the name, he knew Marsh would make quick work of him. "But he's a good kid, Joanne," Cappelli quickly added. "He ran the scripts up to the floor because I knew the doc wanted them stat. He did everything I asked of him yesterday — and he was nice about it, too. You know, no attitude like some of the young guys. He volunteered to restock the shelves without even being asked. He's a hard worker. He's gonna feel terrible when he finds out. He's not devil-may-care about things, Joanne. He takes the job seriously."

Sarah could see Marsh's impatience rising. "You're being far too understanding, Albert. All the techs have had training in using the BCMA. He was instructed to scan every medication before placing it on the shelf. Had he done what he was trained to do, there would have been no way for him to mistake the 10,000-unit vials for the 10-unit vials."

"You're right, but it's not as though a computer system can't have glitches. Name one system that doesn't fail from time to time. We just started it up last week and we're still working out the kinks. When it wouldn't scan for me, that's what I assumed — it was a kink. And maybe Alejandro figured the same as me," Cappelli responded, defending both himself and the young technician.

Marsh had reached her limit. "Albert, the point of the system — when used as designed and as the staff was trained to do — is to prevent careless errors. If the tech had used the system — and if you had, for that matter — we wouldn't have a critically ill baby in the peds wing right now. This was human error — the tech's error, your error and for that matter, the error of the nurse who administered the heparin. None of you used the system as it was designed. And if you had, the error would have been avoided."

Cappelli was in no shape to argue. He accepted his culpability and surrendered. "You're right, Joanne. We messed up. *I* messed up. I'm so very sorry." He turned to leave, shaking his head. Then, as though he'd forgotten something, he turned back and took Sarah's hand in both of his.

"Good-bye, Ms. Abadhi," he said before bowing his head to his supervisor and heading for the exit.

NINE

Alejandro Avila was scheduled to work that day from 3:30 to midnight. Sarah knew Joanne Marsh wanted to hit Avila with both barrels as soon as he walked through the door, but Sarah needed to talk to him before he realized he was in trouble. She told Marsh to hold her fire until the pharmacy tech had a chance to tell his side of the story. Marsh agreed, as long as she could be in the room when that story was told. Sarah acceded to her condition, provided that Marsh remain mum during the interview. They arranged for the pharmacy tech to be sent up to risk management when he arrived.

Sarah answered the knock on the conference room door at 3:35 to find a skinny kid with curly black hair blinking furiously and biting his lip. He reminded her of the high school boy who mowed her parents' lawn. It was hard to fathom that this young man was the pharmacy tech whose actions had caused so much harm. Sarah showed him in and directed him to a seat at the table. She introduced herself and Doris. In keeping with their negotiated deal, Marsh said nothing. As he sat down, the young technician said, "Hello, Mrs. Marsh," without making eye contact.

Before Sarah could give her standard introduction, Alejandro jumped the gun. "Am I in trouble? Did I do something wrong?" he asked anxiously.

"Alejandro — is it okay if I call you Alejandro?" Sarah asked.

"Sure, sure."

"Alejandro, we're investigating a medication error. We would very much appreciate it if you could help us out."

"Sure, I'll help any way I can."

"Good. Do you remember the scripts for baby Ariel Arkin that were filled yesterday?" Sarah asked.

"No. I can't say I do. Sorry."

"Maybe I can help jog your memory. You delivered them in person to the pediatric wing late yesterday afternoon."

"Oh, yeah. Now I remember. Albert — Mr. Cappelli, I mean — said they needed them in a hurry and to hightail it to the nurses' station on Four."

"Do you remember anything else about those scripts?"

"Just that Albert — Mr. Cappelli — said there was a glitch in the computer system, so he had to hand label one of them," the boy explained. At that point Marsh let out an audible sigh, and Sarah gave her a warning look.

"Yeah, I ran up the stairs two at a time. When I got to peds, I handed the meds off to a blond nurse at the nurses' station. I told her one was hand labeled because the computer system wasn't cooperating. She thanked me and I was back in the pharmacy in no time flat."

Sarah could see the boy start to relax as he told the story of how he'd followed his orders to the letter. She was reluctant to question the obviously well-intentioned tech about his method of stocking the shelves, but she knew that if she didn't get to it quickly, Marsh's fuse would likely blow.

"Alejandro, did you restock any medications yesterday?" Sarah inquired, with as much nonchalance as she could muster.

"When I came in at 3:30 yesterday, things were a little slow, so I asked Albert if I could get some of the inventory onto the shelves. He said, 'Sure,' so I did some restocking until things started to pick up."

"Do you recall putting some heparin on the shelves?"

"Yeah, I sure do. It was the last thing I restocked."

"And can you tell me how you restocked it, that is, what dosage it was and where you put it?"

"Definitely. It was a box of heparin, 10 units. I knew it was 10 units because that dose has a blue label. I learned that at my first pharmacy job back in my neighborhood."

"And do you recall on what unit you shelved the heparin?"

"I checked the stocking guide. I don't remember the exact number of the unit but I know it was near the front. Let me see," he said thinking, "maybe on the third shelf. I'm trying to remember. Yeah, one of the units in the teens, like seventeen, eighteen, something like that."

Sarah could see Marsh's impatience grow. She had better ask the critical question. "When you restocked the heparin, what procedure did you follow?"

"Procedure? Oh, you mean the BCMA procedure?"

"Yes, the BCMA procedure."

"Well, that's the thing. For everything that I stocked yesterday, I followed the BCMA procedure just like I was taught and it worked perfectly. I scanned the bar code on the box and then scanned the bar code on the shelf label and everything went great. But when I scanned the bar codes for heparin 10, it wouldn't work. I was trying to figure out why when it got real busy in the pharmacy all of a sudden. It goes like that — quiet, quiet, quiet, then all of a sudden all hell breaks loose."

"So when it wouldn't scan, what did you do?" Sarah asked.

"Well, I left the box on the shelf and took care of an order for Mrs. Pollack. She was one of the other pharmacists on duty yesterday."

"Did you inform anyone of the problem with the scanning of the heparin?"

"No. I mean, I meant to, but as I said, we got really busy and we stayed busy until my shift ended at midnight. I didn't even take a dinner break." Looking at Marsh and then Sarah, he added in an almost plaintive voice, "I guess I forgot all about it. I'm really sorry."

At this point Marsh broke in. "Mr. Avila. What did you learn in the training session about meds that wouldn't scan?"

"Well, they said that if it wouldn't scan it was probably because something was wrong."

"Did you consider that perhaps you were making a mistake when the scanner wouldn't accept the box of heparin on the shelf for 10 units?"

"Well, not really, since the blue label is heparin 10. I'm sure of it. And all week I've been hearing other people in the pharmacy say they were having trouble making the BCMA system work for them, so I figured that was the reason it wouldn't scan," Alejandro explained. It was evident that the logic of his thinking gave him some hope that he was not in trouble with his new boss.

Marsh was outraged. "Mr. Avila. Today we discovered the reason that the box of heparin wouldn't scan." With contempt dripping from each word she added, "And it had nothing to do with a BCMA system failure. The box you left on the heparin 10 shelf contained vials of 10,000 units of heparin."

"It did?" the young man asked incredulously. "No way," he protested. "Heparin 10 has a blue label. Blue is 10 units. It is." He was almost pleading with Marsh.

Sarah jumped in. "Unfortunately, Alejandro, the label of heparin 10,000 is nearly an identical blue. The reason the heparin wouldn't scan was that you stocked 10,000 rather than 10 units on the shelf."

A scapegoat had to be found, and at the end of the interview, Alejandro Avila, the eager-to-please young pharmacy technician — a probationary, at-will employee — was told by the head pharmacist to clear out his locker and hand in his security tag. For good measure, she added that if he even thought of using her or the hospital as a reference, she would make sure he was never hired by any pharmacy in the tri-state area. For the final blow, when Avila opened the conference room door to leave, there was a security guard present to escort him out of the hospital. After he left, Joanne Marsh headed straight for John Mess's office. Sarah guessed she was on a mission to mount an offensive, laying all the blame at the feet of Avila, and absolving the system she touted as foolproof, even in the hands of a wet-behind-the-ears pharmacy technician.

TEN

Sarah and Doris needed a break after the Avila interview. The two women were a study in contrasts as they made their way to the "two holer" down the hall. Sarah, tall, tailored and serious, matched her short, matronly and agreeable colleague step for step.

After coming out of the stalls, they stood side by side washing their hands. It was Doris who brought up Alejandro Avila.

"I know, Sarah. He made a terrible mistake, but I feel sorry for that young man."

Looking at herself and Doris in the mirror, Sarah nodded as she dried her hands and pushed a lock of her dark, curly hair from her face. "He seemed like a well-meaning guy, but he set in motion a terrible chain of events."

"True enough, but it was an honest mistake. His only real error was not asking for help when the labels wouldn't scan. But even then, he explained how they got so busy. He probably figured he was going above and beyond by stocking the shelves when it got slow. He could have just as easily sat there playing with his phone until things picked up. You know, a lot of kids his age would have done just that. Anyway, I feel bad for him…and of course, the poor little baby, too. It's a very sad story, any way you look at it."

"That it is," Sarah said as she and Doris simultaneously took their lipsticks from their purses and each applied a new coat. "I think that will have to do for our beautification, Doris. We'd better head back just in case that Dr. Smith is on time. I know," she smiled, making her dimples show, "it's a long shot, but we can hope, can't we? The faster he gets in, the faster you can go home."

"Frankly, I can't wait to go home. I'm gonna put my feet up, have a glass of merlot and do my best to put what I've heard today behind me."

*****

The women's hopes were realized just a few minutes later when a panting man entered the conference room and introduced himself as Rick Smith. He looked like something the cat had dragged in: unshaven, his dark hair tousled, his blue jeans and Columbia sweatshirt having seen better days. If he had the look of someone who had just rolled out of bed, it was because that's exactly what he had done — just minutes earlier. He'd run all the way to the hospital.

"Would you like some coffee, Dr. Smith?" Sarah asked.

"No thanks," he said, begging off. "I'm hoping to go back to sleep after we're done here." Seeing the quizzical look on the lawyer's face, he added with some impatience, "Look, I was on from noon yesterday until after eight o'clock this morning. I'm behind on my sleep and this interview isn't helping."

"I am very sorry we had to call you in today," Sarah responded. "I'll be as quick as I can so you can get your much-deserved rest." She started the digital recorder and made her standard opening. "The hospital is investigating the medication error that occurred yesterday in the case of the infant Ariel Arkin."

"Damn well better investigate it. Someone nearly killed that baby," the doctor said.

Sarah was taken aback by his blunt, albeit correct, assessment of the situation. "The hospital is eager to find out how the error occurred, as I'm sure you are, Dr. Smith."

"It's obvious how it occurred. Someone from the pharmacy screwed up. They sent heparin with a thousand times the potency I ordered."

"Yes, that seems clear, but I'm investigating the circumstances that allowed that error to be made, particularly given the fact that the BCMA system is in operation."

"Yeah, so much for that. We've been hearing for months how the BCMA was going to make medication errors a thing of the past. Guess that particular emperor has no clothes."

Sarah was eager to hear more. "How so, Dr. Smith?"

"Isn't it obvious? Even with all the scanners in place, the infant nearly bled to death from an enormous overdose."

"Do you have an idea as to how that could have happened?" Sarah was particularly interested to hear his answer since he had played no role in the overdose and had no reason to try to cover his rear.

The pediatric fellow sat slumped in the armchair, his head resting on his hand. He was either very relaxed or dead tired. "How did it happen?" he asked incredulously, suddenly coming to life. "Someone wasn't doing their job, that's how. The manufacturer clearly labeled the vial "10,000 units." Hard to miss all those zeroes — even without a scanner," he said impatiently.

"Apparently the labels for the 10- and the 10,000-unit vials of heparin are nearly an identical shade of blue. It appears that contributed to the mix-up," Sarah explained.

"What, people can't read now? We go by colors? What is this, preschool?"

Sarah was impressed by his forceful condemnation of those responsible for the overdose. She was still looking for the part of him that engendered fondness in the people who worked with him. Perhaps his high expectations for patient care were part of his appeal. And, truth be told, he'd likely clean up nicely. Little doubt about that, Sarah thought, before getting back to the business at hand.

"I can understand your intolerance for this type of error. But it appears there were circumstances that contributed to people making the mistake. One factor appears to be that the hospital was short staffed because of the flu going around. The newness of the BCMA may also be a factor."

"Look, I have some sympathy for the nurses — and all the

floor staff, for that matter. People are being asked to work back-to-back shifts and they're exhausted. And it's not just because of the flu that's going around. Understaffing is a constant problem here. As far as bedside care goes, the administrators are trying to run this place on the cheap. As for the computer system, which I'm sure cost the hospital a bundle, trouble-free it's not. It rejected scripts from me without reason several times this past week. I know a lot of people have found it to be a thorn in their side.

"That being said," Dr. Smith continued, "do you have any idea what happened to that little baby yesterday? It was disastrous. There's no other word for it. I spent an entire night trying to undo the horror caused by simple carelessness. That baby did not have to suffer this trauma. She *shouldn't* have suffered this trauma. So if you think I have, what did you call it, an 'intolerance' for the error, you're goddamned straight I do. I am intolerant of an error that could inflict so much harm on a helpless infant."

Doris coughed. Maybe she had a tickle in her throat, but Sarah took it as a signal that she was impressed by the rumpled doctor's passionate advocacy for his patient. Sarah couldn't take her eyes off him. His unvarnished appraisal was both helpful and refreshing. Maybe that's what people enjoyed about him. There was no bull from Dr. Smith.

"I appreciate your assessment of the conditions that may have contributed to the baby being harmed. I am certain this will be cold comfort, but many of the people with whom I've spoken today are stricken with a deep sense of remorse. No one wanted this terrible error to happen."

"Well, I know Joyce Hilker is a wreck about this. She's a great nurse; don't get me wrong. She trusted the pharmacy's label on the heparin. And she should have been able to trust it. If the pharmacy had done its job correctly, she would never have administered a near-lethal dose of heparin to her patient. But as it stands, she's got to live with the knowledge that she nearly killed a baby."

Sarah thought this would be a good time to get Dr. Smith's take on the rollout of the system lauded by Joanne Marsh. "To what degree, Doctor, would you say the staff believes in the efficacy of the BCMA system?"

"You want the truth?"

"I do."

"So far, I'd say the BCMA has been more trouble than help. If the company who sold the system had flooded the hospital with their own people to debug it as we rolled it out, maybe we would have had a better first week. But that didn't happen. I know that I overrode it when it rejected perfectly appropriate scripts. I can't speak for the others, but I wouldn't be surprised if they did the same."

Bingo. The system had problems. Help was scarce. Maybe most importantly, people hadn't bought into the BCMA. Hence, Alejandro Avila's reluctance to believe the scanner's error message and Albert Cappelli's override of the system with his handwritten label. Joyce Hilker had followed suit, chalking up the failure to scan as a system failure. Sarah would guess Dr. Smith, Avila, Cappelli and Hilker were not alone in responding to the "foolproof" system by blowing it off. In this particular case, however, had everyone involved not overridden the BCMA, Ariel Arkin would likely be healing nicely from the staph infection that brought her to the ER, and the pediatric fellow sitting next to Sarah would be enjoying his day off.

Sarah could see the guy was beat, but there were still some bases to cover. In the event the baby didn't survive, there would be a further investigation into how the staff had responded to the error. So she asked the pediatric intensivist to describe his efforts to stabilize the baby. She knew she could get much of what he had to say from the baby's chart, but she figured she couldn't be too careful. Dr. Smith complied in painstaking detail. When he was done explaining how he had labored through the night to save the child, she shook his hand and thanked him for his help in the investigation.

For Rick Smith's part, he hightailed it back to his apartment and the lure of at least another couple of hours of shuteye. As he left the interview, he toyed with the idea of checking on Ariel Arkin, but he knew that if he went up on the floor, he'd get sucked in for hours. Instead, he jogged home and thought about that good-looking attorney. She was a little uptight, but a beautiful woman. No doubt about that. Once in his apartment, he quickly pulled off his sweatshirt and jeans and got back into bed. He thought about how he wouldn't object to spending a little time alone with that lawyer — and then he was out like a light.

*****

After Doris headed home, Sarah gave John Mess and Julie Bonner a verbal summary of her findings. She emphasized that it was more complicated than just the careless error of a novice pharmacy tech — the story Joanne Marsh had tried to sell earlier to Mess. Sarah told them they would have her written report in the morning. They were both happy — no, ecstatic — to share news on the baby's condition. Her vitals were strong and her infection retreating. She was responding to stimuli appropriately for her age.

After a day filled with graphic accounts of so ghastly an event, Sarah was relieved to know there was reason to hope that little Ariel Arkin might recover.

ELEVEN

Sarah worked until the wee hours of the morning on her report. It shouldn't have made any difference that the injured baby had a powerful father, but knowing the big guns Mark Arkin could aim at the hospital did, in fact, make her even more meticulous than usual. She paid particular attention to writing up her highly strategic — some might say daring — recommendations. She planned to share her work with Harry in the morning. If, after hearing her out, he didn't think she'd lost her mind, they would go to the hospital together to deliver her report to John Mess and Julie Bonner.

She knew she was sticking her neck out on this one. Until now she'd been the ideal protégée on every project, doing what Harry would have done had he had the time or inclination. She read him like a fortune teller reading a palm and often knew his preferences without him offering a hint of direction. That was why he'd plucked her out of the pool of associates and made it his business to groom her for partner.

But this time was different. Her recommendations were based on what she thought was right for all involved, but she knew they might incite an infamous Meinig tantrum. She was willing to chance it, though. If she could persuade Harry to her way of thinking, she had a feeling they could neutralize the "cluster fuck" and actually do some good at the same time.

Another morning without time for a swim or a run. Sarah was in the office by seven, putting the finishing touches on her report. She handed it over to Harry for his review just before eight. He muttered to himself as he read her findings about how Alejandro Avila's initial error had not been caught — and why. The report was as much an indictment of the hospital's staffing policies and half-baked implementation of the BCMA system as it was of Avila, Albert Cappelli and Joyce Hilker, at least one of whom, under different circumstances, might have caught the error. Leaving nothing out, Sarah slammed the pharmaceutical maker for marking such vastly different doses of heparin with a nearly identically colored label.

When Harry turned to the last page of her report — her recommendations — she held her breath. He kept reading, gesticulating with his hands, raising his eyebrows and muttering to himself. She had prepared herself for an explosion, but all Harry said when he was done was, "Are you sure about this, Sarah?"

"Yes, I am. I think this is the best way to go."

"Well, it's a risk. But I've heard about some other cases that were handled this way with good results. I'll back you up on this, Sarah, but don't fuck up. Do me proud."

She couldn't believe what she was hearing. Harry trusted her risky strategy — trusted her. "I promise you, Harry. I won't screw this up."

Within the hour Sarah was handing out copies of her report to Julie Bonner and John Mess. They sat riveted as she described the confluence of factors that had led to the baby's overdose. In terms of the BCMA, she was emphatic that there had been insufficient training and buy-in of the staff, from lowly pharmacy technicians to physicians. The failure to offer onsite tech support from the developer during the critical first weeks of implementation had also contributed to the dosing error. Taken together, those factors had greatly diminished the BCMA's power to prevent medication errors. Sarah minced no words on the role played by staffing shortages. With fatigue being a well-documented cause of performance failures, having tired nurses doing back-to-back shifts was nothing short of playing with fire.

Mess and Bonner took it all in, but said nothing in response. Finally, Sarah came to her recommendations. She took a deep breath and laid them out: Admit fault to the parents; tell them everything that went wrong and why. Offer a sincere apology. Then stipulate in detail what measures the hospital would immediately take to make certain this type of error would not happen again. Finally, make a fair offer of payment for pain and suffering, and a promise to pay for any therapies or remediation the child might need as a result of the medical trauma. Sarah knew that giving these parents money was like giving oil to Saudi Arabia. But it was a necessary gesture of contrition and a required part of the mea culpa approach she was recommending.

Mess could hardly contain himself. "You're kidding, right? Harry, you don't buy into this suicidal advice, do you?"

"Actually, John, I think Sarah's pegged it just about right. Mark Arkin can sully the good name of this hospital in every media outlet from coast to coast and let loose his vengeance via a jury trial. Hell, he can make it his business to bankrupt the hospital. We've certainly given him cause to want to see it brought to its knees. I've seen him when he's out for revenge and it's not something I'd recommend the hospital tangle with — not if there's any way to avoid it. With Sarah's approach, we come clean about the weaknesses in the system, promise reform — we'll have to demonstrate its implementation, of course — and then make a monetary settlement offer. I think it might work."

"And if it doesn't?" Bonner asked with more than a hint of incredulity in her voice. "If Arkin doesn't accept our 'apology' he can take what we've given him and blow us away in the press and in court — and we will have handed him the ammunition with which to do it."

Harry stood firm. "What I'm saying is, he can blow us away, regardless. A two-week-old infant nearly bled to death because of a chain of errors made by hospital staff. Sure, we can pin some of the blame on the pharmaceutical company for labeling two doses of heparin nearly identically. But the lion's share of fault lies with the hospital."

Sarah was emboldened by Harry's support. "Look, everyone I met with yesterday was a good person — well meaning, competent and heartsick about what happened. The baby apparently is making a good recovery, due to the efforts of the medical staff. We need to emphasize that very point. We have a staff that is capable of doing world-class work. But we put them at a disadvantage because of the conditions I outlined in the report. When those conditions are corrected, this type of error — everyone's worst nightmare — will not happen to another infant."

Mess turned to Bonner. "You know as well as I do that most people who sue say they're trying to prevent another person from suffering the loss or injury they did. They say that the money is just a way of teaching the doctors and the hospital a lesson so they won't make the same mistake again. If we can show Arkin and his wife that they needn't sue us to get that outcome, that we get what went wrong and are committed to correcting the weak links in our quality control system, they might just buy it."

Bonner didn't respond right away. Finally, she said, "I'm not saying it couldn't work. The fact that the baby continues to do well, remarkably well, really — I checked with the attending this morning — is a definite plus. And I guess we could document how much this plan for remediation would cost. It'll be a bundle; you and I both know that, John. Each new nurse runs a minimum of seventy-five thousand with benefits. And getting onsite tech support from the BCMA manufacturer is extremely expensive. That's why the hospital passed on it to begin with. We've got to take this to Phil before we can agree to anything."

Sarah guessed Phil to be Philip Kerrey, hospital CEO. Of course, he would have to be consulted before they went into negotiations with the likes of Mark Arkin. But she felt she had to add a final recommendation before they wrapped things up. "It's my feeling that the sooner the hospital stands up and takes responsibility for what happened, the more likely it is that the parents will be receptive to the hospital's offer — particularly if the baby continues to improve. I think timing will be everything in this case."

"Well, Phil is out of the building this morning. I'll get back to you this afternoon," Mess said.

"Good, John," Harry said. "I'd like to reiterate that I think Sarah has shown us the right path out of this mess." Realizing instantly that he'd stepped on the risk manager's surname, he quickly apologized. "Sorry, John. I don't know what I was thinking."

"Oh, forget it. I get it all the time. Half the time I think my name is what got me into the business of risk management: John Mess — manager of all manner of messes. Maybe they'll put that on my tombstone when I'm gone."

TWELVE

Mark Arkin would have given half his fortune to have been spared the events of the prior forty-eight hours. He hadn't been so powerless since he had been a child in Brooklyn, living under the reign of his mother. Trapped in passive misery, he'd had to watch the staff try to undo the unspeakable harm their co-workers had caused his baby. Most wrenching was listening to Catherine berate herself for infecting Ariel with MRSA. He remembered watching a news story about observant Muslim men who flogged themselves until the blood streamed down their backs in rivulets. He had thought them mad at the time, but what Catherine had done to herself since finding out she was a MRSA carrier was worse than self-flagellation. If Ariel didn't make it, he worried she might lose her mind. There was only one way the endless loop of self-recrimination would stop, and that was for Ariel to get well.

The truth was, Mark wasn't beyond blaming himself, either, compliments of his newfound conscience. Though part of him thought it nuts, a little voice kept telling him this was what he got for walking away from Linda and their kids. But if a stiff-necked god was exacting a steep price, it was Catherine and Ariel who were bearing the cost. His special form of anguish was watching them endure agonies his imagination could never have conjured up.

If there was anything that gave him reason to hope, it was that Dr. Smith. He had seemed like a son of a bitch at first, but it had soon become clear that he knew what the hell he was doing. Catherine had it right when she said he was their only hope. Dr. Smith had worked on Ariel that whole first night, making sure to give them continual updates on her condition. He had gotten the bleeding stopped. He had gotten her vitals stabilized. And before he had dragged himself home yesterday morning, he told them he was "guardedly optimistic" that she would make it. Although Mark's first reaction had been to transfer Ariel out of the hospital that nearly killed her, it was Dr. Smith's single-minded efforts that had made him change his mind.

Dr. Smith was back on Ariel's case today and his presence gave Mark some sense of security. That Dr. Cho was good, too, and Ariel had remained stable yesterday when she was in charge. But there was something about Dr. Richard Smith that Mark could lock onto. Dr. Smith might very well be a son of a bitch, but he worked like a dog to win — even when the odds were against him. That was something Mark understood. He was surprised that someone with that kind of drive had become a goddamned pediatrician, of all things. No doubt about it, they'd caught a lucky break with Dr. Smith.

Of course, Catherine had been treated as well. He had to admit that the staff had done a good job getting her MRSA under control. They had gotten her on meds right away and the infection seemed to back off within hours. And they had been gentle with her, too. Catherine had gotten the idea in her head that her milk would dry up once the baby stopped nursing, and became even more distraught. The lactation specialist had gotten her hooked up to a pump to keep her milk supply going. The image of that contraption attached to his wife's beautiful breasts gave him the creeps. But it did the job. Catherine could see she was still making plenty of milk and that reassured her. They had brought in a counselor of some kind, maybe a shrink, to talk with her. That person had ordered an Ambien so Catherine could get some sleep. Sleeping was what she was finally doing now, on the cot next to Ariel's crib. In fact, she and Ariel were both sleeping, a first since their odyssey began. He could hear their rhythmic breathing and it sounded so normal. What a relief it was to hear that steady in and out, in and out.

He dozed off in the chair himself, for how long he didn't know. He was awakened by movement in the room followed by a gurgle coming from the crib. Opening his eyes, he saw Dr. Smith hovering over Ariel. He panicked until he saw that the intern and nurse with him were smiling.

Dr. Smith turned when he heard the baby's father stir. "Oh, good afternoon, Mr. Arkin. Glad you got a chance to catch some shuteye," he said in a low voice, so as not to awaken the baby's mother. Mark was taken with the change in the doctor's body language and attitude, not only from their first meeting but from earlier in the day. Was it possible that he was cheerful? The doctor turned back to the baby and gave an order for something Mark didn't catch. Then the intern and the nurse turned and left the room.

"So how's she doing now, Dr. Smith?" Mark asked.

"Well, I'm actually quite pleased with what I see. You have a little fighter here. She's responding well to her treatment. Her white count is way down, which means the infection is coming under control. Her red blood count is good. Come and take a look. Your little girl is feeling a whole lot better."

Mark could hardly believe the effect those words had on him. His eyes started to burn as he got up from the chair. When he looked in the crib, he saw Ariel tracking the doctor's finger with her eyes, alert and — well, for lack of a better word — happy. She looked at him and held his stare for several seconds. Then she looked at the doctor, kicking her legs and moving her arms. Mark pulled out his handkerchief and wiped his face.

As Ariel grabbed the doctor's index finger, he shared more good news with Mark. "I don't want to wake your wife — believe me, I know how much she needs this rest — but I think that perhaps in a day or two she'll be able to start nursing Ariel again. Let her know when she wakes up. I think she and Ariel will be much happier when they can get back to doing what comes naturally."

Mark could have given him a bear hug. Instead, he grabbed the doctor's hand and gave it a vigorous shake. He dared to wonder if it was possible that the whole nightmare was drawing down. Of all the great wins in his life, nothing could match a good end to this ordeal. He couldn't wait until Catherine woke up so he could tell her the news. He gave a silent thank you to the god he had only recently dismissed as stiff-necked and vengeful. Guilt, helplessness and anguish were joined by yet another new feeling rising up within him: gratitude.

THIRTEEN

Over a lunch of kosher deli, Sarah and Harry hashed out how the apology would be orchestrated if the hospital CEO gave the go-ahead. Sarah argued for having the baby's doctors — and perhaps one of her nurses — apologize to the parents for the hospital's error. The mea culpa would have far more credibility coming from them than from hospital administrators or lawyers. She had a twinge of conscience about roping the heroes in the gruesome tale into admitting so egregious an error, but she knew they were the hospital's best hope.

By mid-afternoon, John Mess called with the okay to proceed. While they were on the phone, Harry strongly recommended that action be taken quickly — before the end of the day, or the following morning at the latest. He also advised that the admission of error come from the medical staff treating the baby. Mess agreed to both. Though he would attend the meeting with the parents, he knew they'd see him as nothing more than a hospital suit. It wouldn't be the first time, nor the last.

Harry and Sarah were back at the hospital half an hour before charge nurse Jeannie Lopez and Drs. Smith and Cho were scheduled to show up for a meeting in Mess's office. As they arrived, Sarah exchanged pleasantries with them until Mess called the meeting to order. After introducing Harry, he emphasized the requirement of confidentiality regarding what was to follow. Then he turned the meeting over to Sarah.

Sarah did a reprise of the report she had made to Mess and Bonner earlier that morning. The doctors and nurse cringed when they heard the string of errors that had led to the baby's overdose, but their responses to Sarah's conclusions and recommendations differed. Lopez became defensive when back-to-back nursing shifts were listed as a factor contributing to the medication error. Dr. Cho was annoyed that she had been taken away from her work to listen to a litany of errors and their aftermath. And Dr. Smith scratched his head in disbelief.

"You're really going to admit fault?" he asked Mess.

"Yes, we feel it's the right thing to do."

"Well, I have to say that I find that refreshing," the doctor said, making no effort to mask his sarcasm. "I applaud your decision to do the right thing."

Mess ignored the pediatric fellow's tone and continued with his mission. "Thank you for your support. But here's the thing, Dr. Smith. We want the three of you to meet with the parents and deliver the following message: first, the admission of our errors. Second, that the hospital takes full responsibility for those errors. Finally, that we propose a rigorous plan of reform to make certain this type of error never again happens to any child in our care."

Lopez looked as though someone had just ordered her to walk the plank. But before she had a chance to protest, the attending doctor got to her feet.

"Oh, no. No, no, no, no, no. You're not going to dump this on us," Dr. Cho railed, her face contorting in indignation. "How did we get selected to do the hospital's dirty work?"

Sarah was taken aback by the defiant attitude the doctors had toward Mess. She knew administrators were not doctors' favorite people, but she had underestimated the antipathy with which they viewed the risk manager. Mess was right about being seen as a hospital suit — and apparently not just by the baby's parents. It was obvious that neither doctor viewed Mess as playing for their team.

"Please sit down, Dr. Cho," Mess said.

"I'd rather stand, thank you," she snapped.

"Suit yourself. I don't characterize what we're asking you to do as 'dirty work.' It's certainly most regrettable that the error happened. However, that error has uncovered critical weaknesses in our quality control system. We aim to develop a plan that will address those weaknesses and improve the hospital's functioning. The three of you are indispensable to making that happen. Since you've been working with the baby and the parents for the last two days — and doing exemplary work, I might add — the parents will be most receptive to a hospital apology coming from you."

"Look," Dr. Smith interrupted, "you don't have to butter me up with how exemplary my work is, John. It's all right to call you John, isn't it?

"Of course," Mess replied, annoyed by the unwelcome familiarity.

Dr. Smith continued, "I'll do it. I'll make the apology for the hospital even if Jeannie and Esther would rather not." Then, turning to his colleagues, he said, "Look, I don't blame you for not wanting to participate. But for me, personally, I like when the administration of the hospital steps up to the plate. After all, it's a rare occurrence that should be encouraged. The hospital screwed up big time and now it's 'fessing up. For once, the powers that be are taking the high road. Me, I'm all for it."

Addressing Mess and the attorneys now, he reiterated, "I'm serious. I'll tell the parents myself if Esther and Jeannie would rather beg off."

Mess smiled and nodded. "That's very kind of you, Dr. Smith, but I think that the presence of the attending and the charge nurse that have been caring for the baby will increase the credibility of the apology and the promise for improvement. I, of course, will be there as well, but I'm certain the parents are far more interested in hearing from you." There was more than a hint of impatience in his voice.

"So in other words, you aren't asking us if we'll do it. You're telling us we have to," Dr. Cho concluded as she bit the inside of her cheek.

"Well, that's true, Dr. Cho. However, the hospital administration greatly appreciates your part in remediating this very troubling situation. I promise you, your efforts on behalf of the hospital will not go unnoticed."

Sarah felt as though she was watching her strategy unravel. If Dr. Cho made the apology to the parents while gnashing her teeth, she'd likely torpedo the plan, even if Dr. Smith played his role to perfection. She had to intervene. "May I, John?"

"Why yes, Sarah, feel free."

"Dr. Cho, a ghastly error occurred that nearly took the life of a tiny infant. Now there are two possible outcomes for the hospital. Both involve money — lots and lots of money. Given the fact that the baby's father is extremely powerful and influential, here's one outcome: The parents go to the media and ruin the hospital's good name and reputation from coast to coast. They institute a suit that will likely take many years to resolve, using the best lawyers money can buy. The hospital will defend itself, both in the media and in the courts, spending millions. Some will go to enriching my firm, some to filling the coffers of the hospital's PR firm. In the years leading up to the trial, you and everyone involved in the case will be called to law offices to give sworn depositions, perhaps numerous times. Then you'll be called to testify at trial. It will be highly unlikely that we will win a case such as this. Our best hope will be to minimize the damages for pain and suffering. These damages — probably in the many millions of dollars — will go to the child of one of the wealthiest men in New York.

"Here's the other outcome — also extremely expensive. The hospital acknowledges its error, using the only people the Arkins trust to make its heartfelt apology — that would be you. The parents agree to entertain a proposal for remediation in lieu of filing suit against the hospital. Within the week, the heads of nursing and pharmacy, the designer of the BCMA system, Mr. Mess, Mr. Meinig and I present the parents with a detailed plan for improving the staffing of nurses and the implementation of the computerized medication administration system. We include contingencies for staff illness, such as when the recent flu decimated the nursing ranks. We offer a reasonable amount to the child for her ordeal and for any therapies that she may need in the event that she has suffered permanent damage. We include guarantees that the improvement plan will be implemented, with oversight by a neutral third party mutually acceptable to the parents and the hospital.

"Both outcomes are costly, but I think you would have to agree, Dr. Cho, that the second one will actually do the hospital, its staff and its patients some good. I wish the error had never occurred. I wish we could avoid a legal and PR disaster without your help. Believe me, I would rather all of you were on the floor now working with your patients. But the facts are what they are. You three alone have the credibility needed to persuade the parents of our earnest desire to make things right."

When Sarah finished laying out her argument, no one spoke. She hoped her two scenarios had persuaded Lopez, who had said nothing so far. But Dr. Cho was the nut she had to crack. Even if Cho wasn't won over by the argument, Sarah hoped the idea of depositions and testimony at trial had made an impression on the doctor who had neither the time nor the patience for meeting with lawyers.

It was Lopez who broke the silence. "Point taken, Ms. Abadhi. I'll do it. If the hospital has to fork over millions to defend itself, that's millions the hospital won't have to actually improve staffing, training and patient care. We certainly could use that money. And I have to say that giving this family millions of dollars bothers me, even though the baby did suffer a terrible trauma."

Now all eyes turned to Dr. Cho. She had stood with her arms crossed throughout Sarah's monologue but something seemed to soften in her body language. "The second alternative is clearly preferable," she said. "I think I'm beginning to appreciate the role I can play in making that happen."

After everyone else left, Dr. Smith stayed behind. Having volunteered to take the lead in the meeting with the Arkins — referring to his role as "apologizer-in-chief" — he needed to study Sarah's conclusions and recommendations. As he read over the report, his appreciation of the attorney's way of thinking grew. He would have no problem delivering her report to the parents the following morning.

Catherine Malloy-Arkin was overjoyed to be given the go-ahead to start nursing her daughter again. When Jeannie Lopez entered the baby's room the morning after her meeting with the hospital attorneys, she saw the father sitting on the armrest of the recliner, gazing lovingly at his wife and baby. Ariel was suckling heartily at her mother's breast, as though making up for lost time. The parents seemed transfixed by their infant. It was a tableau Lopez hated to disturb.

Though her heart was pounding in her chest, the charge nurse did her best to appear calm as she told the Arkins that the doctors wanted to speak with them in a nearby consultation room. Both mother and father leapt to the same conclusion: They had discovered something else wrong with their child. Jeannie took pains to reassure them that the baby — who at that very moment had fallen asleep after taking her fill of her mother's milk — continued to do well. When questioned by the father about the reason for the meeting, she demurred, saying the doctors would meet them in just a few minutes.

The consultation room was a small, windowless affair outfitted with soft lighting, a round table and chairs, a box of tissues and a telephone. All the participants arrived within moments of one another. As soon as they sat down at the table, Mark Arkin cut to the chase. "What's this all about?"

Dr. Smith was ready.

"Mr. and Mrs. Arkin. You know Dr. Cho and Ms. Lopez. This is John Mess, who also works for the hospital. We've asked you to meet with us for two reasons. The primary one is to offer you the hospital's heartfelt apology for your family's ordeal. This has been a terrible time for you. Every person who's worked on this case is remorseful about the mistakes made by our staff that led to Ariel's overdose. We all chose medicine because we want to help, not harm, our patients. So, speaking for myself and my colleagues, we are so very sorry this ever happened."

Mark sat stone-faced at the table. But Catherine's reaction was as swift as it was furious. "The monsters who nearly killed my daughter are sorry, are they? Sorry doesn't cut it, Dr. Smith. You saw her. You saw what happened to my child because of their mistakes," she said, pounding her fist on the table. "Damn them. They can burn in hell as far as I'm concerned."

Mark put his arm around Catherine, but said nothing in response to the doctor's apology. He wondered why the hospital would have him admit to so serious a mistake. He kept his face expressionless and his thoughts to himself.

"If it's any consolation, Mrs. Arkin, I share your rage," Dr. Smith said. "The mistake should never have happened, and yet it did. I believe you both have the right to know how. That's the second reason for this meeting. I'd like to tell you what happened and what the hospital is proposing to do to prevent the error from happening again. May I?"

Catherine looked at her husband and nodded her agreement. Thus began Dr. Smith's full exposé of the staffing shortages and errors that had led to the overdose of their baby. Though it was excruciating to hear how small errors — so avoidable and unintentional — had led to their calamity, both Catherine and Mark sat in awe as Dr. Smith laid it all bare: the days-old implementation of the BCMA system, the novice pharmacy tech's error, the failure of the veteran pharmacist and the crackerjack nurse to catch his mistake.

When Dr. Smith was done, Lopez made her apology for the over-scheduling of the baby's nurse, saying she was hopeful the plan for remediation would address the hospital's nursing shortage. Finally, Dr. Cho weighed in, saying that she had every reason to hope that Ariel's ordeal would not be in vain — that the hospital was committed to learning from the terrible mistake and to correcting problems the investigation had uncovered.

When Dr. Smith, Lopez and Dr. Cho were finished, Mess, who until that point had said nothing, entered the conversation. "I'm here representing the hospital to let you know that it is our intention to do everything in our power to make certain that what happened to Ariel never happens to another patient in our care."

"You're here to head off a lawsuit," Mark shot back.

Mess continued, unfazed. "Of course you're free to pursue whatever course of action you choose in response to our error. I ask only that you give us the opportunity — perhaps next week — to detail our proposal for addressing the weaknesses exposed by this terrible event."

Dr. Smith could tell Mark was ready to blow Mess off as a hospital lackey. He came to his aid. "Look, I've read the outline of a plan for fixing what went wrong here. And I wouldn't be here now unless I was convinced the hospital means business about making sure no other baby goes through what Ariel went through — that some well-meaning novice doesn't make a simple error with such awful consequences. What the hospital proposes is creating a system that will catch a novice's error before any patient is harmed."

Dr. Cho stepped in to bring the point home. "The hospital's proposal will be very costly: more nurses, better training on the new computer medication system and contingencies for staff shortages due to illness. The hospital has promised us that they intend to do whatever it takes to minimize the risk of medication errors. I'm not easily persuaded; I think my colleagues here would tell you as much. But I am persuaded that the hospital has every intention of making something good come out of Ariel's ordeal."

Catherine looked at Mark, trying to get a sense of his take on what was happening in that small room. Unable to get a read on him, she took the lead. "Mr. Mess, you mentioned that you would like an opportunity to detail your plan for improvement. I don't think we would be averse to such a meeting," she said, looking to Mark for approval. He raised one eyebrow as she added, "Of course we will be inviting our legal counsel to be in attendance."

"Naturally. Both you and the hospital ought to have legal counsel at the meeting," Mess responded matter-of-factly. "However, I want to stress that the purpose of the meeting is to share with you our explicit plan to redress our errors."

Mark had heard enough. "Sure. We'll meet with you — but after Ariel is well enough to go home. We've already spent more time away from her than I'm good with. This meeting is adjourned." He nodded to his wife, took her hand and proceeded toward the door. Then he turned back and said, "Oh, and I expect Dr. Smith here to be at that meeting. Consider it a requirement." Then he and Catherine headed back to their baby girl, who was sleeping soundly in her crib.

Ariel Arkin made the kind of speedy recovery for which the very young are famous. On Friday, when all indicators pointed to the trouncing of the staph infection, Drs. Cho and Smith sent her home with instructions to her parents to have a CBC — complete blood count — done daily for the next five days. As a courtesy, they arranged for the physician's assistant who had worked with Ariel to do the blood draws at the Arkin home. The discharge orders also indicated that the parents should not hesitate to call either doctor should any questions arise. To drive home the point, the doctors' work and home numbers were provided. An office visit with them both was arranged for the following Monday.

The moment Sarah got word that the meeting with the parents had gone as she'd hoped, she asked John Mess to assemble an ad hoc committee to hammer out the improvement plan. The directors of nursing and pharmacy were appointed, as was Albert Cappelli. His long experience as a working pharmacist and his jaundiced view of the new computer system provided a perspective Sarah felt was needed. The head designer of the BCMA system, Rob DiPerna, flew in from his Kansas City corporate headquarters. The hospital's vice president for finance and budget, Ted Ainslie, was added to provide fiscal parameters to the group. Mess was nominal leader of the committee.

Their working sessions were long and sometimes contentious. The head of nursing, Aimee Sackoff, though happy about the prospect of hiring more nurses, rankled at the idea of prohibiting mandatory overtime. She argued that even with new hires, unforeseen things were bound to happen, and her charge nurses needed the authority to assign back-to-back shifts. But Sarah had done her homework. The state legislature was poised to outlaw required overtime. She pointed out the benefit of getting in front of the law's passage, making the hospital look proactive — rather than recalcitrant — in dealing with the problem of fatigue in the nursing ranks. Given that, Sackoff got on board.

To her credit, Joanne Marsh threw herself into making the BCMA system live up to her claim of it being "nearly foolproof." Albert Cappelli's sense of having seen it all, as well as his part in the overdosing error, gave him a unique role and a stake in the whole project. When Rob DiPerna espoused the elegance of the program's design, Cappelli was there to remind him of how things really worked in a busy urban hospital pharmacy. And, as Cappelli readily admitted, elegant design meant nothing when hospital staff put more faith in their own judgment than the judgment of software designers in Kansas City.

After two twelve-hour days, the committee's work was done. Its bleary-eyed members bade Sarah good night at seven on Friday evening. As they headed off for the weekend, Sarah still had to put the committee's work-product into a package that would prove compelling to the Arkins and their legal counsel. Harry was coming up with the offer for financial compensation for Ariel's pain and suffering, as well as for compensatory damages. He was also talking with legal counsel for the heparin manufacturer about addressing their confusing labeling, which had apparently contributed to numerous overdoses throughout the country. It was Sarah's job to synthesize his work and the work of the committee for the ten o'clock meeting the following Tuesday. She had just one final thing to do before getting down to work, and that was to get together with Dr. Smith.

Though Mess had invited him to join the committee, Dr. Smith begged off, mincing no words about how ridiculous it was to put a doctor's rear end in a chair for two full days if the hospital was trying to address staffing shortages. However, he did agree to drop in on the deliberations whenever possible. Though his time was short, he was a quick study. And, like Cappelli, he provided a reality check by reminding the committee of the demands of a busy teaching hospital.

Since Mark Arkin seemed to put so much stock in his opinion, Sarah didn't want Dr. Smith coming to the Tuesday meeting unaware of the committee's final recommendations. She asked him to come to the conference room after work on Friday evening. To sweeten the deal, she offered to provide a dinner of his choice. Apparently, he was a fan of Thai food, the hotter the better. She got the name of his favorite restaurant and his order. They decided on seven-thirty for the start of their working dinner. After sitting all day, she looked forward to picking up the food herself, rather than having it delivered.

As soon as she exited the hospital, her senses reawakened. The chilly air on her face and the smell of chestnuts from a corner pushcart re-energized her. Even the blast of the cabbies' horn had a salutary effect. She toyed with the idea of extending her walk before reluctantly heading straight to the restaurant.

As she approached the conference room, dinner in hand, Sarah was surprised to find Dr. Smith waiting, texting on his phone. Then she remembered he had been on time for his interview on Monday as well. Maybe he was one of the few doctors who were habitually on time, or maybe he was just exhausted and wanted to get it over with. In either case, she was happy he was there. She was more than ready to be done with this last task of the day.

The doctor continued texting as she set out the chopsticks, napkins and containers of takeout. As she headed for the office fridge to get some soft drinks, Dr. Smith put away his phone and picked up a brown bag from under the conference table.

"Can I interest you in a beer?" he asked, holding up a bottle.

Known as a cheap drunk in college and law school, Sarah knew a beer would put her under the table. Still, she was impressed that the doctor had thought to make a contribution to their dinner. "Thanks. Very nice of you to provide drinks." Then she added, "But, I'm so tired, I think a whole beer will do me in."

"So I see you're quite the lush," he laughed. "Not to worry. I won't be offended if you don't finish. But I warn you that I'm a man who can't stand to see good beer go to waste. I'll take it off your hands whenever you're ready."

They were too hungry and exhausted to face the task at hand. Instead, they dove into their generous portions with nary a word about the committee's recommendations. They chatted about their off-duty hobbies. It soon became clear they both liked to run and to swim, she at an indoor pool on 90th and he at his alma mater, Columbia. That led to the realization that they had both attended Ivy League colleges and pressure cooker post-graduate schools. Neither had any siblings. And work took up nearly all their waking hours.

Sarah was shocked when she looked up and saw it was past nine. Rick was neither surprised nor chagrined. He was enjoying every minute of getting to know Sarah Abadhi, who wasn't the least bit chilly once she stopped focusing on work. But the clock snapped Sarah back to attention and the pleasant conversation came to an end as she went over every detail of the remediation plan with the pediatric fellow. At midnight, the night custodian asked how much longer they would be.

When it was nearing one, Sarah was satisfied they had covered all their bases and started packing up her bag. Just as the doctor was cleaning up from their dinner, he received a text message. It was Graciela, the pretty nurse on Seven West whom he'd been texting when Sarah arrived with their dinners. Her shift was over and she was headed toward his apartment.

Extending his hand to Sarah, he said, "You're one hell of a task master, and I mean that as a compliment."

Then Rick headed for the door, leftover beer in tow, hoping to beat Graciela home.

FOURTEEN

It was common knowledge at her firm that Sarah's work ethic, legal mind and enormous billables put her on the fast track to partner. She was at her desk early each morning and stayed into the wee hours with the most wired and macho of the male associates. As she approached her thirty-second birthday, her only break from work came from college friends — now scattered all across the country — her parents, Eva and Joseph and the rest of her small family. After living with a man whose betrayal scarred her more deeply than she cared to remember and dating her share of empty suits, she'd given up looking for a life partner. For Sarah, the only difference between the weekend and the workweek was that she could trade her suits and heels for sweats and sneakers.

This weekend was no exception. From the moment she awoke on Saturday, she focused on fashioning Tuesday's presentation for its intended audience. Catherine Malloy-Arkin, reputed to be intellectually quick and tough minded, wrote features for a highly regarded business magazine. Her husband's corporate strategy — leave no competitor standing — was legendary. Raised in a working-class family, the scrappy Mark Arkin had clawed his way to the top. As for the attorney who would accompany them, be it the general counsel of Arkin Worldwide or a malpractice specialist, he or she would be the Arkins' pit bull, safeguarding the family's interests. There was no doubt the small audience would be a hard sell. The stakes were enormous, and given the harm done to the helpless newborn, emotions were raw. This was Sarah's most challenging project to date, and since it was her brainchild, her career might well rise or fall on its outcome.

She took only three breaks during the weekend, spacing them out for maximum stress reduction: one long run along the river, an hour of laps at the pool and a phone conversation with her Bubbe Rivka. Rivka was her mother's mother, a Lithuanian Jew and a Holocaust survivor. At eighty-six, her frail looks were deceiving. The truth was, she had a spine of steel. She was also one of the few people who could send Sarah into fits of laughter. Widowed for years, she still lived in the same Coney Island high-rise where she'd raised her two children. Sarah rarely had time to trek out to the last stop on the subway line, but she tried to call her grandmother every weekend.

This weekend's call featured a blow-by-blow account of the latest *Oprah* show. Rivka recounted the story of a bearded transgendered man who was having a baby with his wife. Apparently, his uterus was intact and his age made him the more fertile of the pair. Rivka was fascinated by the story. She was also fascinated by Oprah, whose rags-to-riches life struck a chord with a woman whose family had emigrated to America with nothing more than two small valises of second-hand clothing.

Rivka adored her granddaughter; Sarah was named after Rivka's mother, who had been murdered by the Nazis during the war. Rivka thought Sarah was both a *shankeit* and a *mensch*, a beauty and a fine human being. Rivka was quick to add that she wasn't the least bit biased, either.

The Tuesday meeting was set to take place on neutral turf: an upscale boutique hotel just a block from the Arkins' Upper East Side brownstone. Sarah got to the hotel hours before the rest of the hospital team, which gave her time to organize the environment to her liking. She arranged the rectangular tables in the shape of a U, so all participants could easily see one another as well as the projection screen. Following the seating chart she had devised, she positioned large, two-sided name cards in front of everyone's place, including one labeled "Counsel for the Arkin Family." She set the dozen printed copies of the remediation plan behind her name card and then distributed paper and pens so they were readily available to each of the meeting's participants.

She took pains to make the room comfortable. The thermostat was set to seventy-two degrees. Sarah adjusted the vertical shades so that the sun wouldn't blind anyone as the morning progressed. She directed the hotel to offer specialty coffees, espresso and chai before the meeting got underway. She awaited a delivery of French pastries from the Meinigs' favorite patisserie. Just as she was putting the finishing touches on the room, the tray of tarts, éclairs, scones and petit fours arrived and was placed next to the hot pots of coffee and the bottles of water, juice and soft drinks.

The hospital's team — less Albert Cappelli — was told to arrive by 9:15 in order to do a final review of the presentation before the meeting got underway. Joanne Marsh, Ted Ainslie, Aimee Sackoff and John Mess arrived together by cab a few minutes early. Rob DiPerna, fresh from LaGuardia, walked in with Harry and Doris, who would be keeping the minutes of the meeting. Dr. Smith, having run from the hospital, came through the door at precisely 9:15. His parka, green scrubs and white sneakers stood in bold relief to the tailored suits and fine footwear worn by the lawyers and administrators in the room.

The team finished its final run-through in less than half an hour and the tension in the room started to rise as everyone awaited the Arkins' arrival. Mess and Ainslie together paced along the length of the room. Sarah took the opportunity to use the bathroom one last time. When the Arkins and their lawyer walked in at seven minutes past ten, Harry muttered a curse under his breath. The Arkins did not, in fact, bring Larry Heidigger, general counsel for Arkin Worldwide, a guy Harry knew to be someone he could work with. No, the Arkins were represented by Reid Baumgarten, famous for winning eye-popping medical malpractice awards. He was slicker than snot and, thanks to the handiwork of his plastic surgeon and cosmetic dentist, movie-star handsome. Plaintiffs loved him for winning them both vindication and a bundle of money for their troubles. Harry figured they were done for. There was no way Baumgarten would let millions be funneled into hospital improvements in lieu of a fat settlement for his clients.

From the get-go, Harry had thought it best to have Sarah run the meeting. Given his history with Arkin, there was no point in picking that scab. And it was Sarah who knew every last detail of the remediation plan. As people started to take their seats and the hotel waiters took everyone's beverage order, Harry leaned over and quietly whispered in Sarah's ear, "Knock 'em dead, kiddo."

Sarah raised an eyebrow and whispered back, "There's only one guy in the room I hope to knock dead." With a little grin, she got up and called the meeting to order.

Sarah had been deliberate in her seating arrangement. She'd placed the Arkins and their attorney at the base of the U shape created by three tables. To Mark Arkin's immediate right, at a table perpendicular to the one at which he was seated, was Dr. Smith. Sackoff, Marsh and DiPerna sat to Smith's right. Harry sat beside the Arkins' legal counsel and opposite Dr. Smith. Sarah, Doris, Mess and Ainslie were to Harry's left.

Thinking back on it later, Sarah didn't know how she remained so cool. She stood in the middle of the room and addressed her remarks to the Arkins, whom she'd previously seen together only in the society page of the Sunday paper. "We appreciate you taking the time to meet with us after the difficult week you've experienced," she began. "We'd like to thank both of you in advance for giving us the opportunity to explain our plan for improvement."

It was clear they were still suffering the effects of their ordeal. Mark looked haggard, showing every day of his fifty-two years. Catherine Malloy-Arkin had her blond hair pulled back in a ponytail;

she appeared tired and wan.

Like the good lawyer she was, Sarah asked a question to which — having checked with Dr. Cho — she knew the answer. "I hope Ariel is doing well?"

"She's better...so much better," Catherine said with a little smile.

"That's wonderful news," Sarah said, genuinely glad for the child's recovery.

"Yes, it is. But I want to make it clear at the outset that I don't want to be away from Ariel for long. Can this meeting be wrapped up in an hour?" Catherine asked, tapping her fingers on the table.

Sarah scanned her fellow committee members and Harry for agreement before responding. "Of course. We understand how anxious you are to get back to Ariel. We'll complete our presentation within your preferred time frame. To make things more efficient, I suggest that you hold your questions until you hear the entirety of our proposed improvement plan. There are paper and pens available if something comes to mind during the presentation."

The Arkins and Baumgarten nodded their silent assent.

"First, on behalf of the hospital, I would like to say how sorry everyone is that your baby girl was subjected to a terrible error at the hands of our staff. I personally interviewed everyone involved in your daughter's care. Each staff member expressed profound regret knowing that Ariel suffered because of our mistake. I want to assure you that this error has had, and continues to have, both personal and institutional ramifications.

"From the institutional perspective, I'd like to emphasize that the intent of the hospital is to leave no stone unturned in its effort to prevent another child from going through what Ariel went through. Its goal is nothing short of the elimination of medication errors. To that end, it assembled this team to create the remediation plan we are about to present. I'd like to introduce the team: Dr. Richard Smith, fellow in pediatric intensive medicine; Aimee Sackoff, director of nursing;

Joanne Marsh, director of pharmacy; Rob DiPerna, chief of the design team for Accumeds, the hospital's computerized medication administration system; Ted Ainslie, hospital vice president for finance and budget; and John Mess, hospital vice president for risk management. Counsel for the hospital is Harry Meinig. I'm Sarah Abadhi, Mr. Meinig's associate. Also here today from our firm is Doris Ostrom, who will be keeping the minutes for this meeting."

"Mr. Meinig and I go way back," Baumgarten interjected. "Nice to see you again, Harry. Too bad it's under such terrible circumstances."

Harry didn't blink. "We can all agree that we're here today to make sure those circumstances are never repeated. In the interest of time, I suggest we let Ms. Abadhi continue." Then he gave Sarah the nod to go on.

"Each of our team members will present the proposed changes in their area of expertise. First to present is Aimee Sackoff, director of nursing." Sarah motioned to Sackoff to begin as she returned to her seat to take charge of the PowerPoint visuals.

"Good morning," Sackoff started. "I would like to reiterate what Ms. Abadhi said. Our entire nursing staff was shaken to the core by the error that was made in Ariel's case. However, we believe that something really powerful, really good, may occur as a result of what your baby experienced. As you may know, your daughter's nurse was working back-to-back shifts last week, due to a staffing shortage. That nurse is one of our very best, most experienced nurses. We believe that fatigue played a role in her not catching the medication error. We are committed to addressing the problem of fatigued nurses delivering beside care. In keeping with that commitment, we propose to be the first hospital in the city to eliminate mandatory overtime for nurses," Sackoff said triumphantly, revealing none of her previously expressed reservations about the proposal.

"This is so important," Sackoff explained, "because we all know that people do their best when they're not tired. This will be a very costly measure. Mr. Ainslie will be able to give you the specifics on that. But to me, as a veteran nursing administrator, this proposal indicates that the hospital is committed to spending whatever it takes to make mandatory overtime a thing of the past." She then elaborated on the numbers of new nurses who would be hired, with Sarah showing the graphics to illustrate the increases in staffing. The head of nursing concluded with a brief discussion of contingency plans for times when illness might strike the nursing staff, as had happened during Ariel's hospitalization.

Sackoff was as concise as she was enthusiastic and, to Sarah's mind, persuasive. Sarah introduced Joanne Marsh next, keeping her fingers crossed that she would do as well.

"Good morning to you all. Before I explain our plan for improvement, I want to give you my personal, heartfelt apology. The error that harmed your daughter originated in my department. Throughout my long tenure here at the hospital, I've made the elimination of medication errors my number-one priority, so when I learned that a brand-new employee in our pharmacy was at fault, I was distraught. Though I know my apology will not put things to right for your family, I want you to know that everyone in my department was heartsick to learn of the error. We have redoubled our efforts to make certain that it never happens again.

"To that end, we propose an intensive training program for every staff member who handles medications. Never again will a novice pharmacy technician — such as the young man I fired last week for causing your daughter's heparin overdose — step one foot in the pharmacy until she or he is completely conversant in the computerized medication administration system we adopted just days before Ariel's hospitalization."

Baumgarten interrupted. "Would have been nice if you'd done that before my clients' baby entered your hospital."

Marsh was not cowed. "We agree with you. We thought our training was sufficient, but clearly, we were mistaken. However, we aim to correct our mistake, and Mr. DiPerna here," she motioned to her right, "will explain to you in detail how we aim to make the system as fail-safe as is humanly possible." With that, she handed off the presentation to the chief designer of the BCMA system. He piggy-backed on what Marsh had said, making a point-by-point case for massive, onsite tech support from his firm. In addition, the BCMA system would be redesigned to add audible alarms when scans did not match. DiPerna closed by saying that such a plan would further reduce the probability of an error such as the one that had affected Ariel Arkin.

Finally, Ted Ainslie explained the cost of all the proposed improvements in staffing and training — over ten million dollars in the first year alone. Maintaining high staffing levels among nurses, and providing training for all new hires, would cost at least as much in each subsequent year. Projected out three years, the bill would top thirty million dollars.

It was Sarah's job to conclude the presentation. Taking the floor once again, she looked directly at the Arkins. "In closing, I want to emphasize the seriousness of the hospital's commitment to eliminate medication errors. We are on a mission. Although we have no power over the pharmaceutical company, we have initiated talks with the heparin manufacturer about a redesign of the labeling for their products in order to eliminate the type of mix-up that occurred in Ariel's case. Those discussions are part and parcel of our overarching goal: that no other patients suffer as Ariel did from a mistaken dosage or from an incorrect medication. We are willing to fund that effort despite, as Mr. Ainslie just illustrated, its eight-figure price tag. And, to guarantee our good faith, should you agree to our remediation plan, we propose that it be monitored for compliance by a neutral third party — mutually agreed upon — for the life of the agreement, that is to say, three years."

Sarah took a sip from her lukewarm latte and continued. "Of course, we want to address the pain and suffering Ariel experienced because of our error. We are offering your daughter a monetary settlement of five hundred thousand dollars as compensation for the trauma she experienced."

Sarah had no sooner announced the figure than she heard Baumgarten remark in a stage whisper, "You've got to be kidding."

She'd anticipated that reaction from the Arkins' representative and remained calm and measured in her presentation. "Though her response to treatment has been so encouraging, giving us all great hope that Ariel will make a full and complete recovery, our settlement has contingencies built in for remedial therapies through age twenty-one in the event of physical or cognitive damage associated with the medication error." Sarah saw Catherine shudder.

She was nearly done. She looked down at her watch: five minutes to eleven. At that point she knew it was time to open the floor to the Arkins and their counsel. "I understand that you are anxious to get back to Ariel. However, I want to give you every opportunity to ask questions about what you just heard."

Baumgarten went first. "Very nice presentation. We appreciate your efforts to prevent another little baby from suffering the way Ariel did. Jesus, you guys nearly killed her. So it's nice that you don't want to kill off any other babies who come in with a simple staph infection. We appreciate that. We really do. But how does your plan do my clients any good? The harm has already been done to their little one. Five hundred thousand? Why, that's chump change. You know that, Harry," he said, turning his attention to Meinig.

Harry could see the storm clouds rolling in. God bless Sarah. Her idea of admitting guilt was a logical strategy given the damning evidence of hospital culpability, but it looked like Mark was aiming to play hardball. He had to try to salvage the plan. "Reid, what I know is that we'd all like something good to come out of what was nearly a catastrophic error. Thank God the error was caught immediately and Ariel was given state-of-the-art treatment by Dr. Smith here and the rest of the medical team. We all hope and pray that she's going to be okay. But as important as making sure she's okay, we want to make sure her ordeal brings about something positive. That's the thrust of our proposal. And we hope you and your clients will give it some thought. That's all we're asking — that you give it serious thought."

Mark had sat stock still throughout the presentation while his wife took copious notes. His face was blank, betraying nothing but fatigue. When he broke his silence, he turned toward Dr. Smith. "My good Dr. Smith. I haven't heard squat from you. What's your impression of this so-called 'plan for remediation?' Is it worth a rat's ass? I'm interested in hearing what you think. I know you work for the hospital, but I also know you're not afraid to call things as you see them. After all, you called me an asshole when I was being an asshole. Not too many people have ever done that and lived to tell the tale. So I figure you'll level with me. What's your take on what you just heard?"

Harry winced when he heard that Dr. Smith had called Mark an asshole to his face, though he couldn't agree more. He wondered where he had gotten the balls to do that. The same question crossed the mind of nearly everyone else in the room. Not Sarah, though. She found herself suppressing a little smile.

Rick colored when he was reminded of the scene in the baby's room — when the father was yelling and he couldn't think straight as he tried to counteract the effects of the overdose.

"Sorry about that, Mr. Arkin. Things were happening pretty quickly at that moment. I apologize for losing my cool."

"I don't give a crap about that. You saved my daughter's life. By my lights, you're a straight shooter. Is this plan the real deal? That's all I'm asking."

Rick had had his share of moments in the sun. He'd been a two-sport varsity athlete in high school. He'd won academic honors in college. Beating out the competition, he'd been appointed pediatric chief resident. Now he was in one of the country's best fellowship programs in pediatric intensive care. But nothing had prepared him for this. He thought for a moment and then sat up a bit straighter in his chair.

"You want the truth, Mr. Arkin? All right, here's the truth as I see it."

The members of the hospital team held their breath when they realized a sixty-grand-a-year fellow decked out in scrubs and sneakers might well hold the hospital's fate in his hands.

"Mr. Mess here will confirm that I just about fell out of my chair when I heard that the hospital was going to take responsibility for the error. Frankly, such honesty is a rare occurrence, Mr. Arkin, and I was happy to hear the hospital was willing to do the right thing. We doctors and nurses — and all the staff — we're just people. We're not automatons. We do our best — and believe me, I work with the very finest people in the field — and despite that, we sometimes make mistakes. Believe me, nobody woke up that morning and said to themselves, 'Oh, gee, maybe I'll injure a little baby at work today.' Just the opposite. The people I work with are driven by the desire to help kids get better. But despite that, a series of circumstances allowed well-meaning people — highly competent people — to deliver an overdose to your baby.

"I've reviewed this plan at length. Ms. Abadhi had me going over it with a fine-tooth comb. I would have to conclude that, using your terminology, this is 'the real deal.' It's a good-faith, comprehensive effort to address the circumstances that allowed good people to make a terrible mistake. If it's implemented, I believe it will go a long way toward helping competent, well-meaning doctors, nurses and pharmacists do their very best for each of our patients, and will get us as close as we can to eliminating medication errors at the hospital."

It was as though every person on the hospital team exhaled at once. The man in the scrubs and sneakers had spoken, giving the plan his seal of approval. Harry thought that after that ringing endorsement, it was possible they might still have a shot at convincing the Arkins to bypass the malpractice route. It depended on how great their desire was for vengeance, since it was clear they didn't need a cent from the hospital. Baumgarten would be key on that point, emphasizing the need to "teach those bastards a lesson," or some such tripe. The question was, would they accept the remediation plan as proof that the lesson was learned?

Catherine had stopped her note-taking to look directly at Dr. Smith. "Thank you, Dr. Smith. As is obvious, we put a great deal of faith in your opinion. My husband and I appreciate your assessment of the hospital's proposal."

Baumgarten, who would have liked to put a sock in the doctor's mouth, cut Catherine off before she could say another word. "Yes, thank you, Dr. Smith. And thank you all for your presentation this morning. My clients and I will be getting back to you after a thorough review of your proposal. I'm assuming, Ms. Abadhi, that you've prepared a document for us to review?"

"Yes, of course, Mr. Baumgarten." She got up and handed each of them a copy.

"I really have to get back to Ariel now," Catherine said as she stood up to leave. "You've given us a lot to think about."

"My clients and I will be going over their options. We'll get back to you," added Baumgarten.

Sarah tried to get a read on Mark, but his face revealed nothing. She had given it her all. Everyone did their part during the presentation, none more than Dr. Smith. Time would tell whether their efforts would pay off.

FIFTEEN

As each day passed with no word from the Arkins or their attorney, Sarah grew more on edge. With Thanksgiving coming up, word from the Arkins would likely be further delayed. She decided to distract herself by spending the holiday at her parents' house in Westchester. During the big feast, Bubbe Rivka regaled her children and grandchildren with tales of romantic intrigue at the Brighton Beach Senior Center, but Sarah was too worried to enjoy her grandmother's storytelling. That night and the next, she slept poorly in her childhood room.

If she'd been a fly on the wall at the Arkin home, she might have enjoyed her Thanksgiving more. Daily life changed after the Arkins brought their baby home from the hospital. Mark lingered in the mornings, not leaving for work until ten. He was back for dinner each night by six. His company had always been his reason for living, but now all he cared about was Catherine and Ariel. He forced himself to show up at the office and put on a good front, so people wouldn't think he was losing his edge. He knew they'd take advantage, just as he would if he sensed a weakness in someone else. But the truth was, all he really wanted to do was stay home with Catherine and help her take care of their daughter. He even changed a diaper or two.

Mark had shoved the hospital's settlement offer to the back of his mind, despite Baumgarten's daily attempts to set up a meeting to discuss it. Mark knew the lawyer's take on it: Let's clean the hospital's clock. Normally, he'd have been one step ahead of him. Vengeance was not only sweet, it was necessary to ensure that others didn't try the same stunt. But the realization that he had no urge to destroy the hospital left Mark confused and worried; so much so, he kept both Catherine and Baumgarten at bay every time they brought up the subject of the settlement offer.

Two weeks had passed since they'd received the hospital's proposal. For Catherine, every day that Ariel awoke happy and healthy was a red-letter day. Although she couldn't forget what had happened, she felt the sincerity of the hospital's apology could be measured in its proposed improvement plan. She thought it well designed, and no one could say that they were trying to do it on the cheap. She'd written a piece on the economics of health care a few years back and knew what hospitals were up against: cuts to reimbursements from Medicare, more uninsured patients turning into charity cases, competitive demands that drove them to keep up with neighboring hospitals — be it with sunlit atriums for their lobbies or the newest robots for microsurgery. She thought the hospital's proposal was on point. And for her, the idea of something positive coming out of their nightmare held great appeal.

On a sunny morning in early December, as she and her husband sat at breakfast with Ariel next to them in her baby seat, she decided to force the issue that Mark had been so artfully dodging.

"Sweetie, I think it's time we talk about the hospital's proposal. I get the sense you'd rather not and I can understand why. The whole experience was...well, we both know how devastating it was. But Ariel's doing well now. I've given the proposal quite a bit of thought and I know you likely have, too. So I think it's time we share our thinking."

Mark had been dreading this. What he shrank from was admitting that he didn't have the thirst for blood that had always driven him. That nice-looking lawyer representing the hospital had made a good case. And, as soon as Dr. Smith had told him the improvement plan was the real deal, he had no reason to doubt it. That wasn't the problem. The question was, would he make the hospital pay for nearly killing his daughter, for making his wife almost lose her mind? To his amazement, the answer that kept coming to him was, "No." He was just relieved that it was over and that they'd had a chance to pick up with their lives again.

"Sorry I've been putting you off. I wanted to think it over." Stalling some more, he asked, "You said you have an opinion. How do you think we ought to respond?"

"Well, I have to admit that as tired as I was that day, I was impressed by that attorney's presentation. What was her name? Something funny, I can't recall. She and the other lawyer made a good point. If millions are going to be spent because of what Ariel went through, let those millions do some good. The truth is, the patients would be the beneficiaries. Better nurse-patient ratios, less fatigue in the nursing ranks, effective implementation of the computerized medication system. The downside, of course, is that Ariel's cash settlement would be much smaller than what she would get if we filed a lawsuit."

"There's no doubt about that, Catherine. The case is worth millions, particularly because they confessed to all their mistakes. The question is, is that the route you want to take? If so, I'll get Baumgarten on the horn and give him the go-ahead to prepare for war."

"Well, how do you feel, Mark? Do you want to go to war? I wouldn't blame you if you do."

Trying not to sound too sheepish, he finally made his admission. "The truth is, I just don't have much of a stomach for it. I can't believe it myself but I just want to put all of it behind us. But I'll go to war with the hospital if that's what you want. I will, Catherine."

"No, I don't want to go to war," she said as she started to well up. "I feel just as you do. Let's delight in this beautiful baby and get satisfaction from knowing that her suffering produced some good. Truth be told, Ariel doesn't need millions from a settlement. It would likely ruin her. She'd become one of those disaffected rich kids getting into trouble with all their money. We don't want that, do we?" she teased.

"We certainly don't want her to fall victim to the corrosive influence of wealth," he said, tongue in cheek.

"No, we certainly don't," Catherine said, smiling. "So what do you say? Can we accept the offer — maybe with a counter that they throw in free medical care for Ariel until age eighteen or something like that?"

"Well," her husband replied, laughing to himself in disbelief, "we certainly don't want to look like a couple of chumps. Let's demand free medical care." Then he added, "Baumgarten's going to think we've lost our minds. He'll be furious when he sees the fees he would have earned from a fat settlement — or better yet, a jury award — go up in smoke. And you know what? I don't give a crap."

Catherine got up from her chair and sat down on her husband's lap. As she kissed him, a feeling of wellbeing flooded over Mark. Much to his surprise, his groin played no role in it. He wondered if he was turning into some blissed-out pansy. But as he kissed his wife back, his *shlong* came to life, restoring his faith in himself as a man's man.

SIXTEEN

Word of Sarah's success spread quickly through the law firm. Harry went straight to the firm's managing partner and lobbied for a substantial raise for his protégée. John Mess, delighted and relieved, passed the Excedrin to Ted Ainslie, whose job it was to find the money to implement the remediation plan. Mess made good on his promise to recognize Dr. Richard Smith, Dr. Esther Cho and Jeannie Lopez. For delivering the apology to the Arkins, they each got two extra weeks of vacation — or two weeks' pay if they preferred. On top of that, Dr. Smith was made an offer to join the hospital as an attending in pediatric intensive care when he completed his fellowship in June. With the single exception of Reid Baumgarten, the Arkins' attorney, all parties involved concluded it was the best possible outcome from the near-tragic medical error.

Rick wasted no time in contacting Sarah to offer his hearty congratulations. He suggested they celebrate at an Asian fusion restaurant and continue their discussion of all things non–work related. Sarah readily agreed. She was fairly certain his endorsement of the improvement plan had tipped the scales in their favor. But beyond that, she wasn't averse to the prospect of spending more time with the doctor. He was not only as tall as she — and handsome in a rough-hewn way — he was also smart, driven about his work and gutsy. Had she met him under similar circumstances before she dialed back her expectations for happiness, a date with Rick Smith would have been cause for some excitement. As it was, she was open to the idea of sharing a meal with him.

After checking their calendars, it became clear that the

upcoming Sunday was the only day open to them both. They agreed to meet at eleven so they would have the chance to work out beforehand, she with a swim at the pool and he with a run along the river.

Rick and Sarah — as they learned to refer to one another over dim sum — talked effortlessly as empty plates accumulated on their table. After a couple of hours, Sarah noticed the maître d' giving them the evil eye, and the long line of people waiting to be seated.

"I think we'd better get our check," Sarah suggested, nodding to the waiter.

"Oh, is our time up? I thought we were just getting started."

"Well, I think our time at this table is up, unless you don't mind the ugly stares from those people over there," she said, nodding in the direction of the door.

Rick turned around and saw the mass of humanity eager to have their go at dim sum. "Oh. I see what you mean." But he wasn't ready to say good-bye to Sarah Abadhi.

"I don't know what the rest of your day looks like, Sarah, but if you have some time, we could walk up to the Met. Actually, if you say yes, you'll be rescuing me from a life devoid of culture. At this point in my training, the only culture I recognize is the kind that grows in a dish of agar."

Sarah hadn't been to the Metropolitan Museum since she'd gone with Alex years before. She generally shunned anything that reminded her of their time together, but she found herself tempted by Rick's suggestion. "Well, I guess you could say I'm equally deprived, culturally speaking. Eighty hour workweeks have a way of doing that to you. I think your prescription to remedy our shared deficit might be just the thing."

The waiter approached with the bill and they both reached for it.

"Hey, this is my treat. Think of it as congratulations on the settlement," Rick said.

Though the fellow made just a fraction of what she earned,

Sarah didn't put up a fight.

The twenty-five-block walk to the museum, the three hours they spent at the exhibits and the visit to a cafe that followed were characterized by nothing if not comfort. Rick and Sarah both found themselves comfortable in their own skin, and unable to run out of subjects to discuss, often with passion. One topic segued seamlessly into the next, and before either of them knew it, the day had turned to night. Rick couldn't believe his good luck. Not only was Sarah hot, she was great company for a cherished day off. Sarah was a bit incredulous herself. She wondered if she might get a break from the narcissists who'd plagued her dating life in the five years since Tom, the last boyfriend of record, had left.

Leaving the cafe, Sarah decided to make the first move. She turned and kissed Rick, lightly at first, and then, when she got a friendly response, with more enthusiasm. He was glad he'd put clean sheets on the bed after his morning run — just in case he got lucky that day. He suggested they go to his place. Sarah complimented him on coming up with another fine idea for spending a Sunday off.

As it turned out, Rick and Sarah fit one another to a tee. They had an equally good time under the covers and out of bed. Since their schedules were hectic, mutually free time was hard to come by, but they let no opportunity pass. They usually met at Sarah's apartment, which was not only habitually cleaner, it was also not shared by — as Rick good-naturedly described him — a hairy ape of an orthopedics resident. When they had more time than it took to have sex and catch some sleep, they worked out together. They pounded out seven-minute miles along the river or swam laps at Sarah's pool. With Rick's help, Sarah mastered flip turns, something that had eluded her for years.

Early on, Rick brought up the subject of commitment, explaining that it was something that held no appeal for him. "Look," he said matter-of-factly, "I have no plans to get married — ever. I don't want kids. I like my work, a lot, and it takes just about all I have to do it well. I don't want to add something into the mix as important as a family, and end up ruining both."

Rick had given this early warning to each of his many girlfriends over the years. Most of the women had tried to change his mind, saying something akin to, "You'll sing a different tune when you meet the right woman." But Sarah was not like any of his previous girlfriends.

"I'm glad you brought this up. Thanks for your honesty. I agree to your terms," she said in a businesslike way. "I understand what it means to have work fill up your life. The truth is, I'd planned on saying something similar, but you beat me to the punch." Then she punched him lightly on the arm and they ended up wrestling on the floor. In no time flat they were in the sack, enjoying each other's bodies with abandon.

A few weeks later Rick broached the subject of getting tested for the standard battery of sexually transmitted diseases, so they could ditch the condoms and switch to some other form of birth control. When he mentioned birth control, Sarah's mood changed.

"Are you okay with that? Getting tested, I mean," he asked.

"Sure. It's a good idea. Let's do it." But the issue of birth control had touched a nerve. Now she'd have to disclose what she'd told only one other lover — Tom — back when she was a law clerk. She took a deep breath and laid it on the table. "But birth control won't be necessary. I'm sterile."

"What? No way. You can't be sterile. You're a beautiful, sexy, athletic, big-bucks lawyer."

That made her smile. "Well, if those were the key factors in reproduction, I guess I'd be one hell of a fertile earth mother. But the fact is…." Her voice trailed off, pained at having to discuss the thing she mourned like a death. "The fact is, I can't have children."

With Tom, a fellow lawyer, she merely told him she was infertile and that birth control was a non-issue. But it was different with Rick.

"You're probably wondering what happened to me," she said, trying her best to sound cool despite the rhythmic pounding in her head.

"As a doc, I am kind of curious. But you don't have to go into it if you'd rather not."

"No. It's okay. I got chlamydia from my college boyfriend, Alex. We'd been together for years. We went to grad school together, planned a future together, you know, the whole nine yards. But, unbeknownst to me, he'd been screwing around, apparently for a long time. I didn't realize he'd infected me with chlamydia until it progressed to pelvic inflammatory disease. The end result is my fallopian tubes are shot."

Rick's first thought was what a shame those terrific genes would not be making an appearance in the next generation. Then he remembered something he'd learned during his gynecology rotation — how infertility often precipitated major depression in women. From the way Sarah's mood had changed when he mentioned birth control, it seemed to be a big deal for her. Even a high-powered attorney probably wanted babies. The drive to reproduce was instinctive to most people, though it was a drive he didn't share.

"I'm so sorry, Sarah. I really am." He put his arm around her and rubbed her back. He kissed her cheek and brushed a lock of hair away from her face. "If you point out the bastard who did this to you — this Alex jerk — I'll beat the crap out of him," he offered, picking up his fists and jabbing the air.

"Nah, no point. He's long gone. And I'm okay, really," she said, touched by Rick's response.

"You know, when and if you ever want kids, the docs may be able to help you," he said. "They've come a long way with IVF — in-vitro fertilization. You're young and otherwise healthy. But I warn you, you may end up with more than you bargained for — triplets, for example. Really, Sarah, you may be able to become a mother if that's something you want."

"You think? Well, it's always nice to have options. I didn't take it well when my reproductive life was extinguished at the age of twenty-three."

"Are you sure your tubes are blocked? Sometimes they're partially occluded but those little spermies don't need a heck of a lot of room," Rick said, trying to make certain there would be no need for them to take precautions.

"Well, two eminent gynecologists feel certain. And I went for a couple of years in a subsequent relationship without using any birth control. I have no children hidden under the couch. Promise."

"No babies under the couch?" Rick ducked down and took a look, bringing a little smile to Sarah's somber face. "You speak the truth," he said. "No babies under the couch. Okay. So we'll get tested and then — if it's all right with you — we'll say good-bye to the condoms."

Sarah caught his gaze and held it. "Sure. But there's one more thing. I'm assuming that you're suggesting we ditch the condoms because you want us to be exclusive. And that's fine with me. And it will be fine until it's not fine with one or the other of us. What I mean is, when you want to be with someone else, just tell me. And I promise I'll be frank and honest with you, too. We're grown-ups. When we're not enjoying each other as we are now, or when something else catches your eye or mine, well, no game playing. Okay?"

Rick was having trouble imagining a time when he wouldn't want to make love to this woman, to run along the river with her lithe figure next to his. For Sarah, he'd willingly drop out of the hunt, for a while at least. He couldn't argue with her terms. No cheating, full disclosure. Always the joker, he stood to attention and put his hand on his heart, declaring, "I promise that when Sarah Abadhi, Esquire, does not sufficiently entertain me in every way, I will hereby say that I want out."

Not to be outdone, Sarah got up and stood face-to-face with

Rick. She placed her hand on her heart and offered her play on his words, "I promise that when Richard Smith, M.D., does not sufficiently entertain me in every way, I will hereby say, 'See ya later, busta.'"

After this perverse send-up on nuptial vows, Rick embraced her and whispered that, at that moment, he wanted very much to be in. Luckily, he still had an ample supply of condoms.

SEVENTEEN

The long winter finally yielded to spring, and Sarah and Rick continued to enjoy one another's company. Given her low expectations, Rick was a ten on the "male-o-meter," a rating system Sarah's college friends used to rate the men they dated. She and Rick had a good time just about every time. They could talk about work, politics, running and swimming. After their discussion about Sarah's infertility, they gave topics relating to their personal histories a wide berth. The only thing Sarah knew about Rick's life story was that he grew up with his single mother in Michigan, and had been in a terrible car accident when he was five, the latter accounting for the many faint scars on his body. They rarely disagreed, and when they did, one was always ready to capitulate to the other. The issues that divided them were never more serious than what DVD to rent or which restaurant to order from, but nonetheless, each was mindful of the other's desires and aimed to please.

Although they never made a conscious decision to hide their relationship, neither did they go out of their way to advertise it. In fact, only two people knew they were a couple: Jeff, Rick's roommate, a.k.a. the "hairy ape" orthopedic head resident, and Devorah, Sarah's best friend who lived in Chicago. If they passed someone they knew while coming off a run by the river, they chatted pleasantly and kept it light, with first-name introductions only. People at Sarah's office saw more of her elusive dimples and figured she'd likely met someone. Rick's reputation as a player was put in jeopardy when he failed to put the moves on any of the attractive female nurses for months, leaving co-workers scratching their heads.

The major exception, of course, was Jeff, who knew precisely what was preventing Rick from maintaining his position as alpha male among fellows and residents. Jeff liked Sarah from the get-go, and the feeling was mutual. They occasionally made a running threesome, with Jeff pushing himself to keep up and Rick and Sarah adjusting their pace to accommodate him. Once every few weeks, Sarah would meet Rick and Jeff for a drink or some supper on a Friday evening before she and Rick headed off to her apartment for the night.

There was no doubt about it: Rick and Sarah were compatible. Just as important, they each refused to give oxygen to the idea that their relationship was anything more than a great time. They were vigilant about not making plans. A week or two into the future was the farthest outpost of their shared horizon.

At the end of their fifth month together, Sarah, who had always been as regular as a clock, was late with her period; first a day or two, and then a week. She was under a lot of pressure at work with an important case: a professional pianist had lost his forearm due to a medical error. Unless they could work out a settlement, the case was going to trial in a few weeks. Though pressure was nothing new, Sarah thought maybe it was wreaking havoc with her menstrual cycle.

When she was ten days late, she began to feel light-headed. Her mind raced to every possibility. Was she coming down with some strange infectious disease? Was she developing a brain tumor? Perhaps it was premature menopause. She'd read about that happening to some women. It would be just her luck to have yet another insult to her damaged reproductive system.

She decided to call for an appointment with her internist. If she had some terrible disease, time might be of the essence. Her period was now two weeks late, but it also felt like it could come any time. She felt bloated. Her breasts ached right up through her armpits. She even had menstrual cramps. What worried her was that little things exhausted her — like going up a flight of stairs. Just the day before, she'd had to turn around early on her run. Maybe it was mononucleosis. How ridiculous would it be to get the adolescent scourge at age thirty-two?

The doctor's office had a cancellation for that morning, and Sarah grabbed it. The doctor, Grace Tanaka, had grown up in a suburb northwest of Chicago — next door to Devorah. She had joined a bustling practice on the East Side after completing her residency at NYU. Sarah had visited her only a couple of times before. Each time they swapped tales of Devorah's parents' gourmet cooking skills and exotic vacations.

That morning Sarah was feeling especially woozy. When she arrived at the doctor's office, she thought about taking the stairs, but then thought better of it. She opted for the elevator, signed in at reception, peed into a cup as requested and found a seat in the waiting room. After filling out the required paperwork, she opened her laptop to make the most of the inevitable wait.

After about half an hour, her name was called and she was shown into a small examining room. Dr. Grace Tanaka followed quickly on her heels.

"Hello, hello," the meticulously groomed doctor said as she extended her hand to Sarah. "It's good to see you. Have you heard from Devorah lately?"

"Oh, yes. We talk at least a couple of times a week. She's doing well, busy with work, like the rest of us."

"I don't doubt it. She was always a worker, even as a little kid."

"She didn't graduate summa cum laude for nothing. She's whip smart and, as you say, a worker," Sarah said, remembering their college days.

The doctor scanned the form Sarah had filled out. "So, I see that general malaise has brought you in today. When did it start?"

"Maybe a week ago. And it's funny because I have no fever, no rash and no sore throat. I just have no energy," Sarah explained. "I can hardly go up a flight of stairs without being wiped out. And I generally swim or run before work, so something is off."

"Do you notice any other differences?"

"Only that my period is late — but I think it's coming any day. I've got all the symptoms: cramping, bloating, sore breasts."

"How late, Sarah?"

"A couple of weeks. I don't know if you remember, but I had PID several years ago. Afterwards, two doctors determined my tubes were completely blocked. So pregnancy is out."

"I see on your form that you're sexually active."

"Yes."

"And are you using birth control?" the doctor queried.

"The one good thing about being sterile, Dr. Tanaka, is the money you save on birth control. To answer your question, after having the tests done for STDs, my current partner and I have not been using birth control."

"Okay, so I'll have to investigate. You get into a gown; take everything off. I'll be back in a few minutes and I'll see what's up."

A few minutes later the doctor knocked on the door as Sarah was arranging her paper gown as modestly as she could.

"Come in," Sarah said.

The doctor began with the usual: eyes, nose, ears, throat, thyroid, reflexes. She listened to Sarah's heart and lungs and took her blood pressure. Then she told Sarah to lie down on the table. She examined her breasts and her belly before having Sarah put her feet in the stirrups. After examining her vaginally and rectally she told her she could sit up.

"Well, Sarah. Everything is unremarkable with the exception of your uterus, which is a bit enlarged. As you expect your period any day, that could explain the enlargement. I won't be able to get to the bottom of this without some lab work. I'm going to order a CBC and some tests to measure your hormone levels. Low thyroid function could make you feel punky. It could also throw off your menstrual cycle. But I really don't want to speculate until I get the results of the blood work."

"Sure. Needles don't bother me. Can you do the lab work right here in the office?" Sarah asked, hoping to expedite the process.

"Actually, there's a lab on the second floor of this building that can do the blood draws. You can use that lab or any other. I'll give you an order and you can take it wherever you like."

"When will you get the results?"

"I could get them within the day if you get to a lab this morning. I'll give you a call — certainly by tomorrow — with the results."

"That's great. I just want to shake this weird feeling. The sooner you know the cause, the happier I'll be," Sarah said.

"It's a deal. Remember, Sarah, you've got Dr. Tanaka on the case now. Together we'll solve this puzzle." The smiling doctor shook Sarah's hand again and said, "Please, say hello to Devorah the next time you talk."

"I certainly will — and thanks. I appreciate you seeing me on such short notice."

After the doctor left, Sarah dressed quickly. As she did the last button on her skirt she was relieved to know that whatever was bugging her would soon be identified. If she was lucky, there would be a treatment and she'd be back to herself in no time.

Sarah was in her office eating Chinese takeout when the call from Grace Tanaka came in around seven. Rick had texted earlier to let her know he was swamped. And from the looks of her desk, she'd be lucky to get out of there by ten.

"This is Dr. Tanaka calling for Sarah Abadhi."

"Oh, hello, Dr. Tanaka. This is Sarah. Thanks so much for calling tonight."

"I hope it's not too late."

"Oh, no, not at all. I'm still in the office. Did the blood work give you any leads?"

"Lots of good news. Your hematocrit and hemoglobin levels are good. Your white count shows there's no sign of infection — so we can rule out mono and leukemia. Your thyroid function is normal, so we're not dealing with hypothyroidism. But there was one surprise in the blood panel. Sarah, your blood work shows HCG — the hormone that's produced during pregnancy."

There was silence for a good fifteen seconds. "Sarah, are you still there?"

"Yes, yes, I'm still here...but I don't understand. How can that be? My fallopian tubes are blocked. Perhaps the lab made a mistake."

"Well, as I said, I'm surprised as well. All things considered, I would say the probability of a lab error is slight. And given your history, we really need to rule out an ectopic pregnancy — a pregnancy that implanted outside of the uterus, either in or near the fallopian tubes. I suggest you follow up on that right away. An ectopic pregnancy can be quite serious if not treated early."

"I don't understand how this could have happened."

"Sarah," the doctor responded calmly, "we don't know exactly what has happened except that it's likely conception has taken place. Do you have a gynecologist I can send these results to?"

"Yes...yes, let me see. It's Dr. Scholl. Dr. Jared Scholl. I'll get his number for you if you give me a minute." Sarah found the number and read off the digits.

"Okay, Sarah. I'm going to call his office and make a referral for you. I suggest you see him as soon as you can. He'll likely do an ultrasound to see where the embryo is growing — and then you'll have the information you need for the next step. I want to reiterate the good news, Sarah: You're healthy and your malaise is consistent with normal symptoms of the first trimester of pregnancy. You are not sick."

Embryo. First trimester pregnancy. Not sick. Sarah was having trouble processing the doctor's words. "Thank you. Thank you very much for that, Dr. Tanaka. I was thinking you might find a brain tumor or some other terrible illness. But pregnancy…I don't know what to say. I'm astonished. But I do appreciate you reminding me that I am, in fact, healthy, and that is definitely a relief." She realized she was rambling and that the doctor likely had other calls to make. "I'm going to call Dr. Scholl's office tomorrow — and I'll make sure he shares his findings with you. Thank you again. You've been a great help."

Rick came to bed after midnight and, for the first time, Sarah turned away when he starting caressing her. She mumbled something about not feeling so great. He said he was sorry, kissed the back of her neck and instantaneously fell into a sound sleep. Sarah, on the other hand, proceeded to spend the night thrashing about the bed, imagining every possible ectopic pregnancy scenario, from dying on the operating table during surgery to suffering so much blood loss that she would be mentally impaired for the rest of her life. She'd handled a malpractice case with precisely that fact pattern. There was a downside to knowing too much.

The early dawn gave her an excuse to get out of bed and do something — anything — to take her mind off thoughts of early death or disability. She decided to clean the bathroom while Rick lay sleeping in the next room. She scrubbed the sink, tub and toilet as they'd never been scrubbed before. When she was done, she was spent.

After Rick got up and out, Sarah called her gynecologist. She was thankful his office started picking up at half past seven, but the call only heightened her fears. She could only guess what Dr. Tanaka had told Dr. Scholl, because his secretary seemed to be expecting her call. She fit Sarah into the gynecologist's invariably jam-packed schedule with the last appointment of the afternoon. The woman told Sarah that it was essential that she come to the appointment with a full bladder, suggesting she drink three to four glasses of water an hour before her appointment.

She could ill afford the time it would take to go downtown to the doctor, but the truth was, her productivity was pathetic. Her mind kept generating one question after another, none related to the work on her desk: How could it be true? Did two esteemed doctors make a mistake when they told her she was sterile? What about the two years she had used no birth control with Tom? And if she had surgery for an ectopic pregnancy and the surgery went well, how long would the recuperation take?

There was also the whole issue of Rick. He had laid out his ground rules at the outset, and they were remarkably similar to hers. How could she tell him she had conceived? What if he thought she'd lied when she said she was sterile? If it was an ectopic pregnancy, maybe he could be a great support for her as she negotiated her way through surgery and recovery. That was, of course, if he'd be willing to wait around for her to come back to herself.

She drank the required quart of water and left for her appointment with Dr. Scholl just after four. When she arrived, the waiting room was empty and it seemed most of the staff was heading for the exit. She was ushered into a room with an ultrasound machine and an examining table. After the technician left, she did as she'd been told. Taking off everything from the waist down, she got on the table and covered herself with the pink paper drape.

When the technician returned, she was in the company of Dr. Scholl, who offered a big hello and a handshake.

"So what's this I hear about an elevated HCG level? Sarah, don't tell me we're going to have to write you up in a journal."

Sarah's hands and armpits were sweating and she had to pee. "Frankly I'm at a loss to know what to think. But I'm anxious to know what you find. Very anxious," she said nervously. After a moment's hesitation, she added, "And I also have to pee, so if we could hurry, that would be great."

"Will do. We need you to have a full bladder in order to get a good image of your uterus. We'll do this as quickly as we can," Dr.

Scholl said, switching effortlessly to high-efficiency mode. The technician put cold, clear jelly on Sarah's flat belly — which only made the urge to pee more intense — and then started moving the ultrasound probe. In no time at all she focused it on one spot. There on the screen for all three of them to see was a tiny fish-like being, smaller than a dime, with its heart rapidly beating. Sarah lay there astonished.

"I'd say that looks to be an embryo at about four to five weeks of development. It's implanted high up within the uterus, a very normal and healthy place for implantation. If you can wait another minute or two I'd like the technician to quickly scan your fallopian tubes and ovaries as well, just to be certain there is no other embryo developing outside of the uterus."

"More...more than one embryo?" Sarah stammered.

"Oh, probably not, but I'd rather we just poke around to be sure," the doctor said calmly.

The technician did a full tour of her left ovary and tube, and then her right. Then she wiped the jelly off of Sarah's belly with a tissue and told her she could use the restroom adjoining the examining room. When Sarah emerged from the bathroom, the woman told her she could get dressed and meet Dr. Scholl in his office.

The five minutes she sat alone in the doctor's office were the longest five minutes of her life. She had a feeling that no matter what he was going to say, her life was about to change. He walked in carrying some three-by-three–inch shots of her ultrasound. He put them on his desk and then sat in his leather swivel chair.

"When you first came to see me — let me see, it was more than five years ago — you brought your records from Dr. Farouzhan in Boston. He is one of the most respected reproductive specialists in the country. It was his assessment that your tubes were completely occluded. My follow-up tests confirmed his original diagnosis."

"You don't need to remind me of the diagnosis. A day doesn't pass that I don't think of its ramifications: I'm unable to conceive. So I don't understand how I could have an embryo growing inside my uterus. I'm not saying I'm unhappy about it. I actually don't know how I feel about it. I'm just trying to figure out how I became pregnant," she said, biting her lip.

Sarah was not alone in her puzzlement. Jared Scholl was equally perplexed, but he made an effort to tame the incomprehensible with reason and probabilities. "There are things that we doctors don't have a complete handle on, and I would have to say this pregnancy is one of them. I can only hypothesize that one of your tubes reopened a bit. You remember that when you had PID, the fimbria — the little arms at the end of the tubes — closed shut in an effort to wall off the infection. It was a survival response that kept the pathogens from spreading to the internal organs in your peritoneal cavity. In that sense, it was a good physiological response. But that closure ruined the functional anatomy of your fallopian tubes. It is possible, however, that a small opening occurred in the intervening years. It's not unheard of but it's very, very rare — highly uncommon," Dr. Scholl explained. "And even if there was a small opening, the chances of the egg being released into that opening without functional fimbria to catch it and sweep it into the tube…well, they're very low. However, it's my best guess that this is the scenario that explains your pregnancy."

"You mean I got lucky?"

"Well, it all depends on how you view this pregnancy. If you want to be pregnant, then I would say you are extraordinarily lucky."

Sarah remembered little of her journey back to her Midtown office. The doctor's words kept echoing in her head. From the time she was seven years old — when her mother had told her she would likely have no little brothers or sisters — she had wanted a baby of her own. When she was old enough to babysit, she became a favorite of the mothers in her suburban neighborhood. She loved babies' skin and smell. She got a kick out of the way children tried to make sense of their world. She marveled at how kids grew and changed. If teaching hadn't been such a low-status, poorly compensated job, and if her parents hadn't shelled out so much for her Ivy League education, she would have chosen teaching over the law in a heartbeat.

So, before the subway doors closed on the uptown train, Sarah knew she would not interfere with the unexpected life growing in her womb.

As she walked into her office, she took stock of where she stood in the firm. She had worked hard and come very far, very fast. Another few years and she had a good shot at making partner. Since Tom had left — jumping ship at the mere suggestion of marriage — being a good attorney had been the driving force in her life. How would a baby fit into that life? Staring at the work piled on her desk, she wondered how she would get everything done with a baby. Other women with demanding jobs had somehow figured it out. She would, too.

But not that night. She couldn't focus on anything other than the embryo growing inside of her. She made a perfunctory effort at getting her desk organized, left a few notes to herself about where to pick up in the morning and walked out of the office at half past seven. As she headed for the revolving doors, the lobby's security guard teased her about skipping out early before wishing her a good night. Picking up some groceries at the market down the block from her apartment, she resolved to eat less takeout and more homemade meals. It occurred to her that an embryo the size of a raisin was already making its presence known.

She made enough primavera and salad for Rick in case he made it over to her place that night. As she ate, she scanned her apartment. Where would she put a baby? It was a decent one-bedroom — particularly for the city, where shoeboxes were called studios and windows, as likely as not, faced a brick wall. Her apartment was a walk-up, true, but it had hardwood floors, new appliances — including a washer/dryer combo — and windows facing north and west with views of the street. The location was ideal, with shops for essentials nearby and the river just a few blocks to the east. When she had time, she could walk to work. Central Park was close by. Could it be that in eight months she would be one of those women wheeling a stroller to the park?

Deep in her reverie, she heard a key turn in the door.

"Hello, Ms. Abadhi. It's your friendly doctor here to make a house call," Rick said before he kissed her hello. "Are you feeling better?"

Sarah panicked. What did he know about her feeling lousy? Had she said anything to him? And then she remembered. She'd refused his overtures last night. "Oh, I'm a little better. Have you eaten yet? I made dinner — hear that? I *made* dinner, homemade with fresh ingredients: pasta primavera and salad."

"That sounds enticing, almost as enticing as the chef." He pulled her to her feet and gave her a more robust embrace.

"You'll have to wait for dessert," she scolded playfully.

"How about having dessert first?" he suggested. "Let's break the rules and have dessert first."

Sarah looked at the man who had done the impossible: He'd made her pregnant. Yielding to his suggestion, she turned down the lights. They stripped off each other's clothes and headed for the sofa.

Sarah made love with an urgency she'd never felt before. She wanted Rick safely within her. Everything else could wait. Rick matched her ardor. He'd never wanted a woman the way he wanted her. Sarah came and then came again just as Rick climaxed. Then they lay entwined on the couch, each lover breathing hard, astonished at the intensity of what had just happened.

After a few minutes, Sarah got up to use the bathroom, leaving Rick naked and alone on the sofa. He smiled when he remembered how he'd thought Sarah chilly when they first met. So much for first impressions. She was nothing if not passionate about the big three: work, sex and working out. Besides that, she was easygoing and easy to be with. Equally important, she wasn't interested in getting a guarantee about the future. She was happy to take it one day at a time, and so far, they'd enjoyed every one. She was the perfect partner. He marveled at his good luck.

As she sat on the toilet, Sarah mulled over the idea of telling Rick her news. Given his take on fatherhood, there would never be a good time. But if not now, when? They had just made each other so happy. Emerging from the bathroom, she decided to bite the bullet. Standing at the living room's threshold, she stared at the man who'd made her pregnant.

"What are you looking at?"

"I'm looking at one naked, sex-crazed guy, that's what," she replied, assuming the role of the irreverent Sarah she knew he liked so well.

"Well I may be sex-crazed, but it's only because you make me cah-ray-zee," he whooped. He extended his hand and, as Sarah approached, he pulled her back on the sofa. "I don't think we need this robe," he said, opening the tie to reveal her beautiful and somewhat-fuller-than-normal breasts. "And I love these. Oh, how I love these," he said, caressing them.

"Rick, can we be serious for a minute?"

"Oh, yes, Frau Abadhi," he said in a German accent, removing his hand from her breast and saluting. "I am now serious."

"I mean it. I got some news today that I need to share with you."

"News? Should I be excited or worried?"

"Well...," she said tentatively.

He couldn't imagine what was going on. Why was Sarah so serious all of a sudden? "Are you okay, Sarah? You said you weren't feeling so great. Is everything all right?"

"I don't know how this happened, Rick, but...." She took a deep breath, exhaled audibly and said, "Somehow I've become pregnant."

In all his many years of enjoying the company of women, no

one had ever dropped that particular bomb. "What? How did that happen? You said you were sterile. You told me we didn't need to take precautions. What the hell, Sarah? What the hell? Were you playing me?"

Her fear was realized. He thought she'd tricked him.

"I'm sorry you think me capable of playing you. I would have hoped you knew me well enough to know I could never do that."

"Well, what happened then?"

"The diagnosis of infertility was given to me by two doctors. I saw one of them today. Even he has no idea how this happened."

Rick's mind started racing to all the possible outcomes. There was only one that he could fathom, and that was erasing the mistake. But what if she wouldn't abort it? Oh, God…what then? He wanted to pound his fist on the coffee table and scream obscenities, but instead he cleared his throat and asked as evenly as he could, "What are you planning to do?"

Sarah took hold of his hand and looked him straight in the eye. "I know you don't want this. You made your feelings about children clear. But I do want this pregnancy. I want it very much. I never thought it could happen…and I may never have another chance. I plan on continuing the pregnancy." Rick grimaced as he pulled his hand away.

"You're a wonderful man, Rick. I really like you. And I'll understand if you get your clothes on, walk out the door and never look back. You owe me nothing. You owe this embryo nothing. By continuing with the pregnancy, I am taking full responsibility for the child, financially and otherwise."

Rick thought this was the worst thing she could have said. If she had chosen to get an abortion, they could pick up and carry on like nothing had happened. If she had demanded he pony up and become a father to her baby, he could rail against her for roping him into something he'd sworn off. But here she was, as ever, the straight shooter: I want it, you don't. I'm letting you off the hook.

"Jesus Christ, Sarah…I don't know…I don't know what to say…," he stammered. "I know it's your body. But don't I get a vote?"

"What would you say if you were deciding?"

"I'd say, 'We're doing fine without a baby. Who needs to ruin this great thing we have?'"

"So you'd abort it."

"Yeah, I would, so we could keep on like we have been. I love being with you, Sarah. I know you've enjoyed it, too. Why mess with it?"

"You say we have a great thing going. But what is it exactly, Rick? What is it we have?"

"What is it? Are you nuts? It's perfect. I was just thinking that a few minutes ago. We get along so well. We like the same things. And you can't deny the chemistry we have, Sarah. You don't find chemistry like ours every day," he said, almost beseeching her to see things his way.

Sarah nodded her head slowly. "You're right about all of that. Up until now we were on the same page about what we wanted and it's been great. But this pregnancy is a game changer. I saw the embryo today on the ultrasound, with its tiny heart beating. I never imagined I'd see a child growing inside me. I never even let myself entertain the hope of becoming pregnant. But now, somehow, it's here," she said as she placed her hand on her stomach.

"I'd wager that as much as I want this pregnancy, you'd like it to go away. You know there's no way to compromise on this, Rick. One point of view has to prevail. I'm sorry I'm making you unhappy. I would never intentionally do that. What I'm trying to say is, if luck is with me, I'm going to have a child next winter…and it would be lovely if we could do this together. But if you decide to beg off, I'll respect your decision."

He was defeated. Tears of anger rolled down his cheeks. "You're right about one thing. This is a game changer, Sarah. I never signed up for fatherhood. You know that and you're still choosing to have the baby."

"I am. I'm sorry."

"I don't want a kid — not now, not ever. I got that out on the table from the get-go. I never misled you."

"You never did. That's why I know what you have to do now. It's all right, Rick. Really, it is."

He put his arms around her and suppressed a sob. Then he kissed her hair, her cheek, her neck and finally her lips. They made love once more, slowly, each savoring every touch, every smell, every part of their lover's body.

When they finally exhausted one another, Rick got up from the sofa, put on his clothes and left the key on the kitchen table where Sarah would be sure to find it.

EIGHTEEN

Susan Smith had two great loves in her life. The first was her work as a professor of health care policy at the large research university down the street from her small, utilitarian home; the second was her only child, Rick. She had nearly lost him when, as a little boy, he had been critically injured in an automobile accident. But her boy had exceeded everyone's expectations, eventually regaining both his health and vigor. He grew up to be the kind of man she'd hoped to raise: devoted to the service of others, intellectually curious and fearless in the face of authority. His sense of humor was an added bonus — she took no credit for it, but still, his irreverent quips gave her great pleasure. So it was with alarm she noticed that, on call after call, her son's usual good humor was replaced by irritability and impatience.

Susan had no idea what had thrown her sturdy son off his game, but, as good mothers are wont to do, she decided to find out by doing some reconnaissance in the form of a visit. A health reform conference provided the pretext for her trip to New York. She sent in her late registration fee and e-mailed Rick her schedule, asking if she might sleep on his pullout sofa for a couple of nights.

Rick agreed to his mother's request, but had mixed emotions about her visit. They were closer than most mothers and sons, maybe because it had been just the two of them after his father left. When he was young, his mother was his rock. During his adolescence, she parted company with most of his friends' mothers by giving him the chance to make mistakes. She offered advice, but sparingly, usually waiting to be asked. Rick learned the hard way that he ignored that advice at his peril.

He knew he probably could use some of what his mother had to offer now, but he worried about her seeing him as he was. She could always read him like a book, and the truth was he was a mess. Try as he might, he couldn't get Sarah out of his head. Beer had become his nightly friend, helping to quiet the demons that rose up as soon as he didn't have work to distract him. It wasn't until he'd downed his sixth bottle — usually while watching some game at home — that he could stand being with himself every night.

On the day his mother was scheduled to arrive, he was thankful he had workups for several new admissions to keep him occupied. He blocked out everything but his patients, including the passage of time. When he looked at his watch, he realized his mother had been on the ground in New York for more than an hour.

It was Jeff who answered the buzzer, letting Susan into the upscale building he and Rick had moved to after becoming attending physicians. Jeff had only met Rick's mother once before — and briefly at that — when she had done some consulting for the city's public health department. That meeting left Jeff wondering how such a small, serious, blond had spawned his tall, dark, smart-aleck friend. He could only guess that Rick took after the other side of the family.

He remembered his musings on Rick's genetic inheritance as the elevator opened to reveal its only passenger. Wearing a battered, tan trench coat and brown flats, the petite gray-blond woman walked toward the apartment door with a brisk step, dragging her suitcase behind her. Though unadorned, except for some earrings Rick had sent her for Mother's Day, she was handsome in the way a healthy, fit, older woman could be. Never a beauty, this was the highest physical ideal she could aspire to, and though she would hesitate to admit it, aspire she did. Her son may have gotten his good looks from his father, but he had gotten his athletic talent and drive from his quietly competitive mother.

"Hello, Jeff," Susan said as she approached the apartment door.

"It's so nice of you to put me up. I really appreciate it, especially with the cost of a hotel room in your neck of the woods."

"We're so glad you could join us in our new bachelor pad," Jeff lied, aware of Rick's ambivalence about his mother's visit. "Come in, come in. Rick is still at the hospital, but he phoned a little while ago to say he thought he could wrap things up by 7:30. Have you eaten yet?"

"Oh, no, no. Not even a complimentary pretzel on the plane. I'd love to take you boys — oh, pardon me, men — to dinner. I'm famished and I'll eat anywhere you suggest, as long as it's nearby and we get there soon."

Jeff took her coat and wheeled her carry-on next to the convertible sofa in the living room. "How do you feel about Japanese food?" he inquired as he motioned to the sofa to offer her a seat.

"I simply love it. And it's so healthy. I think the Japanese have cornered the market on diet. You know, Okinawans have the greatest longevity. We could take a page out of their book."

"You're absolutely right, but I don't think you'll be convincing your son that he should switch to fish and vegetables anytime soon. Maybe he'll go for the Japanese beer and the sake. And he's a fan of sushi, but don't take his beef away from him, especially lately. He's been on a meat-and-potatoes diet of late, but don't tell him I told you," Jeff confided as he sat down in the armchair next to the sofa.

"Oh? Don't tell me he's becoming a fan of the American diet. It must be the stress of the job," she suggested, grabbing the opening for a discussion about her son's change in mood.

"You know health care, Mrs. Smith. We're always stressed. It's the nature of the biz."

"Please, call me Susan. Mrs. Smith sounds like the woman who supposedly makes those frozen pies," she offered. "But in terms of stress, Rick seems a bit more stressed than usual, at least as far as I can tell from our phone conversations. I know that's hardly a reliable metric, but you know mothers, Jeff. We have our antennae."

"Indeed I do. My mother's intuition is uncanny. Once when I was a teenager, she knew I'd been hurt before I even called her from the ER. I'd slipped and fallen on broken glass, cutting my hand and requiring stitches. She didn't know the particulars, but she swears she knew I was injured." Jeff was actually glad that Rick's mother was going down this road. He was eager to talk to someone about Rick's newfound short temper. Just yesterday Rick had railed at him for using the last of the ketchup; this from a guy who never used to eat dinner at home.

"Scientifically, I have no idea if there's a basis for this, but I know that mothers know their offspring. And I sense that something is irritating Rick. I just assumed it was work, but perhaps I'm off base on that," Susan said, fishing for information.

Jeff wondered how much to disclose. He knew Rick was a pretty private guy, but he was worried about him. He'd broken up with Sarah — or she with him, he never did find out who had pulled the trigger — more than three months ago. Since then he'd been off. He still had an occasional one-night stand, but he was home nearly every night. And from the looks of the pile of bottles waiting to be recycled, his intake of beer was impressive. If he wasn't mistaken, Rick was even developing the beginnings of a beer gut — nothing dramatic, but something of note for a guy who had always had washboard abs.

"Yeah, Rick hasn't been quite himself lately," Jeff said honestly, while remaining vague.

"So you've noticed it, too?" Susan asked.

"I guess so. I mean he's fine, but it's just that Rick is usually a laugh a minute — you know, he's a funny guy. And lately he's just quieter, more thoughtful I guess you could say."

"I don't want to pry. After all, I'm well aware that he's a grown man. But did something happen to precipitate the change?" Susan asked. "Of course, I don't mean to put you in an awkward position. I'm not asking you to break any confidences," she added quickly.

"No, no. No confidences. I think he's just...maybe," he struggled, "I mean I'm guessing here — maybe he's in a funk about his love life. It's a common lament among single men our age. No big deal," Jeff said, trying to give Rick's mother some pertinent — if generic — information.

"Oh, I see. Yes, it's a lament common to the human condition, I would say. Is there anyone in particular he's lamenting over?" Susan knew she was pushing the limits of motherly investigation, but she thought it worth a try.

Jeff wasn't sure if he should say anything about Sarah. He figured the breakup had precipitated Rick's edginess. At the very least, it was coincident with his change in mood. He decided to approach the subject tangentially.

"I don't know how active Rick's social life was when he lived at home. But since I've known him, he's gone out with a lot of great women. Only recently he was dating an attorney, as smart as she was good-looking. I liked her a lot."

"And?" Susan asked, anxious for the rest of the story.

"Oh, the usual. Rick enjoys meeting lots of women. He's definitely not a one-woman man. Me, on the other hand, I'm waiting for my one woman to hit me over the head and drag me down the aisle."

Just as they were sharing a laugh about that, they heard the key in the door. A disheveled and out-of-breath Rick made his entrance, having run the three blocks from the hospital. His mother got to her feet and gave him a hug, which he returned in kind. Jeff was impressed by how long they embraced, especially considering how wound up Rick had gotten when he told Jeff his mother was going to visit.

Jeff stayed in his chair, feeling a bit awkward. Just as he was about to excuse himself, Susan released her son from her embrace and declared, "I'm starving!" Rick broke into a broad grin.

"Dr. Smith, the patient is demanding food, and I think it best if we feed her. Perhaps some Japanese would do," Jeff suggested.

"I concur, Dr. Gotbaum. That's clearly the best course of treatment: Feed her. I think an immediate dose of vegetable tempura might do the trick," Rick quipped, relieved and happy that Jeff had initiated the banter.

Susan was only too happy to join in. "Well, after a trip to the john, this patient will be ready to participate in your suggested treatment. And then, stand back. You'll be surprised how much a woman my size can put away. I hope I won't embarrass you in the restaurant."

"Don't worry, Mom, if anyone asks we'll say we picked you up on the street, a hungry Midwestern tourist."

"You won't hurt my feelings if you pretend you never set eyes on me before." With that, Susan excused herself as she went off to the john, which still smelled of the disinfectant Rick had used that morning when he took a rare turn at cleaning the bathroom. As Susan sat on the toilet, she breathed a thankful sigh that she'd come. Rick wasn't himself. If all was well, he never would have let her hug him like that in front of a friend. And he had actually hugged her back.

Susan had not exaggerated her hunger. She ordered miso soup to start, followed by an appetizer of *age dofu*. She polished off a platter of vegetable tempura, leaving not a single grain of the accompanying brown rice. For her grand finale, she had some *mochi* and green tea before declaring herself sated. Rick and Jeff enjoyed both their food and the lively dinner conversation; the hot sake they shared added to their high spirits. The more time Jeff spent with Susan, the more he began to see the wit he knew so well in her son. He decided she must have been quite the firecracker in her younger days. Not so different from Rick after all.

After dinner, the three walked back to the apartment, picking up the pace as the late-summer breeze turned cool. Once home, Rick hung up his mother's coat in the front hall closet, and Jeff excused himself to check his e-mail and make some calls. As much as Susan enjoyed Jeff — she could see what a good friend he was to her son from their earlier Kabuki dance of questions and answers — she was glad to have some time alone to visit with Rick.

"I'm going to have a beer. Can I interest you in one?" Rick asked, knowing what his mother's reply would be, but deciding to err on the side of the good manners she'd taught him.

"Beer? Oh, no, dear. But if you have a tea bag or some decaf coffee I wouldn't say no," Susan said.

"Yeah, I'm sure we have one or both of those. Let me check. Jeff," he yelled, "do we have any herbal tea?"

Jeff interrupted his work on the missive he'd started to a woman whose profile he'd read on JDate.com. He came out of his bedroom, showed Rick where he kept the tea bags and made a beeline back to his laptop.

Rick found a package of cookies to go with the tea. He realized he hadn't been inside a food store since he'd gone shopping with Sarah months before. For years, Jeff had bought the toilet paper and OJ. Now that Rick was home more, Jeff got groceries for both of them, just totaling up how much was owed. Rick had no problem with paying up. He was just relieved to have some food to eat after coming home from work.

"Herbal tea, coming up. And cookies, just to show how civilized we guys can be," Rick said. He brought the tray to his mother, who had kicked off her shoes and tucked her feet under her on the couch. He sat down in the armchair, beer in hand.

"Oh, thank you, dear. You didn't have to trouble yourself by opening the package of Oreos."

"How did you know I opened the package?"

"Oh, my ears are still functioning quite well, thank you. I heard you opening the package in the kitchen," she explained, revealing her secret.

"Really? That would never have registered for me. I guess

women's minds must work in a different way," Rick said. "At least that's what I've come to conclude after my dealings with the opposite sex."

"A revelation for you, dear?" Susan teased. "Yes, we're wired somewhat differently. We're generally better than men at keeping several balls in the air. I believe the perpetuation of the species depends on it."

"You really think so?" Rick asked, interested in his mother's take on the age-old Mars versus Venus dichotomy. "You think men and women are hard-wired differently?

"Well, let me be clear. In terms of sheer intellectual power, I see no difference. So you're a fine doctor and a woman as intellectually endowed and committed as you would be as fine a doctor. However, as she'd be treating her patient she'd have in the back of her mind that she'd better call home to remind the sitter to help Johnny with his math homework. Between patients she'd also call the vet to make an appointment for the cat on her day off."

"Sounds like a miserable way to go through life. As far as I'm concerned, the patients alone provide more than enough entertainment. But I don't think being able to remember to call the sitter and the vet is a sex-linked characteristic. A man could do that if he had to," Rick insisted.

"I think most men wouldn't do it and maybe couldn't do it," his mother countered. "One thing at a time; by and large, that's how men function. I know I am generalizing, of course, and there are exceptions to the rule, I'm sure," Susan said, covering her bets as she sipped her chamomile tea.

"I don't know if I buy that. I have a different explanation. The woman physician will have to make the call to the sitter because she's hard-wired for kids — to make babies and raise kids. That's what women want. It doesn't matter what heights they've scaled professionally, how sexually alluring they are, how smart or how dim-witted they are. They all want babies. Consider it something I've gleaned from my experience with the opposite sex," Rick said dejectedly.

"Is that so bad, dear? After all, where would we be without that drive to reproduce? I think it's instinctual, don't you?"

"It is. But if you ask me, we have far too many people already walking the planet. I've never had any interest in adding to the overpopulation problem. There's nothing so exceptional in my genes that I think they should be passed on to the next generation."

This last comment gave Susan the lay of the land. She guessed that her son had butted up against the drive to perpetuate the species perhaps one time too many — and perhaps most recently with a woman whom he liked but who'd insisted on children. She decided to keep her response light and positive.

"Well, as your mother I might disagree with you on that point about your genes. I think you have exemplary genes. As an only child, you are certainly entitled to reproduce at least once without any guilt about compounding the global population problem. Speaking selfishly, of course, I would hope one day to be a grandmother. No pressure, dear," she said with a little smile. "But all things being equal, I think you would be a fine parent, for a man that is," she teased. "I recommend finding a good woman who can multitask and pick up the slack."

This turn in the conversation was tying Rick's stomach in knots. It made him crazy to think that just blocks away there was a fetus carrying his DNA, a fetus that Sarah had chosen over him. He wondered what his mother would make of that. He decided to mount a preemptive defense.

"I don't know how you can advocate for the whole marriage and babies thing, especially after your experience. Think of how much better your life would have been if you hadn't married him and had me," Rick said, nearly spitting out the last words.

Her son's brutal appraisal took Susan aback. Rick rarely spoke of his father, and she had never known exactly how he viewed their marriage. She knew he still smarted at the memory of the desertion. It had come at a terrible time, just as he was beginning his long recovery from the accident. At the ripe old age of five, he had been assaulted by an oncoming car and by a father eager to shed his family. Still, it stung Susan to think that her failed marriage had soured Rick on the possibility of creating a happy family of his own. She knew he dated extensively, and she had always assumed, wrongly it now appeared, that he would eventually want to settle down. Most devastating was his declaration that she would have been better off had he never been born. She had to set him straight.

Susan put her stocking feet back on the floor. "Rick," she began, "how can you draw conclusions from a sample of one? I'm quite surprised. You're a scientist and know better. For your information, your father and I were happy for several years. Things happened over time. You can blame him for his failings, which I admit are serious, but you can't blame the institution of marriage. Of one thing I'm fairly certain: If you decide to marry, you won't take the road he took.

"As for you, your existence on this earth is the best thing that ever happened to me. Hands down."

Rick wasn't convinced. "How do you know I'm not exactly like him? What? You think me incapable of leaving a wife and child high and dry? For all you know I may be a real chip off the miserable old block."

"Rick, I think I know you. You're not your father. I know he hurt you when you were a little boy. But you can't allow that to influence the choices you make now. You're too smart for that."

"Well, maybe you don't know me as well as you think. Maybe those genes dear old Dad passed on are manifesting in your precious boy. Did you ever think of that?"

Without hesitation, Susan threw the argument back at him. "Genes are just a starting point. What you do with them is up to you, Rick. If you don't like how your life is going, you can do something about it. I didn't raise you to be helpless, that much I know."

"No, you poured your heart and soul into me. I get it. What I don't get is how you can say I was the best thing that ever happened to you. Look at what I put you through, how I changed your life. Once your no-good husband took off, without me you could have enjoyed your career and probably gotten a heck of a lot more recognition. You could have had good times with your friends — male and female — traveling hither and yon, and doing whatever you damned well pleased. I was like a millstone around your neck."

This was not the plucky, determined boy Susan had raised. True, after his dad left, his heart had been broken. But his grandfather — her dad — had jumped into the void, taking early retirement from his job at the auto factory so he could be at his bedside each day. After a long series of surgeries and months of rehabilitation, Rick had rallied. She didn't feel she was sugarcoating things to say that he'd had a happy childhood, too. Now she had to try to get him back to his true self, which she believed to be nothing if not forward-looking and optimistic. She put down her mug and took both of his big hands in hers.

"Now you listen to me, Rick. I'm no Pollyanna and I'm no dummy. I am telling you that I wouldn't trade being your mother for anything. You have been — hear me clearly — the most important thing in my life. I love my work, but the finest moments I have ever known have been as your mother. You have surpassed my every hope, my every expectation for a son. Never, ever think that I would have been better off without you. You are everything to me, and I can't imagine my life without you in it."

As she spoke, tears filled her eyes. To her surprise, her words had the same effect on her son. She kissed Rick's hand and then wiped her face. "Don't you ever doubt what I just said. You are the most important thing — the best thing — that ever happened to me."

She hoped her words had hit their mark, reaching her son's place of vulnerability and offering balm to the wound that made him feel himself unworthy of being his mother's son.

That night was the only time during the visit that mother and son spoke so frankly. The following morning, Rick and Jeff awoke before six to the aroma of freshly brewed coffee, home fries, bagels and eggs. Susan had gotten up at five, assessed the household food stocks and gotten to work preparing a hot, sit-down breakfast. As a mother she saw it both as her duty and her pleasure to provide her son and his friend with this small bit of comfort in their stress-filled lives. As they ate, Susan tried to gauge Rick's frame of mind, but all she learned was that he still enjoyed his eggs over easy.

After they finished breakfast, the three went their separate ways, promising to meet at the end of the day for another dinner out. That night they chose an Ethiopian restaurant. Both the food and the novelty of eating without utensils were to their liking. They spent most of the night discussing the politics of health care reform, a matter near and dear to them all. Jeff and Susan agreed that a single-payer system on the order of Medicare would be the easiest and least expensive way to get one hundred percent coverage in the population at large. Rick protested, pointing out that low reimbursement rates and paperwork were driving good doctors to opt out of Medicare. If that was the single-payer system they were endorsing, he would have to count himself out. The heated but friendly discussion had a salutary effect on Rick. It had been a long time since he had been interested in debating anything.

The next morning Susan did a modified reprise of the breakfast she'd created the day before, substituting croissants she'd picked up at a French bakery for the bagels. The breakfast was a hit and they were all sorry when it came time to leave. As they emerged from the apartment building, Susan reached up and hugged them both, giving each a pat on the cheek for good measure. As she headed down the street toward the subway station, she turned to catch a parting glimpse of her son and his friend as they joined the current of pedestrians.

The couple of days Rick spent with his mother gave him the chance to see her in a new light. It dawned on him that at the very same time she'd had a child on death's door, she had been face-to-face with the crumbling of her marriage. After being tossed aside like last year's fashion, she had made sure that both she and Rick survived; and more than that, she had given him the chance for a good life. After doing that for him, she had actually said he was the best thing that ever happened to her.

He realized that his mother was like some of the parents he'd met at the hospital — parents who had left no stone unturned to help their child survive a medical crisis. His mother was like that. He had been — and still was — one of the lucky ones. The least he could do in return was not piss away his life drinking beer in front of the television. It was time to get his act together.

He started by cutting back on the beer and forcing himself to run every day. He felt more present and alive from just those changes in his routine. He still had no real interest in women, which was a worry. But he mulled over his mother's take on marriage. The fact that someone who'd had such a resounding failure could possibly endorse it made him laugh out loud.

Her endorsement aside, he couldn't imagine how marriage might ever be in the cards for him. There was no way he could see himself as a husband. The word actually stuck in his craw. And if there had ever been a woman he'd consider for a lifelong contract, it was Sarah. But he'd let that ship sail. He knew that the only way to move forward was to somehow come to terms with how much he missed her. He'd just have to follow his mother's example and find his way out of the dead end known as regret.

NINETEEN

One of Sarah's pleasures during her pregnancy was thinking about how to rearrange her apartment to make it ready for the baby. She would indulge in her reverie after returning home from work or while lingering over a cup of tea on a Sunday morning. It was only when she got into bed, in the minutes before she fell asleep, that her thoughts turned to Rick.

Their last night together had been startling in more ways than one. She had never had a lover like him. Their bodies were perfectly suited to one another; their attraction was nothing short of electric. Merely holding hands with him was an erotic experience. But she knew that his appeal went beyond sex, revelatory though it was. She admired the work he did and his dedication to helping extremely sick children. She had to smile when she thought about how he had handled himself in the settlement meeting with the Arkins and their lawyer — how everything had been riding on him and how he had finessed the situation. She thought of their long runs together, and how easy it had been to be with him. Counter to expert prognostication, he'd made her pregnant. It made her happy to think that he was the father of her child.

What brought her back to her life alone was the memory of Rick's reaction when she had told him she was pregnant. Panic had radiated from every pore in his body. It wasn't because he didn't want her; their last time together had made that clear enough.

So, as wonderful a guy as he was, she had to presume he had some major flaw, a flaw that made him poor "marriage material" as Devorah would say. It was a hidden flaw, like a fault line deep beneath the earth's surface that only revealed itself during a devastating quake.

It was the image of formerly intact homes torn asunder by a long, gaping fissure in the earth that took the edge off the longing Sarah felt whenever she thought of Rick.

Pregnancy suited Sarah. She was one of the fortunate women who never threw up their breakfasts as the small life within them grew and took shape. She tired more easily in the first months of her pregnancy, a fatigue made worse by swearing off coffee. Still, she drew energy from her belief that some stroke of astounding good luck had allowed her to conceive a child. The series of ultrasounds showed the baby developing rapidly. The little fish-like being she had seen during the first ultrasound soon grew arms, legs, fingers and toes. After each visit to the doctor, she was so giddy she wanted to sprint the thirty blocks back to her office.

She allowed her pregnancy an exemption from the pall of low expectations. When it came to the baby, optimism had free rein.

Her route to motherhood, however, would have one minor bump. As a single, unattached woman, she was well aware that people would question who had fathered her child. Since she had released Rick from all responsibility, she decided — quite reasonably, in her mind — to keep his identity to herself. Then she came up with a plan for sharing her life-altering news with those who needed to know.

Since her first-trimester lethargy made it hard to maintain her usual pace at work, she chose to disclose her pregnancy first to Harry. She knew telling him might cause him to lose interest in her as a protégée. That made her nervous, not only because she liked him, but also because she needed him. No associate made partner without having a godfather, and Harry was hers. Of the fifty partners in the law firm's New York office, eight were women, and three were mothers. Despite the daunting odds, Sarah had no intention of letting motherhood derail her from the partnership track. She hoped Harry would share her resolve.

She waited until her eighth week and then looked for the right moment to tell him her news. The occasion presented itself around five on a Friday afternoon. They were in Harry's office, just finishing up some work on the case of a hospital accused of turning a blind eye to organ trafficking using donors from third-world countries. At risk was the hospital's accreditation as a transplant center.

"Well, I'm calling it a week. I hope this weather holds. Toby and I are headed to the beach house."

"Sounds great, Harry. I hope you get some time on your boat."

"Me, too. What about you? Any plans for getting out of town?"

"Nah, if I get a chance, maybe I'll catch up on some sleep."

"Well remember, Sarah, all work and no play made Jack a dull boy."

"Thanks for the reminder. I'll take it under advisement."

"Yeah, I know what that means."

"Harry, if you have a spare minute, I'd like to share a confidence with you, something personal," she began, her heart racing in her chest.

"Okay, shoot," he replied as he stopped packing up his briefcase. Sarah rarely gave any indication of having a personal life, so his curiosity was piqued. He sat down and gave her his full attention.

"I've become pregnant, Harry."

He flinched, wondering how the hell that had happened. After cursing silently to himself, he asked diplomatically, "Are congratulations in order?"

"Yes, Harry, I'm very happy. The baby's due early next winter."

He came out from behind his desk, took her hand and kissed her on the cheek. "Then I offer you my heartiest congratulations." Patting her shoulder he added, "That's going to be one lucky baby to have you as a mother." Once back in his chair he asked, "How're you feeling, Sarah? I mean, I remember Toby throwing up her guts when she was pregnant with each of our boys."

"Oh, I'm good. No morning sickness, just not much of an

appetite. The major issue is that I don't have my usual stamina. I understand that should pass in about a month or so," she said, touched and relieved by Harry's response.

"Okay then. It would be a good idea if we got you some help on this alleged organ trafficking case, at least for the next little bit," he suggested. "We've got no margin for error."

"Some extra help might be nice until the fatigue passes," Sarah admitted. "I was thinking I'd like to work maybe ten-hour days for the next month or so. I need more sleep than usual. But the doctor assures me this is very temporary. I should be back to normal soon."

Harry nodded. "Don't worry. Just do what you have to do. Cut back on your hours if you need to. We'll reassess in a month or so. How does that sound?"

"Sounds great. Thank you, Harry."

What he didn't ask was how Sarah came to be pregnant. He figured if she wanted him to know about the father, she would have told him. Regardless of who the bastard was, Harry's crack associate was pregnant. It was all the same to him. He would make whatever adjustments were necessary to have things work for her, including running interference with the managing partner if it came to that. He knew she'd feel punky for a while, but Sarah at half speed was quicker than most associates at full throttle.

Harry acquitted himself admirably that day. The memory of his kiss on her cheek made Sarah smile more than once, especially when she juxtaposed that sweet gesture with his well-earned reputation as a cutthroat legal shark.

Breaking the news to her parents required more thoughtful preparation. Harry's investment in her was nothing when compared to theirs. Born in European displaced-persons camps to Holocaust survivors, Eva and Joseph had come to this country as children. They had married right out of college and grabbed for every brass ring within reach. Joseph trained for a career in medical research. Eva's poetry landed her a teaching job at a well-respected liberal arts college. They named their first child Sarah, after a grandmother murdered by the Nazis. They were soon able to purchase a comfortable, suburban home convenient to work. But one dream eluded them — that of having a large, happy family. After Sarah's birth, despite visiting doctor after doctor, Eva never again became pregnant. Sarah, their first and only child, became the crown jewel of their lives.

As proud as Eva and Joseph were of Sarah's stellar career success, they worried about the long hours that success demanded. It was not only unhealthy — they could only imagine how hard it was for her to meet eligible men. Every month or so, they took the commuter train to the city to meet Sarah for lunch or — a rare treat — dinner and the theater. Whenever they were with her, they chose their words of pleasant conversation carefully, all the while trying to gather bits of intelligence on her progress toward finding a mate. But for several years now, Sarah had made that difficult. While she was open to talking about work, politics and her friends from college, she refused to engage in a discussion about the men in her life. That fact left her parents feeling chastened and bereft.

It hadn't always been so. When she was younger she'd introduced several boyfriends to them, starting with the gangly Solomon Grossman in high school. Her college beau, Alex, had become a fixture in their house during semester breaks and summer vacations. In fact, Joseph and Eva had predicted that the Jewish scholar-athlete would likely become their son-in-law, so inseparable were he and Sarah. They had headed off together to Boston after college, enrolled in prestigious graduate programs and shared a funky apartment near campus. Young love and the excitement of a new adventure had infused every phone call between Sarah and her parents. As far as they had been concerned, it would only be a matter of time before she and Alex announced their engagement.

But it was not to be. At Christmas break during her second year of law school, Sarah had come home alone. She said she and Alex had split and that's all she would say. Eva and Joseph had agreed it best to let her be, expecting she'd eventually talk about what led to the breakup. But years had passed and they remained in the dark about what had come between the two lovers.

Sarah saw her parents only twice during the first months of her pregnancy. She was exhausted, and whatever energy she had was dedicated to the case of alleged organ trafficking. After work, she'd sleep ten or twelve hours a night. She called her parents every day or two so they wouldn't worry, telling them she was buried in work. Even when the threat of early miscarriage had passed, she was in no rush to share the news with them, or with anyone else, for that matter, choosing to savor the magic of her pregnancy for as long as possible, uncomplicated by prying questions and people's judgments.

But by the end of her fourth month, Sarah knew her time was up. She thought it best to share her news with her parents in a public place. Though she felt certain they would love the idea of a grandchild, she doubted they'd be as restrained as Harry had been in asking about the baby's father. She decided to use a Broadway musical as the excuse for a shared day out. After making sure her parents were free on an upcoming Saturday, she got tickets to a matinee of *South Pacific*. Eva and Joseph were delighted when she called to invite them to the theater and dinner. They agreed to meet in front of the fountains at Lincoln Center.

The latest fashion of baby-doll blouses was fortuitous for a woman not yet ready to announce her pregnancy to the world. For her day out with her parents she decided on black stretch leggings with a black-and-white print blouse, which gathered below the bust in an empire waist. With her black ballet flats, red necklace and bangle bracelets and large red bag, she cut an attractive figure. Her parents were already waiting by the fountains outside the theater when she arrived. Just seeing her approach made them each break into a big smile.

"Hello, hello, you beautiful girl," Joseph said as he gave her a bear hug and a kiss. Sarah was a female version of her father: It was from him that she had gotten her height, her athleticism, her large dark eyes and her crazy black curls. Her mother, a fair woman of average height — whose idea of exercise was walking the aisles of the grocery store — often joked that she'd been the incubator for the cloning of her husband. Though Joseph was nearly eligible for Social Security, his closely cropped curls were still jet black. He was beaming as he released his daughter from his embrace.

Eva looked on, *kvelling*. The two most important people in her life were standing before her, and in such high spirits. No one affected Joseph as Sarah did. He was proud of her many achievements, but the truth was, it was her very existence that brought him joy.

Trying not to alert her mother to her changing body, Sarah skipped the frontal embrace, opting instead for an arm around her shoulder and a kiss on her cheek. But it was no use. Eva's quick once-over led her to conclude that her daughter had put on some weight around her middle. But rather than comment on so touchy a subject, she delivered a compliment.

"Where did you get that gorgeous bag? It looks like you could carry half your life in it. I wouldn't mind a bag like that myself."

Sarah made a mental note to pick one up in a different color for her mother's upcoming birthday. "Oh, I don't even remember where I got it. But you're right. It holds a lot." She opened it to reveal a light jacket in case the theater's A/C was too much, as well as her makeup, hairbrush, phone, keys, small bottle of hand sanitizer and other various and sundry items.

Joseph couldn't resist. "I don't know how we men get along without a purse. It's actually something of a miracle. Perhaps some Ph.D. student in need of a research topic will examine how we exist without all the things you women *schlep* around in your handbags. I can see the title of the dissertation proposal now: *The Adaptation of Male* Homo Sapiens *to the North American Cultural Norm of Purse*

Deprivation."

"Go ahead and poke fun all you want," Eva said. "Who do you turn to when you need a tissue? Who says, 'Honey, could you hold my sunglass case for me?' I ask you that. Men are only too happy to benefit from us *schlepping* these bags around and getting back pain in the process."

"True. It's all true. I admit defeat. Sarah, as always, your mother is right," Joseph conceded as he made a small bow to his wife.

Sarah wondered at the miracle of her parents. How was it possible for a man and a woman not only to fall in love with one another, but to negotiate all the twists and turns of a life spent in tandem? To all appearances, Eva and Joseph still enjoyed being with one another. A miracle indeed, and one that Sarah had no expectation of ever experiencing herself.

"Always right? Mom, just a minute." Sarah made a show of digging through her bag. "Too bad I don't have my handheld digital recorder. We could tape Dad's acknowledgement of your infallibility and you could play it back during your next disagreement. Excellent support for your case, whatever it may be," Sarah suggested. "Trust me. That would be powerful evidence in any court of law."

"Sarah," Joseph explained, putting his hands on his chest, "the key to a happy marriage is a happy wife. I make it my job to keep your mother happy. If all I need to do is agree with her, I have no problem doing it."

Eva rolled her eyes as Joseph repeated his oft-stated recipe for marital bliss. "Joe, thank you so much for regaling us once again with how you yield to all of my wants and needs." Then turning to her daughter she asked, "Sarah, how are *you*, darling? We haven't laid eyes on you for, what, six weeks or more? I know we're all terribly busy, but we have to make it our business to fit in a little visit with each other. It's important. Really," Eva added, not wanting to sound too pushy while still getting her point across.

"I know, Mom. I promise that I'll do better from now on. I've just had a lot on my plate the last couple of months."

"It's as much our fault as yours," her father offered, trying to deflect Eva's implied criticism. "We could easily just come down and have lunch with you, or stop on the way to pick up Rivka for the weekend. Just for a sandwich in the deli. It doesn't have to be fancy. Just a chance to catch up."

"Sure, Dad. You're right. We can come up with a schedule or something after the show, over dinner," Sarah suggested. "Given how jam-packed our lives are, I think we just have to block out some time or it won't happen."

"That would be lovely," Eva said, thrilled that her daughter was so amenable. "Ah. I see people are beginning to go in. They must have opened the doors. You know me. I always like to read the *Playbill* before the curtain goes up. Would you mind going in? We'll have plenty of time to talk over dinner."

"I made reservations at a Middle Eastern place nearby. I hope that's all right," Sarah said.

"It's perfect!" Joseph exclaimed. "How did you know I'm in the mood for *tourlou* and falafel?"

"They don't call me your daughter for nothing, Dad."

The Abadhi family made their way into the theater, giving Sarah the opportunity to hit the ladies' room one more time, though she had used the bathroom at home not forty minutes before. Another of the many ways her fetus made its existence known.

Although the Abadhis had seen a number of productions of *South Pacific*, they agreed that this one was far and away the best. It was in a buoyant mood that the three satisfied theatergoers walked up Columbus Avenue for dinner.

"My only regret," Eva said, "is that we didn't think to bring Bubbe Rivka along for the show."

"So how is Bubbe?" Sarah asked. "I'm ashamed to say I haven't called her in…geez, it must be a few weeks."

"Your grandmother is a wonder," Eva exclaimed. "She's doing well. She turns back any suggestion that she give up her apartment in Brooklyn to move closer to us. She's still rolling her shopping cart to the supermarket every week. Her only concession to old age is that she's agreed to let Uncle Max, Aunt Ellen and us give her the gift of a weekly visit from a housekeeper. You know, something's got to give when you're eighty-seven, and in her case, it's cleaning."

"Oh, that's a great idea," Sarah said. "I noticed the apartment was getting a little ripe when I was there last. I actually think a person is entitled to give up housecleaning at Bubbe's age. In fact, I think it should be a national right. We have Medicare and we ought to have Housecare."

"Wonderful. Let's push the federal deficit up a bit higher," Joseph said, only half in jest.

Sarah saw the sign for the restaurant that Harry had long raved about. "I think we're here," she said, both nervous and excited. She had choreographed the disclosure of her pregnancy with precision. She would tell her parents about the baby after they ordered and were enjoying their appetizers.

They were shown to a booth in the back of the restaurant. Their hunger helped them make quick work of the menu. As soon as their *dolmades*, hummus and pita arrived, Sarah inhaled deeply and began. "I have some wonderful news to tell you," she said. When Eva heard the word "wonderful" and saw her daughter's eyes brighten and her cheeks flush, she was sure Sarah would tell them she was dating someone special.

"Oooh, tell us, tell us," Eva said excitedly. "Tell us your wonderful news."

"Well, if all goes well, sometime in mid-January, you're going to become grandparents."

Eva and Joseph sat frozen in their seats. Eva, whose natural element was language, was left speechless.

Joseph slowly started to shake his head from side to side.

"How? How are we going to become grandparents? I don't understand."

"Dad, I'm pregnant."

Joseph and Eva were at a loss. As far as they knew, their daughter didn't date, no less have a relationship that could result in a child. Through her bewilderment, Eva strained to match her daughter's obvious happiness. "You're pregnant? Oh my God. We didn't even know you were involved with anyone. That's why Daddy is so surprised, why I'm so surprised. Who's the lucky man?"

Sarah was ready. "There is no man, lucky or otherwise. I'll be doing this alone."

"What? You went to a sperm bank?" Joseph asked, his voice heavy with disapproval.

"No, Dad, the baby was conceived in the usual way, but I'm having it on my own. This pregnancy was unplanned. The relationship in which it was conceived wasn't serious. The man was very accomplished, very bright. He was a lovely man — really — but not at all interested in marriage and children. He made that clear from the beginning. As I said, the pregnancy was a complete surprise," Sarah explained as she felt the blood pulsing at her temples.

Perhaps Eva and Joseph might have reacted differently had Sarah ever shared the circumstances leading to her breakup with Alex: the STD he'd given her, and the sterility that had ensued. Instead, they had assumed their daughter was healthy and fertile — and savvy enough to take precautions if she was intimate with a man. So all they knew was that she'd gotten herself knocked up by someone who'd left her.

"So let me see if I understand this," Joseph said, indignant. "You told the man you were involved with that you were pregnant and he walked away. Now you're in this thing by yourself. You'll be saddled with a child and he'll be off doing as he pleases. Do I have it right?"

Her father's grim take on her situation stung. She was no

hapless victim. And Rick was not the reptile her father implied. "Your interpretation is completely inaccurate. From the outset, he was up front with me about his intentions. He doesn't want children. Somehow I conceived, despite being careful. The pregnancy was a shock for us both. I told him that I wanted the child, but that I wouldn't force him into a role he had never signed up for. I decided to have this baby on my own. Well, not on my own, exactly. I was hoping that you and Mom would want to be a part of our lives," Sarah said, trying to change the trajectory of the conversation.

Eva was astonished at her daughter's decision to let the father walk away. But, rather than cause a break with her only child, she swallowed hard and put on a good face. "Honey, of course we'll be part of your lives. You know that Dad and I support you in everything you do. If you're going to have a baby, we'll do what we can to help you." It now occurred to her why Sarah had agreed to the idea of getting together more often. After years of shutting them out of her personal life, she would soon need their help. Eva wanted to weep.

But Sarah was oblivious to her mother's distress. "That means so much to me. It would in any case — I mean if I were married and expecting a child — but given the fact that I'm single, it means everything. Thank you," Sarah said effusively. "You're such great parents. I know how lucky I am to have you."

Joseph, however, was not assuaged by the compliment. "Don't you think this child has the right to a father?"

The criticism hurt. "Well, Dad, perhaps at some point the baby will know its father. But at this moment in time, the baby's father has no interest in being a father to anyone. I don't think it's fair to coerce him. Nor do I think the child would benefit from having a father who sees him or her as a liability. Let me be clear. I have no animosity toward the father. On the contrary, I think he's a good man. Luckily, I have the means to support the child by myself."

As their meals were delivered, the conversation came to a halt. As soon as the server turned to leave, Joseph continued. "If the man is as good as you say, how can he leave you in the lurch?"

"You'll just have to trust me on this, Dad. I told him he was free to go, that I would assume all responsibility for the baby. If he'd had his druthers, I would have had an abortion. For me, this is the better solution. I'm delighted by the new life that is growing inside of me. I'm sorry you don't seem to share my happiness."

Eva saw there was no changing the facts. Without asking their advice, Sarah had decided on a go-it-alone pregnancy. There was nothing to be done now but swallow that bitter pill and fall into line. She patted her daughter's hand. "Enjoy your pregnancy. Dad is just worried about you, that's all. He and I will be behind you every step of the way," she said, giving Joseph a gentle kick under the table.

But Joseph would not be hushed. "I realize you're an adult and you get to make your own decisions. Your mother and I have become bystanders in your life. But there was a time when we were more than that. You used to include us in your world. But since you came back to New York, you could have been celibate for all we knew. And now you tell us that out of some casual relationship you're having a child on your own.

"You think you're so independent that you can live your life while keeping the people who care most about you at arm's length. But listen to me, a little advice from your old father: This city is littered with highly successful, miserably unhappy people. If you're not careful, you'll join their ranks."

Sarah was stunned. So that's where her father thought she was headed. She decided at that moment to spend the rest of her pregnancy proving him wrong.

TWENTY

By the end of September, it was impossible for Sarah to find clothes that would hide her pregnancy. The time had come for her to make known the truth. She decided to enlist Doris's help in getting the word out at the office.

Doris received the news with the happy surprise that was due, even though she'd harbored suspicions that Sarah might be pregnant for a couple of months. When she learned that Sarah was going it alone, it saddened her to think the relationship that had led to the pregnancy didn't have the legs to continue all the way down the aisle. But, wanting to be a good friend, she readily agreed to discreetly let the other people in the office know about the baby.

Word spread quickly. Speculation around the water cooler abounded regarding the source of the sperm that had impregnated Sarah Abadhi. People tended to project their own fantasies. Several women concluded that she must have gone the route of artificial insemination. They figured Sarah didn't need to put up with some jerk just because she wanted a baby and her biological clock was ticking. She had the money, the brains and the energy to go it alone. Sarah's male co-workers — a number of whom had tried unsuccessfully to scale her barricade to intimacy — discounted that theory. They figured some lucky dude had knocked her up after an unforgettable one-night stand. Though Sarah would occasionally catch bits of these discussions as she entered the break room, she did nothing to disabuse either camp of their erroneous speculations.

In keeping with her promise to include them more in her life,

Sarah consulted with her parents about how to tell the rest of the family. Together they decided on Eva's birthday dinner as the setting for her announcement. On the morning of the party, Sarah bought a taupe version of the handbag her mother had admired by the fountains at Lincoln Center. Then she headed over to Grand Central and caught a train to Tuckahoe, her hometown just north of the city. Her father and grandmother were waiting for her as her train pulled into the station. Bubbe Rivka, perhaps ninety-five pounds soaking wet, got up from her seat on the bench, stood ramrod straight and made a beeline for her granddaughter. Sarah quickened her step to meet her halfway, fighting off the urge to pick her up and kiss her. Instead, she bent over and embraced her elfin grandmother.

Though Rivka's hearing was failing, her eyes were still sharp. She could tell immediately that something about Sarah had changed. "Bubbela, it's so goot to see you. You're bedda den medicine from de docta for your bubbe, you know dat, don't you?" Then Rivka took a step back and took a good look at her granddaughter. "Maybe I should git my eyes checked, but I tink sometink is different vit you. Eh? Is Bubbe right?" she asked in the singsong voice she had used when Sarah was a little girl.

"It's impossible to pull the wool over your eyes, Bubbe. I have some great news for you. You're going to be a great-grandmother," Sarah announced, glad that her grandmother made breaking the news so easy. "I'm due to have a baby in January." She put her bubbe's hand on her round stomach so Rivka could feel for herself.

"*Gott in himmel*, Sarah. Ven is de vedding? And who's my new grandson?"

"No wedding, no new grandson, Bubbe. Just me and the baby. It's the twenty-first century way of doing things," Sarah explained.

"Believe me. It's not a tventy-first century tink. Girls got in trouble in all de udda centuries, too. But okay, vat's done is done. Ve'll manage somehow." She stopped to think for a minute and then she said, "I'll come and help you vit de baby. You'll see. It vill all vork out." Looking up at Joseph she asked, "You knew about dis?"

"Yeah, Mom. Eva and I have known for a while, but Sarah wanted to wait and tell you herself," Joseph said, trying to sound matter-of-fact.

"Vell, dis surprise takes de cake. You cut knock me over vit a fedda. Ha! I never vut guess dis news. Vell, vell. Let's go see your momma. Ve have lots to celebrate now. Eva's birtday ant a new liddle baby for da family. *Gott in himmel!*"

Sarah was so relieved by her bubbe's take on things — particularly after the painful dinner she'd had with her parents — that she bent down and kissed her again. They walked hand in hand to the car.

Coming through her daughter's kitchen door, Rivka wasted no time in chiding Eva, who was stirring the béchamel on the stove. "You knew about dis ant kept me in de dark? Vat am I? Chopt liver? A bubbe needs to hear dis news. Look. I cut leave dis verlt anytime. You have to let me know ven dere's bik news. I'm serious, Chava!" Eva knew she was. Her mother only used her Jewish name when she was upset with her.

"Momma, I was following Sarah's instructions. She wanted to tell you in person," Eva said, wondering why she had none of Rivka's gumption in dealing with her own daughter.

Sarah came to her mother's defense. "Mom's right, Bubbe. I wanted to tell you myself. And I want to thank you for your offer to help once the baby's born. I'm sure I'll need all the help I can get. I've been reading books but I bet you and Mom have a corner on the market for baby care tips," Sarah said, wondering why it was so much easier to talk to her grandmother about the baby than it was her parents.

"Okay. I forkive you, but you gotta promise. No more secrets," Rivka insisted, pointing her finger first at Eva and then at Sarah. "I'm serious," she scolded them both, though it was clear who she felt deserved the lion's share of blame.

"Momma, it wasn't my news to tell. But I promise to keep you up-to-date on all the developments I know about," Eva said as she turned off the burner and covered the saucepan.

"Vell, okay den," Rivka said, ready to move on. "Sarah, about advice vit de babies, de books can help sometimes. I read Dockta Spock ven I raist your mudda and Uncle Max. But common sense is de best. Today I tink de mommas go a liddle bit crazy vit da babies. I see dem in de elevator in my buildink. Everytink has to be perfect. Dey have to have all de equipment. Dey forget babies have been born for tousants of years, fancy strollas or no fancy strollas. Vit luck, dey all grow up."

"Well, Bubbe, I'll be calling you for the common sense part. I promise not to go too crazy on the stroller decision," Sarah said.

Eva held her tongue and let her mother engage Sarah in the conversation about the baby. She had plenty to do to get everything ready for the family dinner. So far, the preparations had kept her busy enough to keep at bay her worries about how her brother and sister-in-law would take the news of Sarah's pregnancy.

Dinner went reasonably well. Though shocked that the family's golden girl was on her way to becoming a single mother, Max and Ellen offered both congratulations and some baby equipment that was taking up space in their attic. Aaron and David, their teenaged sons, took the news with a mix of embarrassment and disgust. As soon as they sensed they wouldn't provoke their mother's wrath, they escaped to the family room to watch a football game.

Eva loved Sarah's gift and was genuinely touched that Sarah had remembered how much she'd liked that purse. The memory of that breezy, warm, early September day at Lincoln Center was a momentary reprieve from the disappointment and worry she'd felt since. Eva knew she needed to take a page from her mother's book when it came to Sarah's pregnancy. As they were doing the dishes together in the kitchen, Rivka said, "Vat's done is done. *Gott* villing, it vill be a nice little baby. Ve vill all love it. Vun vay or de udda, it vill vork out, you'll see, Eva." Of all of the presents Eva got that day, it was that one she valued most.

Sarah saved her college friends for last. They were scattered across the country, and only one was married and had a child. The rest were toiling in the fields of their respective professions and bemoaning the dearth of men interested in settling down. Upon hearing the news of Sarah's pregnancy, they all voiced their congratulations and support, despite harboring misgivings about managing a job and a baby alone. It was only Devorah — the one friend privy to her infertility diagnosis — who was floored when Sarah told her she was pregnant. With a Ph.D. in public health under her belt, Devorah had found Sarah her doctors, Dr. Farouzhan in Boston and Dr. Scholl in New York. She alone understood why Sarah was having this baby, father or no father. Given the same circumstances, she knew she would make the same choice and said as much. After hanging up from that call, Sarah was certain Devorah was the closest thing to a sister she would ever know.

As the months passed, Eva and Joseph slowly came to accept their new normal. The concerns they had were gradually counterbalanced by a growing anticipation of the baby's arrival. In November, Eva came to the city each week for Sarah's birthing classes. Sarah had asked her mother to be her labor coach, which soothed Eva's pain at being kept at arm's length for so long. Joseph drove her down to the city on Tuesday nights, so he was tangentially needed as well. On their trip back home each week, Eva gave him a blow-by-blow description of what they had covered during the class. It was the first time in a long time that they had been so much a part of their daughter's life. Despite the less-than-ideal circumstances, it pleased them very much.

In December, as Sarah entered her ninth month, she methodically began handing off her responsibilities to the junior associates she and Harry had singled out to carry on her work. She was set to begin the firm's standard three-month maternity leave on or around her mid-January due date. With considerable encouragement from Harry, she also requested a half-time leave for three additional months. He assured her that her place in the associates' pecking order was secure, and that the leave would do nothing to dissuade him, when the time came, from championing her bid for partnership. Sarah could have kissed him, but instead, she thanked him effusively and repeatedly until he finally told her to get back to work or he would change his mind.

Doris hosted a baby shower on the Friday afternoon before Christmas. Sarah asked that her parents and grandmother be invited. Eva was brought to tears by Doris's beautifully hand-lettered invitation. On the appointed day, Eva and Rivka arrived first, welcomed by Doris as honored guests. When the tall, curly-haired Joseph emerged from the elevator after parking the car, there was no doubt in anyone's mind that he was Sarah Abadhi's father.

Sarah had always viewed the showers to celebrate a co-worker's upcoming wedding or expected child as interruptions in her workday. They were routinely held in the firm's largest conference room, with its wall of windows looking out to the East River and beyond. She had always attended, brought a nice gift and stayed just long enough not to be considered rude.

However, it was something of a revelation to be the guest of honor at her own shower. As she sat at the head of the long conference table, her colleagues seemed genuinely pleased to be there. It didn't hurt that Harry had contributed liberally to Doris's budget and that the refreshments were both ample and delectable. Beyond that, Sarah sensed that people to whom she had been pleasant and businesslike over the years had come happily, bearing thoughtful gifts for her baby. Harry's wife, Toby, had hand-stitched a quilt for the baby, starting work on it after learning Sarah was pregnant.

The outpouring by Sarah's colleagues gave Eva and Joseph a

small window into their daughter's life at work. After witnessing the kindness and generosity showered on her, whatever misgivings they still harbored about her pregnancy gave way. The baby gifts filled the trunks of Joseph's and Harry's cars, requiring a second round trip by Joseph to get everything delivered to Sarah's third-floor walk-up apartment.

Although the firm was closed for the week between Christmas and New Year's, Sarah came into the office several times in order to leave all of her projects in good shape — just in case she went into labor early. Afterwards, she went home and wrote heartfelt thank-you notes for the gifts she'd received. She put each present in its appointed place: the wall hanging above the crib, the hooded bath towels in the linen closet. The dresser Bubbe Rivka had insisted on buying for her first great-grandchild was soon filled with tiny outfits that would carry the baby through its first year of life. Joseph and Eva had gone stroller shopping with Sarah and purchased her favorite, a jogging stroller that would allow her to resume her runs after the baby was born. The apartment quickly filled in anticipation of the arrival of its new occupant.

By the end of the week, Sarah had her thank-you notes in the mail and her projects at work ready to hand off. She spent New Year's Eve with her parents, Bubbe Rivka, Aunt Ellen and Uncle Max and her parents' closest friends. She was the youngest person at the gathering by a good twenty years. But being surrounded by people who had known her for so long made her feel safe and secure as she approached the birth of her child. Many of the female guests offered Sarah pointers about caring for the baby. No one woke either Sarah or her bubbe as they dozed off, side by side in their armchairs, long before the crystal ball dropped amid the throngs of revelers in Times Square.

TWENTY-ONE

Ten days before the baby was due, Sarah awakened to the clock radio at five-fifteen. It was a dark January morning and the weather report was discouraging: record-breaking cold for the coming days with highs in the single digits. It was currently two degrees below zero and hours before dawn. Rather than get up and head off to the pool, Sarah rolled her round body over for another hour of sleep. This could be one of her last opportunities to sleep in. Only yesterday Dr. Scholl had declared her cervix to be one centimeter dilated. The Braxton Hicks contractions that came and went made it clear that she was in the home stretch now.

At six-thirty Sarah traded her warm bed for a long, leisurely shower. She emerged from the steamy bathroom and headed to her closet to choose from the lampshades and tents that passed for maternity clothes. This morning it would be the black maternity pantsuit that had lost whatever professional flair it'd had six weeks prior. At this point, there was no outfit that could mask the reality that her time was near.

She paired a mauve maternity turtleneck with the black suit. Though she found her office too hot these last months, a turtleneck was obligatory on a day like today. She'd also have to put on every bit of outerwear she owned before venturing out into the frigid streets: the polypropylene face mask she used for running, her wool scarf, knee socks, high shearling boots, mittens and hooded gray wool coat. She hoped that would be enough to fend off frostbite on the way to the office.

Three blocks from Sarah's walk-up apartment, a different set of preparations were underway. Bobby O'Brien, wearing his thermal underwear, flannel-lined jeans, wool shirt, black fleece neck warmer and tan hooded jumpsuit, carried his lunchbox and thermos as he ascended to the cab of his sixty-five-ton crane. It was a bitterly cold day to jump the crane, but the developer had ants in his pants about getting the forty-three-story condo completed. They were on the eighteenth floor and they had to add two thirteen-foot sections to increase the crane's height. After they got the sections in place they would have to brace the crane by positioning a six-ton steel collar around the outside of the crane's tower at floor eighteen. The riggers would secure it to the tower and then tie it to the building with steel struts. Bobby felt bad for the riggers, who would be out in the open air during the whole operation. At least he'd be inside the cab — cold, still, but out of the wind. What a miserable day to be maneuvering a twelve-thousand-pound collar into place.

If it were up to Bobby, he'd wait for better weather, but he'd been in the business long enough to know that if he wanted to keep his job, he did what he was told. This was not the first time he had thought the boss was taking chances to keep on schedule, come hell or high water. He had made his peace long ago with the risks of his job. The truth was he loved being a crane operator. He'd dreamt of it since he had gotten his first Erector Set when he was eight years old. It was hard, technical work and he couldn't space out for even a second. No matter what he was lifting or moving, he had to keep the crane balanced. There was nothing quite like the feeling of knowing exactly how to use the levers to maneuver the swing, the boom and the hoist. Sometimes, when he was sitting alone in his cab, high above the city, he felt he had the best job in the world. The money was nothing to sneeze at either. For a working stiff, he was doing pretty well: a house in Staten Island, nice vacations, a beautiful wife and two amazing kids. Bobby O'Brien had no complaints.

Sarah felt she ought to eat breakfast, even though her appetite had dropped off in the last week. That morning she decided to make a fruit-and-yogurt smoothie and take what she couldn't finish to the office. She sipped on a cup of hot mint tea, used the bathroom one last time and then began getting ready to face the elements. As she put on one layer after another, she thought about how much easier it would be to be pregnant in a warm climate. As she caught a glimpse of herself in the mirror on the way out the door, she was struck by how little she resembled the woman she'd been nine months earlier. It gave her a moment's pause.

At seven-fifteen she headed down the two flights of stairs to the ground floor. Using all her strength, she pushed against the icy gusts that were forcing shut the front door. As she emerged from the building, she pulled her scarf up to her eyes and headed west toward Park Avenue and the luxury buildings' heated porticos that would provide brief moments of warmth during her mile-plus walk.

There were few people on the streets since nearly everyone had opted for some sort of conveyance to get where they were going. But Sarah was determined to get her daily exercise, below-zero temperatures or no. By the time she took refuge in the revolving door of her office building, her feet and hands were so cold they ached. Still, her discomfort was eased by knowing she'd achieved a small victory over the miserable weather.

Since returning from the holiday break, she'd finished up the policy changes for the hospital accused of complicity in organ trafficking. That case had turned out to be a nail-biter, with Sarah and Harry mounting a defense of the hospital before UNOS, the national administrator of organ procurement and transplantation. The UNOS board had ruled that while the hospital did not knowingly participate in the black market for organs, its donor screening policy was woefully inadequate. They had ordered a complete overhaul and Sarah had been integral to that compliance effort. She was fairly confident that the resulting new policy would keep the transplant program out of trouble for the foreseeable future.

She was also knee-deep in a suit brought by the family of an undocumented worker left with a permanent brain injury after being struck by a car. The firm's client hospital had delivered acute, life-saving care. Then, after being unable to find a single nursing home or rehab facility that would accept her as a patient, it had involuntarily returned the woman to her native Mexico on a private jet. It was a compelling case and one Sarah hated to leave behind.

Harry popped into her office around two as she was cleaning up her computer files. "Hey, kiddo, why don't you call it a day? You should go home and put your feet up while you can. If my memory serves me right, before you know it you'll be at the beck and call of an eight-pound tyrant."

Sarah couldn't repress a grin. "You mean go home? At two o'clock? You're kidding, right? Are you looking for a way to dock my pay and save the firm some money?"

"Nah, you'll be paid the full shot, I promise. Just go home and rest. Take a nap. Do it on the firm's dime. You've earned it."

"Are you inferring that this baby's made me soft?"

"No. It's made you temporarily large, but in no way has it made you soft. You're still the same workaholic you've always been. That's the problem. You need to give yourself a break."

"Well, you'll be happy to know I gave myself a break today and slept in."

"Congratulations. A sign of sanity. I know you were in the office almost every day between Christmas and New Year's. I have my spies, you know." Harry saw her cheeks color, but kept driving home his point. "I mean it when I say you should be nice to yourself in these last days. Go to a spa or whatever women do to pamper themselves."

"Harry, I've never been to a spa in my life and I don't think this would be the time to start. I wouldn't fit in with all the svelte young women and well-preserved matrons."

"Well, suit yourself. But I still vote for at least an afternoon nap."

"That's very thoughtful of you. Really, Harry. You've been the best boss a pregnant woman could ever hope for."

Putting his finger to his lips, he said in a whisper, "Would you keep it down? You're going to ruin an image that's taken decades to cultivate."

"Your secret's safe with me. I'll tell anyone who asks that you're a world-class son of a bitch — who just happens to have a soft spot for pregnant women."

"I'll stipulate to that characterization if you amend it to having a soft spot for pregnant women who generate tremendous billables for the firm. Now go home."

"I will, just as soon as I finish up what I'm doing. Really, I will."

Knowing Sarah, that meant sometime before midnight, and that's what worried him.

By three o'clock Sarah had finished streamlining her computer filing system and was quite pleased with her handiwork. Except for bathroom breaks, she had been sitting at her desk since eight, and her swollen ankles were proof of her inactivity — as well as her salt intake. She'd been unable to resist joining in on the lunch order for Kosher deli delivery. She'd ordered one of her favorites, a hot pastrami sandwich with mustard on rye. She wouldn't win any awards for good prenatal nutrition that day — or the next, since she had put the half she couldn't finish into the break room fridge for tomorrow's lunch.

She thought about what Harry had said. The truth was she could stand a nap. She'd stifled at least three yawns since he'd left her office. Perhaps it was the power of suggestion, but she was suddenly dog tired. Whatever was on her desk could wait until tomorrow. She turned off her computer, wrestled her boots onto her fat feet, donned the rest of her outerwear and headed out, causing more than a few heads to turn as she walked through the double glass doors at a quarter past three.

Sarah hadn't gone two blocks when she surrendered to her fatigue and the frigid headwinds. She tried for a cab, but every passing taxi already had its refugee from the cold sitting comfortably in the backseat. She switched to plan B and headed for the 51st Street subway station on Lexington, just a couple of blocks away. In two short stops she'd be within striking distance of her apartment. She could almost hear her bed calling to her.

Happily, the work of the day was progressing better than Bobby O'Brien had dared hope. That was an especially good thing since the crane operator who was supposed to relieve him had called in sick. He'd have to stay beyond his six-hour shift but, with time and a half, he'd make a pretty penny today. Despite the miserable weather, the riggers had no trouble adding the two thirteen-foot sections to jump the crane. The crane was now twenty stories high, some two hundred feet above the ground. Bobby sat atop it with his jib extending farther yet. Now came the fun part, bracing the crane with the steel collar at the eighteenth floor. By 3:15 the collar was suspended from chain blocks, connected to a higher part of the steel tower with four thick nylon slings. If Bobby had his druthers, they'd be following the crane manufacturer's specs for eight slings, but a lot of people in the trade thought that was overkill. And the truth was that the riggers were doing a good job of moving the collar into place with four. Bobby was thinking that maybe he was too much of a worrywart, always anticipating what could go wrong. Better safe than sorry was his motto and he got a lot of razzing from the guys because of it. But it didn't bother him. He wanted everyone on the job to be able to go home at the end of the day — himself included. If they made jokes at his expense, so be it.

Sarah couldn't believe her good luck when a local train pulled into the station just as she reached the platform. Luckier still, there were plenty of seats in the subway car. As the doors closed, the train ambled slowly down the tracks. No need to hurry at this hour. Even so, it took only a few minutes to reach her stop. It was a good thing, too. Between the rocking motion of the train and the warm air of the subway car, she found it hard to keep her eyes open. When Sarah emerged from the station at 68th and Lexington, the cold air took her breath away. She kept her eyes down and her face buried in her scarf, looking up only when she had to cross the street. As she approached 71st Street she heard a loud noise, then a rumble and then a roar from on high.

Suddenly, there was a tremendous blast. As Bobby looked down he saw that the six-ton steel collar had somehow broken free and was plummeting down the crane's tower. This was a nightmare scenario he had spent his whole working life trying to prevent. The steel collar fell like a ring sliding down a steel tube. At the ninth floor it smashed into the collar that was already in place, clipping it from the struts that attached it to the building. The collar continued to fall, slamming into the last collar at floor three. Now there was nothing attaching the crane to the building.

Sarah lifted her head out of her wooly cocoon. It was then that she and the other brave souls on the street stopped dead in their tracks. High aloft, some twenty stories up, they saw a white crane swaying to and fro, next to a building under construction. There were two workers dangling from a pole atop the building. Sarah stood fixed to the pavement, unable to believe what she was seeing. She'd never given a second thought to cranes. They dotted the cityscape, forever building high-rises where five-story walk-ups had been. When their work was done, they disappeared. But this crane was swinging precariously up in the sky, leaving Sarah both terrified and mesmerized. She stood paralyzed until she felt a hand on her arm.

Bobby's last moments were sheer terror. The spindly structure his cab sat atop teetered. With the crane unmoored, all his efforts to keep it balanced failed. Nothing worked. He called out to his wife, telling her he loved her. A fraction of a second later his cab and the forty tons of counterbalances began toppling hundreds of feet to the ground.

As the crane came crashing to earth, it brought with it everything in its path. The noise of its descent mimicked a series of bombs exploding in rapid succession. Everyone around Sarah screamed as they ran helter-skelter to escape the debris raining from the sky. An elderly man grabbed Sarah by the arm and pulled her toward the wall of the nearest building. Was this the safest place? That was her last thought before the grasp on her arm released. Immediately, something struck her right leg with such force it took her breath away. As she fell to the ground she was bombarded by falling rubble. Suddenly, there was an enormous crash and everything went black. She struggled to breathe, wincing in pain. When she tried to get up, she realized her right leg was pinned.

Anyone witnessing the disaster from a safe distance saw a roiling, spinning, red debris cloud rise nearly four stories above the sidewalk where Sarah lay. Her face mask and scarf were no match for the dust. As she coughed and gagged she felt a big kick from her belly and she started to sob.

Finally the deafening noise stopped. She started screaming for help and trying to move in order to attract attention. But to her horror, only her head could move, and just a few inches from side to side. It was then that she realized she'd been buried alive. It took everything she had to tamp down her panic. She had to try to stay calm. Her mind and her voice were her only assets now. She heard the muffled sounds of sirens, lots of sirens. Help was on the way. But her voice couldn't compete with sirens.

Then there was a lull in the sirens. Sarah screamed for help as loudly as she could, but her efforts were for naught. Had it been deadly quiet on the street, the small sounds emerging from the rubble might have been picked up by the human ear. But the street was anything but quiet. Within five minutes of the accident, the site was crawling with fire trucks, police cars, ambulances and hundreds of rescue workers.

Sarah couldn't tell how much time had passed before she heard voices. It was then that she thought of the other people who had been on the corner with her. Perhaps they were buried, too, and very near. What of that person who had grabbed her arm? Was he still next to her? Another kick and another.

The voices Sarah heard were not the voices of the people with whom she had stood watching the crane. Their voices had been silenced by the falling debris. A woman who'd stood not five feet from her had been struck and killed by a concrete terrace that had been sheared off by the crane's mast. That slab had come to rest at a forty-five degree angle above Sarah, creating a life-saving lean-to with the wall of the building she'd been guided to. Of those corner bystanders, Sarah alone had survived the deluge.

It was rescue workers whose voices Sarah heard, and it was their German shepherd who barked furiously upon picking up her scent. Following the dog's lead, firefighters, police officers and EMTs started digging furiously with their hands. The dog's barks encouraged Sarah to cry out again. The voices were getting louder. Was it possible someone was calling out to her? She strained to make out the words.

"We're digging…tight…we know…."

Her heart jumped. She screamed back, begging for help for herself and her baby. Though the sounds coming from the rubble were faint, the first responders heard them and redoubled their efforts. The terrace slab was leaning precariously against the vertical column of the building. Above and beneath the slab were several feet of rubble. They had to work carefully, balancing the need to get to their victim with the reality of the concrete slab leaning unsteadily above the poor soul.

In less than five minutes, Sarah's mittened hand was discovered in the debris. An EMT, crouching beneath the concrete slab, took the hand in his own and gave it a hard squeeze. Then he yelled out, "We've got you, don't you worry. We've got you." Sarah squeezed hard in return. "We've got a survivor here!" the EMT called out to the others. His co-workers let out a cheer.

They passed buckets hand to hand to carry away the debris. In short order, they unearthed the end of Sarah's wool scarf, caked in dust. They continued digging, until they uncovered a head — Sarah's head — still wrapped in the scarf and encased in her wool hood. A firefighter moved in close and gently wiped the dust from her victim's eyes. She did a double take when she saw the face mask.

"Someone, pass me some scissors," she called out. In no time an EMT pulled a pair of shears from his bag.

Then the firefighter spoke directly to her buried victim. "You'll have to pardon me as I get this off your face." She carefully cut at the mask until Sarah's face — caked with dust, blood and tears — was revealed.

The firefighter tried to assess the condition of the survivor. "My name is Caroline," she said, speaking close to Sarah's face. "And we're doing everything we can to get you out of here. Can you tell me your name?"

Sarah responded in a slow, quavering voice. "Sarah Abadhi — A-B-A-D-H-I — and I'm nine months pregnant. Please, please, help me." She cried again thinking of the baby.

Caroline smiled as she listened to her victim spell out her name. Then she turned to the EMT who was ready to take over. "Did you get that, Tommy? She's pregnant — full term."

"We're on it. Let me start her on some oxygen. It will make things easier for both of them," Tommy replied.

Before the EMT and the firefighter changed places, he radioed to dispatch that a full-term pregnant survivor had been found. He then kneeled beside Sarah, took off her mitten and put a blood oxygen sensor on her finger. He suctioned the dust away from her eyes, her nose and her mouth. Then he got the oxygen mask on her face. Next he tried to get a handle on her condition.

"Hello, Sarah. I'm Tommy, and I'd like to get a little info to make it easier on the docs when we get you to the hospital. When's your baby due?" He took off the mask to hear Sarah's answer.

"Ten days. I have just ten more days. What happened?"

Tommy immediately put the mask back on. "There was a construction accident, but we're going to get you out. Do me a favor and answer a few more questions for me. Can you do that?"

Sarah nodded.

"How old are you?"

Again, he pulled down the mask.

"Thirty-two."

It was like a dance in which the EMT led and Sarah willingly followed. As the other rescuers continued their digging, he'd ask a question and pull down the mask. She'd answer and then he'd firmly replace it over her nose and mouth.

"Very good, Sarah. Do you have any medical problems that we should know about?"

"I have no problems," she said. The irony was not lost on the EMT.

"Great. You're doing great, Sarah. Just a few more questions. Do you have any allergies to medications or latex?"

"No allergies. Please. My baby. You've got to get me out. Call Dr. Scholl, Jared Scholl." She suddenly was gripped by fear when she realized the baby had stopped kicking. "Oh God, the baby's not moving."

Tommy didn't miss a beat. "Oh, babies get quiet. You know that, Sarah. It's probably taking a snooze now," he said, hoping to God he was telling the truth.

"Yes, yes. I forgot."

Tommy persisted with his questions. "Do you have any pain?"

"My leg. At first it hurt so much. Now I can't feel it."

"Can you tell me which leg?"

She closed her eyes and tried to visualize her legs, moving the toes in her left boot. "The right leg."

"Okay, that's great Sarah, you're doing great."

"Are you on any medications?" Tommy asked.

"Prenatal vitamins."

Just then the rescue workers dug out Sarah's left arm.

"Can you move that arm for me, Sarah?"

Sarah moved it across the mound of debris.

"Great, Sarah. Any pain when you move your arm?"

"No, no pain."

"I need to get a blood pressure reading on you, but it means I'm going to have to cut the sleeve of your coat."

"All that matters is the baby. You've got to save the baby. Please."

Tommy called out, "Get me a blanket." In no time, his partner, Ed, was at his side with the blanket so Tommy could wrap her arm once the clothing was cut off. The last thing his patient needed was frostbite.

Using the same scissors Caroline had used to cut the face mask, the EMT sliced through the sleeve of the wool coat, then the jacket of the pantsuit and finally the turtleneck, exposing Sarah's bare arm. He wrapped the cuff around it and covered it with the blanket. The machine read out 90/45 with a rapid heart rate. The pulse ox machine showed a blood oxygen saturation level of ninety-four percent with two liters of oxygen. Under ordinary circumstances that would be fine, but he knew in pregnancy, vital signs were not always reliable. To make things even sketchier, pregnant trauma victims didn't necessarily present with the usual signs of shock from blood loss. Who knew what was going on under that mound of wreckage? She could be bleeding out. He'd better get her started on an IV with Ringer's to maintain maternal and fetal perfusion. As he worked to get the IV started he kept Sarah engaged in conversation.

"Sarah, can you tell me how your blood pressure usually runs?"

"It runs low."

"Okay, that's great. You're doing great. And the guys here are digging you out to beat the band. So, you have no medical conditions that the docs should know about?"

Sarah shook her head.

"You mean to tell me you're healthy as a horse, Sarah?"

"Well," she hesitated, "until now."

Tommy couldn't have asked for a better response. The patient was lucid, that was for sure. "You'll be out of here in no time. In just a few minutes we'll have all this crap — pardon my French — off of you. In the meantime I'm going to save the nurses at the ER a little work by starting you on an IV right here in the field. Hold on. It will pinch just a little."

As he wiped her arm with alcohol he kept up his end of the conversation. "So Sarah, you having a boy or a girl?"

"I don't know. I wanted it to be a surprise." She started crying again.

"Don't worry, Sarah, you're going to have your surprise before you know it."

"Really? You think it will be born soon?"

"Could be," said Tommy as he found a good vein for the IV. Ed worked with him to get the IV taped in place. After the Ringer's was running well Tommy wrapped Sarah's arm with the blanket.

"Sarah, do you have an emergency contact you'd like us to get in touch with?"

"My parents. My mother's my labor coach." Sarah started rattling off their phone numbers.

"Whoa, whoa, whoa. Hold your horses, Sarah. My memory's not the best. If we rely on my memory, likely as not I'll come up with a number from Timbuktu. Just a sec." He reached for his radio to call dispatch with the numbers. Just then an ambulance flew by with its siren screaming, shepherding another victim to the hospital. When it passed he called his dispatcher, put his ear close to Sarah and parroted what she said as she recited the home and work numbers of Eva and Joseph Abadhi.

Just as she finished, she felt a shiver go through her body; a moment later she felt another and then another. Suddenly, she couldn't stop shivering. Tommy was worried about hypothermia given the air temperature and the temperature of all the debris that buried her.

"Okay, Sarah. Are you getting cold?'

"Oh, I'm so cold. I can't stop shaking."

"Okay if I take your temperature, Sarah?

"Why am I shaking?" she asked as she nodded her ascent, teeth chattering like cartoon characters she had watched as a child.

"Well, let's see what the thermometer says and then I'll be in a better position to give you an answer." Tommy reached into his bag for the digital thermometer and then put it into her left ear. In seconds it beeped. Tommy looked at the reading: 94.9 F/35 C. Shit. Now he had to worry about hypothermia on top of everything else. He hoped they got this woman out of her death trap soon. Tommy gave a knowing look to Ed.

"Okay, Sarah, your temp has dropped a bit because it's a freezing cold day and your body is just trying to warm itself by shivering. That's all the shaking means. It's completely normal, a natural response to the cold. That's all it is." Ed radioed ahead to the ER to be ready with warming blankets.

Tommy was right about getting Sarah dug out quickly. Eighteen minutes after the German shepherd discovered her, the rescuers had removed most of the debris from her body. It was then that they saw why she couldn't move her leg. A steel construction stud from the condo project — ten feet long, six inches wide, and nearly two inches thick — was planted across the blood-tinged shearling boot covering her right shin. Her lower leg was lying at an unnatural angle, apparently fractured at the calf by the steel stud. A firefighter with a hydraulic demolition shear was there in moments and started cutting through the steel. As he worked, the others stood back, waiting for the moment when the last remnant of their victim's entombment would be cut away.

TWENTY-TWO

As rescue efforts were ramping up just blocks away, Jeff Gotbaum was finishing a successful surgery on a seventeen-year-old girl who had been injured in a car crash on the FDR Drive. Changing out of his scrubs, he congratulated himself on acing the femur repair. Just as he was tying his shoes his cell went off, alerting him to an incoming trauma. He had been looking forward to grabbing something from the cafeteria after the four-hour procedure. Instead, he pulled a protein bar out of his locker and headed to the ER.

Coming through the doors, he immediately knew something big had happened. The place was hopping. Then he heard the harpist playing, a new initiative aimed at calming patients during their time of distress. It gave him the willies and he guessed he wasn't alone. He made a beeline for the nurses' station.

"I'm Dr. Gotbaum, orthopedics," he said, identifying himself to an attractive ER nurse he had never seen before. He glanced down at her left hand and noticed her ring finger was bare. "You have a patient in need of my finely honed skills and expertise?"

To his disappointment, the pretty nurse's response was all business. "Trauma room 2. A thirty-two-year-old primigravida, full term, open, multifragmentary fracture of the lower right leg."

"Thanks very much." Jeff made a mental note of the nurse's name — Cheryl Aiello — and walked quickly to the trauma room, where emergency surgery could be done if need be. Perhaps they were thinking of delivering the fetus immediately. That would make his job easier.

Trauma 2 was abuzz. He recognized the OB, Dr. Catherine Hanna, but he didn't know the other attending. Probably a neonatologist for the fetus. The ER docs were working to stabilize the patient. From the looks of the monitors, things were okay on that front. She was already getting a unit of whole blood. He motioned to Dr. Hanna to meet him outside so he could get brought up to speed. The OB joined him in the corridor.

"Hey, Catherine. So what have we got here?"

"The woman was hit with falling debris from the crane accident over on Lexington. They had to dig her out. I guess she was buried alive."

"You're kidding. There was another crane accident? Wasn't there one a couple of months ago?"

"Hey, Jeff, one more crane falls from the sky and I'm getting out of the city. What good are lower crime rates and cleaner streets when cranes keep toppling from construction sites?"

"I know, it's nuts. But tell me about our patient."

"She's full term and for the moment the baby is hanging in there with a heart rate between 130 and 140. Jeff, I'm no orthopedic surgeon, but I'm thinking her lower leg may be beyond even your fine surgical powers. I'd like to get that baby out right away and then let you go at it."

"That's fine with me. Do we have any imaging?" Jeff inquired.

"She's been x-rayed and scanned. No internal bleeding to major organs, which is incredibly lucky from what the EMTs told me about the scene."

"So are you thinking of doing the section here, or do we have time to get to the OR?"

"There's an OR ready, so I'd rather do the section there and then just hand her off to you."

"Is the patient alert?" Jeff asked.

"Amazingly, she has her wits about her. She was headed toward hypothermia laying out in the cold under all that debris. But since she arrived in the ER, we've gotten her temp back up to 96.8. She's desperate about her baby. I don't think she has any idea what shape her leg is in."

"Do I have time to take a look before we head upstairs?"

"What kind of time are you talking about?"

"Give me five minutes," Jeff said. "I'd like to introduce myself to the patient and lay eyes on the trauma."

"I'll give you three, and then we're outta here."

Jeff had to make his way through a gaggle of nurses, aides and doctors to approach the patient. What he saw was a very pregnant Caucasian woman, her curly hair caked with reddish-brown dust. Her brow was cut but the rest of her face was pale and smooth. It was a face that seemed somehow familiar. Then he caught it: The woman was a dead ringer for Rick's old girlfriend, Sarah — or her sister, if she had one. It was the patient's wristband that was the stunner: Abadhi, Sarah. The ER doc, Jim McReynolds, snapped Jeff back to attention.

"Hey, Jeff," McReynolds said, beckoning him to the corner of the room. "We've got an open, compound fracture. Pictures show both the tibia and fibula were crushed by a metal construction stud the rescue guys had to cut off her with the Jaws of Life. She was pinned for about thirty-five minutes before they got her out. Circulation was compromised. Some blood loss, so we started her on one unit. The patient is responsive."

"Thanks, Jim. I know her — a friend of a friend. Has her husband — or the baby's father — been called?"

"There's no father in the picture. We asked. Her parents have been called. I guess they're on their way."

No father. What the hell? But he had no time to figure out how Sarah could be ready to deliver a baby. "Okay, thanks, Jim. Let me take a look," Jeff said, trying to sound detached and professional.

Returning to Sarah, he lifted the sterile dressing that covered her right leg. As McReynolds had reported, the tibia and fibula appeared to have multiple fractures. Bones protruded through the skin in at least three places. He found a strong pulse in her left foot and a significantly weaker one in her right, which was no surprise given the magnitude of the injury. With a break caused by such a high-energy impact, it was amazing that major blood vessels hadn't been severed.

This was exactly the type of devastating injury he'd trained for, and as a first-year attending he was already gaining a reputation as something of a miracle worker. He hated to admit defeat and, more times than not, he didn't have to. That doggedness, that refusal to give up until he had tried every approach to the problem at hand, set him apart from other surgeons who lacked the hunger to hit it out of the park every time they scrubbed in.

After covering the injured leg with the sterile dressing, he turned to McReynolds and told him to page a vascular surgeon. He flashed back to the three of them — Jeff, Rick and Sarah — running along the river, with him struggling to keep up. Now he would have to pull out all the stops to save her leg.

His promised three minutes were up and he had yet to share his anticipated treatment plan with the patient. He wondered if she would recognize him — particularly given all that had apparently transpired since their morning runs.

"Sarah. It's Jeff Gotbaum."

Sarah turned toward the voice and opened her eyes to see a familiar face.

"Jeff? What are you doing here?" Sarah whispered. She thought she heard a harp. Maybe she was hallucinating. "Is it really you, Jeff? I feel like I'm in a dream."

"Yes, indeed. You're not dreaming. It's really me. Jeff Gotbaum, at your service. We're kind of in a hurry to deliver your baby, but after that I'm going to be fixing your leg."

Jeff's words about delivering the baby focused her attention. She started to talk, but Jeff couldn't make out the words.

"What was that?" he asked as he put his ear closer to her face.

"You're going to be my doctor?"

"Sure am. Lucky coincidence, eh?"

"That's good. Take care of the baby first," she whispered. "Please, Jeff. That's the most important thing."

"You'll be in the OR in a couple of minutes and Dr. Hanna will be delivering your baby by Cesarean section. After that, you'll be all mine," Jeff said. "Your right lower leg has suffered a high-energy injury. I am going to do my best to fix it. I anticipate that the surgery may take several hours."

"Can I be awake to see the baby born? Can I hold it?"

"I'm not really sure what Dr. Hanna has planned for anesthesia, but it's possible she'll order a general, since we'll be coming in right after her to work on your leg. If that's the case, then you'll get to hold the baby as soon as you come out of recovery."

She started to tear up. "Oh, please. I want to see the baby born. I want to hold it. Please."

Jeff swallowed hard. He would prefer general anesthesia, given the extent of the injuries, but if he had to, he could work with an epidural and have the anesthesiologist give Sarah enough sedation to make her out of it during surgery.

"I'll see what Dr. Hanna says. I'll do what I can. But Sarah, your health and the baby's health have to come first. I promise, if it's a general anesthesia I will personally hold your baby and welcome it to the world. And your parents are on their way, so Grandma and Grandpa will take over after that." He looked up to see the transporters from the OR, ready to take their patient upstairs.

"Jeff. If they knock me out…it's Eric for a boy and Anna for a girl."

Jeff looked at her, confused. Then he understood. "Oh, those are your names for the baby?"

Sarah nodded.

"Got it: Anna for a girl and Eric for a boy."

Sarah nodded again and then gave a little smile. "Thanks, Jeff."

Then she closed her eyes as she was rolled out of the ER and into the waiting elevator.

TWENTY-THREE

It was only because her college was on semester break that Eva was home that January afternoon. She was working in her study on a collection of short stories, her first. She was deep within the world of her characters when the telephone rang. The interruption annoyed her; she was on a roll and the story was almost writing itself. She entertained the idea of letting it go to voice mail before thinking better of it. It could be her mother, felled by some insult spawned by old age. And, of course, Sarah was getting close to her due date.

"Hello," Eva said as she cradled the receiver between her ear and her shoulder so she could finish typing the sentence she was working on.

"I'm calling from the emergency room at University Hospital in Manhattan. I am trying to reach Eva or Joseph Abadhi, parents of Sarah Abadhi."

Eva stopped typing and put the receiver in her hand. "Excuse me. Who did you say you were?"

"My name is Reginald Washington, ma'am. I'm an emergency room nurse calling for the parents of Sarah Abadhi. Do I have the correct phone number?"

"Yes," Eva answered cautiously, afraid of a scam artist fishing for information. "Why are you calling?"

"Am I speaking with Eva Abadhi?"

"Yes."

"There was a large construction accident this afternoon around East 73rd Street and Lexington Avenue and your daughter was a pedestrian in the area. She was injured in the accident."

Seventy-Third Street. Close to Sarah's apartment. But she wouldn't have been there at that time of day. "I'm sorry, sir. What is your name again?"

"Reginald Washington, ma'am."

"My daughter is at work in Midtown, Mr. Washington. I just spoke to her a few hours ago. You must be mistaken."

The ER nurse was patient. It was not uncommon for the news he had to deliver to be received with suspicion or disbelief. He would take his time to get the needed information to the victim's next of kin before ending the call.

"No, ma'am. There is no mistake. The information comes from the EMTs who worked with your daughter. Ma'am, have you been listening to the radio or watching television this afternoon?"

"No. No, I've been working. Why?"

"There's been a major accident in the vicinity of 73rd Street and Lexington Ave. I am sorry to inform you that your daughter, Sarah, was hurt in the accident."

"Just a minute. Let me turn on the television." Eva ran from her study to the family room to turn on CNN. There on the screen was a live report from the scene of a crane accident on the Upper East Side of Manhattan. The aerial view showed devastation on the order of a bomb blast or gas explosion. The natural light was beginning to recede, and the area was bathed in bright, emergency lighting. She couldn't imagine anyone surviving an accident of such magnitude. Eva's knees buckled and the phone dropped from her hand. Sprawled on the floor, she remembered the ER nurse. He had to tell her about Sarah. She grabbed the phone lying beside her.

"Are you still there Mr. Washington?"

"Yes, ma'am. I'm still here."

"Oh my God. Tell me about my daughter."

"Yes, ma'am. The EMTs stabilized her before she was brought to our trauma center."

"And the baby?"

"Mrs. Abadhi, I have no information on the condition of the fetus."

The words reverberated in Eva's head. No information on the condition of the fetus. The fetus she was sorry Sarah had conceived so carelessly. The fetus she and Joseph had come to accept, whose birth they now eagerly awaited.

"Are you still there Mrs. Abadhi?"

"Yes. Please give me the address of the hospital so my husband and I can get to her. Let me get a pen and paper." She got up and raced to the kitchen, grabbing a sheet off her grocery list pad. Her hands shook as she wrote down the address.

"Mr. Washington?"

"Yes, ma'am?"

"Are you really certain this is my daughter — Sarah Abadhi — who was hurt?"

"Yes, I'm certain." Then the nurse broke from the official protocol to relay the story told to him by Tommy, the EMT. "Mrs. Abadhi, apparently when the rescue team reached your daughter at the scene, she spelled her last name and rattled off your home and office numbers. The EMTs said she was completely lucid and cooperative. They said she was an IKE — I Know Everything. They all got a charge out of her."

That started the tears flowing. Lucid and talking and the same know-it-all she'd been since she was little. "Thank you, Mr. Washington. You've been very kind," Eva said, wiping her face with the back of her hand.

"Would you like me to inform Mr. Abadhi of the accident?" the nurse asked.

"No. I'd better do it. Good-bye and…again… thank you."

"Good-bye, Mrs. Abadhi. Best of luck to your family."

Eva's blood ran cold at the thought of telling Joseph. Then she had an idea. As she watched the scene on the muted television, she called Sarah's cell phone. Perhaps it was all a misunderstanding. Maybe Sarah was just on the periphery of the accident. Maybe she had just suffered a few scratches. Sarah's phone rang and rang before going to voice mail. Hearing Sarah tell her to leave a message sent a shiver through Eva. What if she never heard Sarah's voice again? She hung up and pushed the speed dial for Joseph, praying that he'd remembered to turn on his phone. On the fifth ring, he picked up.

"Hi, honey. I'm in the middle of something with Bob. Can I call you right back?"

"No, Joe. Don't hang up. Something's happened."

Eva's voice alarmed him. It was the same voice he'd heard years earlier when her father had suffered a massive stroke. His mind turned immediately to Rivka.

"What happened? Is Rivka okay?"

"No, not her. It's Sarah."

"Sarah? Is the baby coming? Is that it?"

"No, Joe. She's been in an accident."

His chest tightened. "An accident? What sort of accident?"

Riveted by the images of devastation on the television, Eva found it hard to speak.

"Eva. Eva. Are you there? What sort of accident was Sarah involved in?"

She inhaled deeply, cleared her throat and tried again. "There was…there was a construction accident. In Sarah's neighborhood. She's been injured, Joe."

"Do you know her condition?"

Here was a ray of hope she could convey. "The ER nurse said she was lucid and talking. That's good, isn't it, Joe? He said she rattled off our home and office numbers to the EMTs. He even said they got a kick out of that." Eva willed herself not to cry.

"Oh, that's very good, sweetheart. Definitely a good sign. Do you know what hospital they brought her to?"

"Yes, I have all the particulars written down. Just come home so we can go and be with her."

"Eva?" Joseph hesitated to ask. "What about the baby?"

"The nurse had no information on the baby. Joe, if anything happens to it I'll never forgive myself. I was so angry at first. Now I've come to love that baby."

"I know, Eva. I know. We both have," Joseph said in an almost confessional tone. "I'll be home as fast as I can."

"Joe, maybe it would be better if someone drove us into the city. Neither of us will be able to concentrate on the road."

"That's a good idea. I'll see if I can find someone in the lab."

"Joe?" Eva said, almost in a whisper.

"Yes, Eva."

"What if it turns out badly?"

"We can't think that way, Eva. Sarah's a strong girl, a runner, a swimmer. Look, I'll be home soon."

"Okay, Joe."

"Good-bye, sweetheart."

Joseph hung up and put his head in his hands, giving himself permission to be scared for just a moment. He longed for the time when Sarah was young, when he could keep her safe. He'd been helpless on that front for a long time now.

Bob Fong, his colleague and friend, gently asked, "Is there something I can do?"

Joseph looked up and saw the concern on his face. "Sarah's been in an accident. Some sort of construction accident in the city. I've got to pick up Eva and go to the hospital."

"Could I drive you and Eva into the city? Let me deal with the rush-hour traffic. I'd like to help."

"Oh, that would please Eva. She suggested that someone drive us in. Thank you, Bob. Thank you very much."

Bob, Joseph and Eva were surprised by the good time they made. Perhaps the frigid temperatures had kept people at home, or sent them scurrying to the warmth of a Metro North train car. Whatever the reason, the traffic kept moving and in thirty-five minutes, Bob Fong was driving into the circle in front of the hospital's main entrance. He dropped off his passengers and left to search out a space in a nearby parking garage.

Eva and Joseph hurried through the revolving door of the lobby, fumbled to find their licenses to provide picture ID for the security guard and headed straight to the plump, middle-aged Hispanic woman at the information desk.

"We're looking for information on our daughter," Joseph said urgently. "Sarah Abadhi, A-B-A-D-H-I." Spelling out "Abadhi" was a family tradition, since nine out of ten people couldn't guess the correct spelling of the Hungarian surname.

"Abadhi. Let me see." She scanned the computer screen in front of her. "Your daughter is in surgery."

It was as though someone had run an electrical current through Eva's body. "Surgery?" she asked. "What type of surgery?"

"I don't have that information. I'm sorry. But they'll be able to tell you more at the surgical waiting room on the second floor. The elevators are down the hall. Take any elevator to the surgical wing," the woman said in a calm, friendly way.

"Should we wait for Bob?" Eva asked Joseph.

"No, he'll figure it out. Let's go."

The surgical waiting room was large and bright, furnished with teak-framed armchairs and sofas. As Joseph and Eva hurried toward the information desk, they passed a host of distractions for the loved ones of those under the knife: several flat-screen televisions, coffee and tea carafes, Internet stations, local newspapers and stacks of magazines.

They introduced themselves to the older white gentleman manning the desk. "We're the parents of Sarah Abadhi. We were told downstairs that she's in surgery. Is that correct?" Joseph asked.

The man looked at his clipboard and seemed unable to find a match. Once again, Joseph spelled out the family name.

"Oh, Abadhi. I was looking under the Os. Sorry. Yes, she is in surgery with Dr. Gotbaum."

Eva blurted out, "What kind of doctor is he?"

"Why, he's an orthopedic surgeon, and a damn fine one, from what I hear," the man responded cheerily. Looking further at his clipboard he added, "I see here that your daughter is being operated on for fractures of the right leg."

Both Eva and Joseph breathed a sigh of relief. It was her leg, not her head, her spine or an essential organ that was injured. The fact that the man had high praise for the surgeon was a bonus.

Joseph asked, "Do you have any information on the baby? Our daughter was nearly due to deliver our grandchild."

The man flipped to a previous page on the clipboard and then looked up with a smile. "Well, I see congratulations are in order. Your granddaughter was delivered by Dr. Hanna before Dr. Gotbaum began his surgery."

Eva and Joseph didn't know whether to laugh or cry. They embraced each other, fighting back tears. Finally, Eva asked, "Can we see our granddaughter?" It felt strange and thrilling to utter the words "our granddaughter."

"Well, she's been taken to the neonatal unit on the fifth floor. If you want to head over there, give me your cell number and I'll let Dr. Gotbaum know when he's out of surgery."

"Oh, that would be wonderful. Thank you so much," Eva said, amazed to be feeling joy mingled with her fright.

They jotted down their cell numbers and left for the neonatal unit. On the way, they ran into Bob as he emerged from the elevator.

"Sarah's in surgery, Bob. And apparently, they delivered the baby already. I guess we're grandparents," Joseph said bashfully, looking at Eva and smiling.

Bob extended his hand to Joseph and kissed Eva on the cheek.

"Congratulations to you both. Boy or girl?"

"It's a little girl. That's all we know. We're on our way to the neonatal unit. Please, come," Eva said. "We're scared, we're happy. We don't know what we are. We could use someone who's thinking straight. Bob, that will have to be you."

"I'll do the best I can," he said with a little grin.

The new grandparents and their appointed voice of reason took the elevator to the fifth floor and followed the signs to Maternity. The three expected to find a nursery filled with row after row of healthy, swaddled infants in clear plastic tubs — the way babies were displayed when their children were born. But healthy newborns had long since started rooming with their mothers. The only nursery to be found was the neonatal intensive care nursery. A young, African-American receptionist — not much more than a teenager — sat at a desk outside the NICU.

Joseph spoke first. "We were told at the surgical waiting room that our granddaughter had been brought to the neonatal unit. Is this the right place?"

"What name would the baby be under?" the young woman asked.

Eva and Joseph looked questioningly at one another. Sensing their uncertainty, the receptionist jumped into the void. "Generally we use the mother's last name for the baby while it's in the hospital. It makes record keeping easier."

"Oh," Joseph said. "It's Abadhi, A-B-A-D-H-I."

The young woman entered the name into her computer and looked up with a smile. "Yes, your granddaughter was admitted to the intensive care unit about half an hour ago."

Jubilant just moments before, the new grandparents were again filled with dread. Bob stepped in. "What's the baby's condition, if I may ask?"

The receptionist scanned her screen. "According to the information available to me, her condition is satisfactory. If you like, I can get the doctor or the baby's nurse to tell you more."

Eva jumped at the offer. "Oh, that would be so good of you. We would so appreciate talking to someone who can tell us about our baby. Thank you so much."

While keeping an eye on the jittery people on the other side of her desk, the receptionist called into the NICU to summon someone to meet with Baby Abadhi's family.

"Someone will be out in a few minutes to talk with you. We have coffee and tea in the waiting room. It's just down the hall and to the right. Please help yourself."

Eva realized she hadn't gone to the bathroom since long before Reginald Washington's call. She ducked into the ladies' room, and the power of suggestion led the men to find their way into the men's room. More comfortable on one level, they all met at the cheerfully decorated waiting room.

Bob made himself a cup of tea. Then, seeing his friends' agitation, he tried to blunt their worst fears by touting the hospital's excellent reputation. As he was sharing the story of his brother's successful knee replacement performed at the hospital, a tall, slender, gray-haired man in a white coat came into the waiting room. All three got to their feet.

"I'm Bart Feinberg, your granddaughter's doctor." He shook hands firmly with Eva, Joseph and Bob.

Joseph made the requisite introductions and then gave voice to the question foremost in each of their minds. "How is the baby, Dr. Feinberg?"

Eva held her breath and said a silent prayer.

"Your granddaughter was born by Cesarean section a little over an hour ago. She was immediately able to breathe on her own. Her color was good and she scored well on the tests we put every newborn through. She weighed in at a hefty eight pounds, one ounce, which for my practice is a bruiser. She was brought to the NICU as a precaution because of the unusual circumstances that preceded her birth."

Eva allowed herself to exhale, then took the doctor's hand in her own and patted it. "Oh, that's the best news I've heard today. You mean to say, she's doing well?"

"Very well, indeed. And if she continues to do well, I anticipate moving her out of the NICU tomorrow."

Joseph's response was more cautious than his wife's. "We're not privy to the extent of our daughter's — the baby's mother's — injuries. What effect do you think they've had on the little one?"

"It's my understanding that your daughter's injuries were confined to her leg, her lower leg I believe. She had some blood loss and was given a unit of whole blood before the baby was born. Your daughter's injuries seemingly have not affected the baby. There were no signs she was in distress *in utero*. Right now she's pink, she's responsive and she has a good, strong sucking reflex. Everything we like to see in a newborn."

"So it's your best guess that the baby wasn't hurt by the accident?" Joseph persisted.

"She is apparently well and indistinguishable at this point from a healthy newborn whose mother did not suffer trauma before birth," the doctor said, hedging his bets by the use of "apparently."

Now it was Eva's turn. "So, Doctor, when can we see the baby and hold her? A baby should be held and kept close. Don't you think? I'm no neonatologist; I'm just a mother...and, I guess, now a grandmother too," she said, pleased at the thought.

"You're absolutely right. Skin-to-skin contact is very important for newborns. And the bonding between the baby and her family is as important as her medical care. I believe the staff is done with all the admission procedures that are our normal protocol here in the NICU. Assuming you're currently well and not fighting off any communicable illnesses, I think we can arrange a visit right now if you're ready," the doctor offered.

"We're healthy. As for ready, oh yes, I'm ready." Eva looked at Joseph, who nodded his okay. "Yes, we're ready."

Bob didn't want to intrude on his friends' introduction to their first grandchild. "If it's all right with you, I'll head down to the cafeteria and grab a sandwich. I'd also like to call home and let Irma know the good news about the baby. Can I bring either of you anything?"

"Not right now, Bob. But thanks. Thanks for being here. It means so much to us both," Eva said.

"Let me echo Eva's sentiments. We appreciate all of your help," Joseph said. "And if you could, would you check again on Sarah — just in case the message didn't get through to the surgeon on our whereabouts?"

"Sure. That's a good idea, Joseph. I'll let you know if there's any news."

Dr. Feinberg led Eva and Joseph into a room adjoining the NICU, where they could wash their hands and put on yellow paper gowns and masks. As they were about to enter the NICU, the doctor turned to them both and said, "By the way, before your daughter was put under anesthesia, she told the orthopedic surgeon that if the baby was a girl, it was to be named Anna."

Joseph stood motionlesss. Anna was his mother, a woman who had witnessed the slaughter of her first husband and children in a Nazi concentration camp. Because she was tall and strong she had been allowed to live as a slave laborer. Taunted mercilessly by the guards for her strength and stamina, she had been made to strip naked in the dead of winter in front of all the other slave workers — so she could prove she was a woman. Now the good Dr. Feinberg was about to introduce Joseph and Eva to another Anna Abadhi, a fresh, new life, but one that was already marked by trauma and survival.

Once in the brightly lit, noisy NICU, Eva and Joseph could hardly believe the size of the babies they passed. Some of the infants would fit in Joseph's hand. Others were the size of full-term newborns, but were attached to life-sustaining ventilators and nasal tubes. As they came to the last incubator — or "open warmer," as the doctor referred to it — they saw a sleeping, relatively large baby wearing a white knitted cap and diaper. It had a little round belly with a newly tied umbilicus. Electrodes were attached to the baby's chest, delivering information on her vital signs. The baby was asleep on her back with her arms splayed at her sides, blissfully unaware of the hum and activity of the NICU.

"Let me introduce you to your granddaughter, Anna," Dr. Feinberg said. "If you'd like to pull over some chairs, we'll have Anna in your arms in no time."

Joseph spotted two free chairs and dragged them simultaneously across the room. Dr. Feinberg swaddled the sleeping newborn in a white receiving blanket and placed her in her waiting grandmother's arms. Eva and Joseph were mesmerized by the perfect baby.

Being jostled from her comfortable, climate-controlled open warmer made the baby stir. She opened her eyes, big round eyes — Sarah's eyes — and stared at her grandmother's face. That was almost too much for Eva.

"Look, Joe. Look at those eyes. Don't they remind you of Sarah?"

"It's uncanny, really. I feel like I'm looking at the newborn Sarah all over again."

"Dr. Feinberg," Eva asked, "would it be okay if we peeked under her hat to see her hair? Our daughter was born with bunches of thick black hair."

"By all means. Take off the hat and check your granddaughter out." As Eva slipped off the hat, she and Joseph started to laugh. It was clear that, at least in one respect, this baby was not a replica of her mother. Though she had bunches of hair, it was platinum blond.

"One can tell very little from a newborn's hair color in terms of what its ultimate coloring will be," Dr. Feinberg explained, trying to ward off any possible disappointment the new grandparents might have.

"Well," Eva laughed, "I, for one, am rooting for blond. My mother and I were blonds. It's clear that this baby is favoring my side of the family. A very intelligent choice," she said while she gazed lovingly into the eyes of her granddaughter. "Good for you, Anna."

The neonatologist always got a kick out of parents' and grandparents' search for likenesses in the newest member of their family. He marveled at how they latched onto the shape of a baby's fingers or toes, how it made its fist, how it burped — if it burped — as signs that the infant belonged to their clan.

"Well," the doctor said, "she may very well remain a blond, but then again, she may not. I wouldn't bet the farm on it. But hair of any color is a wondrous thing, as far as I'm concerned." He laughed, patting his bald spot.

"Just so," Joseph agreed. "We'll love her no matter the color of her hair." Just then, his cell phone rang.

The doctor jumped in before Joseph had a chance to answer it. "Oh, I'm sorry but you can't use your cell in here," he explained. "It interferes with our telemetry. But you can step outside the NICU anytime and use your phone there."

"Oh, of course, I understand," Joseph said apologetically, sending the call to voice mail. "I wasn't thinking. It's been quite a day."

"Not to worry," the doctor reassured. "Look, I've got some paperwork to get to before I head home. I want to reiterate that Anna is doing well. It's my hope that we will be able to move her to the special-care nursery down the hall tomorrow morning."

Joseph stood up and shook the doctor's hand. "It's been very nice to meet you. And thank you so much for being careful with the baby. In my own work — as well as in life — my philosophy is to err on the side of caution whenever in doubt. I very much appreciate your approach."

"Well, that's what we're here for. Careful is our middle name. We know we have some pretty important patients, and that their families are counting on us," he said, motioning to the fragile babies around the room. "We take our work seriously, but we love what we do. If all goes well, our payoff is a beautiful little kid. Not bad wages, I'd say."

"I couldn't agree more," Eva said, tearing up while rocking the baby from side to side.

The doctor and Joseph shook hands again before he left to face his pile of insurance forms and dictation. Joseph was anxious to get back to Bob to find out where they were in Sarah's surgery.

"Eva, I'm going into the hallway to see what Bob has to say. If the surgery is over, would you rather stay here with the baby while I speak with the doctor by myself?"

Eva was torn. She didn't want to let go of Anna. She was so sweet, drifting off and then opening her eyes and staring at her. On the other hand, Eva wanted to hear what the doctor had to say about Sarah's injuries and the results of the surgery.

"Find out what Bob has to say. If the doctor is ready to meet with us now, I'll leave with you. But if the surgery will go on a while longer, I'll stay here with the baby. She shouldn't be alone, Joe. If all was well, she'd be with Sarah now."

After so many years together, the look on his face told her everything she needed to know. He was relieved he wouldn't have to meet with the surgeon alone.

Eva needn't have worried about being torn from her granddaughter. Bob's message — that the surgery was going to take quite a bit longer — brought the weight of the world back onto Joseph's shoulders. After washing and gowning up again, he went back into the NICU and relayed the message to Eva. The news left her as stricken as her husband.

As he looked at Eva and the baby, Joseph thought of all the photos he was missing, photos capturing the first hours of Anna's life. Instead of framing shots with his old, trusted Olympus, he was pacing nervously, unable to sit in the rocker a nurse had kindly brought over. Eva suggested he head down to the cafeteria to keep Bob company. He agreed, relieved to have something to do.

He joined his friend just as Bob was finishing his lemon meringue pie and coffee. Bob made the suggestion that Joseph get some food to go before the cafeteria closed for the night. Joseph dutifully followed the advice, getting some sandwiches in case he or Eva regained their appetites. By eight, he decided it was time to take care of Bob, convincing him to go home and get some rest so that at least one of them would be fit for work at the lab in the morning.

After retrieving their overnight bag from the car, Bob bade Eva and Joseph good night. It was nearly nine when he exited the parking garage. The car thermometer registered zero degrees. Heading for the FDR Drive, he could see the brightly lit disaster site in the distance. As he entered the highway and accelerated, he felt as though he was escaping the grip of a calamity. Soon he would be home, back within the fold of his comfortable, everyday life. He hoped that in time, his friends would be so lucky.

TWENTY-FOUR

It was nearly eleven o'clock before Jeff Gotbaum finished piecing together what had once been Sarah's healthy right lower leg. He didn't know how much of his angst about the surgery was due to the fact that it was a miserable, complicated injury to repair, and how much was due to the fact that it was Sarah he'd been operating on. One good thing was that the vascular surgeon, Dr. Alicia Lewis, was able to reestablish decent blood flow to the leg. As she left the OR around nine, she was optimistic that her repair had done the trick. He envied her confidence.

Jeff had the OR nurse call Sarah's family to let them know he'd be ready to meet with them around half past eleven. When neither number answered he surmised they were with Sarah's baby, and unable to use their phones in the NICU. A call there proved him right, and the nurse relayed the message.

Jeff willed himself to appear authoritative as he walked through the door to the surgical waiting room a few minutes past the appointed time. The lights had been dimmed low and the coffee pot cleaned out for the day. The receptionist was long gone when Jeff approached the only two people left in the room. They sat holding hands on the sofa in front of a television tuned to David Letterman. Jeff wasn't sure, but they might have been dozing. They startled when he approached.

"Excuse me, are you the parents of Sarah Abadhi?"

Eva and Joseph struggled to rouse themselves. They both pushed off from the sofa at the same moment, still holding hands.

"Please, sit down. I would actually like to sit down, if that's all right with you. It's been a long day for me — and I assume for the both of you."

Eva muted the TV with the remote and Jeff pulled up an armchair so he could sit facing the exhausted mother and father. The parents and the surgeon took the measure of one another. Even in the low light, Jeff immediately saw the resemblance between Sarah and her dad.

"I'm Dr. Gotbaum," he said, extending his hand to them both.

"Thank you, Doctor, for coming to talk with us at this late hour. We're eager to hear how our daughter is doing," Eva said.

"Well, she's been through a lot, but she's stable and doing well in recovery. Apparently the only serious injury she sustained was to her leg. Dr. Hanna, who delivered your granddaughter, said the C-section was uneventful. Did you get a chance to talk with her?"

"No, we didn't," Joseph said.

"Well," the orthopedic surgeon continued, "there appear to be no internal injuries to your daughter's vital organs. In that sense she was very lucky, given the magnitude of the accident she was involved in."

Joseph bristled at the thought. "Lucky wouldn't be a word I would apply to what happened to our daughter today, but I take your meaning."

"We're lucky in another sense," Eva said, trying to soften Joseph's rebuke to the doctor. "We've seen our granddaughter and she's beautiful. Dr. Feinberg, the neonatologist, says she appears to be responding like a normal newborn. We're so thankful for that. The doctor said Sarah told you the baby's name? She'd kept the names to herself throughout her pregnancy."

"While she was still in the ER she made me promise to hold the baby when it was born and call it Anna if it was a girl."

Joseph got a quizzical look on his face.

"I should explain that Sarah and I are acquaintances. She's a friend of a friend and we've gone running together a few times in the past. So we were both surprised to see one another in the ER. She wanted to be able to hold the baby after it was born, but Dr. Hanna and I thought it best to go with general anesthesia. That meant Sarah would be asleep when the baby was born, hence my offer to hold the baby and welcome it to the world."

Immediately Eva started wondering if this Dr. Gotbaum might be more than a friend of a friend. Was it possible that he was the father of her little granddaughter? "Dr. Gotbaum, so you held little Anna first? That was so kind of you. You'll have to tell Sarah when you see her tomorrow."

Generally Joseph enjoyed Eva's ability to make light conversation with anyone under any circumstance, but not tonight. "Yes, that was very thoughtful of you, Dr. Gotbaum, but could we get back to the extent of Sarah's injuries? What exactly happened to Sarah's leg?" There was impatience in his voice. Jeff, who had started to relax, felt his muscles tense up again.

"Certainly, Mr. Abadhi. Apparently Sarah's leg was struck by a steel construction stud. My best guess is that it hit the ground and then bounced up, striking her lower right leg with great energy. It caused significant trauma. Both the tibia and fibula were broken in a number of places. In addition, the bone fragments punctured the skin, making what we call an open, multifragmentary fracture. There was also significant contamination by construction debris."

Joseph's jaw clenched as he listened to the description of his daughter's injuries. He squeezed Eva's hand so hard it hurt, but she didn't pull away. "So what can be done to undo so much damage?" he asked.

"First we irrigated aggressively to clean out the surgical sites. We followed that with debridement of the contaminated tissue to try to ward off infection, which is always a possible complication in cases such as this. Then Dr. Lewis, a vascular surgeon, repaired the damage to the leg's circulatory system. There were some soft-tissue injuries. I repaired those and restored the fractured pieces of bone to their proper positions. I also removed several small bone fragments that would cause trouble later on in the healing process. I decided to do an external fixation of the fractures because of the extent of the injuries and the debris that had entered through the openings to Sarah's skin. Are either of you familiar with external fixation?" Jeff asked, hoping he wouldn't have to go into an extensive description of the repair needed for grade III fractures with contamination and soft-tissue damage.

Joseph and Eva looked at one another and shook their heads. "No, we don't know what that is," Joseph said. "Please, explain what it means."

"Well, you're probably most familiar with casts for immobilizing fractures of the bone. But in this case, a cast wouldn't allow us to care for the wounds to soft tissue. We have to be able to get in and clean out the area of the injury for the next several days. Another alternative is internal fixation, where I would nail, screw or wire together the pieces of broken bone. But given the contamination by the construction debris, I felt that would open Sarah up to an increased risk of infection — and possibly the loss of the leg."

Eva gasped. "Oh my god. Amputation? I had no idea." She thought she might throw up the sandwich Joseph had encouraged her to eat.

"In an injury this severe, amputation can never be entirely ruled out. My approach to the repair was to bring that possibility to a minimum."

"So please, Doctor, explain this external fixation," Joseph pressed.

"I inserted pins through the skin and into the bones to hold them in the correct position. The pins are held in place by an external frame — hence the name 'external fixation,'" Jeff explained. "This type of fixation works best in superficial bones such as those in the lower leg, where the chance of pin-tract infection is minimal."

"I don't believe I've ever seen this, but I'm with you so far.

Please go on," Joseph urged.

"This method allows us to watch the status of the wound sites and continue irrigation and debridement until we're certain the risk of infection has passed. The advantage of this type of rigid fixation is that it lets us aggressively and simultaneously treat both Sarah's fractures and her soft-tissue injuries. It also allows us to have her moving her ankle and knee joints, which is good for edema reduction and the general health of her muscles and joints. We can also elevate her leg without any pressure on the injured soft tissues at the back of her leg. We're actually able to suspend her leg — thus keeping down swelling — by attaching ropes from the overhead frame on her bed to the external frame surrounding her lower leg. We can also get Sarah up and about earlier — with a walker or crutches — without fear of destabilizing the fracture."

"What does this thing look like, Dr. Gotbaum?" Joseph inquired, genuinely curious.

"I won't lie to you. It's a little strange at first glance. It's a round, metal frame that goes entirely around Sarah's leg from her knee to her ankle. The pins go out from her leg bones to the frame. Strange as it looks, it's actually an ingenious invention that's become standard procedure for injuries such as Sarah's. Compared with other types of fixation, the research shows it leads to the best outcomes."

"So you think she'll be all right?" Eva asked hopefully.

This was the question Jeff dreaded. Everyone wanted to be given a worry-free prognosis. He'd try his best. "I don't want to minimize the seriousness of the injury Sarah sustained. But she has many factors in her favor: She's young and otherwise healthy, she's had good nutrition and she's not a smoker. Nicotine impairs bone healing. She's not diabetic, and that's great because elevated blood sugar levels also impede healing. The fact that a single limb was involved and that her joints — the knee and ankle in this case — were not affected are all things in her favor."

"What are you saying, Dr. Gotbaum?" Eva asked. "What's not

in her favor?"

"My biggest concerns now are infection and whether the healing of the bone will proceed and allow restoration of good function. To help her recovery along, we'll start Sarah on physical therapy. Getting her to move — even in bed — will start tomorrow. She won't be able to put any weight on the leg for some time, but since she's so fit, I think the therapists will actually be able to get her out of bed in a day or two."

Eva mustered the courage to ask the sixty-four-thousand-dollar question. "What if things don't go as you hope? What if she gets an infection or the bones don't heal well?" Joseph's face twitched as he awaited the doctor's reply.

"Bone healing is a remarkable process. In most cases the strength of a healing bone is eighty percent of normal three months after an injury. But the next days and weeks will be critical. Should infection set in, we can fight it with IV antibiotics. We've already got her on a prophylactic antibiotic regimen. Other complications could be nerve damage or poor bone healing. And of course, the worst-case outcome would be failures so severe that amputation would have to be considered."

"What type of odds are we talking about?" Joseph asked.

Jeff swallowed hard. "Complications during the healing process can occur in as many as fifty-five percent of cases such as Sarah's. Most of the time, we can address them, either medically or surgically. But there are cases where all our efforts fail and the only option is to remove the leg." Jeff stopped there to gauge the parents' response. They both looked horrified, as was Jeff when he tried to imagine Sarah as an amputee. Now that he had laid out the worst-case scenario he tried to give them some reason for optimism. "While amputation is not out of the realm of possibility, it's my hope that Sarah will make a good recovery because of all the factors I've already mentioned. She's a motivated, bright, healthy patient. I think it's not unrealistic to hope for a good outcome."

"Not unrealistic?" Joseph said. "Well, for Sarah's sake, I hope you're right."

Jeff skipped dictating his op-notes and headed home right after saying good-bye to the Abadhis. He felt like crap. According to the OR nurses, the casualty count from the crane accident was mounting. To add insult to injury, the weather was more like Alaska than New York. By the time he entered his lobby, he couldn't feel his toes.

Now he'd have to cap off the miserable day by telling Rick about Sarah — and her baby. He worried about how Rick would take it. He'd started to come around over the last few months, drinking less, working out again, eating better. Jeff figured he still had it bad for Sarah, but he was getting by, making do — like the rest of the poor, single *schmucks* he knew. Jeff wondered if the news might undo him. He prayed Rick was asleep so he could put off telling him until morning.

As he turned the key in the door he could hear the TV. Shit. Rick was up, probably watching a game.

"Hey bro, long day," Rick said, without looking up from the screen.

"Yeah. You probably heard about the crane accident. I caught an open, multifragmentary fracture and it was a beast."

"Yeah, heard about the accident," Rick said distractedly, with his attention still fixed on Kobe Bryant, who was on a scoring roll. "The city is becoming a dangerous place. Remind me not to walk under any cranes."

Jeff went into the kitchen and remembered he hadn't had any lunch or dinner. He opened the fridge and took out some leftover Chinese, set the microwave for two minutes and opened a beer.

"Who's winning?" Jeff called out to the living room, hoping to buy some time.

"The Lakers, 101 to 83 with a minute left on the clock. Kobe's amazing tonight. Nothing unusual about that," Rick said, more to himself than to Jeff.

When the microwave timer went off, Jeff got his moo shu and took it into the living room. Rick moved over to make room for him on the sofa.

"Aren't you on tomorrow?" Jeff asked.

"I couldn't sleep so I thought I'd watch a game. It's working. I'm beat now."

"Well, I'm beyond beat. This is my first meal since breakfast. And I've been on my feet most of the day."

"You surgeons have it so rough," Rick mocked. "But you also make the big bucks." Then he jabbed his fingers into Jeff's ribs.

"Hey, watch it! I'm in no mood for your razzing. If you'd get serious for a minute I want to talk to you about something."

"Sorry, brother. What's going on?"

"The surgery I just finished — the open, multifragmentary fracture — I was operating on Sarah Abadhi."

Rick felt his face grow hot. Though it had been over seven months since they'd split, he still couldn't get Sarah out of his head. Other women — women who once would have made him perfectly happy — didn't measure up. Hard as he tried, he couldn't stop comparing them to her.

"What do you mean? Don't tell me she was involved in that crane accident."

"I'm sorry, Rick. She was. I'm so sorry."

Rick swallowed hard. "How bad is it?"

"Her right lower leg took a direct hit. She suffered a very nasty trauma. I was in the OR with her for nearly six hours."

"How did the surgery go?" Rick asked in a voice so low Jeff had to strain to hear him.

"Well, that's the thing. I pulled out all the stops, but I'm not certain it's going to work. It may, but I have to be honest. I'm not as sure as I'd like to be."

"What the hell? What do you mean you're not sure?"

"What I'm saying is, it was a very complicated fracture. But I'm on it, Rick. And so is Lewis — you know — Alicia Lewis from vascular. No one's slacking off here. Even so, I'd be lying to you if I said the recovery is going to be a slam dunk."

Rick tried to take it all in. For months he'd worked doggedly — and unsuccessfully — to blot out any thought of the embryo that had caused the split between them. He knew Sarah's time was likely near. Finally, with an edge in his voice, he asked, "What about her fetus?"

"You knew she was pregnant? You never shared that critical piece of information with me," Jeff said, trying unsuccessfully to swallow his sense of hurt. "Did that happen before or after you left?"

"Oh, did I fail to mention that the allegedly sterile Sarah had gotten pregnant? She told me on the night we broke up. She wanted to keep it, I didn't, but my vote didn't count. She told me I could walk away free and clear. She cut me loose in favor of becoming a mother."

Jeff couldn't believe Rick was capable of walking out on a pregnant girlfriend — Sarah, of all people.

"So you just walked away?"

"Don't get all high and mighty on me. I'd told her from the start that marriage and babies were not on the menu. She was more than fine with that. But then, despite her allegedly blocked fallopian tubes, she got pregnant. Anyway, there was no way I was going to be forced into becoming a father." The last words made his mouth contort.

"So you just left her? Pregnant? What are you, some kind of ghetto baby daddy?"

"Don't give me crap, Jeff. I'm telling you, she said it was okay. She knew where I stood about babies and she didn't want to abort it. She said she'd take 'full responsibility' — those were her words."

Neither of them spoke. As hungry as he'd been, Jeff's appetite for the moo shu deserted him. Finally, Rick asked again, "What about the fetus?"

"She gave birth by C-section to a baby girl before Alicia and I started the repair on her leg. The baby was full-term and healthy. Nothing short of a miracle, given the fact that Sarah had been more or less buried alive in the accident. She named it Anna."

Anna. All the months of denial were trumped by hearing the name of the child he'd fathered. But he couldn't give in to his rising dread. His focus had to stay on Sarah.

He got up and headed to his room. A minute later, he came back out, dressed for work. "I'm going over there. I'm going to see her."

"What? Are you crazy? With all the narcotics we're pumping into her, she's barely intelligible."

"I won't talk to her. I just want to see her. What floor is she on?"

"She was in recovery when I left but they'll probably take her to Seven. Wait a minute, Rick. You should give this some thought," Jeff said, imagining the tightly wound Mr. Abadhi's reaction to the guy who had knocked up his daughter and then left.

Without answering, Rick grabbed his coat, ran out of the apartment and down nine flights of stairs to the ground floor.

Rick didn't notice the bitter cold as he raced to the hospital, entering through the ER entrance, the only door open at that hour. When he got to Recovery, the nurse who'd worked with Sarah reported that the parents had seen the patient before she was transferred to the seventh floor. Parents. Jesus Christ. He hadn't figured on having to deal with her parents. He'd just have to pretend he was a doc checking on his patient. No need to go into the particulars. In the meanwhile, he could satisfy his overpowering need to lay eyes on Sarah. He took the stairs to the seventh floor.

There was a male nurse in front of a computer terminal at the nurses' station. "Hey, I'm looking for a patient named Abadhi."

"You'd better spell that for me." After Rick provided the spelling, Sarah's name and room number came up on his screen. "Is it

Sarah Abadhi?"

"Yeah, that's the one," Rick said, his heart racing.

"She's in 7201 and her nurse is Gail. I think you'll find Gail in the break room if you want to check with her before seeing the patient."

"Thanks, I'll do that. Hey, you have a good night."

"This is as good as it gets. Nice and quiet. That's just how I like it," the nurse said as Rick took off toward the staff lounge.

As predicted, Gail was on break. Rick introduced himself as an old friend of Sarah's. The nurse was a veritable Chatty Cathy.

"I guess she lives nearby."

"Yeah, she does. Just a few blocks from here," Rick said.

"Probably how she got caught in that terrible accident today. The parents had a key, so they headed over to her apartment for the night. She's out like a light. No point in them hanging around and watching her sleep. The poor girl also delivered a baby today, on top of everything else," the nurse said with some pity in her voice. "How's that for a full day?" Answering her own question, she added, "I'd say that girl would have been better off if she had never gotten out of bed today…or yesterday…whatever. Sorry, this shift makes it hard for me to keep my days straight. I guess the accident happened yesterday, technically speaking."

"Yeah, right. I know what you mean. I've had my share of working crazy hours. I started my day at 6:30 yesterday morning."

"Oh, that's a bitch," the nurse said. "You a resident?"

"No, attending."

"Geez, that's a long day for an attending."

"Sure is. Hey, I thought I'd pop in and check on Sarah. I'll leave her a note if she's asleep," Rick lied without missing a beat.

"When she wakes up she's going to feel like she was hit by a bus, so a note might be nice. She'll need all the cheering up she can get."

Rick left the break room and had to restrain himself from

running down the corridor. When he came to 7201 he stopped. What if she was awake? What could he say to her? Another thing that hadn't occurred to him before he'd taken off for the hospital. He decided he would tell Sarah the same lie he'd told the nurse, that he was working late. Ready with his alibi, he entered her room.

It was a double, and Sarah had the bed closest to the door. He was relieved to see the other bed empty. He was alone with her. She was asleep, as Jeff had said she would be. No matter. This was the closest he'd been to her in a long time. But as his eyes scanned her body, he was taken aback by what he saw. This was not the picture of Sarah etched into his mind. Her right leg looked like it had been attacked by a wild animal. It was encircled by a metal frame with pins sticking into it in several places. The leg was suspended about a foot above the mattress by ropes hanging from the bed frame. Rick remembered Jeff's uncertainty about the prognosis. Now he understood. Sarah might lose her leg.

As his eyes focused on her midsection, he saw a large bump rising from under the white sheets, making it look as though Sarah was still pregnant. Though it was normal so soon after delivering, it was proof positive of the reason they'd split. Then he turned his gaze to her face. Though the lights were dimmed for the night, he could still make out the face that had haunted him, waking and sleeping, over these last months. Her brow had lacerations; a large bruise was forming around her left eye socket. Her hair was covered by a green surgical cap, probably because it remained contaminated with debris. But it was still Sarah, the same beautiful lips, the same graceful neck. A single curl was visible from under the elastic of the surgical cap. Rick took a step closer. He had to stop himself from taking her hand and kissing it. Then he thought about the baby that she had just delivered. He had to sit down. Suddenly, he realized what was about to happen. He ran into the john and threw up.

He rinsed his mouth out and washed his hands and face. When he came out of the bathroom, he pulled a chair next to the head of the bed. At first he just sat there, listening to Sarah's breathing, but after a few minutes he succumbed to the urge to touch her. He stroked her hand with his index finger. The feel of her skin made him want to put down the bedrail and climb into bed with her. He'd stay there all night, just stroking her and whispering to her that everything would be okay. Even if they took the leg, it would be okay. He'd help her get better. In the midst of his reverie, Gail came in to check on her patient. He quickly pulled his hand away.

"Oh, still here?"

"Yeah, I was actually trying to muster up the energy to head home," he said. "It's been a long day." He surprised himself at how effortlessly he fabricated his lies.

"I hear ya," the nurse said. "I'm on a seven-to-seven shift tonight — and when I get off I have to pick up my three kids from my mother's, feed them, dress them and get them to the sitter's before I can hit the sack."

"Oh, that must be a beating," Rick said, forcing himself to engage with the talkative nurse.

"It is, but there aren't a lot of options. My husband was deployed to the Middle East in November and I'm on my own with the kids. Thank God for my mother."

"That's got to be tough," Rick said, getting up from the chair. "Well, I'm going to head out. Good luck with your kids in the morning."

As he was walking out the door she called out to him, "Hey, need some paper to leave your note?" She pulled a small pad-and-pen set out of her pocket and offered it to him.

"Nah, changed my mind. Thanks, though. I'll stop by again in person when she's feeling better."

"Whatever. It's your call," the nurse said as Rick left the room.

He wondered what he might have said if he'd written that note. If he had any backbone he would tell her the truth: that he had never been with anyone like her, that after they'd broken up, it was an effort just to get out of bed every morning. He'd tell her that if she would let him, he would help her get her life back. He knew a lot about rehab. He'd done it himself after the car accident. He could be a big help to Sarah — if she wanted his help. That was the big if.

He was headed toward the elevator when he saw a well-dressed man in his forties looking lost. At that time of night, the man appeared wholly out of place on the floor.

"Excuse me, I'm looking for room 7201. The patient's name is Sarah Abadhi," the man said.

Rick flinched. It occurred to him that, in the intervening months, Sarah might have found someone who was ready to take his place for daddy duty. "And you are?" he asked.

The man caught Rick's hesitancy. "Oh, I'm sorry. I should have identified myself right away. Strange guys walking around the hospital at this hour are not a great idea. I'm Dr. Jared Scholl. I'm looking for my patient, Sarah Abahdi. I'm her OB and I was going to deliver her baby until she was involved in that terrible accident today. I was just on my way home from a delivery and I thought I'd check on her if I could."

Rick went from wanting to smash in the guy's face to hoping to pick his brain. "I just came from her room, but she's asleep. I'm a pediatric intensivist."

"Don't tell me the baby is critical," the OB said, suddenly alarmed. "The nurse who called for Sarah's history before the birth said nothing about the baby being in distress."

"No, no. Not at all. We're just taking precautions, given the accident."

"Oh, that's a relief. Sarah was so excited about this baby. I don't know what she'd do if she lost it."

"They did a section before tackling the mother's injuries," Rick said, trying to sound knowledgeable. "I believe she named the baby Anna."

"I knew it was a girl, but Sarah told me to keep the baby's

gender to myself. She wanted to be surprised. That's great news. You know, if I ever get the time, this patient's case is worthy of a journal article. She was diagnosed with double hydrosalpinx years ago. According to every test I ran — and the Boston doctor who made the original diagnosis — she had virtually no chance of ever conceiving a child normally. So this pregnancy came out of the blue. After she got over her shock, she was so happy. Talk about bad luck, though. I couldn't believe she was involved in the accident today, and so close to her due date, too." The OB paused for a moment and then added, "That, at least, was a plus for the baby."

So Sarah had told Rick the truth about her infertility. Something inside Rick relaxed, like a rope that had been pulled taut under tension and then was allowed to go slack. "Oh, it's definitely a big plus — the biggest plus. I'm sure the family will be relieved to know that she's all right."

"Well, actually, Sarah's doing this alone. There's no husband or partner in the picture. She said the guy she was involved with when she conceived had no interest in fatherhood. Personally, I find it hard to imagine someone walking away from a woman like that. His loss, I'd say."

Rick felt accused, tried and found guilty. Of what? Stupidity? Being a heel? Cowardice? Probably all of the above. He realized the OB was looking at him for a response. "Yup. Sure is. Look, I've gotta run."

"Of course. If you could direct me to her room…."

"Oh, sure," Rick replied. After pointing the OB in the right direction, he shook his hand and said, "Nice talking to you." Though he was relieved to know Sarah had been straight with him about her infertility diagnosis, the fact was, that was his biggest lie of the night.

It was after one a.m. What could he do now? He was too keyed up to sleep. He decided to confront his biggest fear.

He went through the usual protocol before entering the NICU, a procedure he could do in his sleep. The head nurse for the NICU's night shift was a woman Rick had worked with over the years. After explaining he was a friend of Baby Abadhi's mother, she was happy to point out the infant's open warmer. Rick was as jumpy as a cat when he approached the last incubator.

He tried to view Sarah's baby as a patient. A quick look made it obvious that the infant was, indeed, full term. He checked the monitors above the open warmer. Her vitals were spot-on for a healthy neonate. Finally, he looked down at the infant, who was awake and looking directly at him. She had Sarah's big, round eyes and a cleft in her chin, much like his. It was then that his professional edifice fell away. There was no doubt this beautiful child was on Earth because one of his guys had swum to find Sarah's waiting egg. The child before him carried his DNA in every cell in her body.

Over the years he'd handled too many babies to count, but he was tentative as he lifted this one from her open warmer. He swaddled her in a blanket and sat in the rocker Eva had used just hours before, rocking the baby much as she had done. He remembered what the OB had said about Sarah's tubes and how she'd been shocked when she learned she was pregnant. As the baby grabbed onto his index finger, Rick wondered how in the world this child had been conceived.

TWENTY-FIVE

A few hours after leaving the NICU, Rick called in sick. He spent the day in the john or in bed.

When Jeff came home that night, he found Rick burrowed under his blankets, just as he'd been that morning. It was a first in their years of living together. Had Rick been laid low by a pathogen, he wouldn't have worried. His body could beat back a pathogen. But Jeff guessed it was Sarah and the baby she'd delivered that had caused Rick to take to his bed. There was nothing his immune system could do about that.

Jeff was famished and decided to order a delivery. When he checked with Rick about getting something for dinner, he was met with an emphatic "no food" from beneath the covers. Jeff closed the door and let him be. He ordered a pizza, ate alone and then tackled some of the journals piled on the coffee table. Though he found one article particularly interesting — the one on pilon fractures — he could barely keep his eyes open. No doubt about it, he was in sleep deficit from yesterday's late night. Probably the most productive thing would be to turn in early.

Around half past nine, Jeff started getting the coffee pot ready to brew automatically at 5:30 the next morning. He loved the idea of awakening to the aroma of freshly brewed coffee. To his way of thinking, it was the second best way to start the day. And since the first — making love to a beautiful woman — was not on the horizon, it was his absolute favorite. He usually ground enough beans for the two of them. From the looks of the coffee pot, though, Rick hadn't touched this morning's brew.

He knocked on Rick's door.

"Go away."

"I just have one question for you."

"Go away."

"It's about coffee. Should I make some for you for tomorrow?"

"I said, 'Go away.'"

Undeterred, Jeff opened the door and walked in. He was immediately hit by an overpowering smell of body odor.

"Do you understand English?" Rick asked

"Yes, I do, quite well as a matter of fact. As you know, I aced the verbal on my SATs and MCATs. And furthermore, I can't go away because I live here. All I need to know is if you want coffee. And then, of course, there is the small issue of what's up with you. As a physician, I need to satisfy my curiosity on that point," Jeff said as he moved the clothes on Rick's desk chair and sat down.

"Well, you don't live in my room, so you can leave," Rick said from under the covers.

"True, but if I left I would still be in the dark about the coffee and how you're doing."

"Enough with the fucking coffee. Yes. Make me coffee. I'm fine. Now you can go away," Rick bellowed, turning to face the wall so that all Jeff could see was his dark, matted hair.

"Well, I feel better knowing that. By the way, I thought maybe you'd like an update on Sarah's condition," Jeff said, hoping that lure would do the trick.

Rick sat up in bed. "Tell me."

"Well, much to my relief, it was a pretty good day. As you'd expect, she's in a world of hurt, but on the whole, Alicia Lewis and I were happy with how the day went. Yesterday's radical debridement and rigid fixation seem to have put us on the right track. We're not out of the woods yet — not by a long shot — but a day without complications is my idea of a good day."

"How bad is her pain? Are the narcotics covering?"

Jeff silently congratulated himself on getting Rick to talk. "Well, at first she didn't want the narcotics. She said they would go into her milk and she didn't want the baby to be exposed to them. Then we had to break it to her that her chances for a good recovery would be greatly diminished if she nursed the baby. You and I know that she's going to need as much calcium hydroxyapatite as her body can make in order to mineralize and stiffen the collagen matrix. Without the mineralization she won't form callus and lamellar bone. But Sarah was clueless about all of that."

"What else?" Rick pressed.

Jeff hesitated, unsure if he should tell Rick about Sarah's reaction.

"What else? Don't hold out on me, Jeff."

"Well, she got pretty upset when she realized she had to choose between healing herself and nursing her baby,"

Rather than demoralize Rick further, this news brought him to life. "Did you tell her she might lose her leg if the healing didn't go well? That might persuade her to give up the idea of nursing. Sure, nursing is usually preferable, but in this case, the pluses are dwarfed by the minuses. They'll get the baby on a good formula and she'll do fine. Sarah's body needs to be able to go full throttle into repair mode."

"I explained that to her. I was glad her parents were there when I told her. They were gentle, but they made it clear that the healing of her leg was the most important thing she could do for the baby, you know, so she could care for her later on."

"Did she buy it?"

"Yeah, she did, eventually. She's a smart woman. She got it." What Jeff omitted was the copious tears shed at the thought that she wouldn't be able to nourish her baby from her breast; the self-recrimination at failing her baby yet another way, after not delivering her naturally, not being able to hold her right after she was born, not taking care of her on her first day of life.

Had Rick known any of that, he might not have been so relieved. "That's good. So did she agree to the pain meds? God knows, she's going to need them. I saw that leg last night."

"Yeah, she's on a self-administered morphine pump and the nurses tell me she's using it — judiciously, but she's using it."

Rick stayed quiet for a minute and then he asked, "Has she seen the baby?"

"Yeah, the baby's out of the NICU and they brought her to Sarah. They've also decided that as long as one of her parents stays with Sarah in her hospital room, she can keep the baby with her, provided she's willing to pay extra for a private. Sarah and her parents agreed and they've already moved her to a private room. That lifted Sarah's mood quite a bit."

The news had a totally different effect on Rick. All he could think about was how one or the other of Sarah's parents would always be there, making it impossible for him to see her alone.

"So her parents are with her now?" Rick asked.

"Yeah, that's the deal I arranged with the neonatologist and the head nurse. The ortho nurses don't want the responsibility of the baby's care. The neonatologist said he'll stop by twice a day for the next day or so. But after that, he feels she could be discharged to the grandparents' care."

"He's probably right. Who is it, by the way?"

"Feinberg."

"Oh, he's a good guy. I trust his judgment. I saw the baby last night. I didn't give her a complete exam, but she appears to be a healthy, full-term newborn."

Jeff couldn't believe how clinical Rick was in referring to his own child, but he figured this was not the time to call him on it. "Yeah, she looked good to me when I held her. She stared straight into my eyes, first thing. Maybe they all do that. I don't have much experience with newborns. But she definitely looked like she was no worse for her traumatic entrance into the world."

"Jeff?"

"Yeah?"

"You know, I met her OB last night — not Catherine Hanna. Her own OB."

"You're kidding. After midnight? That's one dedicated OB."

"He came to check on her on his way home after a delivery. He told me he'd diagnosed Sarah with primary infertility and said he had absolutely no idea how she had conceived." Then he stopped and looked directly at his friend. "Her fallopian tubes are totally occluded, Jeff. Double hydrosalpinx. The fuckin' tubes are completely closed. There's no way they could allow conception to take place."

"That's insane. What are the chances someone like that could get pregnant without surgery or IVF?"

"The OB said that according to his tests there was no chance — same conclusion as the doc who made the original diagnosis, some guy up in Boston, where Sarah went to law school."

"So it was a fluke?" Jeff asked.

"Yeah, a fluke that resulted in that baby girl you held. The OB said Sarah was shocked when she found out she was pregnant, but that she really wanted the baby."

"The baby was all she talked to me about when I was trying to explain her injuries to her in the ER. She told me several times to take care of the baby first. It was like she didn't care about her leg at all."

"Jeff?" Rick asked, almost in a whisper.

"Yeah?"

"I've been trying to figure out what to do. I kept going in circles. But now I think there's only one thing I can do, and that's man up — you know — take responsibility for the baby. Even though she gave me a pass, seeing that baby made me realize that only a prick would leave Sarah holding the bag. There's no way I'm gonna be a prick to Sarah. But how exactly I'm going to handle the whole thing, I haven't worked out yet."

"You should talk to her, you know, try to work things out."

"I know. But now I'll have to get past the parents."

"Well, the parents will be there until the baby is discharged, maybe a day or two. Feinberg said as much today. I figure in the best-case scenario, Sarah will be an acute care inpatient for another week or so. Then I'll move her to the rehab wing. That should give you plenty of time to talk to her alone."

"Yeah, but you said it made Sarah happy to have the baby with her in the room," Rick said. "I gotta tell you, separating a mother and a baby is fighting nature."

"But a hospital is no place for a healthy baby. The baby can visit all day long before going back home with the grandparents. I'll let you know when the coast is clear." Jeff got up and moved Rick's clothes back to the chair. "Okay. I'm beat. I'm going to get the coffee ready and head to bed. Yesterday was brutal."

"I'll second that," Rick said. "Thanks, Jeff. You know, for the update on Sarah. I appreciate it."

"No problem," Jeff said as he headed for the kitchen to grind his coffee beans before falling into bed, dead to the world.

Rick had an eventful night, a night filled with dreams so intense they woke him from a deep sleep. He dreamed first that he was swimming in the pool up at Columbia. He was all alone. There was no other swimmer, no lifeguard. He looked at the clock above the pool. It was midnight. It was a beautiful swim, peaceful and relaxing. His pace was good, too, putting him on track for his personal best. Then, as he turned his face up for a breath, he saw someone come through the women's dressing room door. In his next breath he saw it was a tall, slim woman on crutches. When he emerged from his flip turn at the end of the lane, he saw the woman was an amputee. She walked to the lane next to Rick's and let one crutch fall. Then, using the other crutch, she gingerly lowered herself so her one good leg dangled in the water. Just as Rick reached the end of his lap, the woman slipped into the water. She and Rick pushed off from the wall at the same moment.

Swimming side by side, they kept an identical pace, lap after lap. He was amazed she could do so well with a leg that ended below the knee. He looked up at the clock on the wall. It was five o'clock in the morning. Somehow five hours had passed and they had been swimming without a break. Rick thought he had better stop so he could get to morning rounds. As he started to climb out of the pool, he felt a hand on his arm. He turned around and saw it was Sarah. "Help me out?" she asked. Just seeing Sarah, feeling her touch on his arm, excited him. He woke up hard and came almost immediately.

After that Rick didn't want to go back to sleep. He only wanted to remember the feeling he'd had when he realized it was Sarah who had matched him stroke for stroke, lap for lap; Sarah, beautiful and lithe still, asking him for help.

He got up and used the john. Then he went into the kitchen and did what his mother had often done when he awoke from a dream when he was little. He put some milk in a mug and warmed it in the microwave. Unlike those childhood nightmares, this was a dream he wanted to burn into his mind. He feared it would recede into the netherworld that swallowed most ordinary dreams. The feelings this dream evoked — peace, synchronicity with Sarah, sexual excitement — were feelings he didn't want to lose.

The smell and taste of the warm milk evoked memories of their own. He remembered how protected he had felt after a terrifying dream, sitting on his mother's lap, drinking his milk with their golden retriever next to them. He remembered how his mother had told him that nothing and no one was going to hurt him, that he was the safest little boy in the whole world. The thought of his old dog, Hercules, made him smile.

He looked at the clock on the microwave: 3:00. He could catch a few more hours of sleep if he was lucky. Even better would be to dream that dream again. He got into bed and soon was breathing slow, rhythmic breaths. The dream of swimming with Sarah came back to him just as he drifted off, but a full reprise was not to be. In its place was another dream, just as vivid as the first. In it, Rick was dressed in his white coat with a stethoscope hanging around his neck. He entered a patient's room to find a little child dressed as a Buddhist monk. His sleeveless red-and-saffron robe covered his torso and legs, which were crossed as he sat on the hospital bed. Rick looked on the child's chart and saw the name Gyatso, Tenzin. DOB: 07-06-35. Rick did a double take. That had to be a typo. This kid couldn't have been more than nine years old.

"I'm Dr. Smith. I'm going to be your doctor."

"Hello, Doctor. Very nice to meet you. I came to the hospital because I am suffering from a very bad pain in the stomach," the little boy explained.

"When did you start to have pain?"

"Well, I was suffering and fretting for some days and then I thought to myself, 'What exactly is the problem? What is the cause of my suffering?' And then I realized it was coming from my stomach. So I knew I had to get help to end my suffering."

"You're a smart little fellow," Rick said to his young patient. "When you're in pain you should seek help. That's what we're here for."

"Yes, I am very lucky that I am here. It makes me happy. I am very happy now," the little boy said.

"So your pain has gone away?" Rick asked.

"Oh, no, no. The pain is very bad."

"Then how can you be happy?" Rick asked, perplexed.

"Oh, I am so happy because you are going to attend to the cause of my suffering. What a lucky boy I am!" the little boy chortled. "The path to happiness is within us all. Now that I have realized a way to end my pain, I am a happy boy."

"Well, all right then. Please lay down so I can examine you," Rick told the boy.

"Oh, yes, Doctor. Please, whatever you say," the boy said agreeably.

Rick lifted the boy's robe and examined his belly. The little boy cried out in pain when Rick examined his right lower quadrant. He looked at the boy's labs. His white count was sky high. The kid likely had appendicitis.

"So, Tenzin — should I call you Tenzin?"

"Some people call me His Holiness, but you can call me Tenzin if you like."

The kid must have a god complex, Rick thought, but he would leave that for the shrinks to deal with. "Tenzin, if you had to give your pain a score from one to ten, with ten being the worst, what score would you give the pain when I examined you?"

"Oh, yes. Ten, definitely ten," the boy said assuredly.

"Well, I think we will have to take out your appendix. It probably has become infected," Rick explained.

"Oh, thank you. I look forward to my operation!"

"Can I ask you another question, Tenzin?"

"Yes, of course, Doctor."

"You have such pain, you need an operation and yet you are happy?" Rick asked his young patient.

"Decidedly so. Very happy. But I will be even happier when you cut out my miserable appendix."

Then the young boy laughed and laughed, making even Rick laugh. He awoke smiling at six a.m. He had a smile on his face as he showered and dressed. He felt rested and ready for whatever the day would bring. Rick couldn't get over the little boy in his dream, happy because the cause of his pain was about to be rooted out. There was a kernel of wisdom there, he thought. He'd have to try to find the time to write that dream down before he forgot it.

The dreams had a good effect on Rick. He actually whistled as he poured his cereal into the biggest bowl he could find in the cupboard. He wolfed down his breakfast and drank more than his share of the coffee, leaving Jeff scratching his head as he put a bagel in the toaster. Before they headed out for the hospital, Jeff checked the indoor/outdoor thermometer on the kitchen window: a balmy seventeen above zero. Not great, but an improvement over what had come before.

TWENTY-SIX

Rick had a satisfying morning. He transferred a four-year-old girl out of the PICU — a child who had been critically injured when her parents' entertainment center fell on her as she scaled its shelves to reach a toy. It had been touch and go, but on day five after the accident, she began to rally. Now her recovery was exceeding Rick's best hopes. She would need some physical therapy after the casts were removed, but he expected that in years to come, her accident would become part of family lore: the child so rambunctious she had risked death to retrieve a plaything. He also was happy about the two-year-old boy whose pneumonia had overwhelmed his lungs. Rick was able to wean him off the ventilator and discharge him to the peds floor.

But the most satisfying part of his morning was the epiphany he had while getting a cup of joe from the lounge. He suddenly knew he could handle whatever he had to face. So he'd been catapulted into fatherhood against his will. What did that matter now? There was a living, breathing child in the world that belonged to him and Sarah. The dream of the two of them swimming together had only served to make obvious what some part of him already knew: She was the woman for him. For years, he'd mocked the notion that everyone had a perfect soul mate. But now he wasn't so sure something like that wasn't at work.

At that moment, as Rick stirred the poor excuse for coffee, he felt better than he had in months. He knew what he had to do. He was like the little monk in his dream. He'd identified the cause of his suffering. Now he would deal with it. He'd go to Sarah and level with her, tell her he wanted to be with her and their baby. He would man up, take on his new responsibilities and get on with life. Only then, like the little monk *sans* appendix, could he conquer the misery he'd known since leaving Sarah. He laughed out loud just at the recollection of the little boy in monk's robes giggling through his excruciating pain. Really, he thought, he had to write that dream down.

Three floors above him, in Sarah's seventh-floor room, happiness was in scarce supply. Sarah didn't know which was worse, the physical agony or the crushing sense of failure as a mother.

Visitors came in a steady stream and stayed only briefly so as not to tire her out. They offered warm congratulations and promises to help in any way they could. Bob Fong and his wife Irma were first, followed by Aunt Ellen and Uncle Max, Harry and Toby Meinig, Dr. Scholl and Doris. Everyone remarked what a miracle it was that Sarah and the baby had survived the accident. But nothing about the day of Anna's birth seemed miraculous to Sarah.

There was one visitor who provided some relief, and that was Dr. Feinberg. His twice-daily visits brought reassurance that Anna was doing well, reminding Sarah that she had succeeded in one important way: nurturing her daughter for nearly nine months.

On the third day following the accident, Dr. Feinberg came into Sarah's room for his early morning visit. Eva was off warming Anna's breakfast bottle and Sarah and Anna were alone in the room. It was hard for him to tell who was more distraught, his hungry patient or her mother.

"Hello, Sarah. I could hear Anna down the hall even with your door closed. I would say we don't have to worry about her lungs. She's clearly got a good set."

Sarah was on the verge of wailing herself. She couldn't see how he could make light of the baby's distress. Raising her voice over the baby's screams, she cried, "There's nothing I can do for her. She doesn't want the pacifier. I can't nurse her. I can't walk the floor with her. I can't even rock her in a chair. What kind of mother does this poor baby have?"

Eva returned with the bottle in time to hear the last of Sarah's lament. She quickly took the pacifier from Sarah's hand and replaced it with the bottle. As soon as Sarah put the nipple to Anna's lips, the baby began sucking heartily. A look of contentment came over her face.

"There, that seems to be doing the trick," Dr. Feinberg said, thinking it was time for a version of the pep talk he gave parents of his very tiny, very sick patients. "Sarah, this is your first baby. I can tell you from both personal and professional experience that even if you were fit as a fiddle, there would be times when you wouldn't be able to comfort Anna. Babies can often be inscrutable, defying a parent's best efforts to make them happy. I think you'll find that parenthood makes even the most able-bodied and clever among us feel wholly inadequate at times. People wiser than I have said becoming a parent is the great leveler, reducing us all to self-doubt."

"I've read the books, Dr. Feinberg. I understand there will be times I won't be able to figure out what's troubling her. But there was nothing in any of the books about what happened to us."

"Fair enough. You have a unique situation to deal with. But you won't be incapacitated forever. And while you heal, you have expert help here," the doctor motioned to Eva, "a real pro who seems to have done an excellent job of raising you."

Eva piggy-backed on that. "Sweetheart, Dr. Feinberg is right. I know this isn't how any of us imagined the days surrounding Anna's birth. But soon you'll be up and around and you'll be able to send me packing."

It was all too much for Sarah. She'd indulged in such sweet expectations for the arrival of her baby. She could see now what a mistake that had been.

"I don't think either of you can understand how awful it is to be too helpless to take care of your child," Sarah said, trying hard not to dissolve into tears.

"Of course, you're right about that," Dr. Feinberg said soothingly, sensing this mother was close to her breaking point. "Forgive me if it seemed I was minimizing your problem. It's a very real problem. But my hope and expectation is that it will be a self-limiting problem. As you heal, you will be able to do more and more for Anna. Eventually, I feel certain that you'll be able to care for your baby without any assistance."

"But she gets one chance to be a newborn. She's starting her life with a loser for a mother. I might as well still be under that pile of rubble as far as she's concerned."

"Sarah, I want to encourage you to remember that these are just the first days of many, many years of being with and caring for your child. This is a painful time, but also a joyous time. My advice is to try to concentrate on the joy you feel for your daughter. It will make the time it takes for you to heal much more bearable."

She averted her eyes from the doctor, concentrating on Anna, who had dozed off after taking her fill. "Your advice is very logical, Dr. Feinberg, but it's not so easy to follow."

"I know it's not. And if you feel the need for some help with your feelings of frustration, I want you to know that my service has counselors who help new parents who've gone through traumatic births of varying sorts. I hope you'll avail yourself of their assistance. They're there to help, just like the rest of us. And their role in getting good outcomes for our babies is every bit as critical as that of the doctors and nurses."

Eva was worried. Sarah had always been a perfectionist. She was never any good at dealing with disappointment. She thought back to the ceramic bowl Sarah had made in first grade. She had been so proud of that bowl, but when it slipped from her hands and shattered, she had refused to cry. All she said was, "I never liked it anyway." Oh, what a tough nut she could be, always working so hard to be in control. Lying helpless in a hospital bed, needing her mother to take care of her most basic needs and the needs of her baby was probably more than she could take.

"Dr. Feinberg, if Sarah decided to take advantage of the counseling service, whom would she contact?" Eva asked quietly.

Her daughter's response was as instantaneous as it was furious. "Mom, I don't need a counselor!" Her outburst caused the baby to start.

"It was just an idea, sweetie."

"I'm upset for a perfectly legitimate reason. God, I'm not a head case," she pleaded as the tears streamed down her face.

"Sarah, you may be the sanest person in this room," the doctor said gently. "All I'm saying is, you have a lot on your plate and if you would like to talk to someone to help sort it all out, we have staff members who are good sounding boards. But it is totally your call." He traded Sarah the baby bottle for the box of tissues on her nightstand.

"Thank you for at least acknowledging my situation. I know you mean well by your offer...but for now, I think I'll try to sort things out on my own."

"As I said, it's completely your call." The doctor held the bottle up to the light. "By the way, I see Anna downed almost three ounces in just a few minutes. You've got a good eater there. That makes me very happy."

The words had a soothing effect on Sarah. "You really think she's going to be okay? After all she's been through — including a helpless mom?" she asked as she dried her eyes and blew her nose.

"Her exciting entrance to the world aside, she looks to be one terrific newborn. In fact, I was thinking of discharging her from my service later today."

"What does that mean — discharging her from your service?" Sarah sniffed.

"It means she can go home today with her grandparents and come every day to stay with you, but as a visitor rather than as a patient," the doctor explained. "She needn't be hospitalized anymore."

"Oh, I guess that's a good thing, right?" Sarah asked hesitantly.

"A very good thing," the doctor assured her.

After the reception her last question had received, Eva steeled herself before she tried another. "Doctor, how much time could Anna spend here during the day? What I'm trying to get at is, would you limit the baby's hospital visits?"

"Oh, no, not at all," the doctor said. "I think the nurses would probably like to have Sarah to themselves until they're done with the morning routines. I would think that after nine, Anna would be a welcome visitor, as long as she was with you or your husband or another caregiver. And she can stay as long as you like, until visiting hours are over at nine at night. That would make for a long day, of course, but it would be entirely up to Sarah. If she decides that's too long, Anna would be able to go home earlier."

"So are you thinking we should start this tonight?" Sarah asked.

"I'll check back later today, and if all is well, yes, I'd suggest we start tonight."

"I feel torn about it. She has such a beautiful crib to sleep in and I got everything ready for her arrival before — you know, before everything happened. She should be going home like any normal baby would and getting used to her surroundings. But I won't be there...." Her voice trailed off as tears once more started streaming down her face.

It was heartbreaking for Eva to see Sarah so miserable. She and Joseph had both been touched by how beautifully she'd prepared her apartment for the baby: a fully equipped nursery, clothes sorted by size from newborn to toddler two, wall decorations and pictures, whimsical nightlights, photo frames in primary colors. She even had nursing pads to absorb the anticipated leakage from her overfilled breasts. Sarah had thought of everything except, of course, the inconceivable. Eva remembered what her father used to say: "People plan and God laughs." That God could allow Sarah to suffer so made Eva want to scream.

But she didn't scream. Instead, she offered comfort. "Sarah, I'll have Dad take pictures of Anna's homecoming. I know it's not what you hoped for when you made everything ready for the baby. It's all so lovely, so perfect. All I can say is hang on. Everyone — Dad, you, me, the doctors — we're all doing our best for Anna.

"I know one thing for sure: You are going to recover and make a wonderful life for yourself and your daughter. And you will be a terrific mother." She knew that if her mother, Rivka, were there she would add a postscript: "From your lips to God's ears."

Anna had a calm and uneventful day, oblivious to the drama surrounding her. She drank, slept and eliminated on a fairly regular schedule, all of which had a good effect on her mother. After changing a number of diapers and feeding Anna her bottles, Sarah felt more useful. As anticipated, Dr. Feinberg discharged Anna to her grandparents' care at the end of the afternoon.

Jeff and his residents stopped in at the end of the day as well. He was happy on two accounts: First and foremost, Sarah showed no sign of infection; second, she continued to have good sensation and pulse in her lower leg. The folks from PT had gotten her off the bed and into a chair in the morning, and again in the afternoon. If things continued on this path, he could do the last debridement in a day or two and sew Sarah up. Eva, who held her breath and bit the insides of her cheeks as the surgeon examined her daughter's mangled leg, relaxed a bit when he announced his pleasure at Sarah's progress.

Joseph spent his day hunting down the requisite bottles, nipples and formula for Anna's homecoming. He celebrated his success by bringing the family dinner from a favorite neighborhood restaurant. Sarah had little appetite and, by seven o'clock, was so exhausted she gave her permission for Anna to be taken home. She dressed her daughter in the outfit Joseph had brought from the apartment. Using the camera Bob had transported to the hospital, he documented the event with nearly a roll of black-and-white film. He quieted Eva's complaints about running out of exposures by showing her the two new rolls of film in his coat pocket. He would be ready for more picture-taking when they got Anna home.

When the baby was tucked into her winter baby sack, Sarah braced herself for the departure. Tears were shed as she kissed Anna good night. Eva told Sarah she would call her as soon as they got to the apartment, and as often as necessary to give Sarah updates. "Keep the phone close!" were her parting words.

Sarah kept the phone next to her box of tissues, which was, once again, put to use after everyone left. Not fifteen minutes later the phone rang. Joseph wanted to let her know that Anna had the makings of a fine New Yorker: She'd enjoyed her first cab ride, short though it had been.

When Sarah hung up, everything suddenly loomed large — the quiet, the hospital smells and the ghastly apparatus encircling her limb. For the first time she was afraid. What began as an amorphous fear soon fixed on her injury. What if the leg didn't heal? How could she manage to care for herself, her baby, her job? "Oh God," she thought, "If you let me get well, I will never again take the ability to walk for granted."

The last time she'd offered a deal to God was when she had requested an A in seventh-grade math in exchange for picking up her clothes from her bedroom floor. By eighth grade, her negotiations with a higher being had come to an end. Not coincidentally, it was in eighth grade that she read *The Diary of Anne Frank* and became obsessed with reading everything that gave meaning to the numbers tattooed on her Grandma and Grandpa Abadhis' forearms. Her grandparents, tight-lipped about their wartime travails, were of little help, but her parents filled in the rough outlines: how Bubbe Rivka and Zadda Sam had left everything and everyone behind to escape the Nazis, spending the war hiding out in the woods, and how Grandma Anna had been a slave laborer who dug peat for fuel. The hardest to hear was how both she and Grandpa Erich had lost their parents, their first spouses and their children in the Nazi concentration camps.

Even at thirteen, Sarah knew that her grandparents had likely done their share of praying during the war, but to what effect? It was then she concluded that God was probably something like Santa, a fairy tale that brought happiness to people who believed, despite all evidence to the contrary.

She had been steadfast in her skepticism until she became pregnant. It was then that she had reconsidered the possibility of divine intervention in the lives of ordinary people. She had always wanted to become a mother and, so improbably, a baby had come into her life. She had allowed herself the indulgence of thinking that perhaps it was the work of a beneficent god that had allowed her to conceive. But the day of Anna's birth had made short work of that. What kind of god would give her a child and let her carry it for nine months, only to envelop her in a catastrophe just as she was ready to give birth?

Thinking about the accident and living in a godless world was doing her no good. She needed to think about something different, but her hospital room offered few diversions: *People* magazine, the pamphlet on patients' rights, television. She opted for the TV, settling on The Weather Channel. She soon learned the cold snap had finally moved out to sea. Now that was some good news. Anna would have more moderate temperatures for her trips to and from the hospital.

After the weather report, Sarah switched to the local news channel. The featured story was the crane accident. A voice in her head told her to turn it off, but she was spellbound by what she saw on the screen. It was only then that she realized the extent of the devastation the accident had wrought. They showed before and after pictures of an apartment house on 71st Street. It had been leveled by the crane's lattice tower. She thought about how many times she had walked past that building, never giving it a second thought. Now it was reduced to a pile of rubble.

As the newscast panned pictures of the scene, a reporter

somberly read off the casualty count: thirty-one dead, seventy-five injured. He ended his report by stating there was little hope that any more survivors would be found. Then they cut away to an interview with an angry, crying woman named Jennifer O'Brien, the wife of the crane operator. She raged at her husband's boss for jumping the crane in such terrible weather, accusing him and the developer of murder. "They murdered my husband and his co-workers, and all those poor people in their apartments and down at street level. And for what? Just so they could get their project done ahead of schedule and make a few more bucks," the widow railed. The news report ended there, in time for a commercial break.

Sarah suddenly understood what her visitors had been saying. It was a miracle she had survived. For the first time since the EMTs had reached her, she thought about the people who had been standing near her as the crane swayed precariously in the sky. She could only hope that they, too, had been visited by a miracle, if indeed that was what had saved her and the baby.

It was all too much. One moment she was on her way home to steal a little nap, happier than she'd been in years, and the next, her world had turned to dust. Now she realized it wasn't just her world. So many other people had seen their lives come undone. And those were the lucky ones.

Sarah pushed the mute button and found herself in tears again. Maybe Dr. Feinberg was right about talking to one of his counselors. There was only so much a person could handle. Just as she was drying her eyes, the night nurse, Mary, came in pushing her medicine cart. On the cart sat a computer terminal, part of the computerized medication delivery system that had failed so miserably in preventing the overdose of baby Ariel Arkin. More than ever, Sarah hoped the settlement she'd worked on had corrected the problem.

"Hi there, Sarah. How ya doin'?" Mary asked, seeing her patient upset. "Is the pain worse?"

"No. No, it's the same, but I just saw a report on what landed me — and I guess many others — in the hospital."

"Oh, I'm sorry. That must have been so hard to watch. This accident is the worst one I can remember," the nurse said as she scanned Sarah's wristband and then scanned the meds she was preparing to give her. "So many people got hurt. And…a lot didn't make it. It's really terrible."

"I'm ashamed to admit I didn't know the magnitude of it. All I knew about was what happened to me."

"Well, who can blame you? Besides your leg injury, you just had your baby. You don't have anything to be ashamed of," the nurse declared as she handed Sarah a little white cup with two pills.

"What are these for?"

"Oh, the usual for people who are on pain meds. A stool softener and natural laxative. You haven't gone once since you've been here," the nurse noted.

"Oh, that's right," she said. "Since they put the catheter in, I haven't had to worry about getting to the bathroom. But how will I get there if these pills work?"

"Don't you worry. Just ring your bell and we'll put you on a bedpan."

"A bedpan? Oh, I couldn't do that lying in bed," Sarah said, aghast at the thought.

"Well, you may not be able to use a commode or get to a toilet for a few more days, so you'll have to try using the bedpan. Believe me, everyone feels the way you do. But it's just one of those things you gotta do," the nurse said, almost apologetically. "You'll get the hang of it, and if all goes well, you won't be needing it for long."

"Well," Sarah said hopefully, "I haven't eaten much since the accident, so maybe I'll be able to wait a few days. By then I'll be able to get to the toilet."

"Hon, don't quote me on the timeline for ambulating to the bathroom. It's just a guess. But the stuff I'm giving you would loosen concrete, so by tomorrow at this time, I'll wager you'll be happy that someone invented the bedpan." And with that, Mary chuckled her way out of Sarah's room, pushing the cart in front of her.

As Sarah silently bet against the nurse's wager, Rick was wrapping things up for the night in the PICU. His newest patient, a twelve-year-old boy, arrived in the ER that afternoon after being hit in the crosswalk by a cabbie who'd run a red light. He was in serious condition with a long list of injuries. The most immediate problem was dealt with right away: the removal of his spleen and control of the internal bleeding. The vascular surgeon handed the boy off to Rick at a few minutes before seven.

While the boy was in surgery, Rick got a text message from Jeff: *Baby discharged.* Ever since he'd settled on his plan of action, Rick had wanted to run up to Sarah's room and tell her everything. Now that he knew the coast would soon be clear, he could hardly contain himself. He was thankful when the boy came out from recovery so he could focus on something other than waiting for visiting hours to end.

He met with the boy's parents, explaining that their son was stable, the most serious injuries having been addressed. He also told them of the sequence of procedures that would follow. The boy's arm, which had suffered a simple fracture, would be put in a cast. His numerous and deep facial cuts had been irrigated and would be sutured by a plastic surgeon with a great track record for facial repairs. The parents were scared, as were all parents whose children landed on his service. But they understood what he was telling them and voiced their appreciation for all the staff was doing for their son. That was about as good as it got for a doctor explaining to parents, sick with worry, how he and his colleagues were trying to make their child whole again.

When he was done talking with the parents it was only half-past eight. Maybe Sarah still had visitors. He decided to get something from the vending machines and head to his office. A pile of paperwork welcomed him as he sat down with his bag of chips and iced tea.

Filling out insurance forms seemed a surefire way to kill some time. But once at his desk, Rick had trouble concentrating. He moved papers around and nursed his iced tea. He couldn't remember when time had moved so slowly.

Finally, it was 9:15. He tossed out the chips and headed for the stairs, taking them two at a time. He forced himself to walk to Sarah's room at a normal pace. The door was open. He had to take a couple of steps into the room in order to see her. The lights were dimmed; the television was on mute. Sarah was propped up in bed, asleep, with a box of Kleenex next to her. Did she have a cold? Had she been crying?

He went to the side of her bed, took her hand and softly called out her name. "Sarah, Sarah, it's me, Rick." When she didn't awaken, he bent down and kissed her on the cheek. Closer this time, he tried again, "Sarah. It's Rick. I hope you're feeling better. I've missed you." He thought he saw her lips turn up into a little smile. Then he saw her eyes open. What came next was not what he expected.

"Rick? What are you doing here?" She looked frantic.

"It's okay, Sarah. Jeff — your surgeon — told me about the accident."

"Oh. Oh. Of course. I'm sorry. You startled me."

"I just wanted to drop in to see you," he said, still holding her hand.

"Thank you."

"It's the least I can do. It was such a terrible accident."

"It *was* terrible — just so awful. I was coming home early from work and then…I thought I was going to die and the baby was going to die." The mention of the baby reminded her of Rick's feelings about her pregnancy. She pulled her hand away.

"Sarah, I'm so sorry you were involved in the accident. But I hear your recovery has been going well. I'm happy for that," he said in a quiet voice, trying to be as soothing as possible. "And I'm glad the baby is okay. Anna. I like the name you picked for her. It's a palindrome."

"Jeff told you?"

"Yeah, he did. Eric for a boy, Anna for a girl."

"I know you didn't want the baby, Rick, but she's beautiful. She really is."

"I know she is. I saw her the night she was born."

"You've seen her?"

"Yup. I even held her. She looks just like you, except for the cleft in her chin. I guess she got that from me."

"I don't understand. How did you get to see her?"

"Well, one of the perks of working here a million hours a week is I can see a friend's baby in the NICU."

"You went to see her?"

"Went to see you, too, but you were asleep. It was right after your surgery."

She shook her head. "Why, Rick? Why did you come to see me and the baby? You were dead set against me having her. I said you were free to go and I meant it. You didn't — don't have to visit us."

"I know I don't have to. But here's the rub: I've missed you, Sarah."

Another surprise. "Really?"

"Really."

"I never would have guessed. I figured you for an easy come, easy go kind of guy."

"Always was, until I met you. Since we broke up I've had a lot of time to think. I was a jerk — and I was wrong to leave you."

Sarah had to look away.

"Well, aren't you going to say something?"

"I didn't think you were a jerk. Not at all, Rick. We had a deal. No commitment, no babies. Then I got pregnant, and all bets were off. You were free to leave. No hard feelings, really," she said, sounding more like his former business partner than his former lover.

"Well, I had plenty of hard feelings — mostly toward myself. I made a mistake by taking off when you told me about the pregnancy.

It's true that I never wanted the whole commitment thing. I never wanted babies. But I want you, Sarah. I came to tell you that whatever it takes to be with you, I'll do it."

Sarah couldn't believe what she was hearing. "Is this one of your pranks? You know, it's not nice to play with someone as beat up as I am."

Rick touched his fingertips to hers and looked directly into her eyes. The touch was electric. "This is no prank," he assured her, never taking his eyes off of hers. "In fact, I've never been more serious in my life."

Sarah wished she could disappear. She was in no condition to be having this conversation. What could she make of this declaration of — of what? She closed her eyes to avoid his penetrating look. For perhaps a minute nothing was said. Finally, she asked in an incredulous tone, "So you're saying that now you're willing to do the whole commitment thing — and with me?"

Rick didn't miss a beat. "That's right. I'm willing to do the whole commitment thing," he said, gently stroking her fingertips.

Sarah pulled her hand away and put it under her sheet. "Well, I'm at a loss for words. It's such an about-face for you. I can't imagine what led you to it."

"What led me to it was realizing that…." He stopped for a moment, stroked Sarah's arm and swallowed hard. "What led me to it was realizing that I'm in love with you."

"You're in love with me?" she asked, her voice thick with skepticism.

"Yes, ma'am. I am. And if you're surprised, you can imagine my shock. I've never said those words to anyone. I've never even thought them before. But it's the truth. I'm in love with you, Sarah."

Rick studied her face, trying to read her. All their time together, especially their last night, made him certain that she was as drawn to him as he was to her. But now he couldn't get a fix on what she was feeling.

"Sarah?"

"Oh, sorry. I was just remembering how our relationship ended. I guess I'm having trouble getting my mind around what you're saying. Maybe it's the painkillers."

Rick got up and gently kissed her lips. He would have stayed kissing her for the rest of the night if he'd had his druthers, but she turned her head away. Still, he savored that kiss.

"I love you, Sarah. I don't care about the drugs they're giving you or your injury or — or anything. I love you. Take your time to try to figure things out. I'll be here waiting."

The kiss bewildered her further. How bizarre it was to feel physically drawn to a man when her body was so broken and bruised.

"Rick?"

"Yeah, Sarah?"

"If it's all right with you, I'm going to take you up on your offer of time. I'm going to need some time to think about what you're saying. Let me see if I've got this right. You're in love with me and you're willing to do the whole settling down thing?"

"Only with you. I still think it's a crazy idea. But since I'm crazy for you, Sarah, I'll go with it," Rick said, returning with a bit of his normal repartee. "Take as much time as you need."

Then something occurred to her. "Are you doing this out of pity? Because if you are, I don't need or want your pity, Rick."

"Pity? No. No way. Pity has nothing to do with this. I feel terrible that you got hurt, but why would I pity you? You're not someone to be pitied."

"As long as that's clear."

"Consider it clear."

"Okay. But I've got a lot to deal with now — first and foremost, getting back on my feet. If you're willing to give me some time, I promise to give your proposal some thought."

"Proposal?"

"Well, didn't you just propose, what did you call it, doing the whole settling down thing?"

    "Oh, yeah," Rick said, "I guess the word freaks me out. But not the idea of being with you. That doesn't freak me out at all."

TWENTY-SEVEN

Rick left the hospital that night a happy man. What never crossed his mind was that in the months following their breakup, he was not the only one who had changed. He had no idea that as he was licking his wounds, Sarah was falling in love with the child that was growing within her. At the same time that he was struggling to find any comfort in the things he had always enjoyed, Sarah was feeling more alive and more hopeful than she had in years. In his haste to regain control over his life, he had failed to consider the possibility that she might not welcome his return.

Alone again in her hospital room, Sarah marveled at Rick's lousy timing. Where had he been for the last seven months? Throughout her entire pregnancy, there had been nothing, not even a text message, from the man who now professed love for her.

It was all too much. Turning off the lights, she thought back to days earlier, when she was healthy and Anna was still tucked safely in her womb, when all those people killed in the accident were going about their business and all was right with the world. That was her last thought before she drifted off to sleep.

It seemed she had only just closed her eyes when she was awakened by the night nurse who was ready to go off duty. Though the woman said it was time to rise and shine, it was dark as pitch outside her hospital window. Sarah pulled her arm out from under the covers for a blood pressure check and silently mocked her last thoughts of the night before. All was not right with the world. She was lying immobile in a hospital bed, separated from her newborn child. And then, of course, there was the reappearance of Rick. It took courage to face the day, maybe more than she had.

But the hospital operation carried on, oblivious to her outlook on the day. Shortly after the nurse left, an aide came in to gently wash her bruised and lacerated body. Then, just as the sun's rays started to stream through her window, the day nurse dispensed the morning medications. As she left, she crossed paths with the cafeteria worker delivering the breakfast tray. Sarah uncovered a bowl of thick, rubbery oatmeal just as Jeff entered her room. He was followed by an entourage of seven white-coated young men and women who quickly assembled around her bed.

Jeff was all smiles and all business. "Good morning, Sarah. You're looking much better today. How's the pain?"

"I think it's beginning to back off a bit. I actually slept all night."

"A good sign, indeed," Jeff said as he turned his attention to his students. "Dr. Prabhu, would you do the honors of examining Ms. Abadhi's leg? As you do, please explain to the medical students joining us this morning what you're looking for in your exam."

The young East Indian resident checked for nerve sensation, strength of pulse, movement in Sarah's foot and ankle, swelling and for any signs of sepsis in either the open leg wounds or the external fixator's pins. She concluded there was no nerve or arterial damage that was evident upon exam, and that the wounds and pin sites all appeared clean and free from infection. Jeff smiled not only at the facility with which his resident conducted her exam, but at the evidence that pointed to uneventful healing in his patient.

"Thank you, Dr. Prabhu," he said, turning to address Sarah. "Everything seems to be going well. Since the swelling is down, we'll unhook your leg from its tether and start elevating it with pillows. We'll try cutting back on the analgesics a bit and see how you tolerate that. We want you out of bed and upright as much as possible. It will enhance your recovery and lessen the chance of pneumonia and blood clots. To that end, I'll have the therapists help you take some steps today."

"That's fine with me," Sarah said. "I want to try walking."

"I'd like to see how you do using a walker to get yourself around the room and maybe into the hall. If your morning session goes well, I'll leave orders for the therapist to teach you to get on and off the toilet using your healthy leg and the walker for support. Then we'll be able to remove the urinary catheter," Jeff said, genuinely pleased that Sarah had, so far at least, dodged complications. But his pleasure was short-lived.

"A walker?" Sarah asked, scornfully. "You've got to be kidding. My grandfather used a walker after he had a stroke — and he was in his eighties. Surely I don't need a walker to help me get around."

Jeff was used to getting flak from college jocks about using a walker, but he didn't see it coming from Sarah. "Well, you can't put any weight on the injured leg. Not now and not for the foreseeable future. Under other circumstances, you could negotiate with crutches just fine given your level of fitness. But your abdominal muscles were cut during the C-section and they're going to need some time to heal. You'll likely find a walker more comfortable than crutches until they do."

Sarah thought about all the marathons she'd run. Now she was being told she had to use a walker to get around her room. "Well, I'd like to at least try the crutches. Could you tell the therapist to let me try?"

"I'll write the orders as you ask, but I'll leave the final decision with the folks from PT. The overriding aim is to get you moving while keeping you safe. The last thing we want is a fall."

"I can think of worse things than a fall, but I certainly don't plan on falling. I just want to give the crutches a try."

"Sarah, a fall in your condition could be very dangerous. You'll just have to trust me on this. Safety first. It's got to be the overriding goal right now," he said, unable to mask his impatience. He wondered if she had any appreciation for how hard it had been to reassemble her leg and install the external fixator.

Sarah immediately caught his change in tone. Her effort to preserve a scrap of dignity had obviously irritated him. "Of course, you're right, Dr. Gotbaum. Consider me an advocate for safety. I promise not to take any risks."

"Great. We're on the same page then," Jeff said. "We'll check on you this afternoon and see how the new dosage of pain meds is working and how you did with your excursion around the room." As his entourage began filing out of the room, Sarah decided to seize the moment.

"Dr. Gotbaum, could I have a word with you — in private?" Sarah asked. "It will only take a minute."

Jeff had a hunch about what Sarah wanted to discuss. Rick had come home euphoric after "manning up" and telling Sarah how he felt about her. But when Jeff had asked how Sarah reacted, Rick had told him she "just needed some time to think things over." Jeff felt his cheeks grow hot and hoped they hadn't also turned red, as they often did when he got nervous.

He called to the residents and students, "You go ahead. I'll meet you outside Mr. Sullivan's room in a minute."

As soon as the last white coat was beyond the threshold, Sarah began the query she hoped would help her figure out what to make of Rick's apparent change of heart.

"I got a surprise visitor last night."

"I suppose you mean Rick. Well, we're roommates, Sarah. HIPAA regulations aside, I hope you don't mind me telling him you were injured. I didn't disclose much more than what was in the *New York Times* article about victims of the accident," Jeff said.

That was news to her. So she'd been written up in the *Times.* Not the way she'd hoped to make her first appearance in the nation's newspaper of record. "No, I don't mind you telling him about my involvement in the accident. Nor about Anna's birth. Maybe that was in the paper, too, for all I know. But I have a question. How did he seem to you after we broke up?"

Jeff swallowed hard. "I don't really want to get in the middle of whatever happened between the two of you."

"You needn't be an intermediary. I'm just interested in your impression of his state of mind after we split."

"Well, it was my impression that he took the breakup hard. Frankly, he seemed to take it very hard."

Sarah nodded her head, aware of how uncomfortable the conversation was making him. "Thank you. That's really all I wanted to know."

"Okay, then. I'll see you later today, perhaps sitting in a chair or walking in the halls," Jeff said, only too happy to put his surgeon cap back on.

Among the several items on her breakfast tray, only the fresh fruit salad tempted Sarah. The melon and berries actually tasted good to her. She took this as a positive sign, a degree of normalcy reestablishing itself in her body. As though on cue, the physical therapist and her assistant came into her room just as she pushed the breakfast tray aside.

"Well, good morning, Sarah. We just spoke with Dr. Gotbaum and he says this is your big day. We're going to get you walking."

"I'm looking forward to it. I know you wouldn't know it to look at me now, but I'm a runner and a swimmer. So don't hold back. Push me to my limits. I mean it. I really want you to push me."

Just then the phone rang and Sarah picked it up.

"Good morning, Sarah. It's Anna's grandma."

"Good morning, Mom. How is she?"

"That's why I called."

Sarah's heart sank. "What happened?"

"What happened? What happened was that you gave birth to

one peach of a baby. Anna woke up only once for a bottle at 3:30. I changed her and put her back in her crib and she slept until just fifteen minutes ago. Can you believe it? A newborn and already waking up only once in the night!" Eva was ecstatic.

"Wow. I figured she'd go for at least two or three feedings, just as she did here in the hospital," Sarah said.

"I'm telling you. She's a real doll, Sarah. We are so blessed."

"I know, Mom. She's the only good thing...." She stopped before she started bawling.

"She's a wonderful baby — and we'll be bringing your daughter to you after we have a bite and get her dressed. I was thinking maybe we could use the stroller today. It's going to be relatively mild. What do you think?" Eva asked, careful to defer to Sarah.

She steeled herself at the thought of Anna's first trip in the stroller without her. "Sure," Sarah answered as casually as she could, "but you've got to use the car seat and the adaptor since she can't sit upright yet. Can Dad get the stroller and the car seat down the stairs okay?"

"Let me ask him. He's holding Anna." Sarah could only hear muffled sounds as her mother put her hand over the receiver. "Yes, darling. He says to remind you that he was the one who *schlepped* the stroller up the stairs after we bought it."

"Oh, of course. Please relay my apology for doubting his strength and agility. Mom, I bought a lock for the stroller — it's on the table near the door — and when you get home tonight you can lock it to the railing that leads to the basement. I asked the super a few weeks ago and he said it would be fine."

The therapist motioned that she and her assistant would come back later so Sarah could finish her conversation. She wanted to tell them that she was almost done, but they were gone before she had a chance. Then she remembered the return of her appetite. "Mom, would you mind very much bringing me some really good coffee and something for breakfast? To tell you the truth, I think I'm hungry."

That was music to Eva's ears. "You're hungry? Oh, that's wonderful! Would you like me to bring you an omelet? Or I can bring something else. You have a fully stocked fridge. Is there something you have a hankering for?"

"Mom, I trust your judgment. I'm sure anything you bring will be great."

"I promise to come up with something really good. We'll be there in an hour or so."

"I can't wait to see Anna in the stroller," Sarah said, trying to picture her tiny baby being wheeled through the streets of New York.

"I know. Me, too. So many firsts. It's an exciting time."

They said their good-byes. As Sarah hung up the receiver, all she could think of was the many firsts Anna was having without her.

The therapist and her aide didn't come back right away. Sarah regretted not getting off the phone more quickly. Given her luck, she'd likely go to the bottom of the list and get only one session for the day. There was nothing she could do now but wait. As she waited, her thoughts turned to Rick.

If there had ever been a poster child for letting the good times roll, it was him. That he'd taken their breakup hard was surprising, pleasantly so. She thought of his fingertips on hers and the sensation of his kiss. They had good chemistry, there was no doubt about that. But she wondered if there had ever been more than good chemistry. She tried to remember what they did when they were together. Sex, food, verbal sparring, sleep, exercise and an occasional drink. Were those the building blocks of a lasting relationship?

And then she thought of Anna. Defying two expert opinions, Rick had made her pregnant. She remembered how her father had exploded when she told him she'd given the baby's father permission to walk away. But now Rick had come back, saying he was ready to do whatever it took to be with her. How could a man make such a one-eighty? It was hard for her to believe the consummate player had fallen in love with her. Then a thought crossed her mind: Maybe it was Anna that had provoked his visit. A living, breathing child of one's flesh was a far cry from the abstraction of an embryo. Maybe all Rick wanted was a way to get access to his daughter.

Joseph and Eva wheeled Anna into the hospital room in her deluxe jogging stroller around ten, a couple of hours after Sarah had hung up the phone. The therapist and her aide had not returned in the intervening time and Sarah was ready to climb the walls.

"I was getting worried. You said an hour, Mom. It's been nearly two."

"Sorry, sweetheart. Just as we were about to walk out the door, Anna experienced what I can only call a blast. I'd forgotten what happens when a newborn moves her bowels. We had to take her out of the car seat, strip off all her clothes, clean her up and choose a new outfit. I had to wash her bunting and throw it in the dryer. That's what took so much time. I should have called to let you know, dear. I'm sorry."

"No, I'm sorry. I had no idea. Thank you for taking such good care of her. What would I do without you?" And, defying her best efforts, the tears began to well up again.

Sarah's father tried to lift her mood. "Don't mention it," Joseph said. "Anna was cute even when she was full of it, don't mind the joke." Eva threw him a look. "What?" Joseph asked, looking at his wife. "She *was* cute. And very cooperative as you wiped you know what from every crevice. She was very helpful. She lifted her little legs in the air and let Mom get to all the important places."

"Dad, thanks. Really, I appreciate everything you're doing for us. You'll never know how much."

"There's nothing to thank me for. It's my pleasure. I'll get a lot of mileage out of this when Anna's older. This is a story she'll rather I forget when she's…let's say, thirteen or fourteen," Joseph said, chuckling to himself.

"No doubt," Sarah said, unable to imagine her tiny baby as a self-conscious teenager. "Could you hand her to me, Dad? I've missed her something awful."

"Of course. And she's been missing you. I can tell," Joseph said as he carried his bundled granddaughter out of her car seat and into her mother's waiting arms. "Here you go. Madonna and child. Eva, where's the camera?"

"Joe, you packed it — I think it's in the diaper bag."

As Joseph searched for the camera and Eva unpacked her stores for the long day in the hospital, Sarah fell in love with her daughter all over again. She laid the baby on her thighs while she untied the hood and pulled Anna's arms out of the sleeves of her baby sack. "So you were a big poop machine this morning, eh? Made a bunch of work for Grandpa and Grandma, did you?" Sarah asked in a gentle, lilting voice. Anna looked directly at her mother's face as though they were engaged in a conversation of the greatest import.

"Oh, I almost forgot," Eva said. "I brought you a cheddar-and-veggie omelet and Dad just got an extra-large Ethiopian coffee from the shop down the street." Sarah's hunger had left her now that she was with her baby. Without taking her eyes off of Anna she said, "Oh, thanks. That's so nice of you."

"I'll go and heat the omelet. While I'm at it I'll give the coffee a little warm-up in the microwave, too. I'll be right back." As Eva left, Joseph captured a series of shots of the spellbound mother and baby. The therapist and her aide appeared just as Eva returned to the room with Sarah's belated breakfast.

"Oh, can we see your baby?" the aide asked.

"Of course. But I have to warn you that you'd better say she's beautiful because, to my mind, there's never been so beautiful a baby to grace the world."

The women needed no prompting. "Oh my God. She really is," the aide said. "Look at those big, blue eyes and all that blond hair.

She's darling."

"I know. I can't believe how lucky I am," Sarah said, beaming.

"You are — and save that thought, because you may not feel so lucky after we're done with you. We're not called 'the toughies' for nothing. No chickens allowed in our therapy sessions," the therapist warned Sarah.

"Oh, you can't scare me off. I'm game."

"Glad to hear it. You're going to need that motivation," the therapist said, smiling as if to dare Sarah.

"I'm used to pushing myself. I want to try using the crutches. Dad, could you take Anna while I work with the therapists?"

"I'll just save your breakfast, honey," Eva said, trying to stay out of the way.

"Could I have just one sip of coffee before we begin? I haven't had coffee in seven months and just a sip would be great."

"The caffeine won't hurt, either," the therapist laughed, "'cause you're going to need all your energy to keep up with us."

The coffee tasted like ambrosia. Sarah closed her eyes and savored the rich flavor on her tongue. "Oh, that's wonderful. Thank you. Now I'm ready." Sarah hadn't felt so upbeat since the accident.

The aide had brought both crutches and a walker as per the doctor's orders. The therapist released Sarah's injured leg from its tether and helped her swivel her body so she could dangle her legs off the bed. Her pain was ever present, but with both women helping, she stood up and grabbed hold of the crutches. She listened carefully to their directions and then moved the crutches forward. As she tried to move her body toward the crutches, she cried out, "Oh my God, I can't do it! It feels like my insides are falling out. I have to sit down."

The therapist and her aide eased Sarah back onto the bed. "Okay, take some deep breaths. This is common after abdominal surgery, Sarah. We can ask the doctor to order a Velcro-closure girdle and that will help you when you stand up," the therapist said. "But even with that, until your incision heals up a bit, the walker might be just the ticket."

"What happened to me? I can't even take a single step," she cried. "I was walking miles every day until — what — five days ago? I was swimming three times a week, lifting weights. I've become a wreck."

"Think of it as a short-term infirmity; short-term, that is, if you work your butt off. We're going to get you moving again no matter how hard it seems," the therapist said, not the least bit concerned by her patient's self-assessment. "Come on, Sarah; let's give the walker a try."

Eva and Joseph could hardly stand to watch their daughter struggle as she tried to use the walker. She persevered as the therapist prodded her before every step — really more of a hop — with her healthy leg. Every time she made the little jump forward, she was certain her guts would end up on the floor. All the while, she had to keep her injured leg from touching the ground, something made harder by the metal fixator. The therapist kept encouraging Sarah to aim for the doorway of her room. When she reached the goal she was rewarded with a couple of minutes of rest in a wheelchair before getting up and making the return trip to the armchair ncxt to her bed. By the time the session was over, sweat poured down Sarah's face, back and chest.

As worn out as she was by her first outing, Sarah felt good knowing she'd pushed herself to her limit. Before Sarah settled down to breakfast, her mother pulled a lovely winter nightshirt out of Anna's diaper bag. Joseph left the room so Sarah could change out of her drenched hospital gown. The soft jersey felt good on her skin as she enjoyed the omelet and coffee her parents had brought.

Joseph was gone for quite a while. Just as they were beginning to wonder where he could be, he returned, lost in thought and gesticulating to himself. Eva guessed the cause of her husband's distraction: He'd been away from his lab for days and the thought of all he had to do was making him crazy. When she suggested he return to work the following day — and Sarah seconded the motion — Joseph's relief was palpable. A plan was hatched. The next morning he'd drop Eva and the baby off at the hospital and then take the train back to Tuckahoe. Bob would meet him at the station and drive him home so he could pick up his car and some fresh clothes for Eva and himself. Then he'd get to spend the rest of the day where he was happiest — at his lab — before returning to the hospital in time for a late dinner.

Once details of the plan were finalized, the rest of the afternoon dragged on. At one o'clock the orthopedic resident, Dr. Prabhu, did what she hoped might be the final irrigation and debridement of Sarah's wounds. Bubbe Rivka phoned at half-past two, complaining that no one had brought her to the hospital to see her first great-grandchild. At three, Sarah's taskmasters returned for another grueling session, this time taking Sarah to the bathroom and teaching her to get on and off the toilet.

At half past four, Jeff and his entourage returned. There were smiles all around at the news that Sarah had done so well during her therapy sessions. No mention was made of the debacle with the crutches. Jeff said they would remove the IV and the urinary catheter the following morning, right before suturing her wounds. Sarah asked about the girdle the therapist had suggested and he readily agreed.

By the time five o'clock rolled around, the Abadhi family was spent. Even the angelic Anna was a bit fussy, and only her mother's singing and swaying from side to side soothed her. Joseph picked up some pizza and salad and brought them to Sarah's room. Anna downed four ounces of formula as Sarah learned to eat some dinner while feeding her baby a bottle. After Joseph polished off the last slice of pizza, Sarah dressed Anna in her winter sack, telling her to be a good girl for her grandparents. "No more blasts," she ordered. Then she kissed her daughter and watched as Eva and Joseph strapped her into the car seat. As they rolled Anna out the door, the exhausted Sarah felt ashamed that she was actually relieved when they left.

Sarah had just closed her eyes when she heard a knock at her door. "Is this a good time for some company?" She would know that voice anywhere. It was Harry.

"Oh, of course. Come in. Any time is a good time for you."

Harry was encouraged by the improvement in his protégée. Though her face was still bruised — around one eye in particular — and the cuts to her forehead remained, she looked much more like herself than she had just a few days earlier.

"I was on my way home and I told Toby I would just drop by for a few minutes. I don't want to tire you out."

"Oh, no, I'm so glad to see you. How are things at the office? Are the junior associates keeping things under control?"

"Two of them together are no match for you," Harry said honestly, acutely aware of how pleased this would make her.

"You know, I just remembered that I told them to call me if they had any questions. Pretty funny, huh? I have no idea where my phone is — or anything else that was with me that day."

"Forget it, Sarah. They can ask me if they have any questions. It's about time I did some real work around the office. It's amazing I get paid what I do," Harry said, grinning like the Cheshire cat.

"Hey, you had your chance to work like a dog doing the grunt work we associates slave over," Sarah smiled. "Plus, you bring in the big accounts. With your book of business, you're worth your weight in gold."

"Well, that's true. I'm sure the partners would prefer I stay rather than leave and take my clients with me."

"No doubt about it."

"So kid, you're looking good, really good. How's the baby?"

"Oh, she's just perfect." But remembering her relief when Anna was wheeled away made her tear up.

"Hey, it's hard having a baby under any circumstance, but

yours takes the cake. Cry all you want, though I have to admit that I actually hate when women cry."

That made her laugh through her tears. She grabbed a tissue, dried her eyes and blew her nose. "There, I'm good again."

"Good, because I have some business to discuss with you."

Sarah brightened. "Go ahead, I'm all ears."

"Now stop me anytime you've heard enough. I mean it, Sarah. You've had a terrible trauma."

"Go ahead. It's okay. Tell me," Sarah said eagerly.

"Do you have any idea who owned the project that led to your accident?"

"No. All I know is that it was going to be condos. I heard it on the news."

"Well, Mark Arkin was the developer. Apparently — according to the crane operator's widow — Arkin Worldwide pressured the contractors to go full throttle, cutting corners whenever possible to get that building completed and generating revenue," Harry explained in a revelatory tone. "With the economy in the toilet and credit dried up, apparently he was having a tough time. He's not one to suffer alone, so he put the squeeze on the contractors."

"I saw the widow on television. She was beside herself." Sarah closed her eyes and remembered the swaying crane. "I saw that crane cab, Harry. Oh, that poor man."

"Sarah, we don't have to talk about this. I'm a blockhead to bring it up."

"Tell me what you came to say. I want to hear it. I do."

"Apparently, Arkin read about you in the paper. There was an article on the people involved in the accident. It was the worst construction accident in New York's recent history, so the media are having a field day. You know how that goes. Tragedy sells," Harry explained apologetically. "So apparently Arkin recognized your name, did his homework and contacted me today about a settlement."

"A settlement? I haven't even thought about filing suit," Sarah said.

"The bastard's using the approach we used on him. He did everything in hypotheticals, of course, but intimated that if he was indirectly responsible for your pain and suffering, he would want to make you whole. And he added that he'd prefer to 'do the right thing' and 'bypass the whole liability labyrinth.' Those were his exact words. He even paid you a compliment by saying how impressed he was by your representation of the hospital."

"What do you make of it, Harry?"

"Well, you know what I think of him. He's a *schmuck* of the highest order — and he feels the same about me, which is why I was surprised when he called. You should have heard him. He actually sounded contrite. Whether he is or not is beside the point. You'll have to give some thought to his offer though, regardless."

"Did he mention a figure?" Sarah asked.

"Well, he didn't show his hand, but he intimated it would be high six figures. He's got insurance, but still, that's a tidy sum," Harry offered.

"I guess so." Sarah got quiet for a few moments. "I've got to tell you, Harry, I'm not really up to making a decision right now. Is the offer time sensitive?"

"He gave no date but was clear that he wanted this over and done with sooner rather than later — and confidentially. Oh, and there's one more piece I forgot. He said that, hypothetically speaking, if he was responsible in any way for your injuries, he'd want to apologize to you in person."

"Are you kidding?"

"Nope. That's what he said."

"Harry, look, I'm going to need someone to represent me. I'd like you to consider taking that on. I'll understand if you'd rather not. You hate Arkin and the case is out of your area of practice. But please think about it."

"Well, I'd only do it if I could do a good job for you. Let me talk with a guy from the San Francisco office who does construction law. I worked with him years ago on an outbreak case of Legionnaires' disease caused by a hospital's faulty ventilation system. He was a good man to partner with then and he's an overall good guy. Not a son of a bitch like me. I'll see what he thinks."

"Harry, you're the nicest son of a bitch I know. You really are."

"If that's a compliment, I'll take it under advisement."

"I mean it, Harry. You're a great boss to work for. You have no idea how much I appreciate how kind you've been to me," Sarah said.

"Well, I was trying to be a nice guy the other day when I told you to go home early. Look where that landed you," he said, looking down at his shoes. "The one time I play the nice guy and see how it turns out? I should stick with being a son of a bitch."

"No, Harry," she said. "Your suggestion that I go home early was very thoughtful. I was tired and you were thinking of what was best for me. The truth is, I was looking forward to that nap. You were right — like you usually are. I just ran into some very bad luck."

"Well, I think I should just stick with being the son of a bitch I was destined to be and everyone will be safer."

"Have it your way, Harry," Sarah said with a little smile.

"That's the way I like it!" he said. "Look, I'd better go. Toby is going to kill me if I get home late and the steak is like leather. There's only one person in the world I fear — and that's my lovely wife."

"Good night, Harry. Thanks for coming. Please give Toby my regards."

"I will. She's eager for an update on how you and the baby are doing. So now I'll have good news to tell her." He put on his overcoat, picked up his gloves and turned to leave. As he reached the doorway he turned back to Sarah. "Good night to my crack associate. We'll talk again soon." And with a wave of his hand, he was gone.

Sarah couldn't believe Mark Arkin's offer. What could she do with that much money? Her first thought was an apartment with plenty of room for Anna and all of her baby paraphernalia. That would be lovely. As the dollar signs danced in her head, she found herself dozing off. But suddenly the laxatives and stool softeners they'd fed her started to work with a vengeance. She awoke in alarm, and quickly pushed the call button. Mary, who was on duty again, was at her door in no time.

"What can I do for you, lady?"

"Oh, just as you predicted, those pills are working. You know, the ones that would loosen concrete. I've got to get to the bathroom." The urgency in her voice reflected the urgency in her gut.

"Well, if you have to go right now, I'll bring the bedpan, because my partner is at dinner and I can't get you on the toilet by myself."

"No, I want to use the toilet," Sarah insisted, "not the bedpan. I practiced today and I know I can do it."

"I saw that in your chart — but I can't get you onto the toilet alone. It's a two-person job and I'm by myself right now."

"Please, there's no time to argue about this. Please help me," Sarah begged.

"Tell you what. I'll bring you a commode and put it right next to your bed. I think you and I can manage that on our own." Mary was gone before Sarah could say another word. But the cramping was increasing by the moment. She was thankful the therapist had left her leg free from its tether after her afternoon session. She sat upright, pivoted her body and dangled her legs off the side of the bed.

"I'm back," Mary said, out of breath as she positioned the commode next to the bed. "What did you do, swing your legs off the bed by yourself? Don't you know you're supposed to wait for help to do things like that?" she chided her patient as she placed the walker in front of Sarah and helped her stand. Once upright, Sarah realized in horror that she that was powerless to stop what was about to happen. An explosion of feces ripped from her rear end and sprayed across the room.

"NO!" she cried out. "This can't be happening!" Dissolving into tears, she held onto the walker for dear life as the nurse tried to keep her from falling.

"Sarah. We're going to be all right," Mary said calmly. "What's most important now is to stand still. Can you do that for me? Can you hold onto the walker? If you can, I'm going to call the nurses' station for some help."

"Yes," Sarah sobbed, "I think I can hold on. Oh my God. What's wrong with me?"

"It's going to be all right, honey. Just hold on." The nurse kept one arm on Sarah as she stretched to reach the call button. "There, I got it. Someone will be here in a flash and we'll get you all cleaned up," Mary said soothingly.

"Oh my God. I can't believe this. My newborn soiled herself and everything around her this morning. I'm no better than that. I'm as helpless as an infant," she wailed.

The first one to arrive was the aide from next door who had heard the commotion. "Oh my, I see we have a little cleanup in here."

"Hold the commentary, Gina, and get some people in here to help."

"Sure. Sure thing, Mary."

When Gina returned with another nurse, they tried to decide where to begin.

"We've got to get Sarah into a chair. She can't stand like this for much longer," Mary said. As Sarah hung on to the walker, she remembered what Jeff had said about the danger of a fall.

"Right," Gina said. "How about the commode? It's right here and we can get her on it pretty easily."

"Good thinking. Okay, Sarah, on the count of three we're going to pivot you and the walker so you can sit down. Okay?" Mary asked.

"Yes, yes," Sarah said, relieved that there was a plan of action to get her off her one good leg. What was left of her guts felt like they would come cascading through the cut in her belly. The smell in the room nearly gagged her.

Just as Sarah was correctly positioned in front of the commode, the door opened. It was Rick. He took in the scene.

Sarah's mortification was complete. "GET OUT. GET OUT. GET OUT," she shrieked.

"Okay. Okay, Sarah. I'll leave. I'll come back later," he said.

"NO. NO. DON'T COME BACK. NEVER COME BACK," she screamed.

"Doctor, I think you'll do the patient more good by leaving. Please," Mary beseeched him.

"Sure. Okay," Rick said, slinking out of the room.

"Oh my God. I don't think I can take it," Sarah cried. "It's too much."

"Okay girls, one, two, three," Mary directed her comrades as they took position around the patient. "You can sit down now, honey."

It was just in time. Sarah was lowered onto the seat of the commode. Gina handed her the box of Kleenex and then the three women donned their gloves and started to work. They calmly and methodically stripped and cleaned Sarah, then covered her in a fresh hospital gown. Then Mary excused herself for a few minutes, coming back wearing clean green scrubs. There was a man from housekeeping beside her, dragging a rolling bucket and mop.

It took more than half an hour to clean Sarah and her room. Then came the work of disinfecting Sarah's leg wounds, which had been contaminated by feces as well. The ortho resident on call, Dr. Prabhu, repeatedly irrigated the openings in the skin of her injured leg. She also upped her antibiotics as a precaution. Just to be sure, she phoned Jeff Gotbaum, who always said he'd rather be disturbed at home than face a train wreck when he came onto the floor in the morning.

It was nearly eleven o'clock when the resident finally left.

Sarah repeatedly thanked her, the nurses, the man from housekeeping and the aide. She asked Mary to keep the window open a crack to help air out the room. Once she was alone, she turned off the lights, pulled her covers up high and started talking aloud to the god whose existence she had long doubted.

"Are you satisfied now?" she asked angrily. "Some loving god you are. I know I haven't been a perfect person by any measure, but what did I do to deserve this? And what did Mary and the others ever do to deserve having to clean up such filth? Well? I'm waiting. I guess I'll have to wait forever. An answer can't come from an invention of the human imagination."

Alone in the dark Sarah made up her mind: There is no god to implore for relief. We're on our own.

Just then there was a knock on the door. A man entered, silhouetted by the corridor lighting. Sarah knew immediately that it was Rick.

"Please leave. I asked you not to come back," she said icily.

Rick pulled up a chair and sat down in the dark. She turned her back to him.

"Sarah, the same thing happened to me."

That got her attention. She turned and saw the outline of his body in the chair.

"Remember you asked about my scars and I told you about the accident I was in as a kid? I was in the hospital for a long time, and part of my injuries made it impossible for me to control my bowels. I was way past the diaper stage and I was mortified. Of all the things that happened to me in that hospital, all the operations, all the pain, it was shitting myself that was the worst. In fact, I'd forgotten about it — buried it, I guess — until tonight. And when I was sitting in my office just now thinking about you, it came back to me again with all the shame, all the embarrassment. I'm so sorry you had to experience that, Sarah."

She listened quietly. Could this be the same Rick, so full of jokes and bravado? This was a part of him that she knew nothing about.

"Now that I'm a doctor, I know that it happens every day and everyone who works here knows it's just part of people being sick and getting better. As hard as it is to believe, no one here attaches any shame to it. We just deal with it.

"That's all I wanted to say, really. I'm just sorry that you had to go through that. I'll leave you to get some sleep." As he stood up, he kissed the top of her head.

The tears rolled down her cheeks. "I'm sorry I screamed at you. I am. It was very kind of you to tell me what you just did."

"Sarah, you're gonna get better, and you'll be able to bury what happened tonight if you want to — bury it under good times and ordinary days."

Sarah found it hard to imagine. "You think so?"

"I know so. I know you're going to get well. I was there — where you are — but worse off. And look at me today, a well-oiled machine of health and vigor. Want to see me drop to the floor and give you ten?" he asked, smiling in the dark.

"You're a nut, you know that?" she said through her tears.

 "A good nut, I hope."

"Yeah, a good nut."

 "But no kidding, Sarah, I healed up just fine and you will, too. You'll be doing push-ups before you know it."

 "It's hard to believe."

 "I know it is. But I'm not telling you this because I'm a doc. I'm telling you this because I lived it. I know I'm right."

 "Well, I hope so."

 "You can bet your last cent on it."

 "Thank you, Rick. I appreciate you coming. Good night."

 "Good night." He kissed Sarah's hand, made a deep bow and left her alone in the darkness.

Sleep eluded Sarah. She would drop off for a bit and then awaken. She felt as though she was skimming along the top of the reservoir of deep sleep, unable to plumb its depths. Terrible thoughts came into her mind, thoughts about how dying in the accident would have been preferable. But then she thought of Anna. Anna deserved to live.

Finally, sleep came to Sarah, but it brought her back to the terror of being buried under the rubble. She started screaming, "Help, help, I'm in here. I'm pregnant. Save me. Save me." The screams brought the night nurse bounding into her room. When she turned on the overhead light she saw Sarah thrashing violently and the IV pulled out of her arm.

"Hey, Sarah. It's okay, honey. Wake up, Sarah. You're in the hospital and you're having a bad dream. You're safe and I'm here with you," said the nurse. Finally, her patient opened her eyes.

"What's happening?" the panic-stricken Sarah panted.

"You were having a bad dream, honey. I'm your nurse tonight. My name is Gail. I worked with you on your first night here."

"Bad dream? It was awful. I was buried, but I was still alive."

"Lots of people have bad dreams after a trauma. I bet if you go back to sleep, though, you'll be just fine," the nurse soothed.

"I can't take a chance of it happening again."

"Tell you what. I'll get you some warm milk and a fresh gown. This one looks like it's a little worse for wear."

That's when Sarah realized it was soaked through with her sweat. "All right. Whatever you think."

"That's what I think. I'll be right back with Nurse Gail's cure."

When she returned, she helped Sarah get out of her cold, wet gown. She tied the fresh one in the back and then handed her patient the cup of warm milk. She restarted her IV, announcing, "There. Now you're as good as new."

Sarah couldn't remember the last time she'd had warm milk. She took sips out of a sense of gratitude to the nurse. After Gail left,

Sarah put the cup aside and turned on the television. There was no way she was going to risk falling asleep again.

TWENTY-EIGHT

When Jeff came in to check on Sarah the next morning, he brought along only the chief resident, Michael Lyi. Rick had relayed how unglued Sarah had become after losing control of her bowels. Jeff figured she could do without the embarrassment of discussing the ramifications of the experience in front of a gaggle of doctors in training.

"Good morning, Sarah," he said as he walked into her room exuding an air of good cheer. "It's just me and Dr. Lyi this morning. How are you feeling?"

"Okay."

"Just okay? How's the pain today?"

"The usual," she said without expression.

He looked on her chart for her vitals and latest labs. Everything was unchanged from the previous afternoon, but Sarah was changed. Her affect was flat; her face revealed no emotion.

"How did you sleep?"

"Not well."

"If you'd like, I can order something to help you sleep tonight," Jeff offered.

"Okay."

It was like pulling teeth to get anything out of her, and he had yet to bring up the topic she likely had no interest in revisiting. "Sarah, I understand that the laxatives and stool softeners had rather a more powerful effect than we had expected. I'm very sorry about that."

"Me, too. I'm sorry for those poor people who had to clean me up and clean up the room."

"I don't want you to worry about that, Sarah. It happens. Actually, it happens a lot," Jeff said. He looked at Dr. Lyi for confirmation.

"Yes, it's common in the hospital. Not pleasant for the patient, but just part of everyday life here," the chief resident said.

"Well, maybe you all should consider getting another life."

Undeterred, Dr. Lyi continued. "No chance of that. We like it here. We take the bad along with the good, because we get to help people regain their health and send them on their way."

"I guess that's what makes the world go round," Sarah replied, making it clear she was finding the conversation tiresome.

Jeff wondered if he should consider a psych consult. But first he had to get to the business at hand. "Sarah, remember how I said we would close up your wounds and get you off the IV today?"

She nodded.

"Because of the contamination last night, I'm going to have to wait on both of those things. If all looks good in a day or two, we'll stitch you up and move you to oral meds," Jeff explained, hoping to get some response from Sarah. He would have actually welcomed some spirited disagreement.

"Whatever you say."

"And Sarah, we can't have another contamination of the wound sites. I understand it was impossible for you to prevent what happened last night, but I'm going to ask you to think of the bedpan as your best friend until we can get your system regulated."

Sarah sighed. "Yet another endorsement for the bedpan,"

"Let me be clear. Infection is the biggest threat to your recovery, hands down. Anything that can help prevent wound contamination is a good thing. In this case, when you sense that urgency, the safest thing is a bedpan."

"Whatever you say."

"And Sarah, we're going to continue serial irrigation and debridement today and see what tomorrow brings."

"Fine."

"Dr. Lyi, do you have anything to add?" Jeff asked, signaling the need for some backup. The chief resident took the hint.

"Actually, I do. Dr. Gotbaum has outlined a conservative course of treatment that will give you the best shot of healing well. I know this has got to be very hard for you. But if you hold on, the combination of our treatment and your own body's power to heal itself will do its magic."

"Thank you for the pep talk."

"Any time. You have a lot to look forward to, Ms. Abadhi. You just have to give yourself some time."

"Time seems to be the only thing I have right now," she said wearily.

That did it for Jeff. He ordered a psych consult for later that day.

Jeff wasn't the only one worried by the change in Sarah. To her parents, it seemed that her spirit had drained away. Eva noticed immediately that Sarah wasn't wearing her pretty new nightshirt and that it was nowhere to be found in the room. She had no appetite for the omelet Eva brought and the latte was left to grow cold on her tray. Her eyes lit up a bit when she saw Anna, but even the baby couldn't lift her mood. Both Joseph and Eva were at a loss to understand what had happened to their daughter.

With Dr. Gotbaum nowhere to be found, Joseph sought out Sarah's nurse. She assured him there was no change in Sarah's physical status, but she relayed the note on her chart about a nightmare around one in the morning. And then there was the incident of the fecal incontinence the prior evening.

Satisfied that he had some explanation for the change in Sarah, he headed back to her room. He found Eva and the baby in the corridor, evicted by the physical therapist and her aide. While he shared with Eva what he'd learned from the nurse, he watched the therapy session through the crack in the door. To his relief, Sarah was able to get off the bed and do whatever was asked of her, albeit with great effort. Perhaps her change in mood could be chalked up to the rough night she'd had.

It wasn't the best time to leave for work, but Eva assured him the Abadhi women could manage alone for the rest of the day. When at last the door opened, Eva heard Sarah say she was worn out and wanted to get back in bed. Once there, Eva had to encourage her to hold the baby.

Eva knew what was eating her daughter. Even as a preschooler, Sarah had become inconsolable the couple of times she'd wet herself. Just as Eva was about to gingerly broach the subject of the previous night's mishap, there was a surprise visitor at the door.

"Hello, hello. It's your Bubbe Rivka. Hello, hello."

Eva couldn't believe her eyes. There sat her mother in a wheelchair being pushed by a gray-haired hospital volunteer. A small overnight bag sat on her lap.

"Momma, what are you doing here? How in the world did you get here?"

"Some hello dat is! Vat do you tink? I hired someone to drive me since you and Joseph ver too buzy to pick me up and brink me to see my darlink granddaughter and her new baby," Rivka said, her voice dripping with reproach.

"You hired someone to drive you all the way from Coney Island?"

"Vat? You want I shoult push and shove in da trains? Dose days are over for dis bubbe. I got no desire to be a sardine in a tin can," Rivka said, dismissing the mere hint that she might have used the subway to get to the hospital.

Eva cut to the chase. "Who drove you?"

"Who else? Lillian Goldberk's goot-for-notink son. He's back living vit his momma again. The whole vay here I hat to listen to his *schpiel* about how hart it is to get vork in dis economy. But I'd like to know vat he vas doink ven de economy vas boomink. Of course, I kept my mout shut, but it's no secret — a ball of fire he's not."

As entertaining as she found her passenger, the volunteer hinted that it was time she returned the wheelchair to the lobby. Rivka responded, "Of course, darlink. You've been very kint. Tank you for de ride." She stood up, straight as an arrow, and patted the volunteer's hand. Then she put down her bag and proceeded to fulfill her mission of seeing her first great-grandchild in the arms of her granddaughter.

She took a long, hard look at the baby, drinking in every detail of her tiny face and hands. "*Kayn aynhoreh*, she's a beauty, Sarah. *A be kezunt*. Such a *shana maidela*. She remints me of you. Vat a *kleine mamela* you vere ven you vere a baby. *Mazel tov, mein kint*," Rivka said, putting her small wrinkled hand on Sarah's cheek.

Then Rivka took a good look at her granddaughter and realized that something was terribly wrong. When she'd asked Eva or Joseph on the phone how Sarah was, they had repeatedly said she was all right. But she could see for herself that they'd lied. Not only was Sarah's face cut and bruised and her leg encased in a strange contraption, there was a resignation in her eyes that Rivka had seen all too often during the war.

"And how are you, my darlink Sarah? *Vai iz mer*. Such an accident. Who ever hert of such a tink? A bik machine like dat should fall down and hurt so many people. Tsk, tsk, tsk."

"It was a terrible accident, Bubbe, but I'm hanging in there."

"Terrible doesn't bekin to describe it. De pictures alone are terrible. I can't imagine vat it vas like for you. Tsk, tsk, tsk. Vat a *meshugge* tink to happen. It's a crazy verlt, no?"

"Sure is," Sarah said.

" I voult kiv anytink if it voult be me in dat bet insteat ov you. I hat my turn to live," she said, dabbing her eyes with her handkerchief.

"Oh no, Bubbe. Long ago you filled your quota of hard times. Don't worry about me. I'm going to be all right. All the doctors tell me so," Sarah said.

"But I voult do it. I'm a *shtarker* and I can take it bedda dan a sveet young *maidel* like you," Rivka said, correctly sizing up the situation. "Vy should you and de *kleine kint* have to go tru such a terrible tink?"

"I don't think there's any answer to that question, Bubbe. But I appreciate the sentiment, and I'm glad you hired Mrs. Greenberg's son to drive you here. That was very clever of you," Sarah said.

"Goldberk, darlink, Lillian Goldberk's son. Vell, I'm glad someboty tinks it vas a goot idea," she said, glaring at Eva. "If I vatet for your fudder, I'd still be siddink in my livink room chair." Rivka chuckled to herself. "And now I'm here vit you and the *kleine kint*. I tink it verkt out very vell."

With Sarah the most animated she'd been all morning, Eva was beginning to think her mother was right.

At lunchtime, Rivka pushed the jogging stroller with the baby as she followed Eva to the cafeteria. Sarah was left with her hospital-issue lunch, which held no appeal. She covered up all the dishes and pushed away the tray. She was reclining in her bed when a gray-haired man in a turtleneck and khakis invited himself in.

"I'm looking for Sarah Abadhi," the man said inquiringly.

"Yes."

"Dr. Gotbaum asked me to check on you today. I'm Dr. Shulman."

Sarah managed a perfunctory "Hello." She had no interest in another doctor examining her.

"Dr. Gotbaum filled me in on the salient events that have occurred over the last several days. It seems as though you've had quite a lot to deal with," the doctor said sympathetically.

"No more than many of the patients in this hospital."

"True, but of course your story is special to you. Stressful physical events can take a toll on a person's spirit. Call it collateral damage, if you will."

Sarah's interest was piqued. "What department did you say you were from?"

"Actually, I didn't say. I'm a psychiatrist, Sarah. Dr. Gotbaum noted a marked change in your mood today. He's concerned that in focusing on healing your leg, he's been remiss in dealing with the emotional trauma you've experienced. As he told me, and rightly so, his quest to return you to full function will only be successful if we treat all of you, not only your leg."

"The neonatologist already made an offer of counseling — which I declined," Sarah said. "If you're here to offer me counseling, we can make short order of that. No thank you."

"May I ask why?"

"Because I'm perfectly sane. The events of the last week would result in any mentally intact person feeling down in the dumps or blue — call it what you will. I personally think it's a normal response to what's happened," she said defensively.

"No doubt you're correct. However, you have a lengthy physical recovery ahead of you and it would be helpful if your mood worked in service of that recovery."

"What do you mean?"

"You'll need to participate fully in your therapies and treatments. You'll have to push yourself to do what you used to do without giving it a second thought. A person who is feeling low often doesn't have the stamina to do what needs to be done to get well," the psychiatrist explained.

"Well, you needn't worry on that point, Doctor. Stamina's my middle name. I'll do whatever it takes to regain the use of my leg. Just because I'm not happy about it doesn't mean I won't do what needs to be done."

"Fair enough. But I understand that you had a nightmare last night — a flashback of your accident. You've got to be able to sleep in order to heal."

"You have a fix for nightmares? Because if you do, I'd find

that interesting."

"Not a fix exactly," the psychiatrist said, "but we have developed some successful approaches to dealing with the stress that follows a trauma."

"I'm listening," Sarah said impatiently.

"The conflicts in Iraq and Afghanistan have put post-traumatic stress disorder on the front burner of psychiatric research. Many of the returning soldiers experience nightmares, mood changes, anger management problems. As a result, we've made some strides in finding effective treatment for the disorder," Dr. Shulman said.

"So what are you saying? I have PTSD?"

"I wouldn't presume to diagnose you without a thorough exam. But what I am saying is, if you find that you can't enjoy your new baby or good food and company, and that you have trouble sleeping or experience nightmares, we can help you get a handle on those symptoms."

The idea of the psychiatrist's "thorough exam" repelled her. "I appreciate you stopping by, but for now, I think I'm all set."

"Okay then. Just know I'm available if you change your mind. Here's how you can reach me." The doctor handed Sarah his card and left to see patients more interested in taking advantage of what he had to offer.

After getting a heads up from Eva, Joseph arrived at the hospital just before six with enough Middle Eastern takeout for the entire family. He found his mother-in-law dozing in the chair, his daughter in bed feeding the baby some formula and his wife fit to be tied. Joseph identified the problem straight away: Rivka's presence added just enough to Eva's load to throw her off balance. He went to work restoring equilibrium, serving up the food, cleaning up afterwards and making arrangements for Mrs. Goldberg's son to pick Rivka up at the hospital at noon the following day.

Sarah was ashamed that, once again, she was relieved when

Anna was wheeled away for the night. It was additional proof that she was a miserable failure as a mother. In fact, the time when she was good at anything seemed remote. She could no more imagine being the person she used to be, or at least the person she had fancied herself to be — strong, capable, independent — than she could imagine getting up and walking out of the hospital.

Her low expectations for personal happiness aside, she now saw how much she'd expected from her life. It had meant nothing to her to get up and out of bed, throw on her running clothes and do six miles along the river. In terms of her pregnancy, she had expected it to go off without a hitch. It was clear she'd made a mistake in expecting so much, a mistake that left her reeling.

In the midst of her self-rebuke, there was a knock on her door. In walked a smiling Rick, happy he was about to spend time with Sarah. When he pulled a chair up next to her bed, the contrast in their moods couldn't have been more sharp.

"Hey, comrade. How goes it today?" he asked.

"It was a day; nothing awful like last night, and nothing to write home about, either."

"Sarah, when you're recovering from a trauma like yours, that's what we docs call a 'red letter day,'" he said, radiating optimism. "Being medically boring is a thing to love: no infections, no fevers, no other 'excitements.' Maybe you have to know what can go wrong before you appreciate an uneventful day in the hospital."

"I'll take your word for it. I don't want any more things going wrong, but I'm ready if they do. So in a sense, today was a good day. I remembered something I'd forgotten — that expectation is everything. If I don't expect anything good to happen, I won't be disappointed when everything goes to hell."

"You really believe that?" he asked incredulously. "You? Of all people?"

"Why do you say it that way? 'You, of all people'?"

"Because you push yourself to the highest standards in

everything you do. In your work, in your sport, in how you carry yourself — you strive to be the best. And you're damn close to achieving it, as far as I can tell."

"Maybe that was true before everything happened. But that was my error. I limited my low expectations to my personal life — more precisely, to the men in my life."

"Ouch. That's a low blow. So the only reason you liked me was because you expected so little of me?" The idea made his palms sweat.

"As I recall, you exceeded my expectations in almost every way. We had a good time," Sarah recalled in an analytical way, "until the end."

Encouraged by that rather positive, if dry, assessment, Rick pursued the point. "Damn straight. We had a great time."

"We had a great time for as long as it lasted. But when it ended, I had no hard feelings toward you. I knew there was no point in expecting any more than you gave me. Today I realized that I have to carry that attitude over to every part of my life. I used to expect to walk outside without having the sky fall on me. But I was wrong. Anything can happen anytime. Now that I get that, I think I'm going to be okay," Sarah said with some satisfaction.

"I couldn't disagree with you more, Sarah."

"Suit yourself. I think I'm being realistic."

"As a doctor who's had patients with the same diagnosis either live or die because of the fight they had in them, I think your take on things will not serve you well. You have to allow room for hope and the possibility of improvement. Don't ever think you have no right to expect good things out of life. Don't do that, Sarah. Please."

"Did you know that Jeff sent a psychiatrist to see me today?"

"No, no I didn't," Rick confessed, worried that perhaps Jeff had caught something even more alarming than what he was hearing.

"Yes, Jeff ordered a visit from a Dr. Shulman. I guess he's decided I'm a nut job. Maybe you believe that, too. But I know that I don't have to be cheery and upbeat in order to fight to get my life back. I'm going to fight with every ounce of strength I have. It's just that if it doesn't work, I'll be ready," she said resolutely. "Personally, I think that's a healthier way to look at things than to expect a happy ending."

"Sarah, no one is saying you have to be a cock-eyed optimist. But you have to expect things will get better. I give you no argument that what happened to you was horrific. Hell, it was a freaking disaster. But it's over now. Past tense. Now you have the best medical care available. Do you realize how lucky you were to have Jeff assigned to your case? Not every doctor would have worked on you for six hours, expertly putting together the jigsaw puzzle that was your leg. Some would have amputated and gone home early. But you caught a break. On the absolutely worst day of your life, you caught a break. The ambulance brought you to this hospital and you got this surgeon, and because of that, you have a chance to get your life back. But not if you hang on to that harebrained idea of low expectations."

His criticism stung. "We can agree to disagree. To my way of thinking, it's the only sensible way to face the day."

"Okay. But I am going to prove to you that you're wrong. You said you have low expectations of men. When you told me you were pregnant, I certainly gave you more evidence than you already had that we men are a low form of life. I know I ran with my tail between my legs. But that was then. I'm here now and I'm telling you I am not the *schmuck* who left you all those months ago. People can change. I'm living proof."

"I'm having trouble understanding what made you change."

"It was you. You made me change. I tried living without you and the truth is I didn't do very well. When Jeff told me you were hurt, I went nuts. Then I saw you and Anna — that first night after everything happened — and something shifted inside of me. I'm done running. I'm serious, Sarah. If you'll have me, I'll never leave you again."

"But the Sarah you knew…she's gone. Just look at me."

"Sarah, you are still you, busted-up leg and all. I see you even if you can't see yourself right now. And I love what I see."

"That's very nice of you to say. I wish I could believe it's true."

"It is true, Sarah."

"Are you sure you're not saying all this to get to Anna?"

"What do you mean?"

"Well, you've seen her. You said yourself it caused something to shift in you. You have the right to be her father, no matter our relationship."

"I know I do, but she's *ours* — yours and mine. I love that, Sarah. I love that she came from the two of us."

"But you were dead set against having children. That's why we broke up. I didn't imagine that, did I?"

"No, you didn't, I'm sorry to say."

"And now?"

"Now I think I'm getting a handle on what scared me shitless about having a kid."

"What was it? I'd really like to know."

"Have a few minutes?"

"Are you kidding? Time is something I have a lot of," she said.

"Okay then. Here goes." He took a deep breath and began.

"Until now, when it came to women, I was a runner. I went out with a lot of great girls before I met you. And everything was simpatico until they started looking at me as a possible father to their children. The first time it happened it gave me the creeps and I tried to ignore it. But I soon realized that there was no profit in that for anyone. The girl had gone down a path I had no interest in following, and there was no turning back for her. So, after it happened a couple more times, I realized that the only thing to do once a woman had made that turn was to leave, as fast and as cleanly as possible.

"When I met you I thought I'd died and gone to heaven. You

not only accepted my terms of no entanglement, you were a step ahead of me. We had a great time, didn't we?"

"I guess we did."

"I know we did. That last night we had together — before you told me you were pregnant — I couldn't believe my good luck. I was with someone so great who had no designs on me as a potential husband and father. Just as I was thanking my lucky stars, you let loose my worst nightmare: Like it or not, I'd fathered a kid.

"Terror is a powerful force, Sarah. It was more powerful at that moment than wanting you. Remember, I was a runner. So, that night, that's just what I did. I ran.

"All these months I've asked myself why. I'm no shrink, but I think it comes down to this: I had a world-class bastard of a father. He was married to my mother for ten years. My mom is great, by the way. I hope you can meet her sometime soon. You'd like her.

"But my father is another story. I remember thinking as a kid that he knew everything. He was a big shot in his field. But the truth was he was a jerk. You know the car accident I've spoken of?"

She nodded.

"Well, it was my father who was driving — like a maniac. It wasn't until I was in college that I found out his blood alcohol level was .23. He walked away from the accident with a scratch — literally — on his finger. I ended up in the intensive care unit for weeks and in the hospital for months. Oh, and here's the topper. While I was still in the PICU, he packed his bags and left my mother and me for one of his graduate students."

"That's awful, Rick. I had no idea."

"Well, I never talk about it. After the accident, he vanished from my life. Poof. Gone," he said, gesticulating. "My mother made sure he paid child support and his share of the college and med school bills. I'm sure he never missed the money — he's hauled in the big bucks for years. So from the time I was five, I had no father.

"After the divorce, we moved to Michigan, back where my

mother's family lived. My mom changed her name back to Smith, her maiden name. I got the idea to change my name, too. I was carrying around his name: Eric Stavropoulous, Jr. My mom's father was a great guy — a machinist in the local auto plant and a big sports nut. He spent all his free time with me. If I was going to be named after anyone, I wanted it to be him. And his name was Rich Smith.

"I guess my mom checked back with the therapist who had worked with me all those months I was in the hospital. When he gave the okay, my mom agreed. My father didn't give a shit. So we went to court and I became Richard Smith. I still remember that day. It was like with the stroke of his gavel, that judge scrubbed me clean."

"I had no way of knowing, Rick. We never talked about things like this when we were together."

"I tried to put all that crap behind me. But what I didn't realize was that all that crap wasn't done with me."

"What do you mean?"

"Well, the thing I feared all my life was being anything like the man who had fathered me — a man who married and divorced several more women after he was done with my mother. I mean I look just like the bastard — at least from my memory of him. I think I ran away from any woman who wanted to get too close because I didn't want to find out how much my father's son I was.

"The terrible irony, of course, is I did exactly what he did. He left my mother and me high and dry, and goddammit if I didn't do the very same thing to you and Anna. Believe me when I tell you that will haunt me for the rest of my life.

"But I refuse to let biology be my destiny. I *will* be a better man than the guy who fathered me. I want to be a better man for you, Sarah. Please let me. I swear to you, if you let me into your life, and into Anna's life, I will love you both, and care for you both. No more running, no matter what." He took her hand and brought it to his face. With eyes closed he kissed each of her fingertips and her palm, then laid her open hand on his cheek. She offered no resistance.

TWENTY-NINE

Much to Sarah's relief, she fell asleep after Rick left and couldn't remember a single dream. Abdominal cramping awoke her at six. Sarah called the nurse who quickly provided her with her new best friend, the bedpan. As difficult as it was to use the steel receptacle, she knew it was preferable to the debacle of the other night. Her belief in low expectations proved useful, allowing her to do what had to be done without self-recrimination. The nurse who assisted her was calm and efficient. The whole thing was over in a few minutes. Rick and that Dr. Lyi had been right. It was just a fact of life in the hospital.

News of her achievement, as well as her quiet night, was left on her chart, pleasing Jeff. Given her good lab results and physical exam, he decided that today was the day to close up her wounds and move her to oral antibiotics. He and his minions left Sarah's room gratified with their patient's progress.

After the doctors left, the therapists had their way with her. They got her off the bed and to the toilet. There she had another success, which buoyed her spirits. When Eva, Joseph and Rivka arrived at nine, they immediately sensed that Sarah was doing better than the day before. She asked for Anna to be put into her arms, just as Joseph bid everyone a good day. He was a man on a mission: a ten o'clock meeting with a major pharmaceutical company interested in his lab's regenerative medicine research.

Eva asked Sarah if she was hungry and was pleased with her response: "I could eat something." She'd brought her daughter's favorite, a fresh, toasted garlic bagel with butter, and a thermos of some home-brewed coffee. Eva had no idea that it wasn't the return of her appetite — but the knowledge that she needed fuel to recover — that prompted Sarah to chew and swallow.

As she worked on her breakfast, Bubbe Rivka sat beside Sarah, getting vicarious pleasure. "*Essen, essen, mein kint.* You neet to eat and drink and take goot care of yourself."

"I'm trying, Bubbe."

"I know. I know how hart it is for you — all dis *mishegoss* dat's happent to you. You must feel like da whole verlt iz upside down."

"Actually, I do."

"During de var I felt dat vay day in and day out. It vas a horrible feeling. I vas so *farblondjhet*. Notink made sense. Everytink I knew — it vas all gone. So many people lost, dey shoult rest in peace. So many tinks lost. De verlt vent crazy. I almost vent crazy, too. I never talk about it because vat's de use?" Rivka stopped for a moment, eyeing her granddaughter. "Now, maybe der is a use. I vant you shoult know a little of vat your zadda and bubbe vent tru. Maybe it vill help you a little bit now dat you have *tsoures* of your own."

"*Tsoures*?"

"Troubles, *mein kint*."

"Oh. That's a good word to know. I guess I do have *tsoures*."

"*Gevalt.*"

"If it wouldn't be too much for you, Bubbe, I would be interested in hearing how you and Zadda Sam made it through the war," Sarah said, looking at her mother to make sure she thought it would be all right. Eva nodded her assent.

"If it vill help you, den I vill try."

"Thank you, Bubbe."

"Vell, Sam and I ver from Vilna. Ve grew up vit a normal life, a house, parents, foot to eat. Ve certainly veren't velty, but ve hat enough. Ven de Nazis came dey kilt many, many innocent people who vere mindink der own business, doink notink wrong. Dey lined dem up and shot dem deat. Vomen, *kinder*, olt people. Shot dem like dogs in de street. Den, dey roundet up all de rest of us and put us in a ghetto — vit guards and fences and bright lights. It vas like beink in a prison. But it vas in dat prison dat your zadda and I fell in love. Strange place to fall in love, eh?"

"Very strange, Bubbe."

"Vell, Got has his vays I guess," Rivka said, smiling to herself and nodding a bit. "Sam knew some men who hat run avay from de ghetto to join de resistance. He talkt me into runnink avay, too. My parents ver hundret percent akainst it. 'No, you mustn't go,' dey sait. 'Ve'll behave ourselves and dey'll leave us be.' How wronk dey vere."

Rivka stared into space for a minute before she cleared her throat and went on. "So, vun night, Sam and I and some udders escapet tru a tunnel dat de men hat secretly duk. Ve ran like *meshuggenas* into de voots. Ve ran to de Rudnicki forest. I hat never been in de Rudnicki forest or any udder forest for dat matter. I vas a city girl, who likt nice dresses and de cinema. I knew notink about de voods and livink out in de open. Needa did Sam. He vas a scholar, not a voodsman. Luckily, vun of de guys knew de voods like de back of his hant," she said, patting the back of her own hand. "Tank Got for his *seichel.* Ve valked and ran until I tought my feet voult fall off. It raint. Ve got soakt. Ve ran out of foot and vater. But finally, like a miracle, ve came to a little village in de middle of de voots. Jews hidink from de Nazis hat built dat village. And as little as dey hat, can you believe it, dey *velcomet* us. I criet ven dey callt us *landsmen* and tolt us ve coult stay vit dem.

"But it vas terribly hart dere. Ve livt in de bitter colt in bunkers mate from de branches of de trees. Ve drank vater from de svamp. Ve ate anytink, anytink — rotten potatoes, bits of meat left on bones, pits, anytink we could fint or steal from de fielts, Got should forkive us. Durink dat first vinter I vantet to kive up. 'Vat's de point?' I askt your zadda. 'Vy struggle so? Just let me die. Vun less mout to feet.' But your zadda sait, 'No, Rivka. Ve vill survive. Ve vill get out of here someday.' And den he voult tell me stories of how it vas goink to be. How de fightink voult stop and how ve voult come out of de voots, how ve voult have a life again, vit a house, vit a hot stove and plenty of foot to eat. He tolt me ve voult have a veddink and den *kleine kinder* — a little *boychik* and a little *maidela*. It vas like he vas tellink me a fairy tale."

Rivka stopped to blow her nose and dry her eyes. She looked at Eva, and saw she, too, was crying quietly. "But your zadda vas right," she said, nodding her head slowly. "Ve got out of dose voots, but not for a lonk time. It took years, Sarah. Ant durink dose years ve verkt for de resistance. Your zadda vas a very brave man. I don't know if you know dat. He helpt de resistance cut phone lines and bomb de Nazis' trains. Ve vemen sewt and fixt de clothes for de fighters.

"All dat time, ve vere petrifiet for our lives. Ve lernt dat our families in de ghetto had been kilt. My momma, my papa, my liddle sister. All gone. Sam's too. All gone." Again Rivka grew quiet for a moment. "But in de voots, ve hat at least a chance to live and to fight de bastards who kilt dem.

"Finally, vat Sam sait really happent. De bat dream vas over ant ve coult get out of dose voots. But ven ve got back to Vilna, dere ve fount anodder nightmare. Everytink ve knew vas gone. De verlt ve knew erast. Completely erast." Rivka stopped and shook her head from side to side as she dabbed her eyes with a tissue.

"Again, I almost vent crazy. But again, your zadda talkt to me. He tolt me, 'It vill be all right, Rivka. Ve vill make a new life. A bedder life. Ve von't forget dem — our parents, our sisters. But ve have survivet. And now ve vill start again to live. Ve vill make a goot life. You vill see.'"

By now all three women had tears rolling down their cheeks. Even little Anna started to whimper a bit before Eva comforted her with some milk. There was a long silence before Rivka could go on.

"So ve hat to struggle to get to a displacet persons camp. Ve vere starvink and filty. Ve hadn't hat a real bat in years. Ven I tink of it now, I don't know how your zadda coult have lovt me like dat — filty and skinny and half-*meshugga*. But, somehow he dit. And I lovet him

— filty and skinny, vit crazy hair ant a long beart. Ve got marriet in dat displacet persons camp.

"Your zadda never gave up on me. Ant I figurt if he vouldn't give up on me, how coult I give up on me? So I put one foot in front of de udder and kept movink ant doink until, after a vile, I began to feel like *efsha* maybe, der vas a drop of trut to vat your zadda sait. Ven your momma vas born, it vas like sometink inside me turnt on, like a svitch turninkg on a light. I knew vat it vas to feel joy again.

"Ve got to dis country and look at the life ve hat here. Your momma and Uncle Max, so educatet, so successful. A beautiful apartment vit not vun — but two — toilets. All de hot bats ve ever vantet to take. All de foot anyone coult ever vant to eat. Ant a *shana* granddaughter, a fancy schmancy lawyer livink on de Upper East Side, namet after my momma. Who voult have ever tought two skinny refugees from de voots coult have a life such as dis? But your zadda believt it vas possible. In de middle of de vorst misery, he believt in sometink bedder.

"So Sarah, I am telling you dis now, not to make you sat. I see you are crying, ant your momma is crying. I don't vant you shoult be sat. I vant you shoult celebrate. Celebrate because ve survivet. Ant you, *mein kint*, you vill survive, too. Just as you survivet from de terrible accident, a *brokh*, you vill survive all dat you have to deal vit.

"Sveetheart, I'm an olt voman now. Ven I'm not here anymore, I vant you should remember vat I tolt you today. Remember dat as lonk as you are alive, der is alvays a vay out, alvays a chance to make tinks better. Never, ever, ever give up. Promise your bubbe."

Sarah could hardly speak. After hearing of her grandparents' travails, she was ashamed of the pity party she'd been having since the accident. "I promise. And I won't forget, Bubbe. I'm honored you shared what you and Zadda Sam went through during and after the war."

"It's all right. Stop crying now, sveetheart. But always remember who your people are. Ve are survivors. Ant you, my darlink girl, you are a survivor, too. Just as Zadda Sam promist me, I am promisink you — you vill make a good life again."

When Mrs. Goldberg's son arrived at noon to pick her up, Rivka was ready to leave, her mission accomplished.

THIRTY

Sarah took to heart what her Bubbe Rivka had said about coming from a family of survivors. A survivor faced what lay ahead — not with resignation, but with grit and determination. She thought about what Rick had said about the need to fight to recover. Fighting was more than submitting to every treatment and procedure. From now on, she would fight to get her life back.

As a first step she decided to tell her parents about Anna's father. That night, when Joseph arrived — elated with the results of his day-long meeting — his happiness reached new heights when he saw his daughter's dimpled smile for the first time since the accident. When he asked how her day had gone, she responded, "It was a good day today, Dad."

Joseph looked at Eva for guidance. She looked back at him, exhausted but beaming and said, "It's true. Today has been something of a turning point for Sarah. Wouldn't you agree, hon?"

"I would. I had a memorable visit with Bubbe, my wounds were stitched up and it looks like I'll be moving to the hospital's rehab wing in the next day or so."

Joseph was jubilant. "That's marvelous, Sarah. I have good news, too. Bob and I met with Adventa Pharmaceuticals. They were impressed with our work and offered us a deal that will allow us to expand our stem-cell project tenfold."

Eva put Anna down in her stroller and embraced her husband. "Oh, Joe, it's what you've been working so hard for. I'm so proud of you." She kissed both his cheeks before they shared a kiss.

Sarah looked at her parents, so in sync. Then she remembered

Rick's visit the previous night. She wondered if she and Rick could ever be so attuned to one another.

"Well, break it up. There's a small child in the room," she good-naturedly scolded her parents.

"Hey, we're entitled. It's about time we had a good day," Joseph countered.

"I have some more news for you. Maybe you both should take a seat."

Joseph and Eva gave each other a quizzical look before sitting down next to one another.

"Okay," Joseph said. "We're ready. And I, for one, am dying to know your news."

Sarah dove into the deep end of the pool. "Anna's father has come back into my life."

Joseph was quick with a rejoinder. "The same man who was dead set against children? Well, I'm glad you suggested we take a seat, Sarah."

Eva was dumbfounded. "How, how? How did you two get in touch with one another?"

"Actually, he got in touch with me. He and Dr. Gotbaum are friends. He's been visiting me after work," Sarah explained.

Eva flashed back on their talk with Dr. Gotbaum after the surgery, when he mentioned Sarah was a "friend of a friend."

"Where does he work, Sarah?" Joseph asked

"He works here. He's a doctor, Dad, a pediatric intensivist. In fact, he saw Anna in the NICU right after she was born."

"Not Dr. Feinberg?" Eva asked, aghast.

Sarah held onto her abdominal incision and laughed. "No, not Dr. Feinberg. He could be *my* father. Anna's father is Rick Smith, Dr. Rick Smith."

"Well, I guess that's good news, isn't it, Joe?" Eva asked. Her husband simply raised his eyebrows and nodded. Then, turning to her daughter, Eva asked delicately, "Do *you* feel it's good news, honey?"

"I didn't know at first, but last night we had a long talk. He apologized for leaving and explained why he did. He says he wants to be with me and Anna. And I believe him," Sarah said, surprising herself.

"Well, I think we ought to meet Anna's father, don't you, Sarah?" Joseph asked.

"He's said he wants me to meet his mother. I'll discuss getting you all together. Actually, I'll suggest it."

"That's fair," Joseph said. "I'm pleasantly surprised that he's decided to do the right thing. Anna will thank you both someday. She deserves to know her father."

It gave Sarah pause to think about Rick's childhood, devoid of a father — that Anna could have shared that fate. "Of course you're right, Dad. A child needs its father. Rick knows that, better than most people. He has no father in his life and he seems determined to be a father to Anna."

Joseph picked up the baby from the stroller. "You see, little one, you are not a fatherless child after all. And your father is a doctor, no less. Not bad, sweetheart, not bad."

"Joe, what are you saying?" Eva asked, looking dubiously at her husband.

"All I'm saying is, at the very least, we know the man will be able to send her to a nice college when the time comes."

"You're too much, Joe. She's not out of newborn-size clothes yet and you're worried about college?"

"Eva, it's never too soon to start saving."

More good news was shared during dinner. Apparently, Sarah's college friends had found out about the accident from the article in the *Times*. When Joseph stopped by the house after work to take in the mail, he found more than a dozen messages on the answering machine. He called Devorah back and asked her to be the clearinghouse of information for their friends. Devorah not only agreed, but said she would be in New York as soon as she could book a flight.

News of Devorah's imminent arrival further buoyed Sarah's spirits. She couldn't wait to share Anna with her dearest friend.

That night, after her parents took Anna home, Sarah found herself looking forward to Rick's visit. She put some lotion on her dry, chapped hands and scrunched up her curls.

He arrived after visiting hours to find her out of bed. He pulled a chair close to hers. "Hey," he said gently, remembering how delicate she had been the night before. "I hope you had another blah day. No complications, no infections, no new excitements."

"It was anything but a blah day, I'm pleased to say," she said, smiling.

He did a double take. "Really? What kind of day was it then?"

"It was my best day since the accident. I had an exceptional visit with my grandmother, Bubbe Rivka. I wish you could meet her. She's so brave. She's a survivor of the Holocaust. Did I ever tell you about her?"

"No. No, I'm afraid we didn't share much personal information when we were together. Probably too busy having sex."

As soon as the words were out of his mouth, he wished he could call them back. Sarah blushed, as did he.

"Sorry. I shouldn't have said that," he said.

"No, no," Sarah protested. "You're right. I think all we did was have sex. Good sex, too, if I remember correctly, though it's hard for me to imagine, given the state I'm in."

Rick was encouraged. "Your recollection is correct. Very good sex. As for your state, that will pass and you'll be good to go again in no time."

"Good to go again?" Sarah asked, feigning shock. "What am I, a car under repair?"

"Exactly," Rick said. "And you'll be good for the autobahn

before you know it."

"What a relief. That makes me feel so much better," Sarah said, keeping up with the double entendre.

"Me, too."

"Well, I guess we'll have to see how things go from now until then," Sarah said, adding a note of caution.

"I just want you to know I am in no rush. No rush at all. I had, at one time, considered the priesthood, so celibacy is nothing for me."

"I didn't know that. You're full of surprises, Rick."

"Hah! Gotcha!" he said as he took her hand in his. "Somehow the priesthood never made it to my top-ten list of smart career moves. First, I was raised Unitarian. Second, and more importantly, my libido would have disqualified me even if I'd been a Catholic."

"You should have mercy on an invalid."

"I promise to be nice to you." He bent forward and kissed her lightly. Just then an unfamiliar aide came in, pushing a blood pressure machine.

"Sorry to interrupt," she said, though it was clear she was not the least bit sorry.

"Well," Rick warned, "you'd better wait a few minutes or you'll get an elevated heart rate and BP — which will confound this patient's physician."

"I'm not going to fall for that twaddle, Doctor. Move out of the way and let me take care of my patient."

"I'm not kidding. If you take this woman's vitals now you're going to get false readings. I think you should come back later."

"Move it," the aide said as she sandwiched her blood pressure machine between the patient and her visitor.

"Well, I guess you got an A in assertiveness training," Rick said.

"Never needed training. I was born pushy. At least that's what my mother tells me," the aide said, wrapping the cuff around Sarah's upper arm.

"Apparently so. Well, I have to commend you for your efficiency," Rick said.

"Got no time to be any other way. One of the other girls is running late because of car trouble and I've got her load as well as my own," she said as she marked down Sarah's temperature, blood oxygen level, blood pressure and heart rate. "There, that wasn't so bad. You two can go back to doing what comes naturally." She left the room, pushing the machine in front of her, a woman in a hurry.

"Did you hear that, Sarah? Even that battleaxe can tell we were doing what comes naturally," Rick said.

"Well, we never had a problem of desire," Sarah said as she thought back to their time together.

"No problem at all." He kissed her gently again. "But this time, Sarah, I'm here for the long haul. It's not *just* sex that I'm after, though I admit that is a draw," he said, smiling boyishly. "A big draw," he said as he kissed her again. "I want to be your go-to guy for the whole nine yards."

Sarah put her finger on his lips and studied his face. "I can't get over you. You're so different now."

"Different better or different worse?"

"Different better."

"That's a relief. The way I see it, we've got a chance to do things right this time, Sarah. I want us to be friends as well as lovers. Now that Anna's on the scene, I want us to be good parents to that perfect little baby. To that end, I was thinking that I should start contributing for Anna's care."

"Oh, I didn't even think of that," she said, remembering her father's comment about saving for Anna's college education.

"Well, I did. I mean to do the right thing. So maybe you can give some thought to, you know, where I'd deposit the money, how much."

"Oh, I'm not sure. Let me think about it," Sarah said.

"Whatever you think is fair. I'm an attending now, so I'm no longer broke. I can help with the bills, no problem."

"Thank you, Rick. I never in my wildest dreams thought you would be so open to sharing responsibility for Anna."

"Well, see, that's what love will do. It's a great motivator for all sorts of irrational behavior," he said, only half in jest.

They both were quiet for a moment. She marveled at Rick's willingness to put his feelings out on the table. It was probably time for some sort of a response. "I'm so flattered, Rick — more than flattered — by your affection for me. We never said anything about love when we were together."

"No, I think we actively avoided the word. I know I did. But I've tried to outrun it for the last seven months and I couldn't. I'm yours whether you want me or not," he said. "But I have to say I am hoping you do — or at least you'll consider it."

"The truth is, I don't know what I feel. I'd like to see how things develop between us. I'm learning that you're more thoughtful and kinder than I knew. I want to get to know you better. Would that be okay?"

"Explore all you want," he said, grinning.

"There's one thing that came up today that I want to share with you."

"Shoot away."

"I told my parents about you. I'd kept your anonymity because I thought you were out of my life. They were very happy when I told them that you wanted to be a father to Anna."

"Oh."

"Just 'oh'?"

"Well, I imagine your parents might not be thinking too kindly about the guy who got their daughter pregnant and then took off."

"I explained we had a deal and that I had willingly assumed all responsibility for the baby," Sarah said, purposely leaving out Joseph's rage upon learning the father was out of the picture.

"Still, there might be some lingering animus, as the shrinks say."

"They seem anxious to meet you. I mean, they said as much. I know a lot has happened in the last few days. Maybe you'd prefer we wait a while."

"Yeah, I could wait to meet them, but they have Anna, don't they?"

"What does that have to do with meeting them?" Sarah asked.

"Well, if I'm going to see my daughter — which I'd very much like to do — I guess I'm going to meet your parents."

That brought Sarah to the brink of tears. "I can't believe I didn't think of that. Forgive me. What a numbskull I am."

"If you're a numbskull, I don't know what that says about the rest of us. All I'm saying is that I'd like to see Anna."

"I'm so happy you want to get to know her."

"Well, if I'll be paying good money for the little thing, at least I can get to spend a little time with her."

"I guess we have a deal then," Sarah said, revealing her dimples. "Why don't we start with my mother. She and Anna are in the hospital all day, every day. If you want to see your daughter, you can meet her grandmother, too."

"Like a two-for-one sale."

"Exactly," Sarah laughed.

"Okay. I'm in."

"I'll tell my mother to be on her best behavior."

"Hey, don't give it another thought. Mothers love me — or at least they used to when I was in high school. I've studiously avoided meeting them since then."

"Well, I guess your dry spell is about to end."

Before leaving, Rick helped Sarah back into bed. She fell asleep almost instantly and was soon lost in a dream so intense she felt as though she were still awake. She was standing on the corner looking up at the crane. An elderly man took her by the arm, saying, "Dis vay, dis vay."

Sarah turned to see her Zadda Sam in the wool herringbone topcoat and gray felt fedora he had worn every winter of her childhood. "Why, Zadda?" she asked. "I want to stay and see this crane. I've never seen anything like it."

"No, *mein kint*. Come vit me. Come dis vay. Only if you come dis vay vill you have a chance."

"A chance for what, Zadda?" she asked her grandfather.

"A chance to live, *mein shana maidel*, a chance to live. For you and for your liddle vun, come vit me." Suddenly the ground opened up, revealing an earthen tunnel. "Come, come vit me," he said as he led her by the arm into the darkened passageway. "Here you vill be safe."

Sarah followed her elderly grandfather, marveling at his agility in crouching down and crawling on his hands and knees through the narrow tunnel. Then, as soon as her thick, pregnant body was deep inside the passageway, Zadda Sam vanished, leaving her within the earth's protection.

When she awoke she felt the sweetness of being with her zadda again. He'd saved her life and Anna's life, just as he had saved Bubbe Rivka during the war. She wouldn't squander the chance she'd been given. It was on that thought that she fell back into a sound, dreamless sleep for the rest of the night.

THIRTY-ONE

"Eva, Eva," the attractive blond called as she stepped out of the elevator.

Even before she turned around, Eva knew it was Devorah.

"Darling girl. Thanks so much for coming. It means so much to all of us. I know Sarah can't wait to see you," she said as she hugged her daughter's friend. "I was just stretching my legs a little by taking a walk around the floor. Sitting in a hospital room all day can make a person antsy."

"I can only imagine," Devorah said, following Eva's lead down the corridor. "How is she?"

"I won't lie to you, Devorah. She's had a pretty rough ride. But thank God, she's showing signs of coming around. I know your visit will do her good."

"I hope so," Devorah said as Eva opened the door to Sarah's room. As soon as she saw Sarah with Anna in her arms, she dropped her bag and ran to them both. She hadn't known what to expect. Now she could see how much the accident had altered her friend. She knelt down beside Sarah's chair.

"Girlfriend, you are a sight for sore eyes," she said, patting Sarah's arm. And the baby…I can't believe she's really here."

"Take a whiff and all doubt will be erased. This angelic little baby has welcomed you with a substantially dirty diaper. Fine way for her to say hello to her mother's best friend, don't you think?" Sarah said, smiling radiantly.

"Oh, give her to me. Baby poop can't scare me off. Let me hold her. Please," Devorah begged.

"Don't say I didn't give you fair warning."

Eva took in the scene of normal banter between the two friends — another sign that Sarah was slowly coming back to herself.

"I can take care of that diaper before you hold Anna if you'd like," Eva offered.

"No way! It's not every day I get to clean the *tushie* of my best friend's baby. I consider it a privilege, and as an expert in public health, sanitation is one of my specialties. Just show me where the diapers and wipes are and let me go to work."

Devorah was impressed by the volume of poop so tiny a baby could produce. Her Ph.D. notwithstanding, it took her ten minutes to clean, diaper and re-dress Anna. Then she swaddled the baby in a blanket just as Joseph arrived from work. After a round of welcome hugs, Devorah made a suggestion.

"Joseph, I think Eva has earned a dinner date with her husband. Why don't you two take the night off? I can help Sarah with Anna."

"I think that's a great idea," Sarah said. "You deserve a night out. Please go and enjoy. We'll be fine," Sarah assured.

"The girls are right, Eva," Joseph said. "Let me take you out tonight."

Eva could see the friends wanted some time alone. And truth be told, a break from the hospital and takeout dinners held great appeal.

"It would be a pleasure, Joe. Just let me get my coat."

The moment Sarah's parents left, Devorah embraced her friend.

"I am so glad to see you. I was so scared after reading about the accident. I called your cell I don't know how many times. I called your parents' house. I was sick with worry."

"I'm lucky to be seeing anyone — but especially you. It's probably good you didn't come until now. I was quite a mess. But I'm doing a little better."

"You look good, Sarah," Devorah said, stretching the truth.

"Well, I'm getting there. For a while I was headed off in a downward spiral. But a couple of things have helped me. One was my grandmother."

"Bubbe Rivka? I love your grandma."

"I know. She's an amazing woman, and it's as though she gave me an infusion of courage. After listening to her talk about what she and my zadda had to do to survive the war, I figure I can do what has to be done to get through my *tsoures,* as she calls it."

"She had never talked about it to you before?"

"No. None of my grandparents would talk about the war, at least not with me. But she said now it might do some good. And she was right."

"You're going to get through this, Sarah. I know you. I know how strong you are, what you're capable of. Just look at how you picked yourself up after the Alex debacle. A lot of women would have curled up into the fetal position and given up after what he did to you. But you didn't. You picked yourself up and carried on with your life."

Sarah started to well up. "Well, I'm not quite the same person I was before all this. But I am going to fight to get well. And don't mind my tears. I think I've cried more in the last days than I have in my whole life."

"It's cathartic. Cry all you want. Blame it on your hormones."

"That's a good excuse. I'll try to remember to use it."

"Hey, you said there were a couple of things that helped you. What else besides your grandma?"

"You're not going to believe what else."

"Try me."

"Rick's come back."

"No way! Impossible!"

"Well, I was pretty stunned myself when he reappeared at my bedside. I had no idea what to make of it. But he's been visiting me every night. We're sort of getting to know one another in a different way than before. There's a side of him that I never knew, like a kinder, gentler version of Rick. I hope you get the chance to meet him."

"I'd better meet the guy who made this beautiful infant possible," Devorah said, gazing at the baby in her arms. "You know, Sarah, she's a double miracle — a miracle of conception *and* survival."

"I'm so lucky to have her. Rick says he wants to be a father to her."

"Whoa. We'll have to change that boy's rating on the male-o-meter."

That made Sarah smile. "I guess we will. He says he's changed a lot since we split. He's even willing to meet my parents."

"The male-o-meter continues its upward rise," Devorah said, her eyes flashing.

"Well, in terms of the male-o-meter's accuracy, I guess only time will tell."

When visiting hours were over and Sarah was alone, she looked forward to the capstone of her day — a visit from Rick. But by ten o'clock, she succumbed to her exhaustion.

Rick had been held up by his newest patient, a nine-year-old girl who had gone into kidney failure. Her grotesquely swollen face and body were misdiagnosed by her local doctor as an allergy and treated with an antihistamine. By the time she arrived by ambulance in the ER that afternoon, her condition was critical. It wasn't until eleven that he was willing to leave, having finally gotten her stabilized.

When he arrived at Sarah's room, he was disappointed to find her sound asleep. He couldn't blame her. It was late, and she was no doubt beat. He wrote her a note and then sat down and watched her sleep. He couldn't believe how bad he had it for this woman. He would come back tomorrow and meet her mother and hold his daughter. He knew it had to be love that was propelling him forward, directing him to do things he had never imagined. He was willing to go wherever it led.

To Sarah, rehab made training for a marathon seem like a walk in the park. If the therapists on the ortho floor were toughies, those in rehab were drill sergeants. They pushed their freshly traumatized patients to their limits and then they pushed some more. The breaks were infrequent and short. Pity, either for oneself or another patient, was snuffed out as soon as it reared its useless head. Everyone had to get moving, working toward the goal of becoming as independent as possible: learning to bathe, dress and feed themselves despite the impairment that had landed them in the unit. The stakes were high. Those who couldn't cut it would be transferred to a long-term care facility rather than being sent home. Sarah had to tell herself repeatedly that she came from a family of survivors and, if need be, she'd claw her way back to mobility and autonomy.

The rehab regime left little time for Eva, Devorah and the baby to visit during the day. Sarah had an hour break for lunch from eleven to twelve and an hour off from two to three. Of course, by the time the breaks were granted, Sarah and her rehab cohort had all they could do to stay awake long enough to eat a meal or chat with their visitors. Sarah got a roommate, a young woman who had fallen down a flight of stairs. During late-afternoon visiting hours, a bevy of well-wishers surrounded her bed.

It was into this scene that a nervous Rick entered around five. He was about to meet Sarah's mother. Apparently, he'd also be meeting her friend, a woman Jeff had raved about at breakfast — someone from Chicago whom he'd run into the day before. And then there was Anna, the child he would publicly claim as his own. The crowded room was a plus. The presence of strangers would help keep everyone on their best behavior.

Sarah had been on the lookout for him. His note had said he'd try to drop by in the late afternoon. When they saw one another, they locked eyes and smiled like co-conspirators.

"Oh, Rick," she said, in a voice that carried above the room's chatter. "I'm so glad you could visit while my mother and Devorah are here." The discussion Eva and Devorah were having about paper versus cloth diapers stopped in its tracks. They both looked up to see a tall young doctor in green scrubs and sneakers. His dark hair and eyes and intelligent good looks impressed them both.

"Mom, Devorah, this is Rick Smith," Sarah said.

There was nothing in any parenting manual that provided Eva advice on how to meet the man who'd impregnated her daughter. She decided to go with simple good manners. She got up and extended her hand.

"How do you do? I'm so pleased to meet you. I can't say Sarah's told me a whole lot about you, but what she has said has been unfailingly complimentary."

"Well, I'm happy to hear that," Rick said, looking directly at Sarah. "Your daughter can be inscrutable at times."

"Oh, you think so?" Eva asked. "So glad I'm not the only one who finds her so."

Sarah defended herself. "What's this? Time to beat up on the patient?"

"Not at all, sweetheart. It's just that you're a very private person," Eva said sweetly.

"Enough about me," Sarah said, eager to change the subject. "Rick came here to meet you — and to spend some time with Anna." Then turning to Rick, she added, "And we have a special bonus for you: my best friend Devorah, who's here from Chicago."

Now was his chance to do a small favor for Jeff, who had taken a lot of crap from him over the last months. "Nice to meet you. My good buddy, Jeff, mentioned you were here. I must tell you that you made quite an impression on him, and he's not easily impressed," Rick said, slathering on the flattery.

"So glad I impressed a man with such high standards," Devorah replied without hesitation, though her cheeks colored a bit.

"No mean feat and I'm not just saying that," Rick said.

Just then, two more visitors came in to see the room's other occupant. Sarah proposed they relocate to the patient lounge. Now wearing rehab's obligatory "street clothes," she struggled to get off the bed without help. She nixed the idea of using a wheelchair to get to the lounge. Watching her work so hard to produce forward motion with the walker brought Devorah to tears, and a lump to Rick's throat. Eva, Devorah and the baby followed slowly behind as Rick walked with Sarah, taking tiny steps to match hers one for one. It took them five minutes to walk the fifty feet to the lounge, but when they arrived it was clear Sarah felt victorious.

"They tell us we have to push ourselves," Sarah said as she gingerly lowered herself into a chair in the unoccupied lounge. "Please," she panted, "everyone sit down."

"That was amazing," Rick raved, taking the chair next to hers.

"I don't feel amazing, but the therapists say I will feel a little less crappy every day."

"Oh, really?" Eva asked, a bit miffed the staff couldn't think of a more articulate way to express themselves.

"Well, they use more professional terms, but that's the gist of it. Phew. I'm glad we're out of that room. This is a little better for Rick's visit with Anna. Devorah, can you do the honors?"

"It will be my pleasure." Devorah got up and placed Anna in her father's arms. "Isn't she a beautiful baby?"

Although he'd held her once before, this time he was ready to be Anna's father. He stared at her for at least a minute and no one spoke. Both Eva and Devorah felt as though they were intruding on an intimate moment.

"Maybe Devorah and I should give the three of you a few minutes by yourselves," Eva offered.

"Would you mind very much, Mom?" Sarah asked.

"Not at all. This is a special time for you. We'll come back in a little while," Eva said as she and Devorah headed for the hallway.

Once they were alone, Sarah watched Rick stare into Anna's eyes and play with her fingers. The sweetness of the moment was tinged with melancholy, and all the willpower in the world couldn't keep her from tearing up.

When he looked up to see her crying, he was baffled. "Hey, what's with the tears?"

"I'm crying because you came so close to missing out on Anna — and she you."

"Hey, we're going forward now, remember? There's no profit in looking back. We have this beautiful little girl and we're going to do right by her. That's the game plan now," Rick said.

"You're right. Of course, you're right. Just keep talking to me."

"Ah! I knew you would come to see my value." He took her hand and gave it a gentle squeeze.

"Yes, I am coming to see your value, as you put it," Sarah said, wiping the tears from her face with the back of her hand.

"Glad to know I'm growing on you," he laughed. "Okay if I take off her hat?"

"You're the pediatrician. They gave her to me with a hat, and we've been keeping her head covered. Do we have to?" she sniffed, interested in Rick's professional opinion.

"It helps her regulate her body temperature. But it's not necessary every minute of the day." He pulled off the knit cap, revealing her thick, platinum hair.

"You've got to be kidding!" he exclaimed. "She's a blond?"

"I guess it comes from my mother and grandmother. They were blonds in their younger days. She obviously didn't get it from either of us," Sarah said, blushing at the thought that their mingled genes had created Anna.

"We can credit all the grandmothers. My mother is…well, was a blond, too. Her whole family has that Nordic look, you know, the blue eyes, light complexion and hair."

Just then Devorah came into the lounge, camera in hand.

"I'm just here to document the moment. I'll be out of here in no time."

Rick reached across Sarah's chair to put his arm around her while he held Anna on his chest facing the camera. Rick grinned at Sarah. Sarah's elusive dimples made an appearance as she looked at Rick holding their daughter. Two delighted parents and their new baby: a moment savored by people from every corner of the earth across the millennia — and saved for posterity by Sarah's clever friend.

When Joseph arrived at the hospital, he headed directly to the lounge, as per Eva's directions. There he found his family — and the man who'd fathered Anna. Like his wife, he was uncertain about how to handle himself. On the one hand, he was pleased that the man had apparently agreed to take responsibility for his child. But on the other hand, the fact that he'd walked out on Sarah still set Joseph's teeth on edge.

Eva broke the ice. "Joe, come and meet Rick. Imagine. We have our very own pediatrician to consult with now!" Eva exulted. "How lucky can a baby be — to have a father who's an expert in childhood medicine?"

Rick stood up and gave Sarah's father a firm handshake. He was taken by how much the woman he loved looked like the man in front of him. "Very nice to meet you, Mr. Abadhi. I would have to say that you and Sarah share a strong likeness. Those must be powerful genes, because Anna looks like she's going to fall right in line with the two of you," Rick said, doing his best to chat up Sarah's father.

"Yes, and my mother — the first Anna Abadhi — shared our facial features as well. Perhaps you're right. Powerful genes, indeed," Joseph said, trying his best to be agreeable, though unaware of any scientific basis for the idea.

"However, it seems as though Anna's grandmothers won the day on her coloring. My mother, as well as Eva — and I guess Sarah's grandma — have passed on their blond hair and blue eyes. Lucky Anna," Rick said, trying to keep things light. "She's a beautiful baby."

"Rick, did you know that my father works in regenerative medicine?" Sarah interjected, hoping to help the conversation along. "You know, using stem cells to regenerate organs?"

Rick felt like a five-hundred-pound weight had been lifted off his back. Making pleasant conversation with a guy in sales or finance would have been tough sledding. But regenerative medicine, well, that was something else entirely. And, of course, it offered an alternative to the uncomfortable subject of where he'd been until now.

"No, I didn't know that. I would really enjoy learning about your work. Right now I have a young patient whose kidneys are beyond repair. If we manage to get her through this crisis, dialysis will be the only way to keep her alive. She'll be tethered to a machine for years. If she's extremely lucky, someday she may get a transplant. But if we could teach her body to regrow a kidney, now that would be the ticket."

"That objective drives our research," Joseph said. "We're actually working on liver regeneration, but we hope that if we're successful, our research will be applicable to other tissues and organs."

"That's got to be so exciting," Rick said in earnest. "You're on the cutting edge of medicine. I enjoy patient contact, so my bent is toward clinical, but if I were to lean toward research, your field would be hard to beat."

If there was something that matched Joseph's passion for his family, it was love for his work. Rick's enthusiasm for his research provided a channel in which the two men could move while each took the measure of the other. It didn't take either man long to figure out he was dealing with a person of substance. Under other circumstances, they would have instantly taken a liking to one another. However, given the reality that they neither knew nor trusted the other's intentions, the jury was out on whether they would ultimately find a way to get along.

THIRTY-TWO

About a week into the rehab regime, Sarah, Eva and a social worker met to discuss where Sarah should go after discharge. Sarah's vote was to go home, but there were obstacles — namely, she lived alone and had two flights of stairs to negotiate. Her parents' house was more accessible, and, of course, help would be readily available. Given her newfound grit, Sarah knew that if the decision didn't go her way, she would swallow hard and do what needed to be done.

During her lunch break, she was trying to tamp down her excitement about the prospect of leaving the hospital when the phone rang. Thinking it could be Devorah letting her know she'd arrived safely in Chicago, Sarah worked to reach it, grabbing for the receiver on the seventh ring.

"Hello, Sarah, is that you?"

"Harry, how nice to hear your voice."

"How're you doing today? The operator told me you moved to another room."

"That's right. I'm in rehab now and they're trying to kill me. But if I live, they say I'll be as strong as an ox."

"Tough therapy?"

"The understatement of the year."

"You can handle it, Sarah. Remember, you're the health care group's premier marathon runner."

"Actually, it's hard to remember. But I have to tell you, rehab is harder than running a marathon."

"Never having done either, I'll take your word for it. Hey, I wanted to tell you that I spoke with Grant Salbago from the San

Francisco office — the guy I told you about who specializes in construction law."

"Oh, thank you, Harry. I really appreciate it."

"It was no big deal. The good news is he's agreed to watch my back, albeit at a distance, if we decide to negotiate a settlement with Arkin."

"That's good. I know you think a lot of him."

"I do. Now the question is, do you feel up to having a preliminary meeting with Arkin and his lawyer? He's apparently champing at the bit to get the settlement show on the road."

The thought of meeting with Mark Arkin unnerved her. Before the accident, she had always done her homework before entering into negotiations. Appearing cool and self-possessed was indispensable, and her extensive preparation had given her the mojo she needed. But now that would be tough to pull off.

"When does he want to meet?"

"Later today or tomorrow."

"So soon?" Sarah asked.

"Yeah, it seems he's a man in a hurry. Too soon for you?"

"I'm just afraid I'll sound tentative. I'm not quite myself."

"If that's your reason for demurring, forget it. I'll handle the negotiations. You can just sit there and look not quite like yourself — which is the whole point, after all."

"Okay. If you think you're ready, I'll follow your lead."

"Good. I'll get back to you with the where and when as soon as it's nailed down."

"Oh, if I'm not here when you call, you can call my mother's cell and she'll relay the information to me." She gave Harry her mother's number before saying good-bye.

After lunch, Sarah had trouble concentrating on her therapy. She did all the painful exercises, but kept thinking about how changed she was from the time she had last met with Mark Arkin. She remembered she had been nervous that day — nervous, but also ready.

How different this meeting would be.

Eva arrived at two with the baby, in time for Sarah's afternoon break. She put Anna in Sarah's arms and then handed her the message she'd taken from Harry. It read, "They'll be at the hospital at five o'clock. I'll arrange a conference room for the meeting. Don't worry. I've got you covered."

"I guess it's going to happen today after all," Sarah muttered.

"What is Harry referring to, honey? He can't be asking you to work, can he? It's much too soon for that, sweetheart."

"Oh no. Harry's not inviting me to a work meeting. This is about a proposed settlement for my injuries. The developer wants to meet with me — but it's completely confidential, so mum's the word," she said, glad her roommate had gone home that morning.

"How about Dad?"

"Well, of course Dad's okay, but let's keep this to ourselves. I'm not even sure what I should ask for. I'm going to have to rely on Harry to represent my interests," Sarah said.

"Harry's been wonderful to you. Don't you think he'll do a good job?" Eva asked.

"I know he'll do his best," Sarah said. "He's conferring with someone from our firm who specializes in construction law. Together I think they'll be able to offer me good counsel."

"Who was the developer, Sarah?"

"Mark Arkin."

Eva grimaced. "Arkin? That blowhard? I never could stand that man. He's always trumpeting his wealth and power. He's so coarse, so blinded by that enormous ego of his, a real *k'naker*. If he was Joe Blow, no one would listen to a word he says. But in this country, where money justifies everything from bad manners to high crimes and misdemeanors, he's a *macher*.

You'd better keep the bastard away from me, after what happened to you and the baby. If I lay eyes on him, I'll tell him what he can do with himself and his luxury condo towers."

Sarah had never seen her mother so irate. It was true that Arkin provoked strong feelings from almost everyone in the city — either admiration for a guy who'd built a fortune from nothing, or contempt for his drive to win at all costs. As for Sarah, she felt strangely neutral about him.

"Mom, did you know I settled a case with Arkin about a year ago? It worked out well for all parties. When he found out I was among the injured, he called Harry and told him that he was favorably impressed with me and that he wanted to make things right. I guess that's the alleged motivation for the meeting this afternoon."

"No, I didn't know. You've always kept your work to yourself." Eva took a breath and began to build up some steam. "And as for him being favorably impressed with you, he'd be a fool not to be. You're a beautiful, intelligent woman, a top-notch attorney and a new mother who nearly lost her life to his 'development project.' He'd better come up with something that can begin to make amends for the harm he's done you," Eva seethed.

"Well, Mom, we'll find out in a few hours just what he has in mind."

At a quarter past four, when Sarah's hour-long lesson on the care and cleaning of external fixator pin sites was done, she inched her way back to her room, determined to get herself together for the meeting. In terms of clothes, there were few choices. With the bulky metal apparatus on her leg, pants were out of the question. The only clothes that fit since she had delivered Anna were the maternity dresses that Eva had brought to rehab. She selected a black jumper and a gray turtleneck, borrowed some lipstick from her mother and ran her fingers through her hair. When Harry appeared at ten before five, Sarah felt presentable.

"Mrs. Abadhi! It's a pleasure to see you again, especially with Sarah doing so much better," Harry schmoozed.

"Yes, I agree on both counts. Sarah filled me in on your

meeting. Would you prefer that Anna and I leave while you talk?"

Harry looked at Sarah for guidance.

"It's okay if you stay, Mom. Just remember what I said about loose lips."

"Of course, darling. Consider my lips hermetically sealed." Eva pantomimed the locking of her lips and then turned her attention to Anna, who was working herself up into a lusty howl after losing her pacifier.

Harry proceeded with the outlines of his game plan. "Sarah, I think our best strategy is to let them talk — you know, hear them out. We don't have to agree to anything today. You can think about whatever it is they offer, and I can pass it by Grant. We can make a counter offer sometime next week or the week after, if you prefer."

"Given the state of my legal wits, listening sounds about right."

"So we'll just hear what they have to say and keep our cards close to the chest. We'll look clever and shrewd instead of indecisive. By the way, John Mess, our friend in Risk Management, was nice enough to offer us his conference room, but the more I thought about it, the more I figured it might be smart to meet right here in the rehab wing. Let them see where you've been spending your days."

"Whatever you think, Harry."

"I think it's best we use the doctors' consulting room near the end of the corridor. Would you like me to get a wheelchair and wheel you over?" Harry asked.

"Better not. My therapists wouldn't look favorably on me catching a ride. I'll use the walker, but Arkin and his attorney may have to cool their jets while I get there. Speed is not yet in my repertoire."

"All right, then. If you're ready, let's head out. Just remember, Sarah, all you have to do is listen. If you want to look pitiful, you can play that card, too. It's up to you."

"Pitiful? That won't be much of a stretch, Harry," Sarah said with a wry smile. "Consider me one of the walking wounded that keeps the staff here fully employed."

"Fair enough. Walking wounded it will be, then."

As they left for the meeting, Eva called out in a stage whisper, "Give 'em hell."

When Sarah and Harry entered the small, windowless consulting room, they had a surprise awaiting them. Catherine Malloy-Arkin sat beside her husband and his attorney, Larry Heidigger, general counsel of Mark Arkin's development firm. Sarah hardly recognized Catherine. The last time they'd met, the thirty-something new mother had looked strained and exhausted. Now Sarah couldn't help but stare at the pretty woman who seemed to embody an effortless grace. The contrast between her and her husband was striking. Despite the Armani suit and expensive cut to his graying, wooly hair, Mark still had the look of a scrappy street fighter. When they saw Sarah struggle to enter the room, both of the Arkins got up from their seats, and their attorney followed suit. As she approached the table they each extended a hand to her. Sarah accepted their greeting and then carefully lowered her body into an armchair.

Heidigger, an overweight, bespectacled man in his fifties, wasted no time launching into his presentation. "Thank you for meeting with us. I want to take this opportunity to bring you up-to-date on the findings of the initial investigation into the construction accident that occurred at the site of the Arkin Worldwide project. The city hired an independent engineering company to analyze the accident. I have a copy of the report for you," he said as he handed Sarah and Harry the analysis done by C.R. Wilson Consulting Engineers PC.

The attorney continued, "It appears that culpability lay with the crane subcontractor in charge of the rigging who, unbeknownst to Mr. Arkin, hatched a plan to — shall we say — improve his profit margin by doing the job on the cheap. He knowingly and willfully disregarded common industry practice in what is known as 'jumping the crane,' extending its height as the construction proceeded. He used half the usual and customary supports for the crane-jumping procedure, four instead of eight, and one of the four supports — a polyester sling — was frayed. The crane's manufacturer recommended the use of eight chain blocks instead of polyester slings, advice the subcontractor disregarded.

"Apparently there is also some evidence that the subcontractor paid off the city inspector to look the other way while he cut corners on the job site. It appears that the inspector falsely reported inspecting the crane just days before the accident. There's an understandable hue and cry for heads to roll in the city building department, and there's pressure mounting for the building commissioner to resign, given the fact that this is just the latest in a series of construction mishaps in the last year. The upshot of all this negligence and malfeasance was a lack of the required number of supports and a resulting catastrophic failure of the crane at the site of our project. These are preliminary findings, of course, but they not only infuriate my client, they clear him entirely of culpability in the unfortunate incident."

It was hard for Sarah to hear. Could it be true that so many people had been placed in harm's way by intentional recklessness and greed? Now she felt some of her mother's rage.

"Mr. Arkin believes — and I concur — that he bears no fault for your injuries," Heidigger continued. "However, because of the high regard he and Ms. Malloy-Arkin have for you and the work you did when their daughter was injured, he has chosen to offer you a settlement to recompense you for your pain and suffering. This conversation and any others that may ensue are, of course, to be kept completely confidential. And the offer that will be made to you today is unique — that is, Mr. Arkin will not be entering into negotiations with any other party involved in this most unfortunate occurrence."

Heidigger looked at his client and motioned that the floor was his. Mark cleared his throat and began. "First, I want to say how sorry I am for what happened. And I wanted to tell you that face-to-face because I mean what I say. I'm a developer, just trying to complete a project on time and, if possible, under budget. My projects have a good safety record. You can check that out for yourselves. But the reality is, however indirectly, my project led to your injuries. And for that, I am sorry. I am here to offer my apologies — on behalf of my wife and myself — for what you've experienced as a result of the crane rigger's screw-up. Beyond that, Catherine and I feel indebted to you for working up the settlement plan that brought some good out of Ariel's suffering."

Sarah thought back to the injuries the newborn Arkin baby had sustained. She shuddered to think how she would react if something like that happened to Anna. "I trust your little girl is doing well?" she asked.

Catherine, who'd been sitting solemnly, brightened. "Oh yes, very well. I appreciate you asking about her. She's toddling around the house and even saying a few words. As far as the doctors can tell, there is no residual effect from her ordeal. We thank our lucky stars for Dr. Smith. He not only saved her life, but also her quality of life. His actions made all the difference." This unsolicited tribute to Rick pleased Sarah.

Catherine nodded to her husband that he could proceed.

"The settlement you designed allowed us to know that our daughter's suffering led to measurable improvements in how this hospital works. The neutral third party overseeing the settlement has sent us monthly reports detailing the hospital's efforts to prevent another disaster like the one that befell our daughter. He confirms that the promised enhancements in staffing and dispensing of medication are being carried out, just as you said they would be. Catherine and I take comfort in knowing that. So the upshot is, we're both extremely thankful; it was the best possible outcome to the catastrophe that nearly killed our baby."

Sarah was moved by what he said. It reminded her that even as a lawyer, she could make a difference in people's lives. "Thank you.

I'm pleased that the settlement has provided you with some comfort."

It was Catherine who spoke next. She seemed almost meek as she began. "I understand, Ms. Abadhi, that you were pregnant when the accident occurred? That you delivered a child later that day? I hope your baby is doing well."

Out of nowhere, Sarah's heart started pounding and sweat began pouring from her brow. She closed her eyes and gripped the arms of her chair to stop her hands from trembling. She couldn't get enough air.

Everything in the room came to a stop.

Harry put his hand on Sarah's arm. "Sarah, are you okay? Should we get a doctor?"

"No. I just need a minute," she said, trying to catch her breath.

Harry wanted to kick himself for agreeing to Arkin's request. "I'm sorry. This meeting seems to be premature. Ms. Abadhi has suffered a terrible ordeal and it may be too early for her to be discussing the fallout from the accident. I suggest we adjourn and meet again when she's up to it."

All eyes were on Sarah. Her first instinct was to flee the room. But then her mind flashed on the meeting she'd had with the Arkins, just days after they'd witnessed their baby nearly hemorrhage to death. Now she understood what it had taken for them to leave her and meet with the hospital's representatives. She took a Kleenex from the box and wiped her brow.

"I'd like to keep going, Harry, if that's all right with you."

"It's entirely your call, Sarah."

"Then let's continue."

Addressing Catherine directly, Sarah said, "You asked about my baby. She's beautiful. The doctors tell me she is apparently fine. It's kind of you to ask."

"Well, I hope your baby will be the blessing Ariel is for us."

"Thank you," Sarah said.

"Ms. Abadhi, as my husband said, we're thankful to you for

everything you did to correct the circumstances that allowed the medication overdose that harmed our baby. Because of that — despite the fact that my husband's firm is not directly responsible for your injuries — we would like to extend an offer to you. Consider it a token of both our appreciation for your efforts and our regret that you were hurt, however indirectly, by my husband's project. We're prepared to offer you a million dollars for the pain and suffering associated with your injuries."

A million. Sarah wondered if what had happened to her was worth more or less than that seven-figure sum. For that she would have to rely on Harry.

At this point, Heidigger jumped into what appeared to be a well-rehearsed presentation. He handed both Sarah and Harry copies of the settlement he'd drawn up. "Of course, our offer does not prevent you from going after the subcontractor who caused the accident. I'm not your attorney, Ms. Abadhi, but you probably will have a case against the city as well, for their corrupt inspector. This settlement is, as my clients say, a token of their appreciation and an effort to help you in your recovery."

Sarah looked at Harry, who took over. "Of course we'll give your offer careful consideration. Sarah has a lot to deal with right now, but we'll get back to you in, say, the next couple of weeks. If there's nothing else, I think we should let Sarah get some rest." He moved his chair back to get up, but was surprised when he felt Sarah's hand on his arm.

"Just a moment, Harry. I'd like to say something. I didn't think I'd say much at this meeting and I haven't planned this so you'll have to bear with me. Since the accident I've been thinking a lot about the misery that was visited on me, and on so many others. If there is some higher being, I'd say he — or she, or it — is one hell of a lousy manager. It certainly looks as though we're all on our own.

"When you asked me about being pregnant on the day of the accident, your question brought up a lot of images. Terrible images.

That day I was eagerly awaiting the birth of my baby and, in an instant, everything changed. In that way you and I are part of a club we never wanted to join. We had our hopes and expectations surrounding the arrival of our child stolen from us. In Ariel's case, it was due to unintentional errors but, nevertheless, they led to a devastating outcome. According to Mr. Heidigger, my injuries were due to intentional malfeasance fueled by greed. The result was nothing short of a calamity.

"So on the one hand, we have action that can lead to disaster; action which, if left unopposed, creates terrible suffering. But on the other hand, we each can be a force for good, just as you described Dr. Smith. For Ariel, he was a force for good. Perhaps we can all take a page out of his book.

"I appreciate you bearing with me. This is the first time I'm giving voice to the thoughts that have been rattling around my head since the accident," Sarah said. "I guess I'm wondering if there's a way that some type of good can arise out of this disaster. I have no idea what that might be, or what shape it might take. I'm just thinking out loud, but perhaps some sort of safety institute could be established to reduce the incidence of accidents at construction sites.

"You know, when I close my eyes I still see that crane swaying from side to side. I see two workmen dangling from a pole twenty stories up. I keep thinking about the terror that crane operator and those other men must have felt in the moments before they fell to their deaths. They died because someone didn't value their lives enough to protect them. I don't think their deaths should be for naught. I would like to think there is some way to have good come out of this catastrophe."

Heidigger could hardly get the words out fast enough. "All right then. Thank you for your thoughts, Ms. Abadhi, but we've covered what we came here to discuss and I propose that this meeting now adjourn. You have our offer. Mr. Meinig will let us know your decision in the next week or two."

As the attorney started putting his papers into his attaché case, Mark spoke up. "Just hold on a minute, Larry. No harm in talking. Let's hear her out. What exactly are you proposing, Ms. Abadhi?"

"I have no definite proposal. I'm just saying that we each have the power to act and we have to decide whether we'll use that power to improve the world or leave it worse off. If Mr. Heidigger's description is accurate, the subcontractor acted solely to enrich himself, to hell with everyone else. We see the results. I'm sitting here now, luckily only battered and broken instead of crushed to death. In contrast to the subcontractor, there are people who make it their business to be a force for good. They do what my grandmother would call *mitzvahs*."

Heidigger couldn't contain himself. "I don't see what this has to do with the facts at hand. With all due respect, Ms. Abadhi, and I know you've suffered a trauma, this is not Philosophy 101."

"No, it's not. It's real life, Mr. Heidigger. Life and death, good and evil. Just the basics." Sarah was more self-assured than she'd been since the accident. "As you said, Mr. Arkin, you do not consider yourself directly responsible for what happened, and perhaps from a legal point of view, you're not."

Mark looked down at the table for a moment before meeting Sarah's penetrating gaze. "No 'perhaps' about it, Ms. Abadhi."

"Even if that's the case — and we both are well aware of the vagaries of liability law — you've made an offer to me out of your regret that your project indirectly caused my injuries. You want to do something significant to make things right for me. What I'm saying is, further action springing from that same sentiment could offset some of the destruction and suffering caused by the accident."

Sarah's argument made sense to Catherine. She'd long felt it was time her husband used some of his vast fortune for philanthropy, but he always dismissed the notion out of hand. Only one principle drove him: maximizing the interests of Arkin Worldwide. The idea of offering Sarah Abadhi a settlement had been Catherine's and had it not been for her singular power of persuasion, the meeting would not be taking place. So she was intrigued when her husband began to reply to Sarah's proposal.

"I know what a *mitzvah* is. I had a Jewish grandmother, too, Ms. Abadhi," he said in his gravelly voice. "You think I should, out of the goodness of my heart, support construction safety even though I didn't do a goddamn thing wrong? You forget, Ms. Abadhi, I'm known as a heartless man," Mark said, now looking piercingly into her eyes.

"I very much doubt the veracity of that assessment," Sarah responded, not knowing where she was getting the nerve to go toe-to-toe with the mogul.

Her rejoinder led Catherine to suppress a little grin.

Sarah continued. "Just as you're enamored of Dr. Smith because he worked to counteract a terrible mistake he had no role in creating, I think the victims of this accident — and the citizens of the city — would be grateful to you for any action you could take to prevent yet another tragedy. Though I'm no expert, I think the essence of a *mitzvah* is that you do good just to do good. Still, you would get the bonus of excellent public relations for your firm. Perhaps a tax write-off as well."

"A *mitzvah* with benefits? Is that what you're proposing?" Mark asked. The irony was not lost on him.

"You could call it that. I've become aware that you have a PR problem. Whether it's fair or not, I imagine many people attach blame for what happened to you — as the developer. You may not care how you're viewed by the public. But perhaps you do, or perhaps your family does. What I'm saying is, it could be possible for you to do well by doing good."

Harry figured he'd better end this exchange before Sarah pissed Arkin off enough for him to pull the offer from the table. "All right, then," Harry said. "It's time to wrap things up. We have your offer. You have Ms. Abadhi's proposal for construction safety philanthropy, which, we understand, is wholly unrelated to your offer to her. Thank you for your time." He gave Sarah the look that said they were done, and she struggled to get to her feet.

Catherine cringed when she saw how hard Sarah had to work to get up from her chair. She was the last to speak. "We very much appreciate you meeting with us, Ms. Abadhi. We hope you look favorably upon our offer. We look forward to hearing from you soon. All the best to you and your baby."

As Sarah and Harry slowly made their way down the corridor, she turned to her mentor and whispered, "I couldn't help myself. Sorry I didn't stick with the game plan."

"Ah, forget it. No harm done. Who knows, maybe you gave the bastard something to chew on. Bet you feel better having given him your two cents."

"Actually, I do. I feel much better."

THIRTY-THREE

A million dollars was a lot of money. It was during one of Sarah's grueling therapy sessions that she made up her mind about how she would use it. Though she told no one, her decision brought her a sense of peace as she struggled to master dressing and bathing with her leg encased in the external fixator.

Harry and Grant Salbago worked through the particulars of the settlement with Mark Arkin and his lawyer. Both were surprised by how placidly Arkin received their counter. There were no expletives, no histrionics, no arguing. Arkin accepted the first proposal — the installation of a stair lift in Sarah's walk-up building — without argument. He agreed to have his staff acquire the needed permission from her landlord and then supervise the installation. If the landlord wanted the stair lift to be temporary, his staff would remove the device when it was no longer needed. In the interim, it would allow Sarah to go home, as well as get to and from her appointments without giving hernias to the guys from the medical transport service.

Harry had expected pushback from his second proposal: that Arkin Worldwide pony up for medical expenses should Sarah suffer long-term impairment from her injuries. Over his attorney's protestations, Arkin calmly accepted that proposal as well. His acquiescence left Harry scratching his head, wondering if he and Grant had unwittingly left something on the table.

But Sarah wasn't concerned. On the contrary, she was pleased with their advocacy. She followed Harry's counsel and accepted the Arkins' monetary offer. The money was deposited into her bank account within days of her signing the agreement. To make the deal sweeter, Harry and Grant waived their usual fees as a professional courtesy for a valued colleague.

She didn't know if it was survivor's guilt or something loftier, but Sarah was determined to devote the settlement money to helping some of the people who had suffered as a result of the accident. She would set aside a small sum for Anna as compensation for her rocky start to life, and then place the balance in trust for the children of the construction workers who had perished in the crane accident.

But she couldn't fulfill her plan without help. For that, she had to turn once again to Harry. When Sarah told him her idea, he wondered if the accident hadn't injured more than her leg. However, her point-by-point argument for using the money as "a force for good" persuaded him that her wits remained intact. He agreed to contact the families and make them aware of the largesse of an anonymous donor who wanted to honor their loved one's sacrifice and ease the way of their children. Playing the representative of a generous benefactor would turn out to be a singular experience for Harry, and one that, much to his surprise, he would rather enjoy.

As the date for Sarah's discharge approached, Devorah flew back to New York to be her helpmate for Sarah's first weeks back home. That simple act of generosity provided a lifesaver to the Abadhi family, allowing them to sense terra firma for the first time since the accident. Sarah was able to return to her apartment, where she could be with her child both day and night. Eva took up her teaching duties once more, just as the new semester was starting up. Both Eva and Joseph savored the rhythms of daily life they'd abandoned during their family emergency. The simple pleasure of waking up in their own bed allowed them to hope that their terrible siege was coming to an end.

Once Sarah was back in her apartment, Rick became a regular for dinner. More often than not, Jeff tagged along. The two mavens of takeout alternated with Devorah in providing the meal and libations.

The foursome enjoyed many a congenial evening together. It soon became apparent that Jeff had more than a passing interest in Devorah and, much to his amazement, his interest seemed to be returned in kind. That their best friends hit it off delighted both Rick and Sarah.

After dinner one night, Rick and Sarah excused themselves to give Anna her bath. They got set up in the bathroom with everything they needed for their task: towels, baby shampoo, fresh clothes and diapers. They put on the heat light to warm the air as Sarah undressed the unsuspecting Anna. Rick examined her umbilicus and deemed it to be healing nicely. Then, with Sarah seated next to him, he did the honors of submerging Anna's tiny body in the warm water of the oversized bathroom sink. The baby's eyes grew wide and her arms flailed as the water hit her skin.

Sarah took charge of the shampooing, while Rick kept the suds away from Anna's eyes. The baby wriggled and splashed in the sink, sending water to distant corners of the bathroom. Every fold and crevice was washed. Once the joint determination was made that Anna was clean, Rick carefully scooped up her slippery body and deposited her onto the waiting towel draped across Sarah's lap. Anna kicked wildly and looked all around as her parents diapered her and dressed her in a fresh flannel nightshirt. The final step was executed by Sarah, who combed the baby's full head of hair.

Both Sarah and Rick marveled at how hard it would have been to bathe their tiny infant had the other not been there. It struck Sarah that the bath was likely a fitting metaphor for the process of raising a child.

The plan that had been hatched while Sarah was still in rehab was to have a home health agency send aides to her apartment once Devorah returned to Chicago. However, as Rick fed Anna a bottle after dinner one evening, an idea struck him: He could take over when Devorah left. He was eligible for the hospital's childcare leave. He certainly could handle Sarah's medical needs and the care of a healthy newborn. He decided to pitch his idea to Sarah, hoping Devorah and Jeff would rally to his cause.

As the others were collectively solving the Sunday crossword puzzle, Rick cleared his throat for effect and began. "I don't mean to interrupt your weighty collaboration, but I'd like to make a proposal."

Sarah and Jeff looked up while Devorah filled in the answer to a clue, "State capital whose name derives from the French for 'wooded area.' B-O-I-S-E."

"I'm all ears," Sarah said.

"Well, I was just thinking that instead of hiring strangers to come in and help once Devorah goes home, why don't I just put in for a leave and take over for her?"

The question caused Devorah to look up from the puzzle, while Jeff was left speechless. Sarah was intrigued. "You? You want to cook, clean, buy groceries, do laundry, make formula and wash bottles?"

"What? You don't think I can do it? *I* can do it," he said, patting his chest. "What I don't know, I'll figure out. More importantly, I'm a pediatrician who specializes in trauma. You and Anna will have the finest medical care at your beck and call. How can you refuse an offer like that?"

Jeff remained mute, astonished that Rick was willing to take an extended leave from work to do domestic duty. Devorah raised her eyebrows and shrugged her shoulders. "He's right, Sarah. He's at least as qualified as the aides from the agency."

"That's some ringing endorsement. I thought you'd be in my corner," Rick said, doing his best to look wounded.

"I am in your corner. I'm endorsing you," Devorah insisted. "And Sarah, his fee will be much cheaper than the agency's. Think of the money you'll save. What a bargain!"

"That's right," Rick concurred. "I'm qualified and a bargain."

Sarah looked at Rick and then at Devorah. They were both nodding their heads and smiling at her. At that moment, both she and

Jeff had the same idea.

"Did you two cook this up together?" Sarah asked.

"No way," Devorah said. "This is all his idea. But I like it."

"So what do you think, Sarah? Say the word and I'll put in for a leave. I'll do it first thing tomorrow morning."

Jeff finally weighed in. "Sarah, for so many reasons I won't go into now, I never thought I'd live to see this day, so for my sake, please say yes. I can't wait to see him make dinner."

"Well, Rick," Sarah began, "you make a good point about your medical expertise. And I take Devorah's point: The price is right. So, I would say, if you're willing to sleep on the couch — just as Devorah's been doing — you can have the job when she leaves."

The couch. Not his first choice, but it would have to do. "You've got yourself a deal," Rick said. "You won't be sorry. Concierge medicine will have nothing on me."

Three days later, with his application for leave in the works of the hospital's HR bureaucracy, Rick flew off to Michigan to see his mother. It was Susan's birthday and a party had been surreptitiously planned by her friends. When Rick called to say he was coming home for the weekend, Susan was delighted.

She picked Rick up from his early morning flight, and readily agreed to his suggestion that they get some breakfast before heading home. The Neptune Diner would forever be etched in Susan's memory; it was there that she learned she was a grandmother. Rick had to say it more than once and produce pictures before she believed that her son was not only the father of a newborn girl, but happily so. He did his best to convey the outlines of his relationship with Sarah. Susan had only one request: that he promise to arrange a visit as soon as he thought it wise.

News of her grandchild, coupled with the party — which she enjoyed after getting over her initial shock — made Susan's sixtieth birthday a happy one. The following day she went to a baby boutique famous for designer clothing, picked out five outfits in progressively larger sizes, had them gift-wrapped and gave them to Rick as he packed for his flight back to New York.

When Rick returned laden with gifts, Sarah was so touched she wanted to thank Susan herself. Rick checked with his mother, and a visit on Skype was set for the following morning. Sarah dressed Anna in the smallest outfit sent by her grandmother. Rick, anxious for Sarah and his mother to like one another, grew restless as he waited for the appointed time.

He needn't have worried. Their meeting via Skype was a success. For Susan, Sarah embodied her long-held hope that Rick might find someone to make a life with. Seeing her granddaughter on her computer screen was nothing short of surreal — thrillingly so. As for Sarah, she was amazed to see a woman who looked not a whit like her son, but who shared with him the gift of rapid-fire repartee. The short visit featured good cheer all around. Even Anna cooperated by looking directly at the camera and turning up the left side of her mouth. Her grandmother was only too happy to deem it a smile.

Once Rick took up residence on the couch, both he and Sarah took things slowly, fearful of asking too much of one another and running their newfound connection off the rails. Rick concentrated on being a genuine help, following Sarah's directions for shopping, laundry and even cooking. It was a crash course in domesticity, but his motivation made him a quick study. As hard as it was for Sarah to be helpless, she was moved by the way Rick came to her aid. And watching him lovingly care for Anna made her swallow hard more times than she could count.

Rick was pleased with how things were going in every way but one. Early in Sarah's recuperation at home, Eva, Joseph and Bubbe Rivka established the pattern of visiting at least once every weekend. Whenever Joseph was in the three-room apartment, he seemed to keep Rick under surveillance. So when the family arrived, Rick would often excuse himself, going for a long run along the river and buying himself some time away from Joseph's watchful eye.

On one Sunday run, Rick was surprised to hear someone call his name. He looked around. There were no other runners or bikers on that stretch of the path, but there was a man sitting on a nearby bench. Rick did a double take when he realized it was Sarah's father.

"Oh, hello there, Mr. Abahdi. I didn't notice you."

"I thought I'd get some air, and also take the opportunity to catch you before you headed back to Sarah's. Please sit down for a moment."

"Oh, sure," Rick said, trying his best to appear relaxed.

"Look, Rick, I'll get right to the point. I don't relish butting in between you and Sarah, but I have only one daughter. You've been very generous with your time during these last weeks. It's a good start in making up for the way you abandoned her."

Rick smarted at the characterization of their split. "Mr. Abadhi," he began.

"Please let me finish what I have to say," Joseph said evenly, his eyes fixed on his target. "I don't pretend to know what went on between you two. Sarah told me she let you off the hook and you left. As far as I'm concerned, it's all water under the bridge. I'm worried about what happens now and in the future. I've got to look out for the interests of my daughter and my granddaughter."

"Naturally," Rick said, tamping down the urge to defend himself.

"When Sarah told me about her pregnancy, I wanted to take the guy who was responsible and beat him to a pulp — and, believe me, I'm generally a peaceful man. The idea of my single daughter being left with all the responsibilities of raising a child while the *momzer* — excuse me, the bastard — was off living a carefree life...well, it infuriated me. However, since you've resurfaced, you haven't behaved like the lout I imagined you to be. On the contrary, you've been very attentive to Sarah and Anna's needs. Believe me, I've been observing very carefully.

"But here's the point. Sarah's been through a lot. Eva and I have never known her to be depressed. She was a resilient child, not the type to stew over things. But the accident...well, it threw her. Although she's coming around, she can't suffer another blow. Do you understand what I'm saying?"

"Yes, I think I do."

"So here's the bottom line: If you hurt my daughter you'll have to deal with me. Am I being clear?"

As a father now, Rick could understand and even admire Joseph's effort to protect his daughter. Rick would do that and more to shield Anna from harm. Still, Joseph's threat grated on him. The months after he and Sarah had split had hardly been a walk in the park. And, since the accident, he'd done everything he could to make things right. But while he knew he had his licks coming, he also knew he had to respond — respectfully — to Joseph's challenge for going forward.

"Yes, you're being very clear. Let me be clear as well, Mr. Abadhi. I have apologized more than once to Sarah. Regardless of the fact that she released me from my responsibilities, I was wrong to leave her when she told me she was pregnant. You are also due an apology. Now that I'm a father myself, I can only imagine how you felt about the — what did you call me?"

"I believe the word I used was '*momzer*,'" Joseph said.

"I can imagine how you felt about the *momzer* who left your daughter. I'm sorry I caused you so much distress. But make no mistake. I'm in love with Sarah. I hope for nothing more than the day when she will feel the same way about me. We have a lot to make up for. I'm aware of how much. But I'm hopeful that we'll be able to work things out. I'm doing everything I can to make that happen.

"You should know that regardless of whether Sarah comes to return my feelings, I plan on being a father to Anna, not just financially but in every sense of the word. I see what a great father you are to Sarah. For most of my life, I didn't have a father. I can't say I know much about what it takes to be a good one. But if I work at it, and — if I'm lucky — with Sarah's help, I hope Anna will come to feel about me the way her mother feels about you."

Joseph was impressed. Perhaps Rick would turn out to be a *mensch* after all. "Very well, then. I see we understand one another."

"Yes, I think we do."

"Good. I'm glad we had this talk."

"Me, too. But if it's all right with you, Mr. Abadhi, I think I'll get back to my run."

"Of course, Rick. I look forward to seeing you back at the apartment."

The two men shook hands and Rick took off, going north along the river. He was relieved that things had finally come to a head. Maybe now he'd be more comfortable around Joseph. For his part, Joseph walked back to the apartment congratulating himself on having had the man-to-man talk he'd rehearsed in his head for weeks. It elicited the best reaction he'd had any reason to hope for.

The following Saturday, Joseph and Eva dropped Bubbe Rivka off at Sarah's before taking in a matinee in celebration of their wedding anniversary. Sarah chatted with her grandmother for a while but, about an hour into her visit, Sarah excused herself for a nap.

"So Rick, are you in de mood for a cup of tea and some of de *mandelbrot* I brought?" Rivka asked as she sat on the sofa cradling Anna in her arms.

"Sounds like a good plan," Rick said, eager for a way to pass the time. He took Anna from Rivka as they went into the kitchen to boil the water for tea.

Rick had no memory of his own grandmothers. By the time he'd moved to Michigan, his mother's mother had been dead for a couple of years. He had no recollection of anyone in his father's family, most of whom lived in Greece. So as he sat across from Rivka at the kitchen table, he thought that might be a conversation starter.

"Sarah and Anna are so lucky to have you. I never knew either of my grandmothers."

"Tsk, tsk, tsk. A little boy — ant a big vun too — shoult know de love ov a grandmudder," Rivka said. "Der's notink like it."

"I'm sure you're right," Rick said. "But I did have a great relationship with my grandfather — my mother's father. I spent just about every weekend with him. He taught me how to fix cars and play every sport you can imagine," Rick offered, happy just to remember those visits to his grandfather's house. "He died a number of years ago. I miss him a lot."

This made Rivka brighten. "You know, Rick, your grandpa is livink on tru you."

"You think so?"

"Of course! Everytink he taught you, all your memories of beink vit him, dat's how he lives on. You're who you are because of him. Your whole life voult be different vitout him. Am I right?"

"You *are* right," Rick conceded.

"Have you ever hert of Abraham Sutzkever?"

"No, I'm afraid I haven't."

"Ach, it's a pity. He vas a great poet, but also a partisan in de var. He, too, vas from Vilna — vere I come from. He vas a brilliant man, very brilliant. Ant gutsy, too. He testifiet at de Nuremberk trials. He wrote many, many poems. My favorite is about his momma, who vas kilt by de Nazis. At de ent of de poem she talks to him. Translated from de Yiddish, it goes sometink like dis:

If you are still here,
Den I exist too,
As da pit in a plum
Bears in it da tree
And da nest and da birt
And da chirp and da coo.

Dat's de Got's honest troot, Rick. Tru you, your grandpa lives on. I'm tellink you. I know vat I'm saying."

For a man who had until only recently expected to be the last of his genetic line, the poem gave Rick something to mull over. It was true. He was, in a sense, the living embodiment of all the people who had preceded him, including the grandfather he'd idolized. Anna's very existence was a continuation of that heritage. That Anna wasn't just his and Sarah's, but also part of a legacy going back through time, was an idea he was beginning to warm to.

THIRTY-FOUR

The rough terrain of rehabilitation was both humbling and revelatory for Sarah. At some point along the path of healing, she realized it was not bringing her to the place she had been before the accident. She was heading toward higher ground. And, though disabled to the casual observer, she felt fully alive for the first time in her life.

Setting aside her driving ambition, Sarah focused all her attention on both the pedestrian and the sublime elements of getting well. At the very same time she was becoming expert at cleaning the pin sites of her external fixator, she was plumbing the depths of the bond between a mother and her infant. As she put her walker aside and mastered the use of crutches, she gave herself permission to fall in love.

She waded carefully into the river of emotions she had avoided for so long, going deeper and deeper, until she found herself at the point where, if she took one more step, she would be in over her head. With Rick leading the way, she found the courage to enter the current. Together, the two novices swam in the river about which they knew little, trusting and depending on one another as they explored the unknown waters.

One early spring evening, after putting Anna down for the night, Rick joined Sarah on the sofa. They played with the idea of a movie, but realized neither could promise to stay awake long enough to read the credits. The truth was, just being with one another was entertainment enough. Sarah stretched out and put her head in Rick's lap. As he stroked her hair, she decided to broach a delicate subject.

"Rick?"

"Yes, my Venus de Milo, my Marilyn Monroe, my Lady Gaga? Your wish is my command."

"Lady Gaga? I didn't know you liked her."

"I do. I like how she's marketed herself right to the top of the charts. She's one clever girl. Her voice ain't too shabby, either."

"Well, I have trouble keeping a tune. If you want to back out, now's the time."

"Nah, I'll stick around. No one's perfect, though I'd say you come damn close...." His voice trailed off as he started nibbling on her fingertips.

"Rick, could we be serious for a minute? I want to talk to you about something important."

"Uh-oh, to the best of my recollection it was on this very sofa that you got serious about a year ago and then all hell broke loose."

"Well, this is nothing like that."

"Promise?" he asked warily.

"Cross my heart," she said, and she did. "I'm just wondering if it would be all right if I amended Anna's birth certificate. When she was born I was listed as the only parent. I want you to be on her birth certificate as well."

"Is that all?" he asked with relief. "Of course."

"Well, there's also the question of her surname. Would you like Smith to be part of her last name — or the whole thing?"

"No, no. Abadhi's fine. I like your name. It's got character. Plus we'll be continuing the tradition: I have my mother's surname."

"That's true. What do you think about Anna Smith Abadhi?" Sarah asked, motioning as though she could envision her daughter's name up in lights.

"Sure. That would be fine — and another palindrome: ASA."

She sat up and drew him toward her for a kiss. "Okay then. I'll see what I can accomplish on the phone or online to make that happen." Then Sarah took a chance and ventured further.

"Rick?"

"Yes."

"There's something else I'd like to talk over with you."

"Here it comes." He put his arms over his face.

"Oh, stop. It's nothing bad."

"Promise?"

"I do promise."

He put down his arms and looked at her with feigned suspicion. "Dare I ask what it's about?"

"It's about Anna's religion. Technically, she's a Jew — I mean according to Jewish law. A child borne of a Jewish woman is automatically a Jew. I would like to follow the Jewish ritual for naming a child. But I know that's something we have to decide together."

He replied without hesitation, "You can do whatever you want. I'm an atheist, but if you find comfort in the ritual, sure. We can do it."

"You're an atheist?"

"Does that bother you?"

"No. Not at all. I became an agnostic at thirteen. After learning the extent of the savagery let loose on people like my grandparents during World War II, I withdrew my support for the notion of an all-powerful god." She looked at Rick expectantly, hoping he'd share how he'd arrived at his atheism.

He didn't disappoint.

"If you saw what I see on a daily basis — the diseases, the injuries, the abuse that kids suffer — you'd be hard-pressed to believe in a merciful god overseeing his flock. As far as I'm concerned, our fate is in our own hands, and it's up to us to make the best of the hand we're dealt."

Of course, Sarah had come to the identical conclusion while lying in her hospital bed. Still, Rick voicing it so starkly triggered something. Maybe it was her legal training, or perhaps it was the doubt that had lately sprung up, undermining her case for the absence of any god. As soon as Rick staked out his position, she took the opposing side.

"I can understand that. I think about what happened to Anna and me, and how we were nearly killed. But then I think about the miracle of Anna — how she defied the odds on the night she was conceived and how she defied the odds on the day of her birth. When I look at her, it's not hard to believe some divine intervention allowed this child to come to be."

Rick focused his gaze on Sarah, who seemed almost transported by the thought that she'd given birth to a miracle.

"Obviously I'm happy — no, let me amend that, I'm deliriously happy — that you and Anna survived the accident. But what about the two kids who were DOA when they got to the ER after being pulled from the rubble? They were on their way home from school. If there was some type of omnipotent being making miracles, why weren't those innocent kids the beneficiaries?" Rick didn't give Sarah a chance to answer. "No, I think we're all subject to random luck, and all we can depend on is ourselves and each other."

Sarah had had no idea that children had been killed in the accident. That made it hard to claim that a miracle had allowed her child to live. She got quiet as she thought of the two dead children and their parents' agony. Rick immediately sensed his mistake; he wanted to kick himself for being so brutally honest.

"Hey, Sarah. I have no corner on wisdom and you're entitled to your beliefs. They have as much validity as mine. Who knows? Maybe more. And if you want to do the baby-naming thing, it's fine with me."

Sarah knew he was trying to make her happy — but she couldn't get what he'd said out of her mind: All we can depend on is ourselves and each other.

"Rick?"

"Yeah?"

"I was just thinking," she began.

"A dangerous pastime, Sarah," he warned, stroking her hair.

"Yeah, I know. But here's the thing. You say all we have is ourselves and each other. Okay. If that's so — and I'll grant that the evidence is leaning heavily that way — what of all the good works that people do? I'm thinking about all the bravery and extraordinary efforts to save Anna and me, and all the other survivors, from the first responders to Jeff and the other doctors, the nurses and my parents...and you. All that help, all that kindness — couldn't they be expressions of a god? A god who acts through people?"

Rick smiled at Sarah's attempt to keep alive the possibility of cosmic coherence and goodness. "If it makes you feel better to think that way, go with it. You might be right for all I know. People can be kind and generous. Perhaps that urge springs from some deity working behind the scenes. I just don't know." But what he didn't say was that the only things he would put his chips on were himself and the people he trusted.

"Well, I can't say as I know either. Being laid up, well, maybe it's given me a little too much time to think."

"Nah, it makes you deep. A woman with deep convictions is my favorite kind of woman," Rick said as he kissed her. "Still, if you think you have a little too much time on your hands, I can help you out with a little more sex. It might be just what the doctor ordered." He kissed her again and started caressing her breasts.

But Sarah wasn't done. "I have to admit that coming nose-to-nose with your own mortality tends to focus your attention on the big questions."

"Ah, yes. A by-product of the near-death experience. It's a common response, actually," he murmured as he became aroused.

"Rick? Hold on a minute."

"Yes?" he asked, disappointed. "Is there something else we need to discuss beyond the existence of God? I thought this serious talk was going to be different. You even crossed your heart. I see you're just one of those bait-and-switch girls. Start with something light and go straight to theology," he said, only half kidding.

"Really, this is something more mundane," Sarah responded, a bit defensively. "If you're all right with the baby-naming ceremony, I was wondering if we could choose Jeff and Devorah as Anna's godparents. It's not exactly required in the Jewish tradition, but the parents can select godparents as a way of honoring them."

Through his frustration, he could see the wisdom of Sarah's idea. "Count me in. Jeff's been a great friend. After all, he was the first person to hold Anna when she was born. I think he'll be into it."

"So will Devorah. Her religion is a big part of her life. Of course, she'll have to come back to New York for the ceremony. As far as I'm concerned, anything that encourages another visit is a good thing."

"I'm sure Jeff would second that thought," Rick said.

"Wouldn't it be something if the two of them got together?" Sarah asked.

"Couldn't happen to two nicer people — except for us, that is," Rick said.

"Well, if you're right that all we have is each other, it would be great if those two had one other."

"On that point, dear Sarah, you'll get no argument from me," he said as he kissed her again. This time, he found a willing partner.

THIRTY-FIVE

When Anna was four months old she learned to giggle. Her mother traded her external fixator and crutches for a walking cast and cane. And, having used up his childcare leave, her father returned to work.

On one of his first days back on the job, Rick's phone rang just as he was wrapping things up for the day. The ring was "Ode to Joy," alerting him to a call from his mother.

"Hey, Mom."

"Hello, dear. I'm so sorry to bother you. Do you have a minute?"

"No bother. I'm done for the day and heading over to Sarah's. What's up?"

"Rick, I just received a call from your father's wife."

"Which one might that be?"

"She gave her name as Kelly. I believe they got married a few years ago. I'll admit her call threw me for something of a loop. I've had no communication from your father or his lawyer since you finished school."

"So why was she bothering you? Did she call to commiserate? That would be rich."

"No, dear. She called because it seems your father had a stroke today while he was giving a talk in New York. She was in the airport in LA, just about to board her plane. He's in your hospital's ICU, Rick. She asked if you could keep an eye on him until she arrives."

"I think that qualifies for what Sarah's grandma would call *chutzpah*. Surely the woman is kidding."

"I'm afraid she sounded deadly serious."

"Well, I don't recall her husband keeping a vigil at my bedside when I was busted up from head to toe, compliments of his drunken driving."

"I'm just relaying the message, Rick. Of course, how to respond is up to you."

"Damn straight it is."

"The only thing I would say is this, dear: You're a better man than your father. You don't have to make the mistakes he's made in his life."

"Well, I'm doing my damnedest to avoid them. But I think taking a pass on his wife's request is hardly comparable to his abandoning me. I was a little kid — his little kid…and his reckless disregard for my life landed me in a hospital bed for months. I owe that man nothing."

"Please don't misunderstand me, Rick. I know the two situations aren't equivalent. But I know you. You're an ethical person. In that way, and so many others, you're a different man from your father."

"So what are you saying? I should step up now even though he's a *schmuck*?"

"That he may be, but he's also your father."

"I thought you said this is my decision. Are you telling me you want me to go and check him out?"

"No. What I'm saying is that, when all is said and done, I don't want you to have regrets."

"Oh, you think I'll feel bad if he dies? I doubt very much that my checking on him will make any difference in the care he gets."

"That's not where I was going. I'm sure he'll be well taken care of. But his wife has reached out to you. You're a person who goes to work every day to help total strangers. Knowing you as I do, I'm concerned that you may someday regret it if you don't help Eric and his wife."

"Got it, Mom. I'll think it over, but don't pin your hopes on that making any difference."

"My only hope, Rick, is that you be at peace with yourself."

"Yup. Got it."

"Now, quickly — because I know how busy you are — tell me about Sarah and Anna."

"They're spectacular. Really. I couldn't be happier." The words caught in his throat. "Gotta run."

"Okay, dear. Know that no matter what you decide, I love you."

"Me, too."

On that warm spring evening, Rick ran as fast as his legs would carry him toward what he loved most in the world. He raced up the two flights of stairs to Sarah's apartment and found her on the sofa reading Anna an alphabet book.

"Hey, you," Sarah said, tilting her head upwards for a kiss. She saw the sweat on his brow. "Did you run all the way home?"

"Sure did," he panted. "All the way." He bent down and kissed Sarah and the baby. "Good day today?" he asked as he started pacing the room.

"Excellent day. Bubbe Rivka got Mrs. Goldberg's son to drive her here for a visit. We had a lovely couple of hours. How about your day?"

"So-so. Actually, it was fine until just a few minutes ago."

"What happened a few minutes ago?"

"You're not going to believe this, but my father's wife — number four or five or whatever — had the nerve to call my mother to tell her he'd had a stroke."

"Was it a courtesy? You know, as his former wife, she had the right to know? That sort of thing?"

"No such luck. He stroked out here in New York and was brought to University Hospital. The latest wife wants me to make sure he gets the best of everything."

"Really? He's just a few blocks away?" Sarah tried to process the thought.

"Really," Rick said, finally joining Sarah and the baby on the couch. Sarah put the giggling, shrieking Anna in her father's arms. The baby's sweet welcome brought momentary relief. Just looking at her gave him joy. He wondered if he'd ever had that effect on his father.

Sarah asked gently, "So what do you think you'll do?"

"I haven't seen him in decades. And if I never laid eyes on him again, it would be fine with me."

"That's understandable. You don't owe him anything, Rick. Not after what he did."

"You've got that right. But my mother suggested that I could take the high road — despite everything."

"She actually wants you to go see him?"

"Not exactly. She says all she wants is that I have no regrets — you know, later on."

"Oh." Sarah turned that idea over in her mind. "I didn't think of that."

Rick handed the baby back to Sarah, got up and started pacing again. "I don't think I can do it."

Sarah had seen Rick so agitated only once before, and that was when she had told him she was pregnant. Then she had held her ground, despite the fact that it upset him. Now she wanted to help the man who was fast becoming her anchor, the man who wrapped his arms around her on nights when she awoke in terror, heart pounding and in a sweat.

"I don't think you have to do what the wife is asking of you."

"But what if my mother's right? I hate to say it, but she usually is," Rick said, dejected. "I found out the hard way — by ignoring her when I was a piss-ant teenager. The woman has an amazing record."

"So you think she's suggesting that you make your peace with him before he dies? Is that what she means?" Sarah tracked Rick as he paced across the living room.

"I guess."

"Is he in danger of dying?"

"I have no idea what his condition is."

"Well, then, maybe you could find out. That might make it easier for you to decide what to do," Sarah suggested.

"I guess I could do that. I wouldn't have to see him. I could just talk to the docs, see his chart. You know, scope things out from a distance."

"That's a reasonable option. Maybe you should let that idea percolate over dinner. Are you in the mood to eat? I have some gefilte fish, compliments of Bubbe."

"What kind of fish?"

"Gefilte fish. You should try it. It may grow on you," she smiled. "And if you're not in the mood for a food adventure, I also have the salmon you bought yesterday. What do you think?"

"I'm not so hungry, but I'll keep you company."

Sarah locked eyes with him. "Good. I love your company."

Thoughts on Rick's predicament crowded out dinner conversation. As Sarah ate and Anna swung back and forth in her mechanical swing, Rick picked at the food on his plate and dredged up long-buried memories.

As he reflected on his childhood, it was hard to know which had caused him greater pain: the injuries sustained in the car crash, or his father's leaving. Right after the accident he cried out for his father again and again, asking his mother when he was coming to the hospital. Long before he had been discharged, he'd stopped asking. The answer had become all too clear.

The get-well cards his father had sent in lieu of visits were, over time, replaced by checks for his birthday and Christmas. But unlike other kids whose parents had split up, his dad had never called, never picked him up for weekends. He had never taken him for school holidays or summer breaks. After a while, if kids had asked where his dad was, he'd shrug his shoulders and say, "Probably dead."

One chilly autumn day, three years after the crash, Rick went through the photo album of his earliest years. He took a pair of scissors and methodically cut his father out of every picture, returning the altered photos to their places in the album. Then he put all the smiling faces of his father in a shoebox, dug a hole deep in the sandy soil of his backyard and buried them. When he was done, he was dirty, sweaty and elated. He'd gotten rid of his phony father once and for all. As he ate a few bites of Bubbe Rivka's gefilte fish, he remembered the relief he had felt that day.

When Sarah was done eating, he cleared the table and washed the dishes. Sarah put Anna in her front pack to get her ready for bed. Just as Sarah was fastening the snaps of the baby's footed pajamas, Rick came into the bedroom to complete the ritual. He fed Anna her bottle, rocking her and singing until her lids fluttered and her eyes rolled upward. As the nipple fell out of her mouth, he burped Anna and put her down for the night.

When he came back into the living room he announced his decision.

"I'll just go back and scope out the scene."

"It can't hurt to know what's going on. I think you're making the right decision," Sarah said.

"Hope so. I'll be back soon." He kissed her before heading off to the resurrection of a dead man.

Eric Stavropoulous, the telegenic evolutionary biologist, had won a modicum of fame by sharing his awe and knowledge of the natural world with the public. He'd come to New York to give the keynote address at a symposium on the evolution of cooperation. He had been nearly done with his remarks when his speech became unintelligible and he collapsed, knocking over the lectern and eliciting gasps from the audience. An ambulance had rushed him to the nearest

ER. There, doctors had administered the clot-busting drug, TPA, but his condition remained critical. Only time would tell if he would live, and if he did, how much damage his brain had sustained.

Rick was made aware of all this when he introduced himself to the ICU staff as a doc doing a favor for the patient's wife. He was shown the results of the MRI, which indicated a clot in the part of the brain that controlled grammar, vocabulary and linear reasoning. It was clear they'd pulled out all the stops to treat the popular scientist's ischemic stroke. But despite that, the patient had not regained consciousness.

As he headed for the doors of the ICU, Rick passed a small whiteboard affixed to the glass window separating him from a patient. He read the name written in green marker: Eric Stavropoulous. On the other side of the glass was his father. Rick's heart pounded in his chest and, though he wanted to run, he felt as though his feet were nailed to the floor. His eyes scanned the man in the bed. The thick black hair he remembered was now snow white, the formerly trim, taut body fat and bloated. Despite the changes the decades had wrought and the breathing tube in his mouth, Rick recognized the face. It was the face that greeted him every morning in the mirror.

Rick couldn't wait to get back to Sarah's — to her and their baby and everything that was right in his life. As he jogged back he was surprised that he felt better. He'd done what had been asked of him and could carry on knowing that, his facial features notwithstanding, he was not the lout — or, as Mr. Abadhi would say, the *momzer* — his father was. When he went to bed that night, he slept well.

The next day, Rick was determined to put the episode behind him and return to his life, helping Sarah, caring for the baby, doing his best for his patients. But one thing made it hard to move on: every day he came to work, he and his father were under the same roof. His greatest wish was that Eric Stavropoulous leave the hospital, either dead or alive; it was all the same to him.

Late one afternoon, there was a knock on his door as he was reviewing lab reports in his office. "Come in," he yelled. A pretty redhead, maybe forty or forty-five, stood in his doorway.

"Dr. Smith?" she inquired.

"One and the same," he replied.

"I'm Kelly Stavropoulous, your father's wife."

He was trapped. He just sat at his desk staring at the woman.

"I'm sorry to bother you," she said, sensing his discomfort. "I wanted to thank you for checking on your dad while I was in transit from LA. The doctors at the ICU told me you dropped by. It meant a lot to us both."

Both. Had he regained consciousness? Rick felt ill.

"I see you're busy. That's all I really came for. So, thank you again." She hesitated for a moment, turned to leave and then thought better of it. "You look so much like your father. It's uncanny."

"Well, short of surgical reconstruction, there's nothing I can do about that."

"I meant it as a compliment."

"If you say so."

"By the way, do you know how I knew you work here — at this hospital?"

"Haven't the foggiest."

"Eric's told me all about you and your career. When I learned where they'd brought him, I recognized the name of the hospital right away. He's very proud of you, you know."

"Proud of me, is he?" Rick asked with a wry laugh. "So proud he hasn't bothered to call or visit in twenty-seven years."

The woman flushed. Rick could see it was her turn to feel uncomfortable.

"You know why, don't you?" she asked, her voice just above a whisper.

"There's really no good answer to that question. Plus, it's

ancient history, in which you played no part."

"No, I want you to know why he hasn't come to see you."

"No need. I think I've figured it out. It's because he's a son of a bitch who nearly killed his five-year-old son driving with a blood alcohol level in the stratosphere. And then there's that sticky point of leaving my mother and me while I was still in intensive care. I think that about sums it up."

When he saw he'd reduced Kelly Stavropoulous to tears, he felt like a bully. "Look, I'm sorry. This has nothing to do with you and if he hadn't stroked out down the street, we would've never met. I have no right to dump on you."

"It's all right. Your father told me about the accident, how he ran away after seeing what he'd done to you. He ran because he was overcome by guilt. He's still filled with guilt. It's my belief that it ruined his life. He drinks too much, he eats too much. Don't get me wrong. I think the world of him. He's got a beautiful mind. He's very generous to everyone around him. We have — had — a good life together. But he's a haunted man."

"Look, I have no interest in him and I don't want to engage in this conversation. He has his life, I have mine. I don't mean to be rude, but I think it's best if you go and don't come back," Rick said, turning his attention to his computer screen.

"But that's just it, Dr. Smith. He doesn't."

"He doesn't what?" Rick asked, not looking up.

"You said he has his life and you have yours — but he's dying," she said.

Rick turned to her. "How do you know that?"

"His doctor told me today. He's not…going to make it." She pulled a tissue out of her pocket and wiped her face. "He developed pneumonia — they think because his swallowing was affected by the stroke. They've tried everything, but they can't clear his lungs of the infection."

"Well, I'm sorry for you. You seem to like him. But you've got to know that as far as I'm concerned, he's been dead for years."

"I do like him. I love him. And based on the picture of the two of you that he keeps on his desk, I think you loved him once, too."

"He has my picture on his desk, does he? Well, let me assure you, I've kept no pictures of him."

Kelly dropped her voice. "Look, I know I have no right to ask this. But it would mean so much to him if you could visit, you know, before, before…it's over."

Rick looked at her in disbelief. "Do you know what you're asking?"

"Yes. I think I do. I know it would be an act of mercy on your part."

"And you think he deserves mercy?"

"I do. He's a human being who made a terrible mistake and he's suffered for it."

"You must think me a better person than I am. I'm just a regular guy. You know, the kind who holds a grudge."

She was undeterred. "Even though he can't speak, he knows what's going on. He communicates by blinking his eyes or squeezing my hand. If you could find it in your heart to let go of that grudge — even for a few minutes — I would be so grateful."

Rick couldn't believe what this woman was asking him to do. "Can you tell me one thing?"

"Sure. Anything."

"How does Eric Stavropoulous get women like you and my mother to fall for him?"

Kelly smiled ruefully, thinking of better times. "Oh, that's easy. He's funny and bighearted and smart. I've known him for years. I worked for him before I married him. I can tell you, he's not the monster you think he is."

After she left, Rick was as jumpy as a cat. Throughout his life, no matter what had happened, of one thing he had been certain: His father was a bastard. That certainty was the bedrock of his world. Now Kelly Stavropoulous comes along to tell him he's gotten it wrong. Was there a chance in hell that she was telling the truth?

There was only one way to find out. He speed-dialed his mother's number.

"Hey, Mom, is this a good time to talk?"

"Just a minute, Rick. I'm cleaning out files in my office and the radio helps pass the time. Let me turn it off." After a moment she was back. "There. Now I can hear. What is it, dear?"

"You won't believe who just paid me a visit."

"I have no idea."

"Kelly Stavropoulous. She says he's about to buy the farm."

"Oh, is he really dying, Rick?"

"That's what she says. I haven't been keeping track of him, but her account of things is plausible."

"Oh, I'm sorry. He's a young man, at least from my perspective. And I think there's a small child from this latest relationship."

"Jesus fucking Christ. He fathered a kid with this woman?"

"He mentioned it in one of his interviews. I'm sorry, Rick. I thought perhaps you knew. I didn't mean to upset you."

"Well, I don't listen to his interviews and I'm already upset, so what's one more thing?"

"Why? Why are you so upset? Is it because he's dying?"

"Hell no. It's because she just told me what a great guy he is. How he's funny and generous. Is she talking about the same man who walked out on us?"

There was a long pause. Then Susan sighed with resignation. "Yes, I suppose she is. He could be very charming when he wanted to be. He certainly wowed me when I met him. And yes, he could be funny and generous."

"So when did you realize he was scum?"

"Scum? I don't think I ever thought of him that way. He cut me to the quick when he told me about the affair, with a grad student no less. That hurt, I won't deny it, but I thought we could weather the storm. But when he drove drunk with you in the car, I actually tried to scratch his eyes out — not something I'm proud of.

"For some reason, though, I never thought of him as scum. Maybe some part of me still loved him, or loved the life we'd built together."

"What? You mean you loved him and forgave him?"

"Oh, no, no, no. I didn't forgive him, at least not for a very long time. But what I did do — with the benefit of time — was piece together what I think happened. Now I actually feel sorry for the man."

"You feel sorry for *him*? Are you kidding?"

"No. I'm not kidding. I think he lost his way. His career took a turn that he wasn't prepared for. As he got more attention in the media for making complex scientific principles accessible to the public, he started to change. He became vain, something there'd been no hint of before. His colleagues — well, I don't know if it was jealousy or an accurate judgment, but they started to discount his work as popular pap. Their criticism wounded him deeply, that much I know. He had always aspired to be a top-notch research scientist. Then suddenly, the quality of his work was being questioned by people whose opinion he valued most. The more that happened, the more he pandered to the media. It was something of a vicious circle."

"You're a helluva lot more understanding than most ex-wives," Rick said impatiently.

"Well, let's just say that my take on him has evolved. At the time he left, I was too consumed with taking care of you to dwell on the wreckage of my marriage. It was all I could do to keep track of your surgeries and procedures, all the treatments and therapies. I had to take a leave from the university so I could keep up with all of it. But eventually you recovered and I had my boy back. I felt like I'd won the sweepstakes: I got to watch you grow up to be the beautiful man you are. Your father missed out on everything. He lost his son. You notice that despite his many marriages, he never had any more children until now. I think that speaks for itself."

"Well, his current wife says he's 'filled with guilt' about the car accident or some such crap," Rick said, mocking Kelly Stavropoulous's words.

"I often wondered how he lived with himself. Even if he didn't love me anymore, he seemed to love you. What he did to you must have eaten away at him. From the pictures I see of him, it's obvious that he's gone to hell with himself. And all those failed marriages. Not exactly the sign of a happy man."

Rick finally got down to what was tormenting him. "Mom, she wants me to visit him before he dies. She calls it an act of mercy. You're in a position to know. Does he deserve mercy?"

"That's a hard question to answer. If I were confronted with your situation, I wouldn't hesitate to say my good-byes. He has no hold on me anymore. I could find it within myself to perform that merciful act, if indeed that's what it would be. After all, it's because of him I have you.

"But," his mother continued, "I'm not you. You have to decide whether you can forgive your father enough to spend a few minutes with him before that's no longer possible. No one can decide that for you, Rick."

"And if I don't do it?" he asked, seeking absolution before the fact.

"I'm sure only the saints of this world would fault you."

The conversation with his mother only muddied the waters further. So the bastard could be charming. And he'd once been a serious scientist before becoming the darling of amateurs and the media. Maybe his wife was telling the truth. Maybe he was haunted by what he had done. Damn it, he deserved to be haunted. But what now, now that the show was almost over?

His mother had said he had no hold on her anymore. Was that

true for him? Did his stroked-out father have a hold on him? Rick looked up. It was six o'clock. He turned off his computer and headed for the doors. He needed to get out of the hospital.

As he headed to Sarah's, he wondered if he was hallucinating. Down the block from where he stood was a tall, curly-haired woman making her way slowly down the street with a cane. Then he recognized the back of the baby carrier the woman wore. It was no mirage. It was Sarah and Anna. His heart jumped and he picked up his pace.

"Hey, you New York City pedestrians," he said, putting his arm around Sarah's narrow waist and matching her step for step. "Out for a stroll?"

"Hey, yourself. Indeed we are. We came out for a walk with the therapist, and when our session was up, I thought I'd just keep on walking. The therapist says I'm ready and she's right. I love being outside — on my own again. What is it, nearly five months since I've been able to do this?" As soon as she asked the question she realized that Rick was only half listening. "Hey, is everything okay? You're heading home kind of early."

"Oh, man, I couldn't wait to get out of there today," he said.

"Tough day?"

"I got a visit from my father's wife."

"Oh. That must have been a little sticky," Sarah said.

"You could say that again. You should see this woman, Sarah. She's got to be twenty years his junior. She's attractive, seemingly nice, well-spoken. The works. How the hell he gets these women, I have no idea."

It occurred to Sarah that the son might have inherited some of the father's magnetism when it came to women, but she kept the thought to herself. "What did she want?"

"Well, she started out slow…thanking me for checking on him. That wasn't too bad. She turned to leave and I thought, 'All right, I'm home free,' but then she started in on how the old man had told her all about my career, how proud he is of me, how sorry he is for what he did to me, how he's weighed down by guilt. The whole nine yards."

"Had you any inkling about any of that?"

"It was news to me."

"He hasn't spoken to you in years, right?"

"Decades."

"But he's proud of you?"

"So she says."

"And drowning in guilt?"

"That about sums it up, at least according to the wife."

"Did she sound credible?" Sarah asked, attempting to weigh the evidence.

"I didn't know what to make of it, so I called my mother to see if any of it made sense to her."

"And?" Sarah asked.

"And she thought it could be — what word did you use?"

"Credible."

"Yeah, she thought it could be credible."

"So maybe that's not so bad. It makes him sound more like a human being than the ogre I'd imagined. And he did father you, after all. He must have some good in him," Sarah said.

"That's not the end of it. His wife wants me to see him because he's dying."

The two of them stopped walking and looked at one another. With Anna between them, Sarah took hold of his hand. "Listen to me. Whether or not you decide to comply with her request, know this: You're the love I never expected to find in this life. You're the father of this child who was never supposed to be. By my lights, you're a hero. You're my hero."

"Well, I don't feel like a hero. I feel like a five-year-old kid who'd like to pummel his no-good father for leaving him high and dry."

"Is it okay if we sit down for a bit? I think we're blocking foot traffic here in the middle of the street. And Anna would likely enjoy a break from the carrier."

"Sure," Rick said as he took the baby in his arms and walked with Sarah to the ledge of a concrete planter. They sat down and grew quiet, each watching the pedestrians pass before them and mulling over Rick's options.

It was Sarah who finally broke the silence. "You know, just the other day I learned a little something about one of my physical therapists — the one I told you about with the glass eye?"

"Yeah, I remember. But what does this have to do with what we were just talking about?"

"Hold on a minute. It connects. I promise."

"Okay. I'll bite. So what did you learn about your therapist with the glass eye?"

"I learned how she lost her eye. She was six years old and a teenage neighbor was playing around with a BB gun. She was just sitting in her backyard — on her swing set with her little sister — when she took a direct hit to her eye."

"Are you telling me this to somehow make me feel better?"

"I'm telling you this because she told me how she came to forgive that neighbor boy."

"And how was that?"

"She said if she hadn't forgiven him he'd still be living rent-free in her head. Something about that image really struck me. What do you think about maybe freeing up some of the psychic real estate taken up by your father? We could use it for our life together. Remember what you told me when I was in the hospital? About things being in the past tense and how we're moving forward now?"

"Me and my big mouth."

"I love your mouth. I love all of you," Sarah said. Then she kissed Rick just as a taxi blasted its horn and a man yelled out, "Hey, watch it, buster." That set Anna on a crying jag. Any further discussion of Rick's dilemma had to bow to the needs of their hungry, tired baby girl.

Rick had a restless night. He finally dozed off just as the sun started streaming through the bedroom window. When he awoke he knew what he had to do. He got up, went into the living room and called the ICU. Though his condition was grave, Eric Stavropoulous was still alive. Rick went back into the bedroom and threw on some clothes.

Sarah opened an eye and asked in a sleepy voice, "Hey, where are you going? It's Saturday. Aren't you off this weekend?"

"Yeah, I am, but I've decided. I'm going to see him."

She bolted upright in bed and threw off the covers. "Oh, we'll come with you. Just give me a few minutes."

"No. I think I'd better do this on my own. Let Anna sleep. You go back to sleep, too."

"Are you sure? I want to help."

"Thanks. That means more than you know, but I think I'll just go and do the deed. I'll be back soon." He sat down on the bed and kissed her. "Really. Thanks for the offer."

"I know how rough this has been on you."

"Well, his organs are failing, so it's almost over."

"Oh, I'm so sorry. He's still your father. I'm glad you're going."

"I wish I was. It's something I just have to do."

When Rick got to the ICU he found Kelly Stavropoulous asleep in the chair next to her husband's bed. What he didn't expect was the small, red-headed boy sleeping in her lap — the half-brother he hadn't known existed. The monitors indicated that the patient's blood pressure, respiration and heart rate were perilously low. Time was short.

Rick went out of the room and got a folding chair. He'd seen people die many times before, but he had to steel himself to approach the bed. What now? Dare he touch him? He knew that even at the end, people can sometimes sense touch and hear voices. He set up the chair close to the bed and took his father's hand. It was cold.

Keeping his eyes focused on the floor, he began. "Eric. This is Rick. I came to say good-bye." He couldn't be sure but he thought he felt two fingers squeeze his hand. "Your wife tells me you feel bad about the accident all those years ago. Well, I don't want you to worry about it. I recovered. I had a happy childhood. I have a good life now. A very good life. I'm in love with the mother of my child. I'm passionate about my work as a doctor. From all indications, I'm pretty good at it, too. Everything worked out okay for me. More than okay. I'm sorry things didn't work out for the two of us. But I see you have your wife and little boy right here. I'm sure they love you very much.

"So if it's your time, go in peace."

Rick hadn't planned on what he was going to say. It just came to him. And when he looked up he saw tears pooling beneath his father's sunken eyes. Rick patted his hand and got up to leave. It was then that he saw Kelly looking at him. "Thank you," she mouthed as he left the room. Two hours later, Eric Stavropoulous was dead.

THIRTY-SIX

The summer and fall that followed would long be remembered by Rick and Sarah as one of the sweetest times of their lives. Despite each learning of the other's flaws and fears, they were in love. Together, they thrilled at watching Anna grow and change. Fortified by happiness, they found the courage to start cutting their demons down to size. Sarah began weaving the accident and its aftermath into the tapestry of her life. Though his father's abandonment was tattooed on his soul, Rick experienced something of an epiphany following his death: Eric Stavropoulous was just a guy, a guy who'd made an unholy mess of his life.

The lovers delighted in knowing that being together made them better and stronger. They decided to celebrate their union when Sarah was at last able to walk without the assistance of crutches, canes or casts. They chose an inn on Cape Cod for their wedding ceremony, which would be led by the rabbi who had conducted the service at Sarah's Bat Mitzvah and Anna's baby naming. Joseph insisted on picking up the tab for their wedding party, adding that it was a father's pleasure to see his daughter well married. Rick reveled in the knowledge that he had earned what he thought of as "The Joseph Abadhi Seal of Approval."

So, on a warm, sunny September day, surrounded by their supportive families and closest friends, Sarah and Rick celebrated the joyous confirmation of what they already knew: Neither could imagine life without the other.

Rick generally got up with the baby around five and cuddled her while she "took some swigs" from her morning bottle. It was their special time together and he savored it. He couldn't believe how fast she was growing. She'd been sitting up and crawling for months. She could coast around the living room while holding on to the furniture. They'd had to baby-proof the apartment because she was so quick and curious. He figured that within the month she'd be walking. Then all bets were off.

It was dark in the morning now, and he had to turn on the kitchen light to do bottle duty, his first act of the day. This morning he'd gotten up before Anna, taken his shower and found her standing up in her crib waiting for him when he emerged from the bathroom. He threw on his tee shirt and briefs and picked up the baby from the crib. They made their way to the kitchen to warm the waiting bottle, then headed for the sofa. Rick turned the lamp onto its lowest setting and covered them both with the hand-crocheted quilt Bubbe Rivka had given Rick and Sarah as a wedding present.

As she drank her morning milk, Anna used her fingers to explore her father's face. She poked his ears and pulled his earlobe, then stuck her index finger between his upper and lower teeth while Rick pretended to bite her. Rick loved looking into those ocean-blue eyes, compliments of her grandmothers. He wondered what else she had inherited from the family. Only time would tell.

Rick sang to Anna every morning — just the two of them in the quiet apartment before the crack of dawn. His repertoire was eclectic, everything from children's classics and Jay-Z raps to old Beatles songs. This morning he broke into a rendition of "Eleanor Rigby." It was there on the sofa, while he was singing about the poor, lonely Eleanor, that his eyes were drawn to the envelope on the coffee table. He focused on the return address: The Estate of Eric Stavropoulous. When Sarah had handed it to him the previous night, it had seemed radioactive and he'd dropped it unopened on the coffee table. But now it seemed to have lost some of its menace. It was as though Anna was his shield, and with her in his arms he could face its contents, whatever they might be.

He picked the envelope up with his one free hand, curious now, and tore it open with his teeth. He removed the first enclosure. It was from a lawyer, explaining the steps involved in settling the estate. The second was a handwritten note card. When Rick opened it, a check fluttered out, landing on Anna, who was all too eager to grab it. Rick gently slipped it from her grip without looking at the sum, and put it face down on the table. Then, with some trepidation, he began reading the note.

Rick,

I was granted the gift of being your father for just a short while. For five years — the best five years of my life — I was able to love and nurture you, to share amazement and delight with your mother at your quick mind and your sense of humor. But then I ruined everything. My recklessness caused the accident that brought you such unimaginable suffering.

I was solely to blame but I didn't have the strength of character to face what I had done. Instead, I ran away. It meant losing you, but at the time it seemed only fair that I forfeit the right to be part of your life. Over my lifetime I've done many things that I regret, but all of them pale next to that fateful decision.

When you chose to cast off the name we shared, I was certain that you hated me and that there was no hope our relationship could ever be repaired. I was brokenhearted. But every day I thought of you, loved you, missed you more than you'll ever know.

You grew up without me. Your mother has my greatest respect and undying gratitude for doing what I was unworthy of doing: helping you become the fine, capable man you are today.

If you are reading this letter, I have passed from this life. Know that it was stupidity and cowardice, not a cold or callous heart, that kept me from you. I am so very sorry that I was not the father you deserved.

Eric Stavropoulous

Rick sat motionless, face wet, cradling the baby in the crook of his arm. There was one part of the note that he kept rereading: *It seemed only fair that I forfeit the right to be part of your life.* Having earned the right to be Anna's father, Rick couldn't imagine giving her up. Now he understood why his mother felt sorry for Eric Stavropoulous.

Anna grew ready for action when the last ounce of her milk disappeared from the bottle. She pulled it from her mouth and would have flung it to the floor had her father not caught it just as it became airborne. There was no time to dwell on what he'd read. He put the letter, the card and the check back in the envelope. Then, as he took Anna back to the bedroom to relieve her of her sodden double diaper, he placed the envelope on top of the refrigerator, safely out of reach of his ten-month-old world explorer.

The baby babbled and chortled as Rick cleaned her bottom and tried to get the fresh diaper on. She kicked her legs wildly, almost daring her father to get a diaper on her rear end. The thought crossed Rick's mind that perhaps the kid had some of his defiant streak. If she did, it probably served him right.

When at last he had the diaper on and her legs back in the footed pajamas, he put the baby in bed with her mother. "Wake up, you loafer. Get to work mothering your child," he teased as he kissed Sarah. She reluctantly roused to see Rick looking at her, his eyes shining. So far there hadn't been a single day when she hadn't gotten a thrill out of seeing him first thing in the morning. Today was no different. They both savored their morning hello before it was rudely interrupted by Anna, who climbed atop her mother and grabbed her lips with both of her hands. It was her newest trick. Rick had laughed the first time she did it. Now it had become part of her daily routine.

"Hey, bud, those are my stomping grounds," he said as he loosened her surprisingly tight clutch. "She's had her morning swig. Her bottom's clean and dry for the moment."

Sarah grunted and closed her eyes again. "Oh, God, I'm sleep deprived. She was up again in the night. The nurse practitioner at the pediatrician's office thinks she's teething."

"That's a bunch of baloney. Just a catchall for everything we don't understand about babies," Rick groused good-naturedly.

"You're probably right," Sarah said, pulling herself up and leaning against the headboard. "My theory is Anna is just angling for some company in the middle of the night. If I had my druthers, I'd let her cry it out, but I can hardly follow those instincts while she's sleeping in our room and you have to be up at five."

"Good point. Thank you for catching the graveyard shift. I owe you big time. Let me show you a token of my gratitude," he said as his hands moved under her pajamas.

"Hey, Dr. Smith, don't you have some place to be? Like work? Don't you have patients who need you?" she teased as she put her hand on his and kissed him.

"Aw, shucks," he said with a slow, Southern drawl. "Gotta go out into the hard, cold world and bring home the bacon. Otherwise, I'd be all over you like ugly on an ape, you lucky thing. Keep your motor runnin' till tonight, sweetheart."

"That's a date," Sarah said, laughing, while Anna blew spit bubbles into her ear.

Rick reluctantly got up and dressed quickly. He ran a comb through his hair — which lately had sprung a few gray strands — tied his sneakers and then kissed Sarah and Anna good-bye. As he got his coat out of the front hall closet he called back to the bedroom, "Short day today, promise. See you for dinner." And then he was out the door.

It was 5:51 on that dark November morning. Sarah sat in bed, holding the babbling Anna. She put on the radio to catch the weather. Instead, there was something about Mark Arkin. The reporter explained that the real estate titan and his wife were bankrolling a new charter school that would open the following fall on the West Side: The Arkin Career Academy for the Construction Professions. Its mission would be to prepare high school kids either for college programs in architecture and engineering, or the construction trades. The chancellor of the New York City school system lauded the couple's generosity in providing a new option for city youth. Then Arkin's voice came on — not his in-your-face voice that let everyone in the room know that he was the alpha male, but the more restrained voice he had used when he apologized to Sarah for the accident. "Our hope — my wife's and mine — is that this school will help prepare youngsters from all five boroughs to be New York's next generation of construction professionals. Consider it our gift to a city that has been very good to us."

Sarah thought this was likely a maneuver by Arkin to get some much-needed good press. A thorough investigation into the crane accident revealed that he'd put the screws to the general contractor to bring his condo project in under budget. And charter schools were the new darling of the billionaires' club, a good place to aim his philanthropy. Given the vagaries of the tax code, it probably didn't hurt his bottom line, either. Sarah wondered if what she'd said to him all those months before — about doing well by doing good — had played some role in his beneficence. She'd likely never know.

When the piece concluded, the newscaster's mellifluous voice reported that it was going to be another unseasonably mild autumn day, with temperatures reaching the low sixties. At the moment, it was fifty degrees with calm winds in Central Park. Perfect. While holding Anna, Sarah put both feet on the floor and arose from her bed. There hadn't been a day since her cast had been removed that she hadn't given thanks for being able to accomplish that simple maneuver. She knew it was possible that as life moved on she might forget — first one day here and there, and then, perhaps, more often. But for now, she remained in awe of her ability to move unencumbered and take care of herself and her baby.

Sarah moved quickly to implement her early morning routine. Anna knew the drill: crib for a few minutes with a favorite bunny while her mother disappeared into the bathroom for a quick shower. Once the shower was done, Anna got to crawl around the apartment while Sarah filled her diaper bag with supplies and goodies for the day's adventures. Sarah threw on some jeans and a sweater before she dressed Anna from her repository of baby gifts. Today was a purple fleece outfit from Aunt Ellen and Uncle Max. She tied the laces on the baby's sneakers — a gift from Doris — and put Anna on her hip. They stopped at the refrigerator for the insulated breakfast bag that she'd packed the night before. Sarah nuked the bottle to take out the chill, and then tucked it in the bag's side pocket. Coats on — and then they set off. Sarah put the diaper bag on the stair lift and walked down the two flights, right hand on the railing, left arm holding Anna tight.

Sarah got the baby in the stroller, which they kept locked to the railing of the basement stairs. She stowed her bags in its storage racks just as a neighbor came down the stairs. He held open the doors, allowing her to negotiate the stroller through the entry foyer. Sarah and the baby emerged onto the dark street at 6:25 and headed west. The radio hadn't lied. The wind was calm. There was a glimmer of light emerging from the east. When they got to Lexington Avenue they headed north.

Along the way Sarah noticed little bundles on the sidewalk — plastic grocery bags filled with leaves. She had to smile as she thought of the enormous plastic bags her father needed every autumn when their massive maple and oak trees let go of their leaves. As a child, she had reveled in those leaves. When she had been drafted as a teenager to help her father gather them into huge piles, she had cursed them. City born and raised, Anna would have to depend on weekend visits to her grandparents' house for opportunities to jump into a mound of dry, crackling leaves. On the other hand, she'd likely never spend a Saturday afternoon raking until blisters formed. Such were the pluses and minuses of a childhood in the city.

She stopped at the cafe on her route and got a paper and a large dark-roast coffee to go. She stowed the paper and put the coffee in the cup holder before proceeding west to Central Park. The light was quickly changing. She hurried to get to her favorite bench so she and Anna could take in the sunrise over breakfast. As they arrived at their destination, Sarah organized their morning repast. Anna watched her every move, kicking her legs in excitement as she saw her mother open the container of yogurt. Sarah alternated a spoonful of yogurt for the baby with a sip of her coffee. The next course was Cheerios on the tray so Anna could pick them up one at a time while her mother enjoyed a yogurt of her own.

These early morning breakfast picnics were savored by mother and baby alike, but their days were numbered. The Indian summer they'd enjoyed would inevitably come to an end. But even if, by some miracle, the weather remained mild, the outdoor breakfasts would cease when the calendar year drew to a close. Two more months. That's all the time they had together before Sarah went back to work full time. Just the thought of it gave her pause. It wasn't the prospect of being elbow deep in legal work that sobered her. On the contrary: Part of her was itching to get back to the office, to have a reason to wear the suits hanging in her closet and to work with Harry and Doris again. What troubled her was the idea of being away from Anna for so many hours every day. She wondered if she was entering into a bargain with the devil in order to regain her professional life.

She and Rick had talked about getting a nanny to come care for the baby, but he felt uncomfortable handing his daughter off to a stranger who would be alone with her all day. He preferred a setting where Anna would be around other children, with lots of adult oversight. The hospital's childcare center had an opening in their one-year-olds' class after the first of the year. They'd visited in October. It was clean, bright and institutional. Sarah had to take a deep breath every time she thought of Anna being there from morning until night. One saving grace was that Rick could drop by for lunch every day. Another was that Grandma Eva had arranged her spring teaching schedule so that she could watch Anna on Fridays.

Sarah felt like their little family was on the cusp of a big change. Next month they'd be moving to a two-bedroom apartment on the eleventh floor in the building next to Jeff's. It was an elevator building and the location was great for Rick. But she'd miss her apartment where their baby had been conceived and their love affair had begun. Still, there were practical considerations. The new apartment was larger, closer to daycare and the hospital. The elevator would make climbing stairs optional — an alternative form of exercise on bad-weather days when a run by the river was less than ideal. And of course, if Devorah moved to New York to be with Jeff — which apparently was under discussion — Sarah might soon be living on the same block as her best friend. By any objective measure, the benefits of the move outweighed the drawbacks. Still, she would miss that one-bedroom walk-up.

Then there was the question of more children. On their honeymoon Rick had suggested that they stop using birth control and "live dangerously." That had made Sarah laugh until she cried. So far their dangerous living had resulted in nothing more than two ordinary menstrual cycles. Sarah knew it sometimes took normal women months to conceive. But her reproductive tract was anything but normal. What if Anna was, as Devorah had said, a miracle baby? What if there was never another child for her and Rick?

The baby brought Sarah's brooding to a halt. She was demanding to get out of the stroller. Anna loved to "walk" between her mother's legs while Sarah held her hands. This, too, was part of their morning routine. This morning Anna was more emphatic than usual about getting up and out. As Sarah lowered her to the ground, Anna stood motionless without reaching out for her mother's hands. Then, with great concentration, she moved her right foot forward, then her left and then fell on her bottom. She wasn't down long. She clambered to her feet and then, holding her arms out for balance, took several steps before landing on her derriere once more. Sarah called to Anna and stepped back a few feet. The baby got up, and this time made it all the way to her waiting mother. When she arrived at her destination, she received a welcome worthy of so great an achievement.

Sarah couldn't wait to share the news with Rick, their parents and Bubbe Rivka. But that would have to wait. It was a little early to phone them, even about something as exciting as this. For the moment, Sarah would hold on to her delicious secret. As the sun rose above the buildings east of the park, Sarah knew that whatever else happened, she had a daughter who could walk. And that was no mean feat.

Acknowledgements

Many of us have friends or family members who have suffered when unable to have a child; some have experienced that agony firsthand. Infertility's pervasiveness does little to reduce its sting. *Fertility*, a labor of love, has allowed me to explore the many dimensions of a rich, fruitful life, one of which springs from having and raising a child.

Being able to cultivate bonds with other human beings is a kind of fertility. At the outset of the novel, our main characters, Rick and Sarah, are paragons of professional success. Despite their many accomplishments, their personal lives are anything but rich or fruitful. They have each erected protective walls to keep at bay anyone hoping to get close, allowing them to live safe — if barren — lives. But as their story unfolds, both Sarah and Rick are forced to slowly tear down those walls. The dismantling process is painful, and they become vulnerable to both the dangers and possibilities that intimacy can bring. Theirs was a story I enjoyed telling.

As I wrote *Fertility* I had the help of early readers. Melanie Novello, Cindy Seltzer Pollard, Joan Cappione, Kathy Kelly and Elsa Wilson generously shared their astute feedback. I am indebted to my old friend, Cynthia Frankel, for her careful reading of multiple drafts. She is a proofreader par excellence. Without the insights of my dear colleague and friend, Susan DeWinter, Sarah and Rick's journey would have taken a different path. Her appraisal and analysis of an early draft was our last substantive conversation before her untimely death. *Fertility* is a better book for her thoughtful critique. Erica Midkiff's excellent copy editing skills and acumen improved the manuscript beyond measure.

To write with some authority about medicine and the law, I sought help from experts in both of those fields. Many thanks to attorneys Alan Kusnitz, Cathy Frankel, Grant Gelberg and Vincent Capuano for helping me learn about the working life of an ambitious law associate. Drs. Marguerite Uphoff and Harris Gelberg assisted in my understanding of the ramifications of heparin overdoses in infants. Pharmacist Joseph Muench offered his expertise on the workings of a busy hospital pharmacy. Shelley Dillon, a floor nurse in a university hospital, provided insights into the bedside care of severe trauma victims.

Finally, I gained an understanding of the physics that can lead to disaster when a heavy object falls from a height of twenty stories from my husband, Charlie Wilson. His doctorate in plasma physics notwithstanding, his clear, simple explanation — replete with diagrams — made it possible for me to describe the accident that turns the lives of our protagonists upside-down.

Of course, I take full responsibility for any errors in my portrayal of law, medicine and physics that appear in this book.

Lastly, I am indebted to my mother, Rebecca Gelberg. The idea for this novel came shortly before her ninetieth birthday celebration. She was the Rivka of my life and her spirit was a constant presence throughout the writing of *Fertility*. It is to her that I dedicate it.

Denise Gelberg

Ithaca, New York
December 2012

About the Author

Writer, teacher, Brooklyn native, Ph.D. in labor relations, gardener, wife and mother are some fitting descriptors of Denise Gelberg. Since leaving the classroom in 2006, she has devoted herself to writing about the things that occupy her thoughts during long swims and runs. An advocate for children, she has written about the current state of education reform in the United States, including the book *The "Business" of Reforming American Schools* (SUNY Press). *Fertility* is her debut novel.

Denise Gelberg lives with her husband and two dogs — Sophie, a standard poodle and Rowdy, an aptly named wire fox terrier — on fourteen acres of rolling hillside ten miles west of Ithaca, New York.

Readers can reach Denise Gelberg at denisegelberg@yahoo.com.
Check out her Facebook page and follow her on Twitter.

CPSIA information can be obtained at www.ICGtesting.com
Printed in the USA
LVOW12s0007241213

366661LV00014B/186/P